I0787963

HEIRS OF ALEXANDRIA

Book Two of The Alexandrian Saga

Thomas K. Carpenter

Heirs of Alexandria
Book Two of The Alexandrian Saga

Hardcover Version

by Thomas K. Carpenter

Copyright © 2023 Thomas K. Carpenter
All Rights Reserved

Published by Black Moon Books

Cover design by
G&S Cover Designs

Chapter Headings design by Aleks49011

Discover other titles by this author on:
www.thomaskcarpenter.com

ISBN-13: 978-1-958498-12-5

This is a novel work of fiction. All characters, places, and incidents described in this publication are used fictitiously, or are entirely fictitional.

No part of this publication may be reproduced or trasmitted, in any form, or by any means, except by an authorized retailer, or with written permission of the publisher. Inquires may be addressed via email to thomaskcarpenter@gmail.com

ALEXANDRIAN SAGA

Fires of Alexandria
Heirs of Alexandria
Legacy of Alexandria
Warmachines of Alexandria
Empire of Alexandria
Voyage of Alexandria
Goddess of Alexandria

Other Books by Thomas K. Carpenter

The Dashkova Memoirs

Revolutionary Magic
A Cauldron of Secrets
Birds of Prophecy
The Franklin Deception
Nightfell Games
The Queen of Dreams
Dragons of Siberia
Shadows of an Empire

The Kingmaker Saga

The Stone Tree
The Crystal Bard
The Ghost Tower
The Champion's Prophecy
The Shadow Labyrinth
The Autumn Empire

The Hundred Halls Universe
SEASON ONE

THE HUNDRED HALLS

Trials of Magic
Web of Lies
Alchemy of Souls
Gathering of Shadows
City of Sorcery

THE RELUCTANT ASSASSIN

The Reluctant Assassin
The Sorcerous Spy
The Veiled Diplomat
Agent Unraveled
The Webs That Bind

GAMEMAKERS ONLINE

The Warped Forest
Gladiators of Warsong
Citadel of Broken Dreams
Enter the Daemonpits
Plane of Twilight

ANIMALIANS HALL

Wild Magic
Bane of the Hunter
Mark of the Phoenix
Arcane Mutations
Untamed Destiny

STONE SINGERS HALL

Song of Siren and Blood
House of Snake and Tome
Storm of Dragon and Stone
Sonata of Shadow and Thorn
Well of Demon and Bone

THE ORDER OF MERLIN

The Order of Merlin
Infernal Alliances
Tower of Horn and Blood

HEIRS
OF
ALEXANDRIA

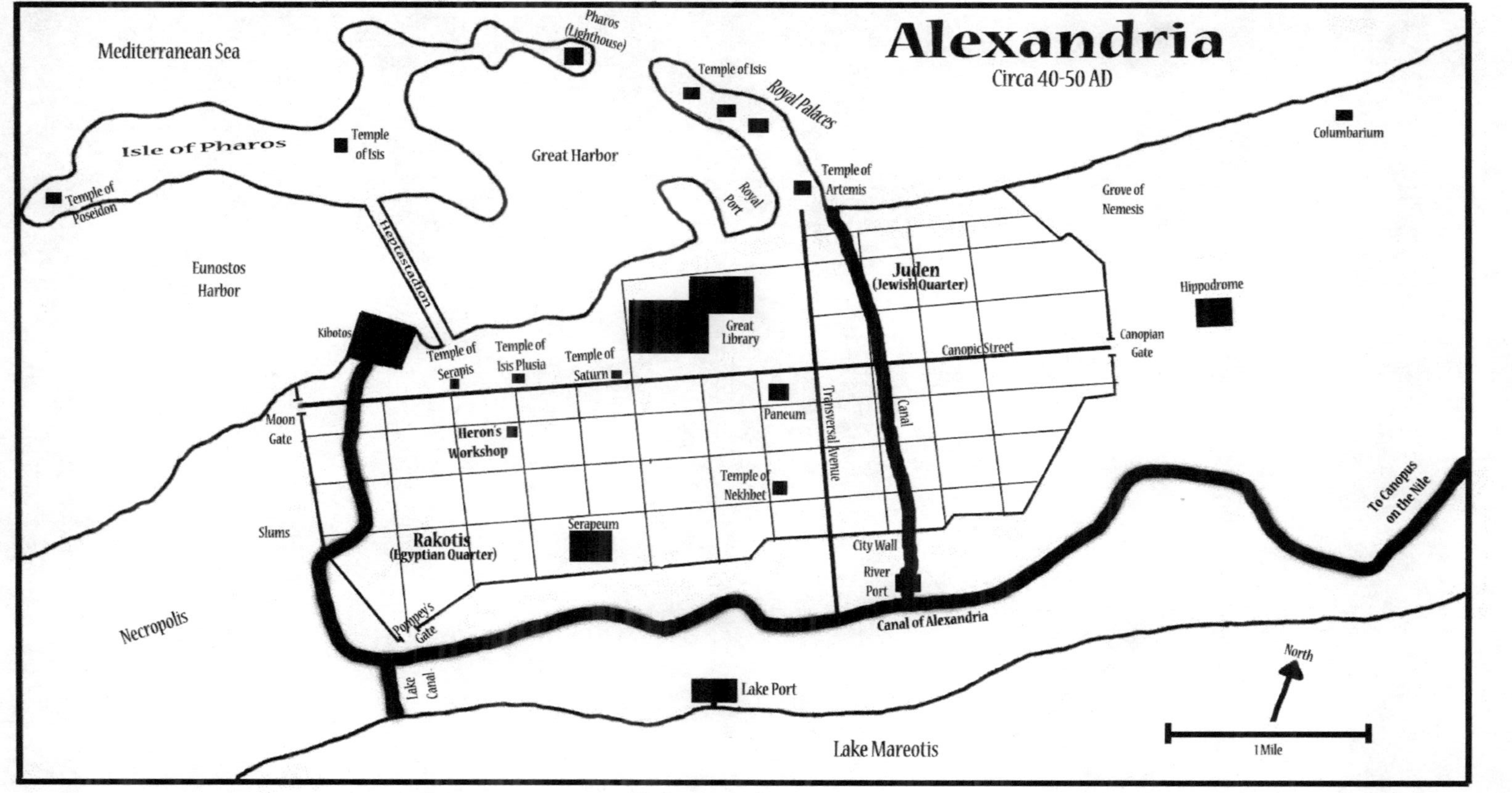

Alexandria
Circa 40-50 AD
Mediterranean Sea
Pharos (Lighthouse)
Isle of Pharos
Temple of Isis
Great Harbor
Temple of Isis
Royal Palaces
Royal Port
Temple of Artemis
Columbarium
Grove of Nemesis
Juden (Jewish Quarter)
Hippodrome
Canopian Gate
Canopic Street
Temple of Poseidon
Eunostos Harbor
Heptastadion
Kibotos
Great Library
Temple of Serapis
Temple of Isis Plusia
Temple of Saturn
Paneum
Transversal Avenue
Canal
Moon Gate
Heron's Workshop
Temple of Nekhbet
City Wall
River Port
To Canopus on the Nile
Slums
Rakotis (Egyptian Quarter)
Serapeum
Pompey's Gate
Necropolis
Lake Canal
Canal of Alexandria
Lake Port
North
Lake Mareotis
1 Mile

ONE

An hour after the last curfew bell had rung, an Alexandrian soldier died on a secluded street corner near the Canopian Gate. Radric regretted the necessity of it, but the individual he was going to meet had requested complete secrecy.

The soldier hadn't been much older than a boy and had been easy to take, not that an older one would have caused him trouble. Now maybe one of those Northmen would have given him pause. They were tall, broad-shouldered, and coarse like an animal.

A few days ago, Radric had watched a trio of the Northmen eating and drinking in an outdoor café. They'd broken a half-dozen earthen mugs in their revelry and scared off the clientele. He saw how the citizens of Alexandria watched them. They won't survive much longer, not even with the miracles of the *Michanikos* giving life to metal.

A week before that, Radric had paid a man a ha'penny to examine one of the mechanicals that made the miracles run. He'd never been one for the gods, but he wasn't sure about a device that didn't serve any. The heavens were full of jealous folk.

Still, he couldn't understand how it worked, either. The man he'd paid told him that it was fed with wood and fire and water, and breathed like a dragon when it was full.

A brief search of the boy soldier's pockets returned more than a few ha'pennies and a Roman denarius. Radric bit down on the coin and shoved it into his purse. The irony of the Alexandrian soldier carrying a Roman coin amused Radric.

The boy soldier was Egyptian with a smooth, hairless face. Probably drawn to the Northman's army because of the miracles. The Egyptians were a superstitious lot. They saw favor in the new Satrap, but if the winds soured, he'd be dead before dawn.

Radric tucked the body into the dark shadows of the alley and moved to a more advantageous position. It was a pity the boy had chosen this alleyway to take a piss.

That was the problem Radric saw with the Northman's army. Too many boy soldiers and not enough of those steam dragons or Northmen. The Roman army supposedly had a million men. Words were thick that they'd be marching on Alexandria by the spring.

A shape bled around the corner toward his position. The Noric steel blade slipped into his hand in readiness. The hood was pulled high and over the face, but Radric could tell it was a slender person and most likely his contact.

"Aite," whispered the shape.

Radric was standing to the right of his contact. He could tell by the whisper that it was a woman. If it weren't for the size of the promised payment, he might have considered other entertainment for the evening.

"Hermes," was his reply.

Another reason he stayed his blade was the choice of meeting word. Hermes was the messenger god of travelers and thieves. Radric always gave a ha'penny at a temple of the trickster god. The goddess Aite was unfamiliar to Radric, but now he knew the reason for the choice.

"Have you been seen?"

Radric's own hood was up which hid his scowl. He wanted to hiss back - *of course not* - but then he remembered the soldier and stayed his tongue.

"No," he replied, resisting the urge to glance back at the body.

"Can you do it?"

The woman had a hard, but seductive voice, and Radric found himself growing excited.

"You wouldn't ask me here if I couldn't."

Radric heard the sound only a moment before it would have been too late. He yanked the woman against the wall and reflexively threw his hand across her mouth. She bit down on the meat of his palm and he had to do everything he could not to knee her in the stomach.

"Soldiers," he whispered through gritted teeth.

She stopped struggling and stayed pressed against him. The thump of soldier boots passed. In the moonless night, he saw vague shapes reflected in distant lanterns. Flashes of steel and oily leathers that absorbed light.

Radric was holding his breath, but he was also acutely aware of her soft, feminine shape. He squeezed a little tighter.

Once the soldiers were safely down the street, he loosened his grip, only to find a shiny blade tucked under his chin.

"I thought we were friends?"

"Only if you want to live your life as a eunuch."

Most folk who carried a blade didn't have the stones to use it. Except for whores, Radric didn't think a woman could. The woman didn't smell like a whore, she smelled like lilacs, in fact, but Radric didn't have any question in his mind whether or not she'd cut him from gap to gullet like a gutted fish.

"I'm strictly a business man."

Radric released his grip and the blade disappeared. As she backed away, he thought he saw a brooch beneath her cloak. It was only a glimpse, but it looked like a sunburst.

She stepped away and stared back blankly in the dark. Radric wished he could see her. He hoped she was beautiful, expected it.

"What's the job?"

"You're a messenger, right?"

Radric chuckled. "I guess that's one way to put it."

She didn't seem to agree with his sense of humor. "You take things from one location and put them in another. A simple messenger."

He perked up at the last bit. "Simple? You'd best not think my services are cheap." He found his voice rising at the end, much louder than he intended.

Then he sensed a subtle shift from the woman. "Apologies. My intent was not to insult."

But you did, he wanted to retort, but kept his mouth shut. The price for his services were not cheap, but he was low on funds, despite the denarius he got from the boy soldier. Living his lifestyle required a steady income.

"So what's the job? This delivery you want."

She shoved something into his stomach. She moved quicker than he expected. A wooden box of some sort. It fit in his hand and was rectangular. There was just enough light present that he could tell it was painted, but he could tell nothing else. Something shifted inside, maybe more than one object, or a material. Dust, maybe. Did she want a poisoning?

"You'll be taking it to the palace."

It was Radric's turn to get angry. "Palace? I may not be a simple messenger, but that's impossible. Those Northmen would cut me open and put a rat in my belly if they caught me."

"I thought you could do it?" There was a hint of playfulness in her tone that he didn't like.

"I can, but do I want to?"

"What if I can get you past the outer guards and payment is triple?"

"Triple?" When he said the word, he knew he would do it. His fee was high enough, but triple would set him up for a year. Radric thought of all the whores he could have for that fee.

But then he realized the implications of what she'd said. If she could get him in, then she was royalty of some kind, or at least a noble. And he didn't like the sound of that. Radric played the games he knew, the royal's game was not one he cared to play. For all he knew, she could be using him as bait, so she could get credit for catching him, to gain favor with the Northman Satrap they called Agog.

But triple the fee was...

"Will you do it, or not?" He could hear the finality in her tone.

"Yes," he answered as his balls cinched against his groin. Her tone and the job cured him of his lust.

"When?"

"Five days hence, mid-morning. Meet me at the Temple of Artemis near the pier and dress like a well-kept slave."

"Five days? I know what's going on in five days." Triple the fee wasn't going to be enough.

"Don't back out on me now. It's a simple job. Just a delivery."

Radric was thinking of far off cities he'd always wanted to visit when she added, "If you're not there, then I'll double what I'm paying you as a bounty on your head."

She shoved another object into his gut. Coins clinked together.

"A little upfront to keep you happy while you wait. I'll give you the rest of your instructions and your fee when I get you in. Don't forget to bring the box."

Radric opened his mouth to answer, but she was gone, like a shadow fading into the night. He'd never felt so confused by a woman in his life, another reason he stuck strictly to whores.

Five days. He knew what was going on in five days and didn't like it. He never minded being used for the right price, but he suspected that he wasn't getting paid enough, but there was no backing out now. In five days, he would make his delivery for the mystery woman, and after five days, anything could happen.

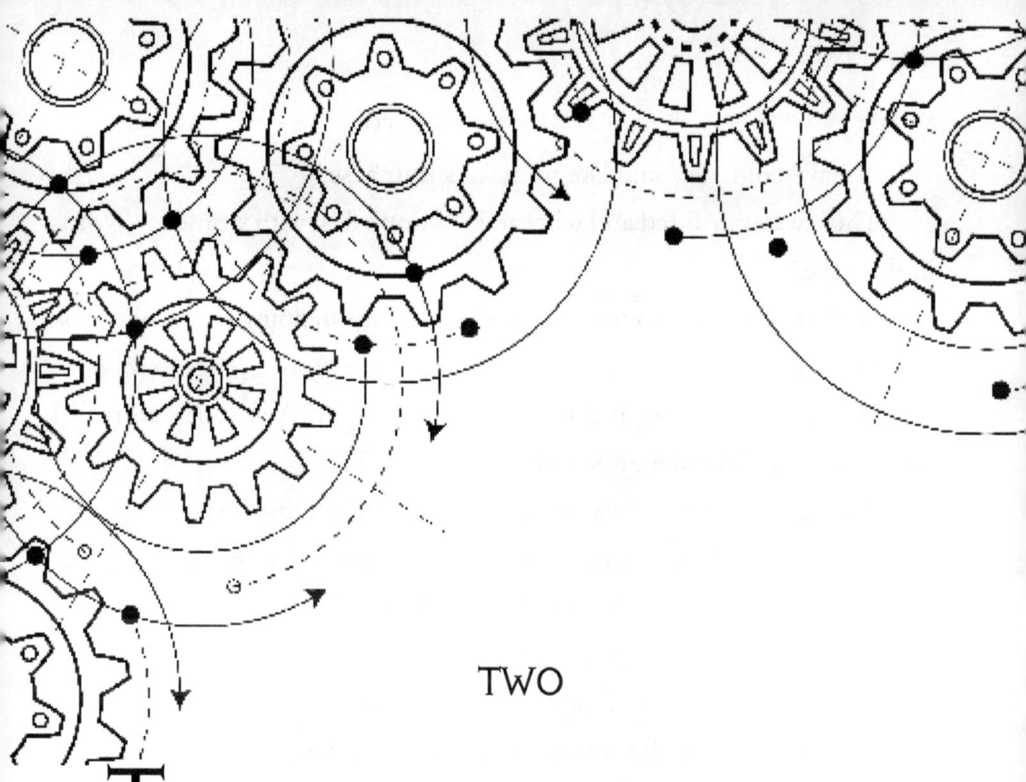

TWO

The door squealed as Sepharia entered The Opal Eye. An Egyptian man in tan robes hunched over the counter with a carving needle. The faint smell of chemicals hung in the air. The merchant's head bobbed up briefly and his eyes hardened, deepening wrinkles.

"You're in the wrong place." He buried his focus into the mounting plate. A cranberry agate fit into the slender base.

She stepped to the counter. The man wheezed slightly, an affliction common to jewelers.

"I need to purchase zinc and nickel. Just a sextula's worth." In preparation for the visit, Sepharia had worn her soldering leathers.

He glanced at her tunic before returning to his work. "There are no women jewelers."

The shop was smaller than most. A scale sat next to a locked cabinet. Tiny weights were lined up like soldiers. A curtain blocked the back room. She'd picked this shop because it didn't get much business and might be inclined to deal with her. She had to start somewhere.

"I have coin. I would like to make a purchase."

The jeweler grunted and wheezed. "I don't deal with women. Or girls in this case."

Sepharia took a step toward the door before stepping back. She took a deep breath.

"Only a bit of zinc and nickel, if you have it. A sextula's worth. I have coin and I'm not a good barterer."

The second grunt was a version of the jeweler's dismissive laugh. He nodded towards the door, not even bothering to look at her as he spoke, "Selling you those minerals would be a waste. I'd rather make less profit on someone who can properly use it."

Sepharia bit back the responses that flew through her head. She stayed at the counter despite the additional clearings of the throat.

"I'll just have someone else come back and purchase these minerals for me," she said.

He chuckled. "And I'll know it's you by the request made. Logic flees from womanly endeavors. Stick to what women are good at, having babies and spreading their legs."

The comforts of the workshop seemed so far away. The sounds of the carving needle shaving lines into the agate could be heard over the noises of the street. A horse-drawn wagon rattled past. She could hear the warp in the axle, probably bent from having too much sulfur in the iron.

"Breeders acid and extract of lemon," she said firmly.

The jeweler's forehead knotted. "I said there are no..." He tilted his head. "What did you say?"

"Breeders acid and extract of lemon. You're cleaning the lime from carnelian stones." She indicated the cranberry agate in the mounting plate. "That is a *glyptic* stone and it appears you're carving a scarab into it. Possibly to sell to the Egyptian nobles who wish to court longer life, since there's going to be a war with Rome."

The jeweler stared for a good long while, dark eyes blank with thought. Sepharia was about to leave when he pulled a key from a chain around his neck and unlocked the cabinet. He measured out strips of zinc and nickel, placed them in a wrapping of leather, and gave her the price.

She paid without bartering, quickly collected the minerals, and left the store. The jeweler never stopped staring at her. Down the next street, she imagined he was still looking at the door.

With the purchase safely tucked into her belt, she practically skipped back toward the workshop. The streets echoed the few travelers upon them. The Rhakotis District had few jewelers, most resided near the Emporium. The Opal Eye was right near the district slums. Sepharia went well around them to avoid trouble.

A heated bartering session between a merchant and a fair-skinned slaver with a trio of Gauls on his chains took up the middle of the street. Sepharia hugged the wall. The distraction kept her from noticing the two men following her until one grabbed her by the hair.

Sepharia was yanked into the alleyway. Her scream was stifled by a calloused hand over her mouth. She bit down on the palm, tearing flesh.

He hit her with a short club upside the head. Her ear exploded in pain. Spots formed across her vision as she crumpled to her knees.

A knife whispered from its sheath. The second man advanced. He wore a tunic but no other discernable markings. Sepharia tried to scramble to her feet, but she was kicked in the gut and thrown backwards onto the cobblestones. Her hair yanked upward as the man with the knife set the blade against her neck.

"The gods see fit to judge you for your father's crimes," said the man. "The world will fall to chaos without slaves to oil its gears."

Sepharia grabbed his wrist, but he was too strong. He looked upon her like a priest over a sacrifice. Blood ran into her eyes.

The muscles in his arm tensed. Sepharia expected the blade's kiss.

His arm loosened and she pushed him away, confused.

When she looked up, she saw a bolt sticking from his neck. Swords rang with purpose. A man grunted and died. Sepharia wiped the blood from her eyes and tried to stand. Her legs were watery.

"This girl should know she is safe now," said a voice in Greek with a particular Egyptian accent. It was lyrical and calm.

"Thank you." A man helped her to her feet. Not the man who spoke, but one who appeared to be his bodyguard.

"I am Ramses and you are Sepharia, the *Michanikos'* daughter." He wore a traditional Egyptian tunic under a long cloak. His bodyguard wore light leathers and had the hardened eyes of a mercenary.

"How do you know me?" she asked.

Ramses glanced at the dead men. "Let us be away from here. While my station protects me from events like these, I'd prefer not to cause entanglements. Take my arm and I will escort this girl to her home."

Walking eased the shaking in her legs. She held a strip of cloth to her head to staunch the bleeding.

Ramses spoke, "This girl is well known to me. I am an advisor to the Satrap and it is my business to know people. I only wished to have a brief conversation and then we saw those men following. Did they say anything of importance?"

Sepharia explained. Ramses nodded along, concerned.

"Yes," he said. "This girl's father garners much dislike for his stance against slavery. Egypt was built upon the might of their labors. He might as well wish to divert the Nile with his boot."

"My father wants the Satrap to change that, but he won't listen to the arguments anymore," she said.

Ramses nodded regretfully. "Ruling is an exercise in compromise. The Northman is wise. He needs the support of the city so he cannot change their ways too much."

"If he makes it a decree then they would have to do it," she replied.

Ramses shrugged. "And lose the support of half his nobles. The *Michanikos* is loved by the people but despised by those same nobles. Especially when he allows his daughter to do a man's work." Ramses raised his eyebrow.

"If I can do the same work as a man, why should I not?" she asked.

He patted her hand. "This girl does not have to explain to me. I understand these pains. But it is the way the world works. Only women like Cleopatra can do as they please."

"But common women like myself must hide our abilities." The words stewed in her mind.

"Ahh..." said Ramses, "we are here. Safe as stone, this girl has returned home."

Sepharia touched her belt. "By the gods, I lost my purchase. It must have fallen out when they attacked."

"A minor inconvenience easily remedied. This girl should be pleased to still be breathing."

"Apologies," she said, feeling foolish. "You saved my life and I'm complaining. I am in your debt."

Ramses scoffed. "It is my pleasure. Your father has done much for Alexandria, freeing it from the yoke of Roman rule. I would still be exiled in the south if it weren't for his efforts."

She paused before going in. "Apologies. I have another favor to ask."

"Please." He indicated she should speak by lifting his hand, palm up.

"Do not tell my father, or anyone, about what happened. I would lose what little freedom I have," she said.

Ramses smiled. "This girl should not worry. I will keep this secret."

They gave their farewells and Sepharia entered the workshop. She snuck into her room after grabbing a pail of water and a clean rag. Once she'd removed the blood from her hair, she changed clothes and thought about what Ramses the exile had told her.

Only women like Cleopatra can do as they please. While her father pushed the nobles to renounce slavery, she would always be in danger. As much from the nobles as from Agog, who could trade their allegiance for Heron's life. And she would never be able to live the life she wanted without power of her own. Thoughts coalesced around a plan, one which would only put her in more danger.

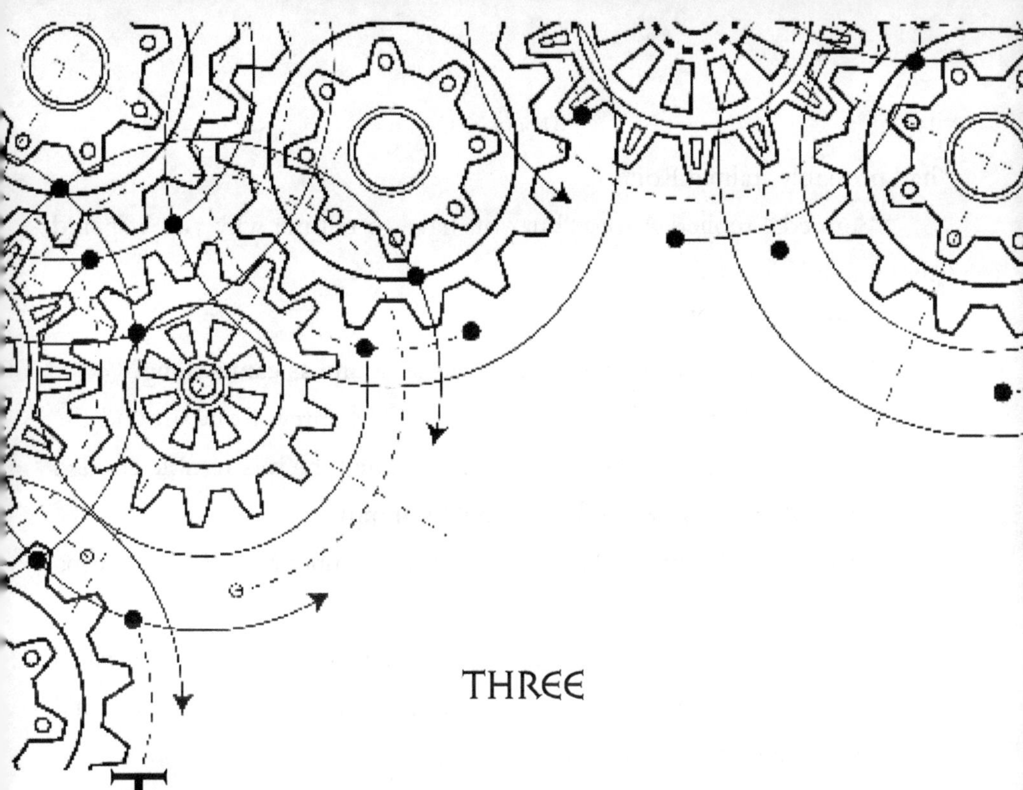

THREE

Two men grappled in the dirt while Agog looked on. He sat upon a smooth marble wall enjoying wine from a goblet. His attendants would silently scold him for spilling wine on his tunic, but getting on top of the wall had been more difficult than he planned.

"A talent on the tall one," said Agog between drinks. "Byrge, right? He looks like he's handling that chubby cousin of yours quite well."

Jarngard nodded. He was perched across from Agog on a squat pillar, cross-legged and rolling his bone dice between his legs. Years of war and adventure were marked on his friend's face: broken nose, nicked ear, a faint scar across the forehead where a jarl had tried to take his scalp off with an axe. Jarngard's cold, blue eyes flicked up briefly before returning to the dice. The laugh from his friend was rooted in anything but mirth.

"Make that five talents," said Jarngard.

Agog narrowed his gaze, trying to figure out why Jarngard would risk so much when it was clear his cousin, Rone, was losing the wrestling match. He considered that Jarngard himself was a superior wrestler and had probably trained Rone.

"Agreed," replied Agog, "but you have to tell me why you wagered that much if you win."

"Only if I win?" Jarngard winked.

"If you lose, then your judgment was as sound as camel dung."

The taller Byrge had a longer reach and he threw Rone around the field. Rone was on his back half the time, though he was nimble enough to roll out of the way before Byrge could pin him.

Agog glanced at his soldiers standing on the upper row of seats. Agog had been drinking with his Northmen in the agora when the two men had challenged each other to a wrestling match and though wrestling was a time honored tradition that the Greeks and Romans respected, he could see the sour looks even from this distance.

He'd been speaking in Greek to test his companion, but switched to Germanic so that even if the wind carried his voice, the soldiers would not understand.

"They think they're better than us," said Agog, sipping from his goblet.

Jarngard pointed toward the two combatants as if he were cheering them on. "I hope so."

"Why, friend?"

Jarngard nodded toward the wrestlers. When Byrge shuffled forward, readying himself for a throw that he'd performed a couple of times already in the match, Rone leapt to the side, and grabbed Byrge in an unorthodox arm lock. No sooner was the taller Northman's arm captured, did Rone roll onto his back, flipping Byrge over. Dust puffed out from beneath the taller man as he hit the ground like a brick. Rone casually put his hand on Byrge's barely moving chest. He was stunned by the impact and Jarngard's chubby cousin had won.

Agog pulled the coins from his purse and threw them haphazardly in Jarngard's direction. His companion caught a couple and threw one to Rone.

"They will underestimate us, just like Byrge did Rone," Jarngard said after a time.

Agog shook his head. "Not a second time. The only thing keeping the Romans from rushing down here and putting a stop to our uprising is having their troops committed in the Britons."

"We have the miracle worker." Jarngard raised his eyebrows, which Agog found comical. His friend's normally straw colored hair had turned chalky white in the southern sun.

"Heron's talents will mean nothing if the city turns against us. I wish Rome would send another army our way so we could defeat it. Strength begets power."

"Your marriage?"

Agog knew Jarngard's opinion on the upcoming wedding. He didn't see the need for marrying a strange southern woman.

He switched back to Germanic. "It will help with the Jewish quarter, but the Egyptians want to bring back the pharaohs, and the remaining Romans, though they have dutifully professed their allegiance, would rather offer my head to Claudius."

"Then remove theirs first," said Jarngard with an eager smile.

"I would, but I need them. When Alexander the Macedonian took his empire, he used those that pledged their fealty to his cause." Agog took a long drink and then wiped his mouth on his arm. "However, if Titus Claudius Vestalis gives me any reason to doubt him, I will send in the royal torturers."

Jarngard seemed genuinely surprised. "You have royal torturers?"

"No, but for that man, I would gladly anoint some. He vexes me at each turn, though I cannot prove it so. If it weren't for his riches and connections, I would have had him killed when I took the city."

"Why don't we just take his gold?"

"He moved it right after the war," said Agog. "Now he just uses it to buy influence with the others."

His companion started humming to himself and then the humming turned to a melody and then it slipped into laughter. Before long, Jarngard was practically rolling off the top of the pillar.

"What is so funny?"

"Nothing, o' King of Kings."

Agog narrowed his gaze. He didn't know what Jarngard was getting at, but he knew what would end his mood.

"I have an errand for you."

Jarngard tucked his dice into the leather bag around his neck, hopped onto his feet, and bowed with a keen smirk on his face.

"What is it, Your Grace?"

"We have an old friend and ally coming to visit."

Jarngard's face brightened like a light had been shone on it. "I thank the gods for this news. There aren't enough of us in this odd city. I have little hope for these people when they have statues that spit water when they could spit beer. Who comes?"

Jarngard's smile faltered when Agog spoke. "Hoth the Black."

"Hoth?" Jarngard stomped his foot and nearly fell off. "You said friend and ally and that man is neither!"

"He's an ally if he has brought me his ships," said Agog through tight lips. "When the Romans turn their attention to us, we'll need his ships if we want to survive."

Jarngard turned back and forth on his pillar, since he didn't have room to pace. If blue eyes could burn red, his would have. Agog waited for him to settle down.

"Can't we buy ships? Commandeer the traders?" asked Jarngard. "Anyone but him."

"We don't have enough gold for that, unless we can turn Vestalis to our side. The Phoenicians are the only ones with enough ships to matter and if the Romans send the fleet down, we'll find our harbor empty."

Jarngard gripped his dice bag and shook his head, looking like he was trying to dislodge some internal demon.

"I know I ask much of you, my friend."

"You remember he took my wife?" It was both questioning and accusatory.

"I do," said Agog. "Which is why I need you to go to him and delay him from entering the city. He's camped a day west of here with a few of his ships."

"Send one of the others: Grimm, Quadi, or Agnar."

Agog shook his head regretfully. "Hoth will run them over with words. I need cleverness, not rage or intellect."

"Then why do you need me to keep him from entering the city if you need his help?" His companion's eyes were glazed with pain.

"I don't want the Romans to know we have ships." Agog paused, the next part would be more difficult to hear, and he didn't know how his friend would take it. "And I don't want him to be in the city during the ceremony. You know how he is, he'll cause problems."

"Of course, *Your Grace.*" Jarngard bowed, low and dutiful.

He hated doing this to his friend, but it had to be. Hoth wouldn't listen to anyone else and the history between the two men would ensure the sea captain would stay in camp. After all, he'd taken Jarngard's woman after a great battle when Hoth's ships had saved them from the Gauls. Hoth had been drunk on victory and Jarngard recovering from a spear wound.

When Hoth's ships set sail for the Balts, she went with him. His friend had taken up the bone dice after that and Agog never dared to ask why he hadn't killed Hoth and taken her back.

"Care to bet again," asked Jarngard after a time, the earlier jovial mood absent. "Ten talents this time."

Agog clicked his tongue in agreement. "Of course, my friend."

Before the match, Jarngard motioned to Rone and whispered in his ear. Then the combatants faced off, circling around each other with arms wide, ready to engage.

Agog glanced to his friend, who wasn't even watching the match. He was staring towards the sea. Agog turned his attention back to Rone and Byrge, thinking it was going to be a long match, when Rone nimbly shuffled forward and nailed Byrge between the eyes with his fist. The taller man crumpled into a heap.

"You'd better do that to the Romans when they come."

Jarngard hopped from the pillar and stormed off, without getting paid. Rone followed his cousin while Byrge lie knocked out in the dirt.

The soldiers along the outer ring of the agora seemed confused by the punctuated match.

Agog nodded to no one in particular. *Yes, I'd better. Or we'll all end up much worse than Byrge.*

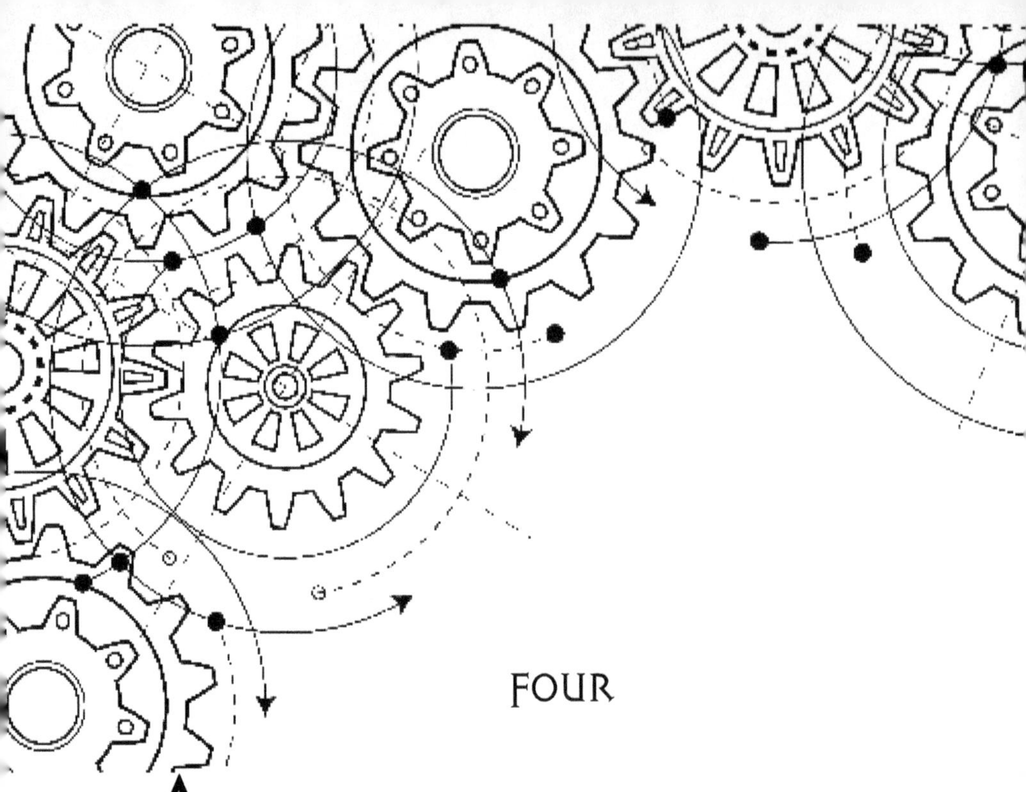

FOUR

Autumn breezes spun the bronze wind catchers, as workers toiled beneath the famous workshop's tarry roof. The interior matched the city of Alexandria in its bustle and confusion, as men scrambled over scaffoldings with hammers gripped in fists and fasteners clenched in teeth.

Heron tugged at her ink-stained tunic and glared at the frustrating hunk of metal on the table. It was supposed to be the newest version of the steam mechanic. During the last test run, the protective casing had belched out a geyser of steam, roasting the tender thigh of one of her workers. Plutarch had rushed the man to the apothecary, but she could still hear the screaming in her head.

She tugged again at her tunic, chaffing against the binding beneath, the one that held her womanly breasts back, and kept the secret of her gender safe. Normally, she didn't think much about the bindings or the fake genitalia between her legs, but the problems of the workshop knocked her thoughts off course, and she found herself annoyed by even the smallest things.

The barbarian's demands were at fault. *The Satrap of Alexandria*, she corrected herself. Agog wasn't the barbarian anymore. By Plato, he wasn't even Agog to his men. They kept calling him Wodanaz.

But no matter what he was called, he'd been furious when he learned Rome had acquired a number of intact steam mechanicals. Her clever protections had been undone by someone more clever than her. Even after the purges, Agog admitted that the city was ripe with Roman loyalists.

But that didn't protect her from his wrath. She'd liked him better when he wasn't the Satrap. He wanted the steam mechanicals outfitted with her newest design, one that she was entirely not pleased with.

Heron preferred her designs to have a certain efficiency of motion. Too much complexity would only introduce variables that she couldn't control. Not with the precision of her tools. And despite her high standards, the newest design was as elegant as an elephant dancing to Dionysus' flute.

Despite her foul mood, the work continued around her. The workshop had never been filled with so many projects. Half the time she couldn't remember designing them, even when they were almost complete.

A pair of golden lion statues that roared were in the final stages. Agog wanted them placed at the entrance to the palace to impress dignitaries. A new automata play was being constructed near the courtyard. It told the story of Agog's conquest to the commoners in the streets. A counting machine was ready to be delivered to the Library along with a bronze statue of Alexander on Bucephalas that was being assembled in the workshop annex.

There were other contraptions scattered around the room, most of them personally requested by Agog. Normally, she wouldn't mind applying her creativity to such projects. The designs she'd labored over should fill her with joy, except that it felt like a different version of the same thing she'd been doing for the temples.

Last time she'd spoken to the Satrap, she'd argued for building more war machines like the steam chariots, but he wouldn't hear it. He kept telling her that Rome was busy fighting a war in the Britons Isles and he needed to focus on the loyalty of Alexandria.

In truth, she liked making war machines as much as she liked making the other oddities, but her head was on the chopping block as much as Agog's. Her status as a renowned inventor would help about as much as it helped Archimedes when Rome invaded Syracuse. He ended up dead on a soldier's spear.

"Heron! Father!" Sepharia's lyrical voice could be heard over the clanking and banging. Her daughter, wearing glass blowing leathers, floated through the clutter like a winged goddess, albeit a dirt-smudged one.

Sepharia relished the changes in the city. The demise of Roman rule, and especially the customs collector Lysimachus, freed her from being sequestered in the workshop. Though the city wasn't as safe as her daughter believed. Heron worried every time the girl left the safety of the workshop.

"You're nearly taller than I am now."

"Almost, Father."

Heron hugged her daughter and smiled at the title. Since saving Sepharia from the Cult of Ur, she'd never faltered from calling her that. Whatever conflicts they had before had been wiped away.

"Can you come look at something for me?"

Heron tensed. Sepharia had a certain sparkle in her eyes that Heron didn't trust. "Only if you can show me your progress on the lelathon cabinet."

Her daughter led her to the craft room. This was Sepharia's domain. Three Egyptians - two women and a man - and a nimble-fingered boy worked at the tables, using delicate hammers on tiny objects.

A kiln rested along the wall. Massive brick-lined ducts led from Punt's foundry next door and could feed the glass oven with heat when Sepharia removed the shutters.

Resting on the far side of the room, well away from the warping heats of the oven, the lelathon cabinet seemed out of place. Her workshop had not made the delicate woodcraft, but the modification made it a prized possession of the noble class.

A bust of Artemis was painted on the front. The goddess was leaning on her bow amid a lush forest. Heron looked inside, feeling around the dark wood.

After her inspection, she turned to Sepharia, who had been watching quietly. "Either your mechanism failed or you hid the trigger well."

Sepharia stepped to the cabinet, put one hand on either side of the inner walls and pushed outward. There was an audible click and the back of the cabinet swung open. A space to hide jewelry and valuables was revealed.

Heron moved to the back of the cabinet. Gears and sprockets filled the space. Her eye was drawn to a double lever attached to two gears. She poked the brass lever with her finger before addressing Sepharia.

"Your gear craft has grown cunning. That was an ingenious way to link the two sides of the cabinet trigger," said Heron.

Her daughter was beaming but it didn't seem to be about the lelathon cabinet. "My thanks, but..."

"But, what?"

Sepharia handed Heron a piece of folded cloth. It held an object that could fit in the palm of her hand. Heron unwrapped it, keeping her gaze on her daughter the whole time. Sepharia looked ready to burst.

Heron gasped when she saw the golden scarab in the middle of the cloth. The look of victory on Sepharia's face was troubling, but Heron ignored it for the moment to examine the brooch.

Instantly, Heron knew the exquisite brooch was Sepharia's best work.

The scarab was realistic yet stylized, making it appealing the eye. Heron had never liked the insects but they were sacred in Egypt so she kept her opinion guarded.

Behind the scarab was a sixteen pointed starburst that Heron recognized from her childhood in Macedonia. It was the Vergina Sun, a symbol of Alexander not normally seen in Alexandria. A subtle nod to the city's founding.

Heron could feel designs on the back with her fingertips, so she flipped it over to find a symbol she'd never seen before. A fully-formed leafless tree with all its branches splayed out like a lightning burst took up the back of the circular brooch. Its branches were etched in white-gold.

"And what is this?"

Sepharia touched the etched tree. "Jarngard told me about it. Said it was an important symbol for Agog."

Heron raised an eyebrow. "And what does it mean?"

"Other than its name, Yggdrasil, he wouldn't say."

"It's dangerous to make symbols you don't understand."

Sepharia nodded. "That's why I put it on the back. It's for Agog only."

"So you mean to give it to him?"

Sepharia nodded again and Heron could sense that whatever stratagem her daughter was employing was coming to a head. Sepharia's face practically twitched with excitement.

"And when do you plan to do this? The Satrap of Alexandria is very busy these days."

"At the *Erusin* ceremony."

There. Now she knew what her daughter was getting at. Heron led Sepharia to the foundry's pattern storage room so they could have a private conversation.

"For you to give it to him, you would have to be present."

"Yes." Sepharia grinned wickedly.

Heron glanced at the brooch again. It was of the highest quality. To deny her daughter the chance for royal acknowledgement after all that work would be shameful. But there was a question of safety and also...

Heron narrowed her gaze at Sepharia.

"Why did you make this? I know your orders are overflowing. This would have taken considerable time and effort to make. I do not believe that you made this brooch, however skillfully, just to watch our barbarian Satrap be engaged to that Jewish woman." Heron tapped a finger against her lips. "And I'm not even sure how such a gift from a beautiful young woman would be received. I am unfamiliar with this Jewish custom of engagement."

When Sepharia smiled and her ear twitched, Heron knew that whatever her daughter was going to say next would be a lie. "I just want to thank him for freeing us from the Romans."

"Hrmph." Heron studied Sepharia's womanly curves and the way her chest wanted to burst from the glass-blowing leathers. "Or is it a ploy to remind our Satrap that you are a beautiful young woman?"

A moment of conflict passed across Sepharia's eyes. "But what's wrong with that?"

Heron resisted the urge to shake Sepharia. It would do no good to battle with her on this subject.

"Besides that, we are not royalty."

"That didn't matter for Agog," said Sepharia. "He took the city by force. Why shouldn't he get to pick who he wants? And who better than the daughter of Heron the inventor."

"Our barbarian has to pick the person that best shores up his support. He's playing the game of royals and he needs the Jewish quarter. Plus, Princess Shayna is said to have connections to an old sect of the Jewish Exilarch, so she's important beyond the walls of Alexandria."

Sepharia turned her back and walked a few steps. Her shoulders were hunched over.

"Do you really want to give up your freedom?" asked Heron. "Here in the workshop, you can do what you want. A princess or a queen must constantly be on her guard."

Heron put her hand on her daughter's shoulder. A flinch made Heron frown. "Power and freedom are like a balancing scale. Put too many weights on one side and the other goes in the opposite direction."

Sepharia spun around. Her eyes blazed. "I know, *Father*. But for us women, it's different. We have neither power or freedom."

Heron took a step back. The words were a spear in her gut. Her daughter wasn't wrong. Otherwise, she wouldn't have to be Heron and could have just been Ada.

Sepharia's barb hurt because she'd insinuated that Heron was no longer a woman. Beneath the bindings and the fake genitalia she was still a woman, but in practice and station she was not. Heron enjoyed most of the benefits of being a man while her daughter would have to be subjected to the trials of being a woman.

Was it so wrong that Sepharia wanted to play the royal's game? Heron looked her daughter up and down. Physically, she was old enough, but could she survive the scheming? Either way, no lecture would dissuade Sepharia, Heron could see that in the way her daughter's shoulders were pulled back and her chin was held high. Sepharia would have to see it for herself to know. There would be no harm in the gift.

Heron closed her eyes for a moment. She couldn't believe she was saying this. "You may attend the *Erusin* ceremony and you may give your gift to Agog, but you must do it at the proper time and not in front of Princess Shayna."

Sepharia hugged Heron. "Thank you, Father."

Heron sighed. "Maybe at some later date, we can find you an appropriate husband, who will appreciate your unique skills. But until then, you need to learn a few things, especially before you attend the ceremony."

Heron found herself standing in the formal lecture pose of the Great Library, and in that moment, she thought she heard a loud noise from outside the workshop. Maybe the ground had shaken too, but she was so focused on Sepharia she wasn't sure. Probably someone had dropped an ingot in the foundry.

"Anything," replied Sepharia, clearly not noticing the noise either. Her student was eager, at least. She wondered how long that would continue.

"I'll send a runner to the Library to fetch some scrolls for you to read. A history of our Macedonian ancestors will be a good start. And the Egyptian Ptolemies. The Ptolemies did an excellent job of co-opting local customs, a skill our barbarian Satrap has learned well."

Heron continued for a few minutes, listing various scrolls of history that detailed the scheming, murder, and backstabbing that went along with trying to rule. She wanted her daughter to have no illusions about what she was asking. When Heron was done, Sepharia was still smiling eagerly.

"And all these scrolls need to be read before the ceremony."

To her credit, Sepharia only flinched slightly. They hugged again and Sepharia returned to the craft shop.

Heron would need to get the request for scrolls sent to the Library right away if Sepharia was going to have enough time to read them. Even then, that really wouldn't prepare her for life in the Palace, and Heron figured that after she spent time there with that bevy of self-serving nobles, she'd want to return to the workshop and enjoy the freedoms provided.

But Heron didn't have long to think about her daughter when a runner came in sweaty and worry-faced.

"*Michanikos.*" The runner bowed.

"Out with it. I sense the graveness of your need."

"Nektam's workshop," he said, eyes darting with concern.

Heron dug her fingernails into her palm. She could sense what he was going to say next. Nektam was well-respected in the city for his industrious workshop. While they didn't always see eye-to-eye, his support of her newest steam mechanicals had eased grumbling from the lesser shops and gotten them to accept the design.

"Plato have pity, speak, boy."

"His shop," he said apologetically, "it's gone. Something blew it up."

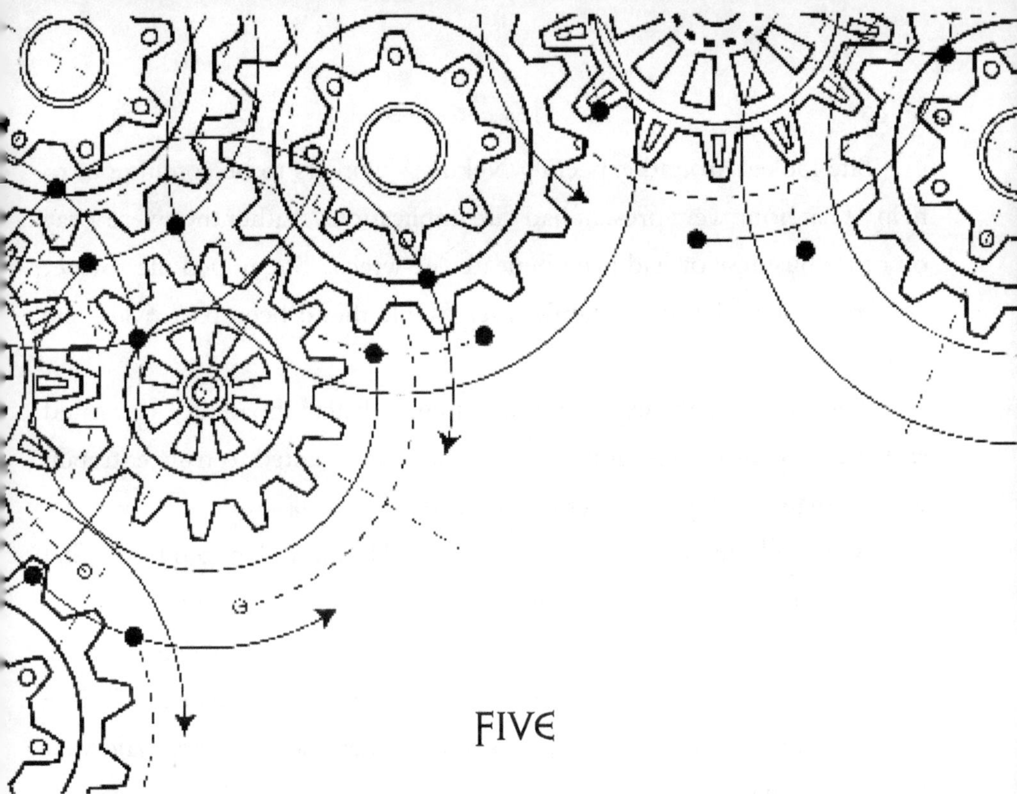

FIVE

Nektam's workshop was a smoking ruin when she arrived. Half the roof had collapsed. From her vantage point on the street, Heron could see at least two bodies. Moaning came from the rubble, though she couldn't pinpoint their locations.

Iron supports creaked with implications. The remaining roof teetered, bits of stone breaking loose.

"Some are still alive," said Punt gruffly.

Even a gentle breeze could collapse the final structure. Stepping through the ruins, Heron could see the injured men, lying in blood beneath the swaying roof.

"That's going to fall," she said, glancing around. "Punt, find me a rope or chain. One taller than this roof."

Punt moved through the broken building, digging through stone and metal. Heron approached the structure carefully. A twisted beam connected the broken portion to the rest of the workshop.

She looked around expecting Nektam's workers to be coming out to help. That none were present had dire implications. Either they were away on other business or had been beneath the wreck. She hoped the former was true, especially in Nektam's case. While they'd been past rivals, she respected his work.

The source of the explosion wasn't immediately apparent. Her mind reeled with possibilities, none of them ones she wanted to truly entertain with Roman sabotage numbering the worst.

A snap alerted her to the shifting roof. Heron took a step back. She wasn't entirely out of the danger area. Injured moaning continued from the wreckage. Punt returned with a long bark rope coiled around his arm.

"Give me an end with enough length to tie around this beam." She surveyed the area behind them. "Take the other end over there and wait for my command to pull. If we do this right, the roof will fall away from those men."

Punt's forehead was knotted with concern. "The roof might fall while you're tying it. Let me do that."

"No time," she said. "You don't know which crossbeam to throw it over. Go quickly."

He unrolled the rope as he stepped backwards. Heron took the slack and hefted the end. The rope was too light and flimsy to make it over the crossbeam. She found a piece of steel in the wreckage. It looked like a construction rod and would have to do.

While she tied the rope around the rod, the pillar groaned and whined. The roof looked ready to fall. Heron swung the rope in a circle once and launched it up and over. The rod clanged against the beam and fell down.

"Plato have pity."

Heron reeled the rod back and swung again, this time it flew over the crossbeam. She gave it slack and collected the rod, stepping beneath the crumbling roof.

With the care of a midwife, Heron wrapped the rope around the beam and cinched the knot. She stepped back through the wreckage toward Punt. Gawkers joined them near the rope.

"You three," she commanded, "grab that rope with Punt."

There was some hesitation, but the look she gave them snapped them to order and they filed in behind Punt like soldiers. The structure groaned and a sub-beam snapped somewhere.

"Pull now!" she yelled. "Pull hard and run backwards."

They nearly tripped over themselves, but were able to pull the line taut. More beams snapped and tarry stone chips fell like rain.

"Harder! Now!"

When the crossbeam snapped, she thought the men beneath were going to be crushed. The roof teetered and swayed, finally moving in the direction of the rope. The crash was deafening and dust billowed out.

Once the crashing had subsided, she listened for moaning. She was rewarded with a cry for help. At that moment, men from her workshop finally arrived, she directed them into the wreckage to help the fallen.

With the workers directed, Heron asked Punt a question, "What do you think caused it? At first I thought it might have been a steam mechanical, but even when mine blew, it didn't cause that much damage."

Punt nodded his head. "That's true." He pointed to a blackened wave of metal that was still faintly glowing on the far side. "The foundry is gone."

Heron nodded. "You know your craft best, what do you see?"

She tried not to think about the possibility that it was sabotage. The Romans still had many spies in the city. But having knowledge and opportunity enough to disrupt one of her steam mechanicals was difficult.

"See how the metal shoots away from the melting furnace?"

Heron nodded again. Like long black fingers, the hardening iron had shot from the metal bath.

"Water had gotten under the surface of the metal." Punt grunted, probably a moment of empathy for the foundrymen, for water and liquid metal don't mix. "When it turned to steam, it threw the bath everywhere."

"If the steam mechanical was somehow thrown into the metal bath, would that have caused it?"

Punt crossed his thick arms in thought. "Aye."

A scream of frustration erupted nearby. Nektam had returned to his workshop. The streets surrounding the fallen workshop were filled with onlookers. They backed away as Nektam flew like a spear at Heron.

Nektam was a towering pillar of muscle. He'd been a blacksmith before he started his own workshop. Nektam jammed a meaty finger into her shoulder.

"Your cursed steam mechanical did this!"

Heron took a deep breath. She needed the facts, but Nektam was clearly not in his thinking mind.

"Were there any witnesses to the explosion?"

Nektam jabbed his finger again. Punt stepped forward, angling so he could intervene but Heron gave him a sideways glance to tell him to keep back.

"Of course there were, but they're all dead!"

In the Alexandrian sun, and with his rage, Nektam's bronze skin was steaming.

"Not all are dead, a few survive and I will petition the Satrap for funds to compensate your losses."

"Losses? Funds?" Nektam threw his hands toward the heavens. "Petition the gods to return my workers. I cannot replace their knowledge, their skill, the memories of their craft that go right down to their bones!"

Heron knew he was right. She couldn't imagine if she ever lost Punt or Plutarch, or many of her other skilled workers. While she created the designs, they made them happen. Too often she'd made a design that she thought impossible, until her workers conjured it with steel and wood and sweat.

"I will lend you my workers and help you hire new ones. I promise I will find you the very best. Even if we have to bring them all the way from Persia or Parthia."

Nektam scoffed. "They will not come here. Not when Rome will soon be at our door." He pointed his finger at Heron's chest. "You will be the first one they kill after they gut that barbarian of yours."

Heron was glad all the Northmen were busy preparing for the ceremony. If one of them had been present, they would have taken great offense to Nektam's words.

"Nektam. Friend. I know you are angry. Deservedly so." Heron took a steadying breath. "But I need to know what caused it, so I can fix it. What were you using the steam mechanical for?"

The tall Egyptian's eyes glazed with thought while his mouth was still drawn tight in anger.

"The bellows," he said after a time. "We used it to stoke the fire blazing hot to make a special Noric steel."

Punt made a noise of appreciation next to her. Steel required specific ores and was harder to make than simple iron.

"Pump bellows?" asked Punt.

Nektam shook his head. "A pump bellows doesn't get the right air for good steel, nor does it make the metal hot enough. We need fresh air. So we pulled it from above the workshop, using a piston design to draw down the air through a long pipe."

Heron could envision the setup in her head. Including the placement of the steam mechanical.

"It was right next to the metal bath?"

Nektam's gaze flitted past her. He probably wouldn't acknowledge it, but she could see he had the same thought she had.

"The air velocity had to be high for the steel and we had to put it as close as we could."

Heron leaned on her cane and carefully considered her response. While Nektam had made a mistake in placement of his equipment, she couldn't fault him, either. Stronger steel would be a boon for the city. Even a modest increase in strength would allow for many new inventions. Her many failures had come from pushing her team to try new things. This could have just as easily been her failure.

And she was the Chief Engineer of Alexandria, tasked with the co-ordination of the workshops. She'd been so busy with her own work that she'd been neglecting to tour the city and confirm the safety and progress of the others.

"The explosion is my fault," said Heron finally. "The newest design of the steam mechanical is unstable. I'm certain the unbalancing caused by the shielding created a wobble that eventually threw it into the metal bath."

Nektam had lost his earlier rage, but he still smoldered, as did the remnants of the foundry. "And what will you do about it?"

"I will speak to the Satrap about the new design. We cannot have that instability, even if it protects the steam mechanical from Roman spies." Heron sighed ever so slightly. "And I will pay for the damages to your workshop and foundry myself until I can get the Satrap to pay for it from the royal coffers. And as I said earlier, lend you my workers to rebuild."

In truth, the royal coffers were empty. She knew that much. Even if Agog agreed with her request, he had no gold to pay her. Any gold he did have was being used to prepare for war. He didn't even have the gold to pay for the projects in her shop. But it would do no good for Nektam to know that and she certainly didn't want that knowledge to get to Rome.

Heron glanced around, almost expecting to see Roman spies watching. But there were no eyes on her except Nektam's. The onlookers were staring at the destruction. Her destruction. Born from the failure of her design.

"Send your men," said Nektam, "I begin rebuilding today."

Heron contained her sigh and nodded. Her work would grind to a standstill while his workshop was being rebuilt.

Nektam left, yelling commands to his surviving workers picking through the rubble.

"Master Heron?" asked Punt.

"Yes?"

The glistening head of her blacksmith was beaded with sweat. A rivulet shot down the side of his bronze head.

"What happens when Rome besieges us?"

Heron shrugged. "I don't know. But I do know we need gold. Both wars and workshops run on gold and we have none."

Punt glanced up. "What will you do?"

"I need business for my counting machines."

"Who will buy them?"

Punt grimaced when she said the name. "Titus Claudius Vestalis. He's the largest trader in Alexandria. If he buys one, then the others will as well, for fear of his advantage."

Heron turned and began walking back toward her workshop a few blocks away. She didn't need the cane as much these days, but her knees never felt quite right, either.

"But the counting machine doesn't work yet," said Punt, catching up to her.

"We'll send Plutarch with the workers to Nektam's. You and I have some work to do."

Punt nodded. And when they returned to the workshop, she'd send a runner to refill her box. She'd been trying not to rely on the violet dust so much, but she wouldn't be seeing much sleep in the next few days. She had to get the counting machine working before the ceremony so she could sell it to Vestalis there. Otherwise, without a new source of gold, all their plans would begin to unravel.

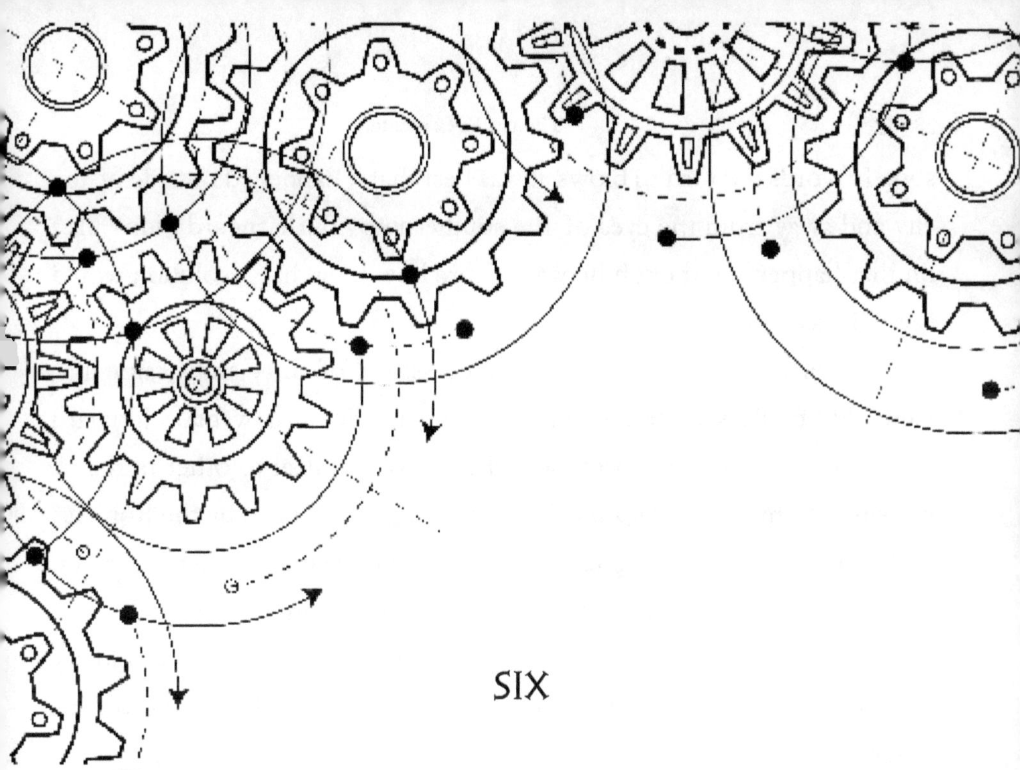

SIX

Dust and sand and shit. The gods must be japing, thought Jarngard, to send men to live in a land filled with bounties of all three. He missed the high country of the north, the green trees, the smell of pine, and the cold kiss of snow on his face.

Now he lived in a city packed with people, and though he was truthfully amazed by the sights, it was still built upon dust and sand and shit. He laughed because laughing was the only thing left he had these days.

Squeezing his thighs, he directed his mount off the trail to the north. He rode alone for speed and to enjoy a moment of desolation away from the city.

The ride also gave him space to think and to figure out how to keep Hoth the Black from wanting to march into the city and spoil Agog's engagement. Jarngard touched the leather pouch around his neck. Gods be damned, he whispered to himself, just as well he had to figure out how not to run him through when he saw him.

It occurred to Jarngard that Agog had sent him precisely for that reason. If words did turn to blows, it was best that it happened outside of the city and away from the eyes of the southerners. But Jarngard didn't plan on that happening, though he wasn't sure how long that resolution would last if he saw Nessa.

Cresting a rise, the tall masts and crosstrees of three ships came into view. He could see tents along the water in the shallow bay. Jarngard was glad that Hoth had wisely sent the rest of his fleet to other ports. A massing of ships near Alexandria would not go unnoticed by the Romans.

The wind was blowing into his face. Jarngard could smell roast rabbit and the crisp sea air. He could also smell another familiar sharp odor. As he neared a natural break in the earth, a place the commoners would say was from the gods dropping a knife from their dinner table, he slowed his horse.

"Ho, brothers! Why sail over that much water if you're never going to wash in it? I promise the seas are much warmer here than home."

Two men with bows stepped from behind the earthen break. On approach, he realized how young they were with light blond fuzz patchwork on their faces. Newer recruits that had probably never fought even one battle.

"We could have feathered you with a chest full of arrows," boasted the taller of the two.

Jarngard smiled at the speech of his folk. He'd grown tired of speaking in Latin or Greek all the time. Agog had been making him practice and they only used their own language when they wanted to keep something secret.

"Not likely with your stench," laughed Jarngard. "The occasional bath is the key ingredient to a good ambush. You might know that if you'd fought before."

Jarngard could see the truth of his words in their slumped shoulders. He began to worry that the ships he saw were the only ones that Hoth had brought.

"And how many battles have you fought?" the youth bravely asked.

The number was too high for him to quickly count. It might have been better to count the campaigns he'd been on.

"Enough times to have been near dead on more than one occasion. But enough talk, the Satrap's business is pressing. Which tent is Hoth the Black's?"

The bold youth pointed his bow toward the camp. "The far tent, upwind."

"Good lads. And next time when you pull your bow on a rider, keep your shoulders set straight. You would have both shot wide and I would have put my axes in your skulls before you could have reloaded."

Jarngard rode past and steeled himself for the reception he would receive in camp. The two youths didn't know him by face and he hadn't given them his name.

A clump of men were seated around a fire pit, pulling roast meat apart with their fingers and washing it down with mugs of beer. Some of them half-rose when he approached.

Jarngard took a deep breath and hopped off his horse, handing the reins to a sailor walking over to greet him. Jarngard recognized the man, though he couldn't remember his name.

Then he heard his own whispered name grow in volume like crickets at dusk. A rough hand clasped him by the shoulder, stopping him.

"Jarngard?"

He turned to find a familiar scarred face greeting him. "Tormod."

"Aye, friend. It's good to see you."

They grasped forearms. Jarngard had fought with Tormod before. He was a fearsome fighter with more bravery than sense. A scar traveled the length of the man's jaw where half his face had been torn off by a screaming Thracian.

"It's good to be seen, but I must be on my business." The others were gathering around. Jarngard wanted to get away before Hoth had been warned he was coming.

Tormod's forehead knotted with question. "Why would Wodanaz send you?"

"They call him Agog here and that's not for me to explain. I was sent, so here I am."

He pushed through the sailors, headed toward the largest tent on the far side of the camp. Jarngard hadn't seen any officers, so he assumed they were meeting with Hoth, which would only make his job harder.

When he pushed his way through the tent flap, the first thing he heard while his eyes were adjusting to the dim light was a sword being drawn. Jarngard didn't bother going for his axes. If they thought he was here for revenge, then he'd be dead before he reached them.

When his eyes finally did adjust, he saw many men he knew standing around a map on a table. Hoth the Black had changed little since he'd seen him last. He was not particularly large or skilled in battle, but men - and women - flocked to his side, or bed in the latter case.

Hoth, without breaking eye contact, motioned for his officers to leave. Jarngard braced himself as they left. Someone slammed a shoulder into his as they moved past.

"Did she put that in your hair?" They both knew exactly who *she* was.

Hoth touched the streak of black in his long blond hair. "This? No. When we burned down a Celt village, a burning beam fell against me and seared my hair. I became rather attached to the look." He seemed to shrug away his words.

"Is she here?" Jarngard tried to keep his tone level.

Hoth shook his head. "Nessa left me a year ago for a rich merchant. Said she couldn't live on a boat her whole life." The sea captain narrowed his eyes. "Still carrying those dice with you?"

The leather bag felt strangely cool to his touch. "The gods owe me." Nessa. He tasted her name on his lips.

"I did you a favor, you know. She was a fickle woman, full of pride, and gold ran through her fingers like water."

Jarngard noticed for the first time that Hoth was unarmed. It wouldn't take but a twitch of the arm to throw an axe into his skull.

"She was my wife."

Hoth stared back unflinchingly. "And I thought we resolved that."

His side ached where the spear had caught him, even though the wound was years old. He'd been wound weak when he had confronted Hoth. Things would have been different if he hadn't been injured in battle.

"You can't come into the city."

Hoth, who'd been pensive before, bristled like a badger. "Then why did he ask me here? I'm not his lieutenant to be given orders like a common dog. He's gotten my letters, he knows what I want."

"Agog needs the fleet to stay hidden for a while longer. It'll take time for you to contact your ships with the new plan." Jarngard threw a scroll onto the table. "His orders."

He knew he shouldn't be taunting him like this, but he was enjoying it.

"It won't take me any time at all to round up my ships and Wodanaz needs me more than I need him," said Hoth. "And besides my curiosity to view this City of Wonders and explore its magics, I wanted to see his woman before he bedded her."

Jarngard moved to the side of the table. "You'll get your chance. This is just the ceremony of engagement. The wedding will come in a month's time."

"A month? He should have his seed in her belly before then. The Romans won't be long after that."

His gut clenched. He could tell Hoth had news. "Is the Roman fleet moving?"

Hoth had a secret smile. "When we passed the Britons, I raided inland near the Romans and caught a pair of soldiers out whoring the countryside."

Jarngard could only imagine what Hoth had been raiding for. His black hulls were feared in the cold seas of the north.

"Did you not fear a battle?"

Hoth smirked, and Jarngard hated him for it. "The gods favored me with a dense fog. I brought the *Cloud Giant* an arrow shot away from their edge boats and they never saw us."

"A foolish endeavor." He said the words, but he did not believe them. Jarngard knew that Hoth took risks, but battles were not won by the timid. Hoth was unmatched in the fogs, through some sorcery he kept secret.

"The Britons aren't taken yet, but it appears Claudius doesn't want to wait. He's outfitting the navy for a southern jaunt. They plan on cutting off trade to Alexandria. Without the sea lanes open, the city will be withered by the time he brings his army for the siege."

Jarngard nodded. It made sense. "How long until the fleet arrives?"

Hoth shrugged. "Maybe three months, maybe less."

"The orders still stand." Jarngard tapped the scroll on the table. "We can't let them know we have any ships."

Hoth began laughing earnestly. "What does it matter? Their fleet is twenty times the size of mine. Unless your Satrap can shit out a navy, I won't be wasting my ships on his cause."

"The *Michanikos* has tricks for us." Jarngard knew of no new tricks, especially for a sea battle, but Hoth didn't have to know that.

Hoth's eyes lit up. "Yes, this miracle worker of yours. Metal soldiers that can fight and ghost horses? What gods does he follow so I might make an offering."

"None that I know of."

Hoth screwed up his face, visibly disturbed by the news. "No matter,

I still want to see these tricks."

"After the orders."

While picking up the scroll, Hoth smirked. "I suppose. But don't expect that I will wait much longer. I didn't sail past those blasted isles and the Roman fleet just so I could sleep on a tent in the sand."

"A room at the Palace awaits once the ceremony is done."

Jarngard turned to leave when he heard Hoth laughing quietly behind him. Jarngard paused at the tent flap.

"I plan on attending the ceremony, unless you'd like to roll those dice again?"

Jarngard closed his eyes momentarily, then he turned around and stormed back to the table, pulling out the dice in one smooth motion.

Hoth met his gaze with a steely one of his own. "Same numbers as last time?"

The dice tumbled over the map and landed next to Agog's scroll. Jarngard snatched them up and shoved them back into the bag once they'd both seen the numbers.

"I'll see you *after*," said Jarngard before he left the tent.

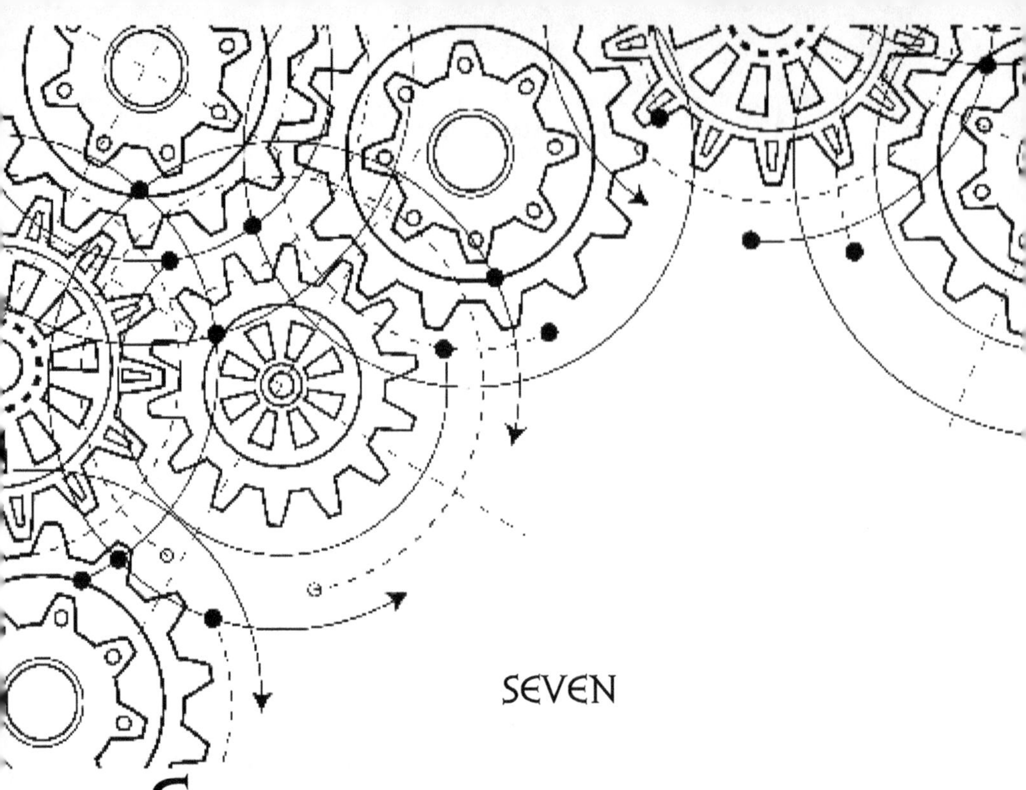

SEVEN

Sepharia clutched the brooch as she moved through the marble hallways of the palace. The nobles were gathering and she wanted to give Agog her gift before he was swarmed. Heron had warned her not to give it in front of Shayna's family.

So she'd snuck away from the reception halls in search of Agog only to get lost. She'd never been past the throne room and once she'd turned a few corners, every new room looked the same.

At least the breezes carried away the Alexandrian heat. The finger of land that stretched out toward Pharos island captured the Mediterranean winds and the palace builders had faced windows and open arches in that direction.

A particularly vigorous gust flapped the hem of her aquamarine chiton and blew her blond curls into her face. A wide, columned atrium led from the main section of the palace back toward the servant's buildings.

Sepharia stepped into a cubby to get out of the wind when she heard voices. She pushed her back against the wall and hid behind the corner.

The voices were coming from a side door.

"It's the other way. This way is too open," said a woman's voice in Greek.

"Fine." The man's voice was rougher. Sepharia heard a commoner's accent in the reply, even though it was in Greek. "But how do I get out?"

"Can you swim?"

Sepharia didn't hear an answer, the wind gusted at that precise moment, but she assumed it was a 'yes' by the woman's next command.

"Once you're done with the delivery, sneak down to the water's edge, and swim to the cliffs on the north side of the city. Our business will be concluded then."

By the hushed tones and covert talk, Sepharia assumed their purpose was nefarious. She wanted to see who was speaking but didn't want to be seen by them. Sepharia edged out of the cubby, trying to get a glimpse of either conspirator.

The man hissed a response. "By the gods, I have to swim out? I don't want to tempt Poseidon with my role in this."

The woman, who had been speaking in hushed tones, almost seductively, switched to a growl. Sepharia could practically hear the woman grinding her teeth. "Take the package and make the delivery. If you get caught and speak my name, my friends will make sure you die a very slow death."

Sepharia edged farther into the atrium. She stopped when she heard the woman's words. If she was seen, could she get away in her chiton? The tube of azure fabric bound her legs together. Normally, Sepharia was used to wearing a man's tunic in the workshop. She could run like an antelope in one of those.

More words were spoken but Sepharia couldn't hear them over the wind. She froze when it appeared the woman was entering the atrium, but she was only turning around. The folds of her crimson cloak flapped like a flag. Sepharia thought she saw a flash of jewelry on the woman's breast.

She didn't have long to consider the implications when she heard hard soles from the other direction and hurried into the nearest doorway. Sepharia scurried through the hallways until she found somewhere vaguely familiar.

Several statues lined the vestibule and between each statue was a painting. Sepharia leaned against a wall and caught her breath. Even after reading the scrolls that Heron had procured for her, she hadn't believed that palace intrigue was all that vicious. She thought most was made up by historians wanting to inflate their status so they would be remembered along with the people they chronicled.

After hearing the woman in the crimson cloak giving orders, she had a different take on the readings. And why shouldn't she, she realized. After all, the cult of Ur had tried to kill both her and Heron for investigating the fires of the Great Library. Certainly, control of Egypt was worth more than that?

Then again, was it her imagination making out the woman's words to be more sinister than they were? Maybe reading those scrolls had just attuned her mind to hear nothing but schemes and backstabbing.

Sepharia didn't have much longer to think about it.

"Admiring Alexander's victory over Darius the Persian?"

Sepharia found herself confronted with a pair of merciless gray eyes. The man was bald and wore the chlamys of a soldier.

She tried to speak but found her throat dry and dusty. "Yes."

His gaze traveled over her and Sepharia felt like a cow being examined for the proper amount of udders. "And what does a fancy little thing like yourself know about it?"

Sepharia knew about Alexander's conquests, including the great battle over King Darius, which lead to his eventual victory over the Persian Empire. She knew about that and much more, for she loved reading the adventures of Alexander more than the ballads of Homer or Euciphydus. But then she remembered she wasn't supposed to be so knowledgeable as a woman.

"I like the colors of the horses and the flags at the end of their spears," she said.

He kept his gaze upon her and though she knew she wasn't supposed to, she matched it for as long as she dared.

When she finally looked away, he asked, "What's your name, child?"

"Sepharia."

"And I am Titus Vestalis." He raised one eyebrow. "You're the miracle worker's daughter, aren't you?"

Sepharia nodded.

"A clever man," said Vestalis, "almost too clever. I can't say I'm fond of him." He smirked at her, a taunt. "What do you think about that?"

"My father *is* very clever."

"And so you must be clever, too. What are you doing all this way from the party?"

"I got lost." She hewed as close to the truth as possible.

"What's that in your hand?" He grabbed her wrist before she could pull away. The golden brooch was in his grasp in a blink.

"Interesting." He flipped the brooch over and ran his fingertips over the etchings. "An engagement gift, I presume?"

"Yes."

Sepharia felt naked under his gaze.

"Powerful symbols you've chosen, girl. I hope you know what they mean." His lips formed a tight line. "And what an odd thing for a pretty young girl like yourself to give such a valuable present."

Sepharia met his gaze. "Apologies, may I have my brooch back? I really should get back to the party."

Vestalis dropped it into her hand and she took off toward an open doorway, hoping it would lead her back. She kept waiting for his stern voice to explain she was going the wrong direction.

Eventually, the rooms grew familiar and she found her way into the party. In the short time since she'd left, the party had tripled in size.

Sepharia paused at the doorway and considered the change. A cluster of noble women near her shrieked and cackled as they spilled goblets. Slaves blotted dribbles of purple from the exquisite marble flooring before anyone noticed.

The men gathered in their own clusters. Soldiers in one group, the higher nobles in the other, each by their people. Egyptians, Jews, and Romans made up the three largest groups. Technically, the Romans were Alexandrians, as most were born in the city and had pledged their loyalty to Agog, but even Sepharia knew they had close ties to family in Rome.

A large man in a purple-trimmed toga bumped into her as he stumbled past. Sepharia wanted to chastise him for not apologizing, but then she remembered she wasn't in the workshop, so she went looking for Heron instead. She needed to tell Heron about the conspiracy in the atrium. As she moved past a particularly braying group of women, Sepharia suppressed the urge to choke from their cloying perfumes.

If this was what all the women nobles were like, then she might have to rethink her request to Heron. But Sepharia knew better than to take the women at their cackling. Even Alexander's own mother, Olympias, had been integral to his empire with her scheming.

Sepharia found Heron in the open ceiling room with her counting machine. She could see her father visibly mumbling, clearly lost in thought about the machine.

Punt was inside the box, adjusting gears and sprockets. She could tell it was the master blacksmith by his broad shoulders and shiny bronze head.

The box itself was unremarkable except for its size. The machine took up the whole cart it rested on, longer than Sepharia was tall, and almost as wide. Various levers stuck out of the box on the end near the eye piece. The eye piece was used to orient the box to Zeus' star. Combined with the distance counter connected to the gears, the machine could help navigate on land just as ships did at sea.

Sepharia had made many of the delicate gears for the machine. She didn't understand exactly how it worked, only that Heron hadn't slept in days while finishing it.

"Apologies, Father." Sepharia touched Heron on the shoulder. "May I speak to you?"

Heron gave her a questioning eyebrow, but did not protest as she brought her to a quiet space along the wall. Her father looked thinner than she'd seen last. Late nights with the machine had drained her.

"What ever this is, please hurry, I must finish preparations so I can demonstrate the machine." Heron glanced around the room before nodding for Sepharia to continue.

She told her tale, trying to convey the seriousness to Heron, but her father looked distracted. Sepharia wasn't surprised when she heard the next comment.

"Apologies for giving you those scrolls from the Library. I did not mean to put these conspiracies into your head. Only instruct you on the possibilities."

Sepharia gripped Heron's arm. "They sounded like they were doing something wrong. What, I don't know."

Heron paused. "Then what does this woman look like?"

"I didn't see either of them. Only the woman's crimson cloak." Sepharia thought back to the atrium. "And maybe she had a piece of jewelry on her breast."

Heron glanced at the room full of party-goers. "I don't see a woman in a crimson cloak and that hardly sounds like the dress of someone trying to be stealthy."

Sepharia didn't see the woman either, but she knew what she heard. "I promise you they were up to mischief of some kind. I could hear it in their voices."

Heron patted her hand. "I'm sure you think you heard something, but maybe it was just the wind. But I really need to get back to the counting machine."

"But you don't understand—"

Heron cut her off. "Yes, I do understand, but there's nothing I can do about it and I don't see a crimson cloak, anyway. If you see her, let me know, otherwise, I have work to do."

Heron pulled away and marched back to the wide room. Sepharia was going to follow her and protest when heralds announced the Satrap was entering the room with his future bride.

The princess Shayna wore a golden gown with heavy Egyptian influences, even though she was Jewish. Clearly, they were playing to the history of the region. She had silky ebony hair that reflected light like black jewels. Sepharia was taken aback by how delicately beautiful the princess was.

The brooch in Sepharia's hand felt like a meager gift compared to Shayna's beauty. Though Sepharia never truly believed that Agog would throw away his kingdom for the daughter of the *Michanikos*, she at least wanted the recognition of his notice.

How she could be noticed next to a beauty such as Shayna seemed comical. Sepharia was rethinking giving Agog the brooch when she saw the woman in the crimson cloak across the room.

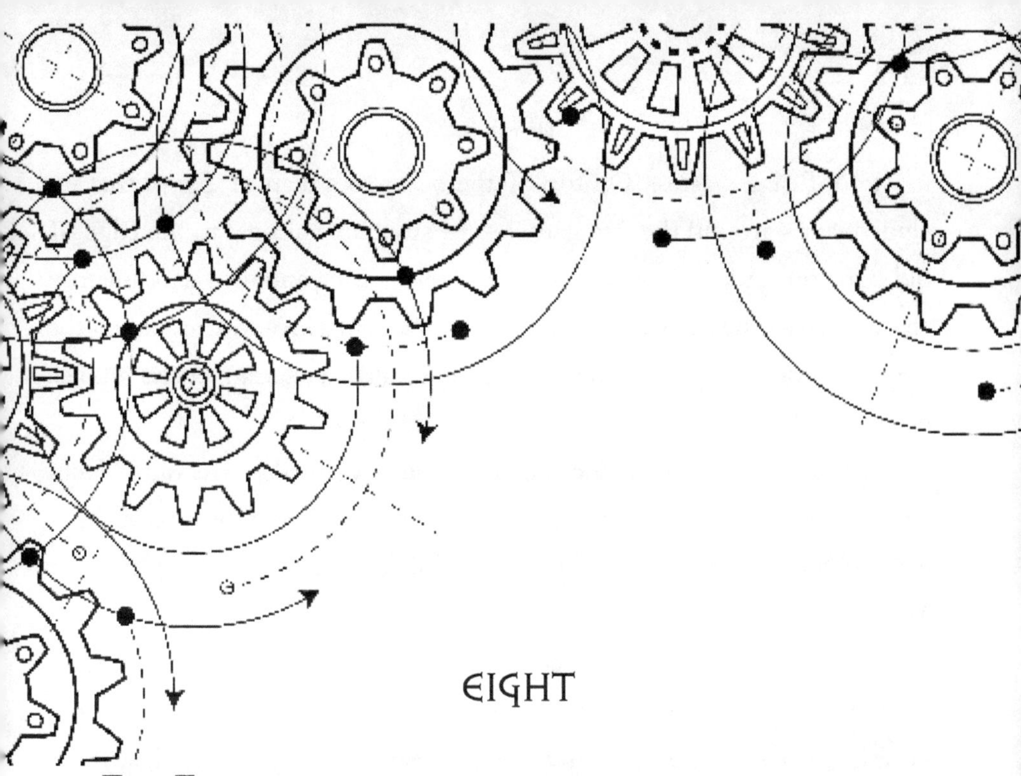

EIGHT

While the chaos of the party whirled around her, Heron pondered the faults of her counting machine. The truth was that counting was the least of its functions. She'd built a specialty machine with tightly fitting gears for the Great Library to aid its discovery of prime numbers, but the monstrosity of sprockets and interlocking gear trains beneath the simple brass box made it a toy in comparison.

Even the task of proofing the steam engine was orders of magnitude different. She wasn't sure how she'd cobbled it together in time for the ceremony and questioned her own wisdom for bringing it.

Heron coughed and found pink spittle on her palm. The violet dust had done its job too well, she thought. But even her exhaustion did not stop the images of the counting machine from marching through her head. She hated the name, though.

It counted distance and reverse calculated the position of the device based on the stars, doing the job of an astrolabe but without the complex manual calculations, allowing even a simple caravan driver to navigate the most confusing wastes. On top of the box was a map of Egypt that included lands around the Arabian Desert, stretching almost to the edge of old Babylon. A lodestone connected to the gearing and moved a tiny iron chariot across the map, theoretically showing actual location, assuming the map was correctly sized. Right now, the miniature chariot sat on a black dot notated with the Greek word for Alexandria.

The root of her machine was based on Archimedes' Heavens Mechanism. She'd seen one at the Astronomical Society in Corinth, but seeing it hadn't been as instructive as Archimedes' text on the subject in *On Sphere-Making*.

The problem hadn't been constructing the device, since she'd made a working Heavens Mechanism and taximeter before. She had those functioning devices in the back of her workshop and only had to dust them off to get them to work. The crux of her problem, besides the lackluster name, had been how to get each piece to work together and to calibrate it precisely.

She knew that technically it did not work. The gears would move and the taximeter could count distance. Even the little iron chariot would march around the map when she moved the internal workings by hand. But she had to estimate the exact positions of the stars from scrolls in the Library, so she had no idea if it would actually give correct position, especially if the map was wrong, which it most likely was.

In addition, the sun, stars, moon, and five planets changed regularly with position and time. All those changes added complexity to an already overwrought idea. Really, she would have to take the counting machine on an extended journey to find out if it worked, but she didn't have the time.

"Look, Shayna, my Chief Engineer toils all day and night, and even when there is a festive occasion, in service of my growing empire," said Agog, breaking her from her thoughts.

A quiet laughter followed as Princess Shayna and her family looked on. Punt, whose face was hidden from the onlookers by the box, rolled his eyes at Heron.

"I relish my service to the people of Alexandria, my Satrap." Heron bowed and smiled.

Agog was like a great bear surrounded by attendants. Even his Egyptian garb didn't remove the image of the barbarian for Heron, but she'd seen him in battle and knew how fearsome he was.

Princess Shayna stepped forward with an inquisitive look. She studied the brass box earnestly. She seemed so soft and beautiful that she carried an inner light. The golden gown added to that image.

"What do you call it, *Michanikos?*"

Heron bowed, dipping low enough for a future queen. "An excellent question. My blacksmith, Punt, called it the Infernal Machine during construction due to its complexity."

The Jewish contingent laughed politely, including her father, Baruch Tanzen. Princess Shayna smiled graciously and clapped her delicate hands, before looking back to Agog.

Agog smiled at Shayna, but Heron thought she saw a resignment in his eyes, but of course, she knew about his first love Aurinia. The conquest of Alexandria would have never happened if it weren't for Aurinia's death.

He was set to marry Shayna, not because of her beauty, for she had beauty to spare, but for her political connections. The saying, *a bound stallion hesitates at the mare*, had much meaning in that brief glance.

"But what about you? What do you call it?" asked Shayna.

"By Plato's words, it has no name, only a purpose at this time."

Shayna stepped to the box and peered over the top at the tiny chariot. As Punt adjusted gears, the chariot moved the length of a hand. Shayna squealed and clapped her hands again.

"You should call it a Miracle Box." Shayna smiled. "What is its purpose, or are we spoiling a surprise?"

Heron opened her mouth to answer when she saw Titus Claudius Vestalis watching her from the open doorway. He wore his tunic and hair in the Roman equestrian style, despite his alleged allegiance to Agog.

Behind Vestalis stood his man servant, a slave-scholar from the Library that Heron had seen a time or two. He was quite distinguishable by the chemical scar across his eye that had blinded it. Heron thought of him as One Eye.

Heron chose her words carefully, knowing that Vestalis was listening. Princess Shayna wouldn't understand technical details so Heron kept her answer light. "It should give our traders an advantage by helping them travel across desolate wastes without getting lost."

Shayna's brow knotted with thought. "Hrmph."

Heron knew she was losing the princess. "It should help Alexandria make more gold than our neighbors, especially if we outfit our traders with steam chariots."

The frowning gaze of Agog could be felt, even though her gaze was on Shayna. He believed the steam chariots should be kept strictly as a military vehicle, for he feared the Romans capturing too many steam mechanicals.

An authoritative voice, one of a captain in battle, sung out from the doorway. "Ave, Heron. A steam chariot would be a boon to my caravans, but not this star-finding box. A good road and durable horses are all my traders need."

Agog grumbled but did not voice his opinion. He needed Vestalis' support. But the way Agog looked at her said she was supposed to deal with it.

"With this box—" Heron cursed that she didn't have a name for it. "—you can take a direct route across the Arabian desert and cut weeks from your journeys."

Vestalis strolled near, holding a goblet of wine in his hand, though she had not seen him drink from it. "And tell me, Chief Engineer, will the sands of the desert not interfere with your gearings?"

His steely gaze drilled into her. Her stomach twisted and she cursed his mechanical knowledge. Of course, he was correct. The box would have to be carefully sealed to protect against dust and sand. And the methods of construction meant it couldn't be used on the open seas due to the corrosiveness of salty air on brass.

"It sounds like our revered friend is afraid of a little sand? Maybe I will sell it to one of the other trading houses and they can cross the desert in record time."

She was familiar with the oratory tricks of the Senate, but hated using them.

"And then I will be rid of one of my competitors when they die, lost in the desert or killed by warring nomads." Vestalis left the room with a righteous smirk.

The light mood that had been prevalent during her conversation with Shayna was burst. Her family left, headed back into the main rooms for entertainment. The scents of burning lantern oil suddenly became pungent and she could taste the oil on her tongue.

Heron did not want Shayna's pity, even though she knew Vestalis would not purchase her machine. Before Shayna left, she touched Heron's arm. "I would call it the Hermes Machine."

With a polite parting smile, Heron nodded. Shayna left to follow her family. Agog moved near.

"It might be too much for the traders to accept," said Agog. "This Hermes Machine looks complicated."

Heron blew air through her nostrils. Her exhaustion was replaced with anger.

"Complicated like the protections you made me put on the steam mechanicals." She kept her voice low so no one outside of the room could hear. They were the only three in the wide hall, ringed with silent statues of the gods.

"I don't want to face my own steam mechanicals on the battlefield. If we're to beat Rome, we cannot let them nullify our advantage."

"We won't have an advantage when all our mechanicals blow up and destroy the very workshops that should be making them." Heron knew she should not be speaking to the Satrap in such harsh tones, but she didn't care. "Work in my own is at a standstill while I rebuild Nektam's."

Agog's eyes glistened with import. "We can't. The steam mechanicals must be protected."

Heron ground her teeth. "Then compensate Nektam for his losses."

His gaze flitted to hers. "You know the answer to that. I wouldn't need all of this if we had enough coin." He gestured to the party.

"Then let me—"

Agog growled. "No. Enough, and that's final."

The Satrap growled and marched back into the other room, leaving her with her box of gears. She had a name for the box now, at least.

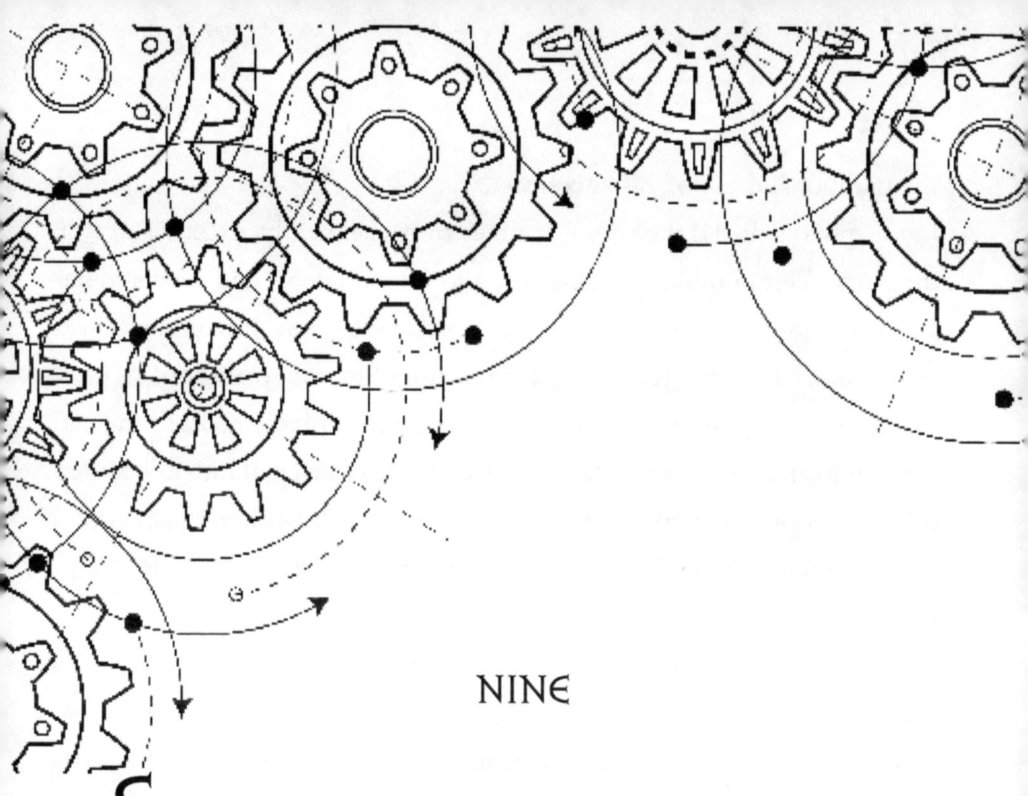

NINE

Sepharia followed the woman in the crimson cloak as she meandered through the party. Sepharia found it odd that the woman did not stop at any of the clusters of nobles spread throughout the hall. She appeared to be alone and without any slave attendants, practically a crime by the nobility's standards.

Slaves in white linen loincloths moved amongst the groups, bringing wine and food. Soldiers stood guard at the doorways, looking every bit like their Roman counterparts, minus the Seal of the Empire normally pressed into the leather.

Light filtered in through high windows. The salty sea air washed away the overpowering scents of the noble women as long as she didn't move too close.

Through a gilded archway decorated with pictograms of pharaohs, the Egyptian district leader Ramses held council with Agog. Ramses was Agog's biggest supporter, having been exiled by Governor Flaccus for disparaging Emperor Claudius. The man was shorter than Agog and wore the traditional dress of his ancestors.

Sepharia circled the room, at times overwhelmed by extravagance of the party. Her humble workshop life and Heron's debts had sheltered her from the noble quarter. Even when times were good, Heron had never spent wildly, focusing funds on her inventions and the workshop.

When she passed through a garden atrium, Sepharia realized she had lost the woman in the crimson cloak. The party stretched into at least ten different rooms, including the throne room, which Sepharia understood would be the location for the engagement. She continued searching, hoping to find the woman before she left or caused trouble.

The Green Room had tables filled with trays of food. Mostly slaves picked through the edibles, readying plates for their masters, but the occasional noble drifted through, examining the wealth of food. Sepharia recognized the Magistrate of the Rhakotis district, a particularly large man in a purple-trimmed toga, eating from a tray of honeyed cakes.

There were endless trays of figs, marinated in various oils or wines or spices. Breads waited on terra cotta plates, cool and hard, as the warm breads were immediately snatched by waiting slaves and hurried into other rooms. Bowls of fruity opsuns, to dip the bread in, tickled Sepharia's nose with sweetness. She wrinkled her face at a pot of lentil soup, before moving to the far side.

Through the columned wall on the other side, Sepharia thought she saw a flash of red in the Sun Chapel. The room had a wide circular hole to let sunlight in: sparkling the surface of an ankle deep pool of water. A couple of nobles rested on the edge, sipping wine and cooling their feet in the pool.

Sepharia was about to leave the Sun Chapel, thinking the woman had moved to another room, when she heard a voice from a cubby to her right.

"You're a Macedonian, aren't you?"

The woman in the crimson cloak was sitting on a cushioned bench. A painting of the god Helios, piloting four fire-breathing horses across the sky, made a fitting backdrop for the woman. It almost appeared the horses were burning her crimson cloak.

"I'm an Alexandrian."

Even sitting down, Sepharia could tell the woman was shorter than most. But her stature didn't take away from her intensity.

"They call me Polyxena." The dark-haired woman patted the cushioned bench next to her. The motion felt like a command.

Sepharia took a steadying breath, tucked the brooch into a hidden fold in her chiton, and sat down. Polyxena took Sepharia's hand within her own and gazed into her eyes. One was faintly blue and the other brown, making Sepharia slightly dizzy. The woman smelled like lilacs.

"I'm Sepharia," she finally blurted out.

"Yes, you are, aren't you? Daughter of the great inventor."

Sepharia nodded. "My father was from Macedonia before he came to Alexandria to make his name."

"I can see that," said Polyxena. "You could be a descendant of Alexander." She had a hypnotic quality.

"You're from Macedonia."

Polyxena's face brightened as if sunlight had been cast upon it. "And how did you know?"

Sepharia pointed to the brooch, half-hidden beneath the crimson cloak. "The sunburst." Sepharia tilted her head. In the center of the brooch was a coiled creature. "But what does the snake mean?"

Polyxena narrowed her eyes, the look was both threatening and admiration. "A symbol of my own devising."

The woman smiled and Sepharia's heart doubled its rate.

"Why were you following me, Sepharia?"

Sepharia blinked twice and thought hard for an answer, but nothing came. Then she put her hand down to push herself away, wondering if she could get off the bench without being stabbed by some hidden knife, when she bumped the brooch in the fold.

"I..." Sepharia let the lie settle in her mind, so she could own it. She could tell Polyxena would sniff out any half-formed deception. "...saw the sunburst and wanted a closer look."

Polyxena didn't seem to accept her answer, so she started fumbling for her own brooch, the one she'd made for Agog.

"I make jewelry," she said, hearing her voice shaking still. "And I made..."

Sepharia shoved the brooch into Polyxena's hands. A long pause followed, during which Sepharia's heart threatened to drum her ears to pieces. Polyxena turned the brooch over in her hands. Her face was creased with a few wrinkles, minor at best, and they hardly marred her beauty, but they did mark her age. The crease at the corner of her mouth deepened at first, a thought or maybe disappointment. Then it was wiped clean by a smile and Sepharia let her breath out.

"What exquisite workmanship," said Polyxena. "How did you know to use the Vergina Sun?"

"I...well, my father brought me scrolls from the Library," lied Sepharia.

Polyxena paused and with what had to be a flash of a thought responded, "You snuck into the Library yourself, didn't you?"

How Polyxena knew that Sepharia had snuck into the Library dressed as a messenger boy, she would never know. The exit looked so far away and Polyxena must have realized Sepharia's concern, because she put a hand over her arm and whispered, "Do not worry, I will tell no one."

Her strange eyes sparkled with the import of a shared secret. Sepharia's relief was mixed with dread. She rapidly regretted allowing herself to be ensnared by Polyxena.

"And the scarab," continued Polyxena as she placed the brooch back in Sepharia's hands, "how perfect a symbol. Though I am unfamiliar with all its meanings, its existence on this brooch can only mean you intend to give it to one person."

"I...well, he's the Satrap...and my father, and I wanted..." Sepharia fumbled through the words until she realized Polyxena was smiling again.

"Girl," Polyxena patted Sepharia's hand, "I understand. And now the mystery is solved. You should go back to the party and enjoy yourself."

The Macedonian woman stood up. "I myself am growing tired and need to retire to my quarters in the city. The journey here was long and I have not recovered yet. I thank the gods for allowing us to meet. May your gift to the Satrap bring what you hope."

Sepharia was stunned when Polyxena gave her a brief hug, a gesture normally reserved for family.

"We Macedonian women need to stick together." Polyxena winked and left the room, leaving Sepharia more confused than when she came in.

Polyxena left through the Green Room, so Sepharia entered an arched hallway filled with frescos detailing the story of Gilgamesh. Sepharia hardly looked at them, though she had read the tales extensively, until she exited into the throne room, bumping into a bear of a man in Egyptian dress.

"Do you have a habit of getting lost, girl?" said a second, familiar voice.

It was the Satrap that she'd bumped into and he was talking to Titus Claudius Vestalis.

"Sepharia."

She could hear the slight annoyance in his greeting. He was clearly talking about serious matters with Vestalis.

"Ave, Satrap. Ave, good Vestalis. Apologies for my carelessness. I shall go around the other way." Sepharia planned to exit the throne room as quickly as possible. Not only was the Satrap speaking to the most powerful merchant in Alexandria, but the family of his future wife was standing not too far away.

Shayna had her back to Sepharia. The princess was speaking to her father. From Sepharia's vantage point, Shayna's golden gown and mane of ebony made her appear divine.

"Girl," said Vestalis. "Sepharia." He rolled her name over his tongue, as if he were tasting it. "Do you not wish to give the Satrap your gift? It's quite the offer."

Mention of a gift brought Shayna around, along with her family. Any chance of fleeing was lost once the princess met her gaze. "Dearest Wodanaz, does this *common* girl offer a gift?"

Sepharia was going to deny and say she'd left the gift at the table. The lie would cover her retreat, but the princess' dismissive gaze and the way she'd said the word "common", as if the word burned her tongue, stiffened Sepharia's resolve.

"I brought a token for the Satrap." She handed the brooch not to the princess, who waited with her hands outstretched, but to Agog. "I made it for you."

Shayna snatched it from Agog's hand before he could examine it. A flicker of annoyance passed across his gaze. Shayna's father, Baruch, watched with half-lidded eyes, a twitch at his lips.

A host of nobles watched as Shayna examined the gift. Agog glanced once - only once - down at Sepharia and she could sense his concern.

"What an ugly tree on the back," said Shayna. "How could she be a proper Alexandrian without knowing our symbols?"

"It's the Tree of Life from Agog's lands," said Sepharia, trying to coach her voice respectfully. "I believe it's called Yggdrasil."

Agog cleared his throat. "It is. How did you..."

Princess Shayna held the gift out as if it were a poisonous snake. "Is this proper for a commoner to give such an expensive gift? It's enough that she should even be allowed here."

"It is the *Michanikos'* daughter," said Agog. "She suffered as well under Roman rule."

"That does not make her royalty, only a dupe," said Shayna.

Agog glanced at Shayna's family, especially her father, Baruch, a stern man with a clipped beard. The Satrap took the brooch from Shayna's outstretched hand.

Sepharia grimaced when he turned it over to examine the tree. He lovingly traced the outstretched branches with his fingertip. Shayna scowled.

"The work is excellent," said Agog, ignoring his fiancée.

Sepharia rushed the words out. "The scarab symbolizes your eternal rule." She nodded towards both of them. "I meant to give it later during the proper time."

Agog stepped forward, putting his enormous bulk between her and Shayna. "Well, it *is* a lovely gift. I shall put it with the others."

The Satrap tossed the brooch to a slave and headed out of the room with his arm around Shayna's waist. The family followed like a dutiful herd of sheep. Sepharia caught more than one nasty glance from the lesser members of the family.

When Sepharia turned to leave, Vestalis grabbed her arm, squeezing until it hurt. "You shouldn't play games you don't understand. You're just going to get you and your father hurt."

From anyone else, it might have been an honest suggestion, but from Vestalis, it felt like a threat. Sepharia did not let him stare her down and matched his gaze until he let go of her arm. Then she walked as calmly as she could back to the Sun Chapel, knowing she had to get to Heron to tell her what had happened.

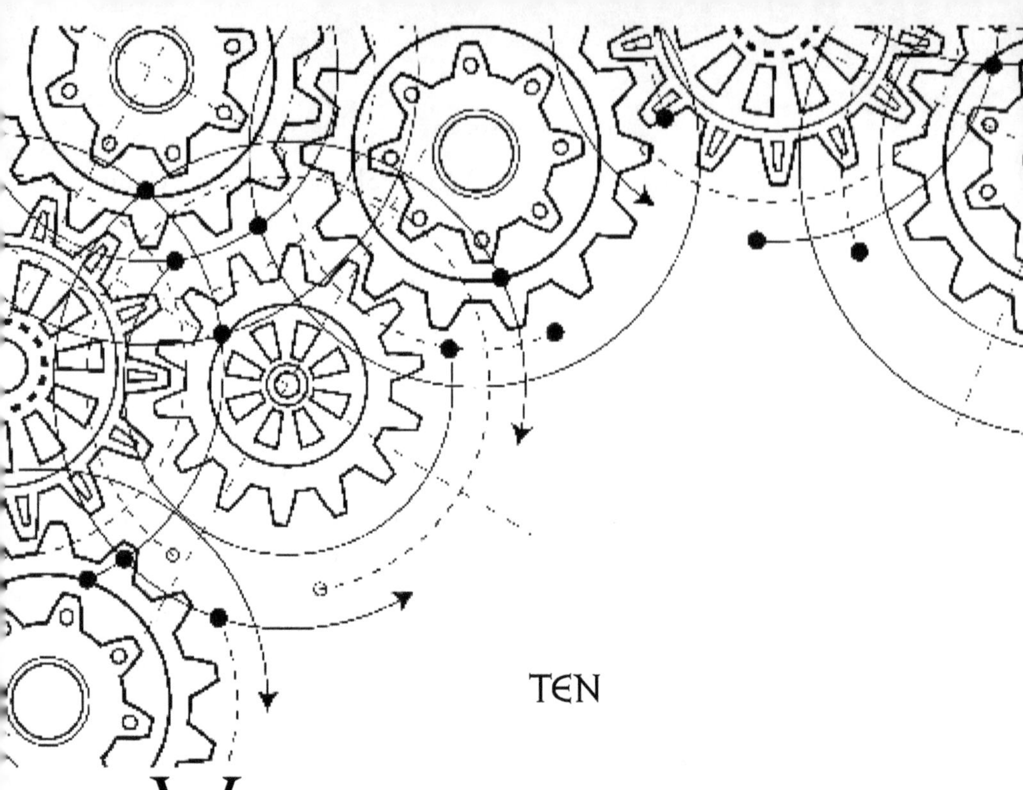

TEN

When the call came to join the *Erusin* ceremony, the act of engagement between the Satrap and Princess Shayna, Heron found herself lingering at the now named Hermes Machine. Punt placed his calloused hand on her arm and nodded toward the throne room.

She knew what he was saying. He would take care of getting the machine back to the workshop. She should take her place at the ceremony. It would be expected.

As Heron left the wide room, Punt hefted the hitch of the wagon and pulled it toward a gilded archway molded with ravens. His thick shoulders flexed with effort, but he made no sound, nor did the iron-banded wheels as they rolled across the silver-inlayed marble floor.

When she joined the ceremony, Agog was speaking to the guests, noble and otherwise. He was thanking them for attending, lavishing attention on his most important guests: Baruch Tanzer, who was Shayna's father, Titus Claudius Vestalis, the exiled Egyptian Ramses, and of course, Shayna herself.

Heron could hardly pay attention. Her mind was on her disaster of an invention. Even if it worked, the complexity would keep anyone from using it, let alone paying good gold to own one.

She spied Vestalis near the front, looking self-righteous. If she weighed his allegiance against his mood, she would have long ago suggested to Agog that he have the merchant beheaded, but Vestalis had always been that way, even to the Romans. The man loved gold more than the Roman Empire and she presumed that he saw his chances with Alexandria. Of course, he could also be eyeing the reward for killing the barbarian invader. Heron had seen the parchments sent from Rome with Emperor Claudius' signature. The reward was astronomically high.

Standing at the edge of the dais, Agog and Shayna began giving gifts to their guests. Heron was called early and accepted it, thanking both the Satrap and his future wife. Heron was confused by the strange glance from Agog and the terse greeting from Shayna, a marked difference from their earlier encounter.

The gift she received was a map made during Alexander's conquest, a valuable piece of history if she was willing to sell it, but she knew she would give it to the Great Library as its historians could make better use of it than she could. Heron assumed the gift came from Shayna's father, despite the dour look she received from him upon walking back to her place.

Heron watched as each gift was given, while her mind patiently worked on the problem of the machine. Gifts to the guests would happen before the ceremony and gifts to the engaged couple would occur after. Heron hoped that Sepharia would give her brooch with delicate care. Shayna's father was a prickly man and his daughter was cut from the same cloth.

Then Heron noticed a flash of rapid movement from the back of the hall. Sepharia was anxiously standing on tip-toes and motioning for Heron to come closer. Heron tightly shook her head. Now was not the time for discussions. But the look of need on Sepharia's face gave her pause.

Heron focused her attention on the Satrap and his bride. It would be unseemly to be caught inattentive, and truthfully, she was curious about this mix of culture traditions.

The Egyptians, surprisingly, did not have elaborate weddings, despite their endless parties. Heron found them the most likely to marry for love, mentally citing Punt and his wife Astrela as an excellent example.

This engagement was new to Heron, for the Greeks did not bother with it. They went straight to marriage, after which the woman cut her hair to show her virginity, which made Heron wonder if she'd married herself when she cut her hair to pose as her dead twin.

The Romans brought the law to marriage, as they did with everything else, adding legal papers that had to be signed by both parties. Heron knew that Agog had entered such an arrangement with Shayna's father long before the engagement had been announced.

The rest of the ceremony would be a mixing of each. After the gifts, there would be words said, blessings from some book the Jews held sacred and then a consecration and drinking of wine to celebrate the moment and ending with the gifts to the couple.

A hand touched her arm, startling her. Heron found Sepharia at her side, clutching the azure chiton as if she'd been wounded. Heron couldn't help but think something was wrong.

Sepharia tried to whisper into her ear, but Heron cut her off with a tight-lipped shush. Then she checked back to the ceremony to make sure no one had noticed.

Fingernails dug into her arm, almost bringing a cry of pain. When she looked down, Sepharia was mouthing words, but Heron couldn't understand.

So she pulled her daughter out of the room. "Enough about the woman in the crimson cloak," Heron whispered through gritted teeth. "It doesn't matter now."

Sepharia shook her head. "The brooch. The brooch," she whispered back.

Heron was about to ask what had happened to the brooch when Agog's deep baritone voice called out, "Bring wine for my guests!"

They hurried back into the throne room before it was noticed they were gone. Slaves in tunics and wraps streamed in with trays stacked with wine goblets.

While the slaves winded through the guests, Sepharia tapped on Heron's chest, right above the breastbone and pointed toward Agog. Heron realized what her daughter was trying to say. She'd given Agog the brooch, though she didn't seem happy about it. The news made the treatment she received from Shayna's family clearer.

"Friends, family, nobles, Alexandrians!" Agog's voice cut through her thoughts forcing her to pay attention.

Heron gripped the wine goblet and cast her gaze across the party. Between Vestalis' rebuke, the incident with the brooch, and Sepharia's report of a conspiracy, Heron began to suspect that her daughter might be right.

She glanced around for the woman in the red cloak as Agog held his cup high. He had a cup twice the size of Shayna's that was encrusted with gems. Hers was a delicate flute of a cup that sparkled in the light from the upper windows.

"Together we are free from the Romans!" shouted Agog. "And together we shall set a course to change this world with Alexandria as its capitol!"

There was cheering, but there had been ample wine, and everyone was drunk on the celebration. Heron took a second look around to see if there were any faces she didn't recognize or that were not happily smiling at the speech.

Vestalis she didn't count, because even he had sort of a grin, maybe more of a smirk, but it was more than he usually cared to offer. Plutarch's sometimes companion, Hortio, was kissing a new partner in the back, but that was no concern of the moment (though she did wonder if she should tell Plutarch).

Besides those two, every other face in the throne room was beaming at Agog, holding their cups high, and readying to drink at his command.

"The conquest of Alexandria was not my conquest, but your conquest!" continued Agog. "So I have chosen to find my wife amongst your nobility, to bind my ties deep."

Agog took on a mischievous cast, which was difficult given his enormous size and bearded face, however neatly trimmed it was.

"But it is not just my ties that will go deep!" When he glanced back to Shayna, the crowd howled. Shayna's father smiled and clapped along with the others. He was giving away his daughter and gaining a piece of the new Alexandria.

The more Heron watched, the more she sensed something was wrong, but she didn't know why. As the moments passed, she decided to dismiss it. She had no proof other than Sepharia's alleged conspirators, who weren't even present at the ceremony. Heron relaxed and held her cup a little higher.

"Good Baruch." Agog motioned to Shayna's father. "He has only agreed upon this marriage if I quickly produce a heir." More laughter followed, though not as vigorously as before.

"Beautiful Shayna," Agog turned to her, "while our upcoming marriage is a binding of ties, I am doubly blessed by the gods of both the northern snows and the southern sands, that you are the most beautiful woman in Alexandria."

Polite murmurings of agreement passed through the assembled. Shayna held her hand demurely over her mouth and tilted her head forward.

Agog, ever the showman, spun toward the crowd and thrust his hand into the air. Wine splashed out of his cup and onto the marble, but no slave dared to clean it.

"In a month! We shall be married!" he shouted feverishly. "And then we shall strike down those dung-eating Romans in battle!"

Everyone cheered, some more loudly than others. Vestalis still had that rueful smirk on this face. "*Yimas!*" Agog yelled the traditional Greek command to drink and then he brought the cup down to his lips, only to be stopped by Shayna. The crowd stopped itself from drinking. Tittering laughter followed.

"Wait, my beloved. It is my people's tradition, that we who will be married, should drink from each other's cups."

Agog let a wide grin form on his lips. "Only if you finish the cup!"

Everyone laughed, including Shayna, who was nodding. Heron couldn't imagine the slight girl consuming the whole cup, but she seemed eager to try. Heron caught a glimpse of Sepharia watching the proceedings with tight lips. Heron elbowed her in the ribs to remind her that it was a festive occasion.

Agog and Shayna entwined their arms, giving the other access to their cups. Everyone else had put their arms down and were waiting for the couple to finish.

With a cheer, the couple tipped their cups and began drinking. Agog quickly finished, as his cup was only a fifth of the size of hers. Shayna, to her credit, kept drinking even when it was clear that she'd never consumed that much liquid in one go before. Her eyes watered, but she seemed determined to drink the whole cup.

The crowd began to clap, which only encouraged her. Shayna clearly had been struggling with the volume of liquid, but once the crowd began cheering, she doubled her efforts. Heron chuckled at the size of the headache the girl would have tomorrow. She just hoped Shayna wouldn't get too sick before the end of the party.

When she finished the goblet, everyone cheered and were bringing their cups up to salute the couple when Shayna brought her hands to her throat. A gasp followed and Shayna fell to her knees, gagging and convulsing.

Even the Satrap did not look well. His hand was on his belly and he was shaking his head. He'd gone from energetic to sallow in a blink. Out of the corner of her eye, she saw Sepharia move to take a drink from her cup. Heron knocked it from her hand.

"Don't drink it! The wine's been poisoned!"

When the Northmen came running to their captain's side, hands on swords, Heron quickly pulled Sepharia away. If Agog died today, then the Roman loyalists would rise up and wipe the Northmen from the city. She had to get herself and Sepharia back to the workshop to have the best chance of surviving the night.

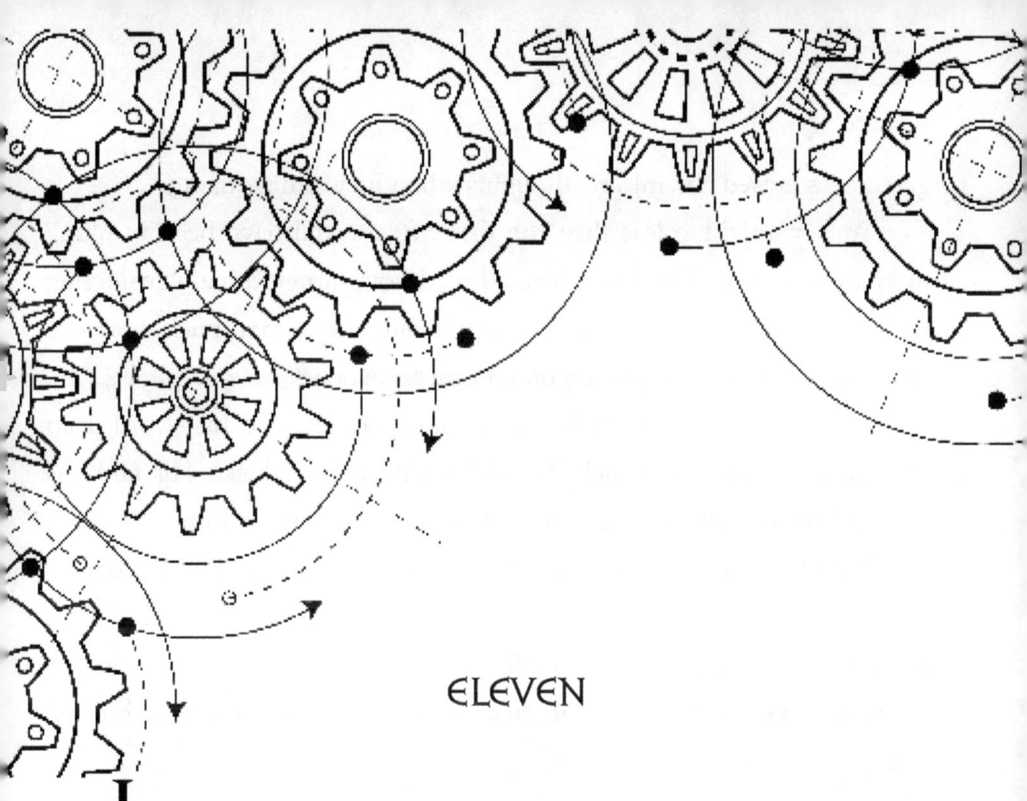

ELEVEN

Jarngard had never been one for weddings, even before his own to Nessa. Pausing as a procession of chain-bound slaves wound through the path between the tents, Jarngard took a backwards glance at the white walls of Alexandria.

On the north side of the city, Agog would be getting engaged to his future bride. To Jarngard, weddings and engagements were the same thing, and he had no intention of attending. His captain had been disappointed, but Jarngard had told him he could 'eat fire from a bull's ass' if he thought he would be there after being sent to treat with Hoth the Black.

Agog had nodded and let him leave. Officially, Jarngard was rounding up contracts of the various mercenary companies outside the city, but the truth was mere avoidance. They had no gold to pay these mercenaries, not yet anyway, but Jarngard collected them regardless, giving token payment before placing the official seal on the document.

His own wedding to Nessa had been a joyous affair, despite the ridiculous bride price he'd paid to her father. Nessa's snowy white hair and lush green eyes erased any miserly thoughts when he was negotiating.

To pay anything less than the first offer would have been insulting to Nessa's beauty. Though it seemed mad now, Jarngard had considering increasing the bride price, even though he didn't have that much money at the time and had already taken on considerable debts.

On the day of their wedding, Jarngard had plunged his sword deep into the ancestral tree, which should have been good luck. His faithless wife had been anything but. Another debt the gods owed him.

With the slaves past, he touched the leather bag around his throat and continued, keeping watch for the sea green tents of the Thracians. After passing a man beating his wife, he found them near a cluster of mushroom eaters that were writhing in the dust around a fire pit long since burned out.

The round Thracian tents were set in a circle. Their construction reminded Jarngard of the mud and grass huts used on the plains east of his homeland seas. They'd picked a good spot, far from the cesspits, and one that collected a sea breeze. The Thracian horses were kept on ropes between the tents.

The sea green flags showed a blank white square in the middle as they snapped in the winds. The empty space in the middle of the flag was intended to show changing allegiance, so they were named the White Company.

A Thracian guard in leathers, Phrygian helmet, and carrying a sword, two javelins, and an oval shield stopped him from entering the circle. Jarngard noted the red tassels on his sword which indicated they were available for hire.

"I come from the Satrap," Jarngard growled in Greek.

When the guard stepped aside, Jarngard asked him. "Who leads the White Company?"

"Teres."

Jarngard found the man easily. Men always situated themselves around their captains, so he only had to look to the center.

Teres was a broad-chested man. Probably used a two-handed sword or something to cleave with. The big weapons were as much about fear as they were killing. In the thick of battle, when one saw a large man with a huge weapon coming your way, if you're a simple infantry, you found someone else to stab with your fragile spear.

"The Satrap wishes to hire the White Company," Jarngard said when he approached, not caring to bother with formalities.

Teres was sitting on a camp bench, naked except for a whore sitting on his lap. She was more clothed than he. His men looked up from their mugs of beer with half-grins and curious stares.

"And why would we want to do that when the Romans will pay us more." Teres squeezed the breast of the whore. "Your captain's like this tit. Looks good enough to suck but you can't get a drop of milk out of it."

Calling Agog a captain rather than the title of Satrap told Jarngard how tenuously they held the city. If even common mercenaries questioned their rule, then trouble could not be far behind.

"We have the miracle worker's machines and more Northmen coming every day." Jarngard crossed his arms. "And Rome is busy in the Britons. They won't be able to bring their armies until next year and when they do, we'll crush them on the field like we did the first one."

Teres raised an eyebrow and playfully squeezed the whore's tit again. "I would like to see these machines. I hear they spit fire and scream like a god enchained."

"And they're faster than any horse and can smash an infantry line in seconds," finished Jarngard.

"But what do the gods think of them? Who gave this miracle worker his secrets? Zeus? Ammon? Hermes?"

Jarngard shrugged. "None of them. All of them. Who gives a shit when you're winning? Some say the gods favor the strongest, just like they did Alexander the Macedonian."

"The Romans still pay more."

"And how much can you spend when my steam chariot has run over your corpse." Jarngard smirked. "Sign with the Romans and I'll make sure we bring our machines against your flank, scattering your company, and pissing on your flag when the battle's done."

Teres scowled and his men put hands to weapons. He might have pushed them too far. For a long, tense moment, Jarngard thought they were going to kill him. They could have their company long gone before anyone found his corpse.

When Teres smiled, Jarngard blew a breath out his nose. "I'll sign with the Satrap if I can ride one of these..." Teres searched for the word. "...steam chariots into battle."

Jarngard was about to agree when Teres held his hand up. "And we get to keep it afterwards along with our normal fees."

"Done and done." They clasped forearms. Jarngard made a mental note that when they met the Romans in battle, he'd put the White Company into the teeth of the Roman army. If the White Company survived, which he doubted, they could keep their steam chariot, for they would have earned it.

Only steps outside of the Thracian tents, one of his Northman cousins, Glartoën, came running up. Jarngard knew it was bad by the fear in his cousin's eyes.

Before his cousin could speak, Jarngard dragged Glartoën away from the Thracian tents in case they were listening.

"What? Speak quickly."

Glartoën swallowed and then spit the words out. "Wodanaz has been poisoned. The physicians say he'll be dead before nightfall."

Jarngard took off toward the city gate, leaving his cousin behind.

If Agog died, then they were lost. He'd have to gather the men and find Hoth and then they would sail back north, hoping to avoid the Roman fleet, and forget this southern adventure. Of course, Claudius would not take this conquest lightly. He'd probably bring his armies north and burn every village he could find. No, if Agog was dead, then the north was lost. If he was lucky enough to make it back north, Jarngard decided he'd probably head east past the Finnish tribes and contend with the people of the steppes.

Jarngard was coated in a fine sheen of sweat when he reached the Palace. The Alexandrian guards wouldn't meet his gaze when he passed, glancing at the marble floor. His Northmen brethren gave him grim nods.

There was no sign of the nobles when he reached the Palace proper. Slaves nervously cleaned the scattered spilled goblets with hunks of purple soaked rags. Jarngard went straight to Agog's chambers. He found the large man propped up on the bed with attendants and physicians surrounding him. The exile Ramses was there as well, worried to the point of grief.

Agog was pale, even for a Northman, and sweat glistened across his brow though they fanned him liberally. His skin had a slight greenish cast and his eyes were closed. Agog's chest was heaving long, slow breaths like the rising and falling of the ocean. His breath sounded shallow, almost raspy.

"It was poison," said the first physician. "We're trying to leech it from him."

Black lines covered his arms. Another physician applied leeches to Agog's leg.

Jarngard growled. "Get out! All of you!" He said the words in his native tongue, but they understood him anyway.

Ramses began pushing them out for good measure. "Give the Satrap his rest. He will recover."

As the men streamed past Jarngard, he grabbed the physician who had spoken.

"Do you have any chalk?" said Jarngard, switching to Greek.

"Why yes, but..."

"Get it. Now."

While the physician retrieved the chalk, Jarngard cleared the leeches off Agog. When the physician appeared with a jar filled with white powder, Jarngard grabbed it, dumped half into a mug of beer and mixed it.

"Help me give this to him."

The physician held Agog's head back and Jarngard poured it down the throat. Immediately, Agog began choking, his eyes fluttering open. Then with a surprising rage, Agog threw both the physician and Jarngard off the bed. Jarngard's shoulder slammed into a column. Ramses hurried to his side and helped him to his feet.

Sitting up, Agog kept coughing which turned to convulsing.

"What have you done?" asked the physician. "Did you poison him again?"

Jarngard shook his head, keeping his gaze upon Agog. "In the north, on cold days when there's nothing else to do and we stay in the mead halls drinking and playing games until the sun comes back, which it doesn't do for many days, occasionally a man drinks too much."

Jarngard climbed upon the bed and began hitting Agog in the back. He could hear liquid sloshing in the great man's belly.

"When they do, we give them chalk to clean out their belly. It might work for poison, too." Jarngard shrugged.

When Agog finally let loose, he vomited a blackish chalky liquid over the floor and the physician's sandaled feet. Agog heaved three more times, spilling more liquid on the floor. The physician smartly moved away, though he'd probably need to burn his sandals.

After a few minutes, in which Agog kept heaving nothing but spit, he finally relented and looked up at Jarngard, eyes blistering red from the effort.

"Jarngard," Agog whispered. "I hate you." His great bearded face twisted into a grim smile.

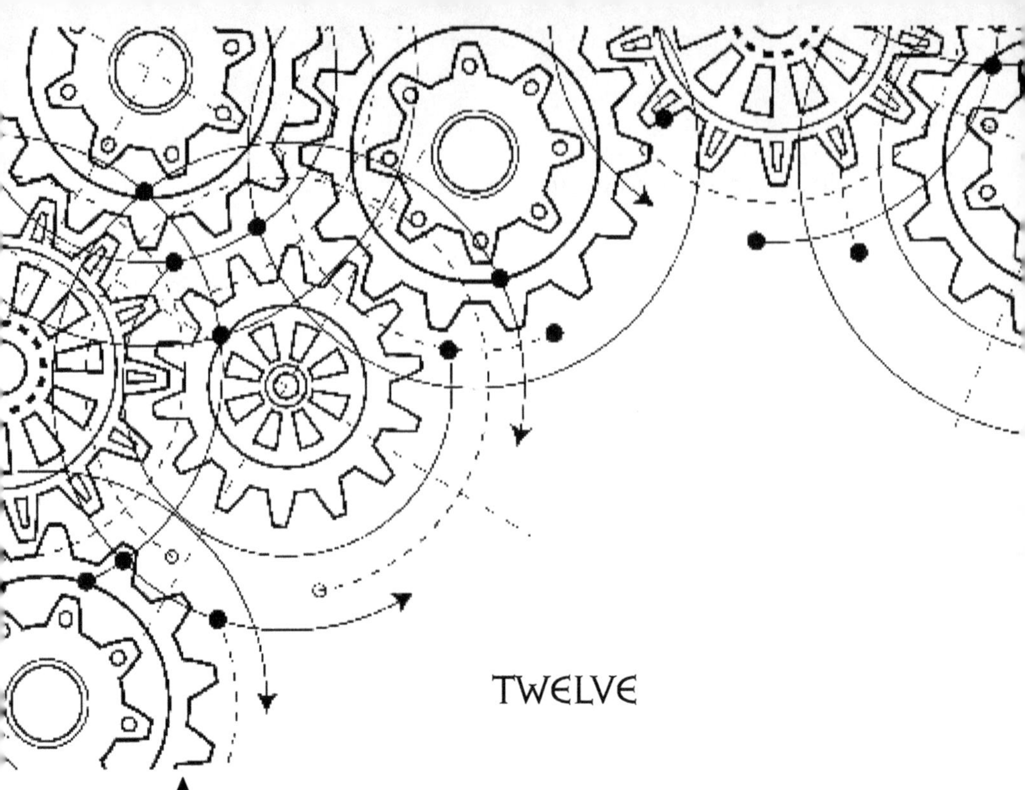

TWELVE

A week after the incident and two days after the burial, the city of Alexandria barely acknowledged anything had happened. Riding to the Palace on her mare, Heron watched the streets teem with activity.

She crossed Canopic street, edging around a group of Bantu traders. Camels stunk of dung and dust from the heavy traffic stung her eyes. The traders were engaged in a shouting match with a team of Persian mercenaries. Heron noted the lack of red tassels and wondered if Jarngard had hired this company.

Over the city, on the island of Pharos, the Lighthouse blazed its fires across the sea. Even in stark daylight, the light could be seen for hundreds of miles. When she was in the city, she often found herself looking at the tower.

An old man in a wine-stained toga bumped into her mare. She had to yank on the reins to keep him from being trampled.

Nearing the Palace, Heron paused at an automata play. A scattering of dirty sewer workers lounged on the dirt and watched while they ate dried fruits and charred meats wrapped in fig leaves. The play was one of her designs. A "Claudius" figure in a Roman toga did awful things like killing a baby and stealing from an old woman, before the "Agog" figure swept in and killed him.

The workers seemed more interested in their meals than the play. It could easily have been a blank wall they were sitting by. Once the automatas had run their course, a pair of children began winding the ropes back up and resetting the figures.

Heron wondered if she should tell Agog what she'd seen, but she doubted he had time for trivial details. He was still recovering from the poison. Today was the first day she could see him.

The last week had been tense, crouched in her workshop, ready to take to the east in a steam chariot should the Satrap die. That he lived only lessened the danger, a little. With Shayna dead and buried, the fragile truce of nobles had splintered, and now there was practically open rebellion in the eastern districts.

She finally reached his quarters after leaving her horse at the stables. The marbled halls seemed empty and the guards and servants she encountered anxious, as if they were expecting the Roman army to come sweeping into the city at any moment.

The few Northmen she saw smiled. Though she shared languages with few, they treated her like a brother. Heron wondered what they would think of her gender. It appeared the northerners gave more freedom to their women. She recalled her thoughts on the ride to the Oracle of Siwa, vacillating between revealing herself and keeping her gender hidden. She wanted to tell Agog, and let him know the true her, but those thoughts were naïve, she realized. Every choice could lead to death. Even the sparring she had with the Alabarch over her debts seemed trivial compared to the looming conflict between Alexandria and Rome.

When she reached the Satrap's office, he was seated behind a massive solid sycamore desk. Its size matched the man seated behind it, though Heron found it odd that a man that studied in killing, could also look like a scholar at the Library.

Agog was reading a folded parchment and holding a small object in his other hand. Heron could not see it clearly, but it appeared to be no bigger than a nut. As Agog visibly realized she was in the room, Heron got the feeling his mind was still working on some problem and probably had been for some time. She knew that feeling well, when she found herself locked in a stasis, holding her quill out, while working through a problem.

The Satrap placed the object into a box, closed the lid, and then he turned the parchment overtop like a tent. The box had been painted but the angle was wrong and the sunlight coming in through the windows created a glare. It could have been a sun or sunburst.

"How is Nektam's workshop?" Agog's gaze was weary and it appeared he'd lost a little weight from his poisoning. She could see it in his cheeks.

"It'll be a month before he can make even the simplest items, but, Plato have pity, at least the foundry was mostly intact. Rebuilding the furnace would have been laborious and expensive."

Agog nodded somberly. "And the engines?"

Heron's stomach tightened. There had been two more accidents, neither as disastrous as Nektam's, but they showed the instability of the newest design.

"There have been difficulties."

"Explosions, you mean? I'm recovering, I'm not blind or deaf."

Heron clasped her hands in front. Given the recent events, she didn't want to battle over the engines, but she couldn't ignore the problem, either.

"If you don't let me remove the protections, there will be more accidents." Heron took a deep breath.

Agog waved his hand, dismissing the thought. "You're the inventor.

Figure out a solution. I can't win a war if the Romans have the steam chariots."

"You're asking too much of my designs."

Agog raised an eyebrow. "I never knew you as one to give up so easily."

His words hit her right in the gut.

"I'm not giving up," she growled right back. "You ask the impossible."

"But the impossible is what we need if we're going to beat the Romans."

Heron slammed her hand on the desk. "I never asked to fight the Romans. While I bear no love for them—" Heron paused and collected a breath. "—and I was happy to foil them when I could, I wasn't stupid enough to pick a fight with them."

"And I am?"

She knew she'd gone too far.

"Apologies, Satrap. I chose my words poorly."

Agog shook his head and a strange, soft smile appeared. "No, the apologies are all mine. In the final reckoning, the historians may call me stupid and reckless, sticking my neck so far out to be chopped off by the Romans." Agog leaned forward, placing his forearms on the table, and gazing directly into her eyes. "But I don't believe it's impossible."

"You're right, Satrap, these things you ask are not impossible."

Agog slapped the table, startling her. "Freda's frozen tits, stop calling me Satrap. You used to call me *the barbarian*, you know."

Heron grimaced, but she realized he was playing with her. And that he knew that she called him *the barbarian* was an interesting insight.

"Impossible," he laughed. "When Alexander of Macedonia conquered the Persian empire and spread Greek culture across the lands, he did impossible things all the time. In truth, it was these impossible actions that kept him winning. If your enemy thinks it's impossible and you can do it, then you have the advantage. Just like Rome let its hold of Alexandria slip, thinking it was impossible for anyone to take it from them."

There was truth in his words. Many of her inventions or "miracles" were considered impossible. She delighted in doing something when others thought that it couldn't be done.

"You know the story of the Gordian knot, right?" asked Agog.

Heron chuckled, finding it amusing that the Northman was lecturing her on history.

"I do, but I want to hear your version. Stories change their meaning depending on who tells them."

"Well said."

Agog turned inward for a moment, gathering the story in himself.

"In the land of Phrygia, which lies east of Thrace, and between the two seas, there was a wagon tied to two prophecies. The first led to the rule of King Midas, and that story, while interesting, only leads to the second."

In Agog's voice, Heron could hear the tone and tenor of a performer. He looked like he could be just as comfortable on a stage.

"The second prophecy stated whoever undid the knot at the wagon's yoke, the one originally brought to the city by King Midas, that person would rule all of Asia.

"Now a story like this would surely be heard by Alexander as a boy, especially one taught by the great Aristotle in the Gardens of Midas. For it was implied that Midas had been a Macedonian before he came to Phrygia and maybe even an ancestor.

"When Alexander came to these lands, he found the temple in which the wagon was kept and tried his hand at untying the knot. Now, in everything he did, Alexander succeeded, so when he approached the wagon, he drew a great crowd, wondering if he would defeat this simple knot.

"But the rope was made from rough bark wound, and no ends were visible no matter how Alexander tugged and pulled at the knot, and it was so tight it seemed there was no logical way to work on it.

"Of course, a problem like this would only encourage Alexander, since no one before him had figured it out. Throughout the day, people came and went, watching the king study the knot and when it seemed that any normal person would give up, he pulled out his sword and cut it in two."

Heron drummed her fingers on the desk. "Well told, but I know a different ending, though I have heard that one before."

"Maybe I've heard the same," said Agog. "Go on."

"In my version, Alexander pulls the lynch pin out of the yoke, which loosens the rope, allowing him to eventually untie it."

Agog taunted her with a smile. "I much prefer my version."

"And I, mine," said Heron, bowing slightly at the waist. "For the answer to every problem is not a sword."

"Which is why I have a Chief Engineer."

Heron bowed again. "Which is why I am here. To attempt the impossible at your command."

Agog's smile diminished, mixing with concern. His eyes gathered distant storm clouds. "Yes, I need more of your miracles than just the engines."

"The poisoner? I have an idea."

Agog seemed genuinely surprised by her revelation. "It was not the question I intended to ask, but it is just as important."

"There was a woman seen wandering around in areas she should not have been. Sepharia overheard her and her slave." Agog flinched when she said Sepharia's name.

"My daughter later met her. She's a Macedonian noble named Polyxena. Sepharia heard the woman commanding her slave to 'make a delivery' and if he didn't complete the job or got caught, her friends would 'ensure his slow death'. I can fathom no other reason that this woman would be sneaking around except to poison the wine."

Agog paused and appeared conflicted about what he had to say next. "It wasn't the Macedonian noble, no matter what it sounded like. And she was never seen near the wine cellar, nor this mystery servant of hers."

Heron slammed the table with her fist. "How can you so easily dismiss this fact? Her words are damning and she was not seen during the ceremony. Why else would she leave?"

"It doesn't matter who you think poisoned me—" Heron noted his lack of mentioning Shayna, though she realized it should be no surprise. "—it only matters who the nobles think may have done it, especially Baruch."

"Who do they suspect? Vestalis?"

Agog glanced at his table, and Heron guessed who was implied.

"Not Sepharia," said Heron.

Agog cleared his throat. "She was seen wandering the halls and after the gift of the brooch, Baruch suspected she had designs on me. Removing her rival would give her a clear path to ensnare me."

Heron pushed the rage she felt in her throat back down. He was still the Satrap. "Sepharia had no intention of giving you the brooch in that manner."

"I know," said Agog. "Remember, I was there, too."

His eyes told her she was pushing too hard, too far. But it was her daughter.

"Have they accused her?"

"No, not yet," said Agog. "But I suspect they will."

"But why would she poison you, too? And the whole engagement party?"

"Jealousy? Rage at being spurned?"

"But she's none of these things."

Agog only nodded which led to a long bit of silence.

Heron remembered what he had said earlier. "This is not the impossible thing you want me to investigate?"

"No."

Heron steadied herself. Her anger was interfering with her thinking. There were clear answers for his behavior, she just had to figure it out. A simple Gordian knot, perhaps.

The answer, once she had calmed, was staring her right in the face. "Forgive me, you are the Satrap and also a victim."

Agog nodded. "This matter is political, not a crime. I would not allow them to bring her to a judge. There is no evidence other than jealousy."

"Then how will you deal with the Tanzens? Baruch is a powerful man and you need him as an ally," said Heron.

"That is why I need you. There are more ways to gather the nobles than through men like Baruch and Vestalis. Other allies wait to rush to our cause, just like Ramses, if it is proved worthy."

His earlier cageyness became clear. "And who are these allies?" she asked.

"I don't know." He grinned. "But I suspect we'll lure them out with the right scent."

Thoughts and ideas rushed around in her head, but nothing made sense. What impossibility would bring hidden allies to their cause? And why hadn't they come already? It certainly wasn't the Hermes Machine and she didn't have a single other invention brewing that sparked the mind. Her energies had been focused on protecting what she'd already made rather than exploring new possibilities.

"Your words are far too cryptic for me today. My body is tired and our sparring has only reduced me. Please explain this task so that I may focus on that," said Heron.

Agog leaned forward and she found herself being pulled in his direction. His eyes studied her. In the distance she could hear bells clanging, and could see the parapets clearly in her mind's eye. Agog's musty male aroma surrounded her.

"Find your voice, Satrap, or I shall have to build a machine to have it say what I want."

"You'd like that," he replied.

"I would."

Agog grinned, the beard bunching up around the corners of his mouth, and Heron realized it was as much a grimace.

"Without Baruch's support, my hold on the city is tenuous. Mere political alliance is frail and too beset with traps. I need a bold change to bind the city to my cause and solidify my rule." Agog furrowed his brow. "I want you to find the heirs of Alexander the Macedonian."

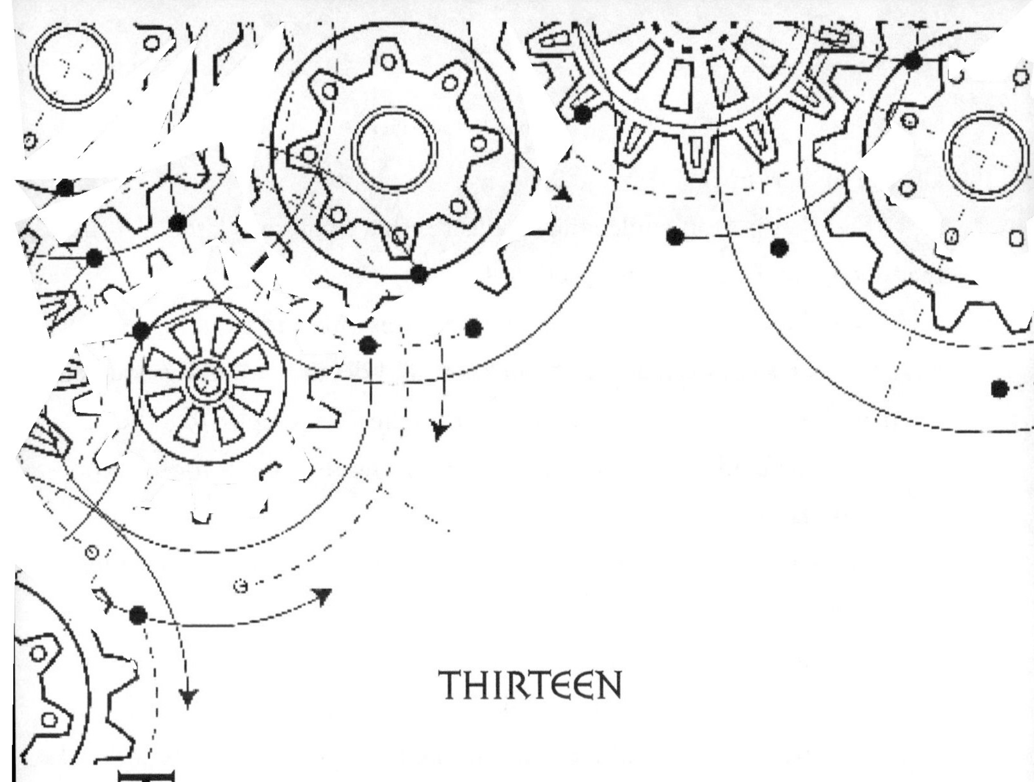

THIRTEEN

The word impossible rose to her lips, but she'd just spent the last twenty minutes discussing the importance of doing impossible things, so she didn't want to remind him. But then it occurred to her that he'd lured her into that discussion to preempt her potential line of argument.

Agog had his arms resting comfortably on the desk and he seemed to be trying not to be smug about the way he'd outmaneuvered her, but she saw right through him. She had an itch to scream the skin from his face, but that would only endanger her disguise as a woman.

No, she was Heron of Alexandria, the great inventor and Chief Engineer. A challenge like this should be greeted with open arms. But the logical side of her, the one that knew Alexander's history, had read the *Alexandrian Romance*, had heard stories of the great man time and time again, knew one important fact. An important fact that everyone knew, one that even a hermit in the Saharan desert would know. That Alexander the Macedonian had no heir. His only child had been murdered in the power struggles after his death. The request wasn't impossible, it was foolish and a waste of her time.

"Did that poison addle your intellect or have you recovered histories that detail other heirs?" she asked dryly.

"No," he said, all traces of his smugness disappeared from his face, or it'd only been her imagination. "You know all I do and more. I've studied the man, but only his war tactics and how he held his empire together."

"He only held it for a dozen years, including the time it took to conquer those lands."

Agog's eyes were wide and he seemed less affected by his poisoning then he had when she'd first came in. "But what he put into place has lasted for hundreds of years, and even to this day, dozens of cities still bear his name. I've read the works of Diodorus of Sicily and concur with his opinions. Alexander spread Hellenic culture throughout the known world and for that, even I, a barbarian of the north lands can be thankful." Agog winked at her.

"Must I revise my definition of barbarians based on your eloquence, or are you an anomaly?" asked Heron.

"I will not rise to your bait, *Michanikos*. But I will admit, even speaking or thinking of Alexander stirs my blood to action. Even Caesar wept upon first seeing the statue of Alexander in the Temple of the Seas." The fire in his eyes burned away all traces of the poison.

"While my blood grows as cold as the trail you set me upon," said Heron.

"You solved the mystery of the fires."

Heron crossed her arms. "A truth you cared nothing about. While the cult of Ur eventually proved responsible, you still blamed the Romans to further your cause. History will only remember your convenient lie."

"You're free to write your version of history." Agog nodded to the south, in the direction of the Great Library. "I will not stop you."

"But I'd be sure to wake the cult of Ur from their slumber and we have more pressing matters."

"Then what stops you?" asked Agog.

Heron paced back and forth, spitting out each word like throwing daggers. "Three centuries of time? The fact that Alexander is the most well studied man of our time or any time, perhaps? The Romans at our gate? The divided nobles? My workshop in turmoil?" Heron put her fingertips on the table and leaned forward. "Or maybe the fact that his only heir, Alexander IV, was murdered in a power struggle, a highly documented moment of history, I might add, ten years after his own death!"

Agog tried to speak, but Heron cut him off, resuming her pacing and tapping her fingers together abruptly. "Not only was the man a legend of history, but that history has become a myth. Even the various writings do not agree on his life. When I researched the fires in the Great Library, I only had to go to one place, but Alexander? Every civilization since his death has written about him. Even in the Mausoleum, they have whole rooms dedicated to Alexander. The Curiosity Rooms were created when Alexander sent back trinkets from his adventures to his mentor, Aristotle. Do you not see what you are asking? I do not have time, nor the energy for this endeavor!"

Heron slumped against the desk, feeling spent from her outburst.

"Are you done?" he asked as if she were a petulant child. He cut off any retort from her by raising his eyebrow playfully. The barbarian could be an infuriating man.

"No," she said as calmly as she could. "But if I am to embark on this foolish adventure, I have certain requests."

"Speak."

Heron took a deep breath. Her only hope was that her requests were so outrageous that he would refuse.

"First, I need your word that nothing will happen to Sepharia. I cannot work on this problem if she is in danger. Second, I need gold and men to rebuild Nektam's workshop and permission to remove those cursed protections from the steam engines so no more accidents happen."

Agog, to his credit, did not flinch at her requests and stared back with a slight smile on his bearded face. But she wasn't done yet, not by any measure.

"Next, I need twenty of your fastest couriers. While the Great Library contains much of Alexander the Macedonian's history, some was lost in the fires and others have been corrupted. I want the original sources and I need messengers to take those requests far and wide." Heron paused. "Do you need this investigation to be secret like the fires?"

Agog nodded.

"Then I need one of your Northmen. One who can read and write and help organize this insanity you have beset me with. I would prefer it be Jarngard."

"Are you done?" he asked sweetly.

Heron searched her mind for a request that would make him balk. She was afraid he would accept everything she'd said so far. When the answer came to her, she felt elation for thinking it and what it would mean if he did accept.

"Lastly, if I succeed, I want you to free every slave in Alexandria and ban their use in your lands."

For her inventions to truly take hold and change the world, people needed a reason to use them. Half the workshops in Alexander had gone slaveless and she knew the workshops and the freed slaves were better for it. The rest of the city was the next step, though the cries from the nobles would surely strike her deaf in their volume.

Agog waited only a few seconds before calmly replying, "I accept."

Heron choked on her words, while the Satrap continued.

"With a few conditions or changes, but I think you will agree with each one."

Heron nodded.

"Of Sepharia, I will bring her to the palace and give Jarngard as her guard and Ramses as her sponsor. The former can protect her from accidents while the later is already working to keep charges from being brought against her. While she is in my care, nothing will happen. Next, men and gold will run like water to Nektam's workshop or any other that should suffer from his fate since I cannot allow for the protections to the steam engine to be removed, but lay any responsibility on my great belly—"

"—how can you promise this when you have no gold?" she asked.

Agog held his hand up, indicating that he would explain. "I assure you that I now have additional funds available. No tricks."

Heron didn't believe him, but let him continue.

"My messengers will be at your disposal, whenever you need, and any other resources." Agog paused and Heron did not like the look of the thought that crossed his eyes. "Since Jarngard is now your daughter's protector, I cannot spare him, and he would have been a poor choice. Instead, I will give you Hoth the Black. He's more learned than I and a quick study. I believe he knows a thing or two about Alexander, as well."

Agog leaned over the desk. "And last, yes last. I will agree to your request, but not when you find the heir, but when together we beat the Romans, for I need their backs to build my empire."

Heron vehemently shook her head. "Then I cannot. When I find the heir or nothing. I will not compromise on this."

Agog sighed. "I would give you the Lighthouse of Pharos instead, but you already own it."

"And so I will not compromise. You've cheated me out of my payment once already."

Agog thought for a moment and when he said the words, she was not surprised, for in him, she could see how far he'd come, and how far he was willing to go.

"I accept your terms." Agog took on the face of a Satrap, one of power and authority. "Now go and find me the heirs."

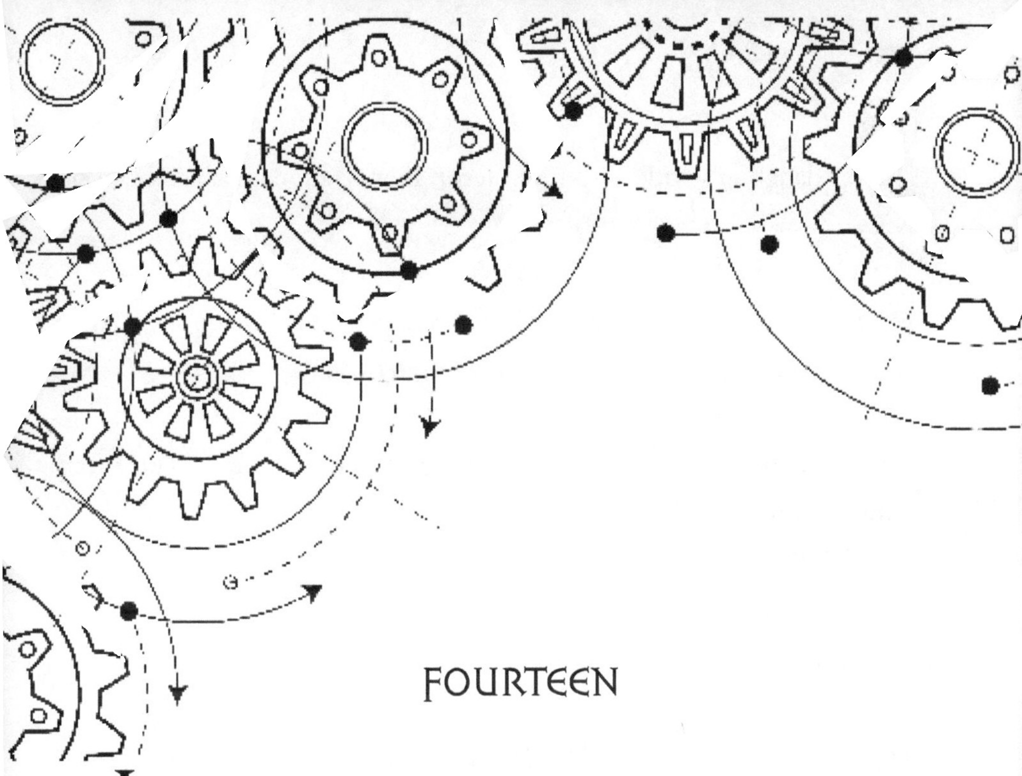

FOURTEEN

In the days that followed her meeting with the Satrap, the workshop returned to its former busy state. Nektam's place rose from the ashes and her debt to the man had been wiped clean. Heron didn't know where Agog had gotten the gold, but he'd paid as promised.

The Hermes Machine was in pieces before her. She'd torn out the guts. Gears and sprockets were scattered around the area. Workers gave wide berth when passing. She almost felt bad for the tongue lashing she'd given the craftsman that had knocked over a stack of brass connecting plates.

The plates were the diameter of her hand. Cut outs and notches in the thin circular sheets actuated gears and levers when turned. Heron thought of each plate as an instruction manual for the rest of the machine. The only problem was that she couldn't verify the instructions were correct.

No, she lamented, Vestalis had been right. The machine was too complex for the sandy roads that spread from the walls of Alexandria.

"Father," said Sepharia tentatively.

Her daughter's wide eyes told Heron how irrationally she'd been be-having.

"The steam barge has arrived."

Heron blinked once, remembering the deal she'd made with Agog. "Yes, the palace, you're going there now, aren't you."

Sepharia made no motion and, "Yes," was all she said.

Heron gathered Sepharia in her arms. "Do not worry. The Satrap promised your safety."

"Will Baruch demand a trial?"

Heron didn't know where Sepharia had heard it, but it explained her tepid behavior.

"It is possible, though Agog has promised me it will not come to that," said Heron. "The exile, Ramses, wields enough influence to keep that from happening."

Sepharia's brow furrowed and her lips drew a thin line. "But he needs Baruch and Vestalis? Why wouldn't he turn me over in exchange for their help?"

Heron couldn't tell her the full reason, but she could calm her fears a little. "If he sacrifices you for his cause then he will have no Chief Engi-neer." Heron tried to give her daughter her best smile. "Would I send you to the palace if I did not have his word?"

Heron put her arm around Sepharia's shoulder. "I'm sorry I had you read those papyrus about royal intrigue. Your mind is beset with worry."

A voice called out from the archway. It was one she was unfamiliar with, but the accent was clearly northern. The man spoke almost as well as Agog. "I could relieve your daughter of her worries if she stayed with me."

A Northman in an azure blue patterned wrap-over and long blond hair stood in the doorway. The streak of ebony in his hair matched his eyes. He was nothing like what she expected. Heron would have just as likely expected him to be carved into a statue next to the gods rather than a flesh and blood being in her workshop. Heron did not have time for the stirrings of her womanhood, but even this Northman made her wonder.

"I am Hoth the Black," he said as he strolled into the room with a grin, eyes firmly on Sepharia. "Scourge of the icy seas. Slayer of giants. And soon to be the Savior of Alexandria."

Hoth's attention on Sepharia stripped any lust she felt in her heart. Heron narrowed her eyes. She noticed the way Sepharia was returning his gaze. Heron was suddenly thankful that her daughter would be moving to the palace.

Sepharia gave a petite bow in her saffron chiton. She practically giggled out of her clothes at Hoth as he captured her hand and bowed. Heron noted the brush of crimson paint along his ear.

"I asked for an assistant, not a whore in men's clothes."

Hoth ignored the comment. "As the *Michanikos'* daughter, you must be Sepharia." His honeyed words made Heron grind her teeth. A whiff of perfume set her nose to itch and beneath that she caught something else, more natural.

"He will be your assistant?" Sepharia asked expectantly. "I could stay and help."

"Your place is in the palace," said Heron. "Jarngard will be your protector during your stay."

Hoth laughed, a sharp and cutting sound, and Heron could hear the history between the two men in that brief noise. "That luckless fool? If your daughter was assaulted, he'd have to stop and pull out his dice to decide if it were prudent to defend her. Pardon my words, but Wodanaz is thick between the ears for giving him her guard. Keep her here and I will keep her safe."

"Sepharia, on with you. The steam barge awaits."

Her daughter dutifully nodded and scurried out of the room, glancing more than once at Hoth the Black on her way.

Hoth made a repentant noise. "Apologies for my behavior." He smiled and Heron realized that the man had been playing with her. He might have been interested in Sepharia, but really he'd been interested in baiting her.

Though it was not the proper way to start, she had to respond. Heron clucked her tongue, mimicking Agog when he became annoyed. "Why would my daughter care for you, if you spend your time and gold in the Temple of Hathor?"

Hoth appeared genuinely surprised. He glanced over his shoulder. "Does the Chief Engineer of Alexandria keep spies?"

Heron scoffed. "I have no need of trained eyes when I have two of my own."

"What magic do you practice that allows sight into the past?"

Heron frowned and gave the man a second look. His mention of magic made her wonder if he was the right Northman to be her assistant. While Jarngard's obsession with his dice was troubling, she'd always sensed a deeper affliction than he let on, always laughing when he rolled them, which to Heron felt deeply tragic.

"I practice no magic. Only the rigors of the mind live here." Heron casually strolled to Hoth. "For example, I know you were at the Temple of Hathor because of the red lip paint on your ear. Only the sacred priestess-es wear such colors, along with their blue faience-beaded dresses."

Heron poked Hoth in the ribs. "Right here a bit of coloring from the clay beads had worn off on your tunic." Heron sniffed. "I can also smell the sycamore incense that the temple burns liberally."

Hoth's mouth hung open. He glanced again behind him.

"As for the priestess you visited, it was Nephthys, and you were drawn to her because of the bleached streaks in her hair. You thought it was a fitting sign, given your choice of hair color."

He touched the black streak in his hair like it had betrayed him. "What sorcery is this? You cannot know those things."

Heron let the smile linger on her face. "I can and do, and it is no sorcery. I am only using my senses and my mind."

"But the priestess. I came to the temple late and no one saw me enter. There were four priestesses and I chose her, exactly for that reason."

Heron pulled a long half-white and half-dark strand of hair from his shoulder and handed it to him. "I have spent time in the Temple of Hathor, goddess of love and beauty, and I know this Nephthys. And now you have, too."

The bravado Hoth displayed when first entering her workshop was now absent. He stared at the strand of hair as if it were a viper ready to strike him.

Her earlier concerns that Hoth was not the right assistant doubled. Like everything Agog did, there were probably other reasons he'd sent Hoth to her. Possibly it was to keep him and Jarngard from crossing swords, but at expense to her needs.

"Keep this in mind if you have designs on my daughter," said Heron. "I will know."

After a moment of thought, Hoth flicked the hair from his fingertips. He looked strangely repentant. "Apologies, *Michanikos*, I have behaved poorly in your workshop."

Heron eyed him carefully, unsure if this was a new ruse. "We must learn to work together if we are to solve this conundrum."

Hoth sighed. "Truthfully, I thought Wodanaz was sending me to you because he did not want me in the palace. A strange way to treat your allies, I considered, and this thing about the heirs of Alexander, while I do have knowledge of the man's history, it seemed a will o' wisp designed to lure me into the swamps to drown." Hoth bowed deeply. "But after your display, I can see why he sent me to you. Maybe after three centuries we can find Alexander's heirs."

"Doubtful, but I am willing to give it a try. The problem with the Satrap's request is that it has been so long and so many have too much to say on the subject of his life. The trail has been trampled by the historians of each time."

Hoth raised an eyebrow and a hint of smile rose to the corner of his lip. "Then maybe what I know might help find the scent. Before I was a captain, I was a fearsome tracker."

"And what is this knowledge?"

Hoth shook his head and his hair danced. "Not yet. I would first see your workshop and these miracles. It is your handiwork that drew me here as much as Wodanoz's request."

The range of emotions on display from Hoth made Heron justifiably apprehensive. Was he just playing her again? Heron detected other reasons for his support of the Satrap, though his interest in her workshop seemed genuine.

Heron led him through the building, pointing out each work and giving its purpose. Hoth was a good listener and asked questions about the machines, especially the ones made for war. He also spoke to the craftsmen and though normally they did not like to be bothered, especially while she looked on, Hoth drew them out like bugs at dusk.

The roaring of the gilded lions amused Hoth when she had the workers actuate it. The lions were ready to be shipped to the palace where they would be placed near the columned promenade. The pair would sit on either side of a set of bronze-covered steps and the top step would be converted to a pressure plate. Climbing the steps would trigger the lions to open their mouths and roar. The sound came from a mix of air shooting out of a billows and iron beads falling on a metal sheet. Heron had designed it so it would roar randomly, keeping spectators guessing.

Hoth climbed under a lion to inspect the inner workings. His face was eager and curious going in and stone-faced when he returned.

Next, Heron brought him to the courtyard where Plutarch was testing her newest war machine. Plutarch's eyes sparkled with interest when she introduced them.

"And what does this do?" asked Hoth, walking around the wagon. A steam mechanical sat on one end connected to a fly wheel. A stone ball about the size of a man's head sat in a metal cup. The wagon was placed before a chipped and cracked stone wall. Plutarch used this location for testing projectiles.

"Nothing right now," complained Plutarch.

Heron squeezed Plutarch's shoulder. "The fault is not yours, good friend. My design is faulty."

"What should it do?"

Plutarch smiled. "A better question in this instance. Heron is improving upon the catapult."

Heron laughed. "I'm improving on nothing but your patience. No matter how the wheel spins, the stone ball either stays in the cup or is not thrown very far from the wagon. But I expect my foreman to figure it out soon enough."

Plutarch bowed and they left him, returning to the scattered innards of the Hermes machine.

"And what is this?"

"A machine that knows your location." Heron sighed. "Or at least that was my intention."

"A useful tool if it works."

Heron quietly appreciated his opinion, but of course he would understand the importance of navigation. On the seas there were no landmarks.

"I've shown you my workshop," said Heron. "What is the information you possess?"

"Apologies, but I don't think I am ready to tell my tale. I'm sure you have other leads to follow first." Hoth looked to her with aplomb. "And if I am staying here, then I must return to my ship and gather my things."

Hoth soon departed and Heron was left alone with her thoughts. Like Agog, she found the ship captain a contradiction. Easy to dismiss at first, but seemingly more interesting and probably as deadly as each layer was pulled back.

Having Hoth stay in her workshop was going to be convenient but complicated. With Agog, she sensed she could one day reveal her gender without issue, but Hoth was different. Besides, she knew that Agog did not entirely trust Hoth the Black. He was necessary for the defense of Alexandria, but came with his own dangers. Heron promised herself she would not trust him, either.

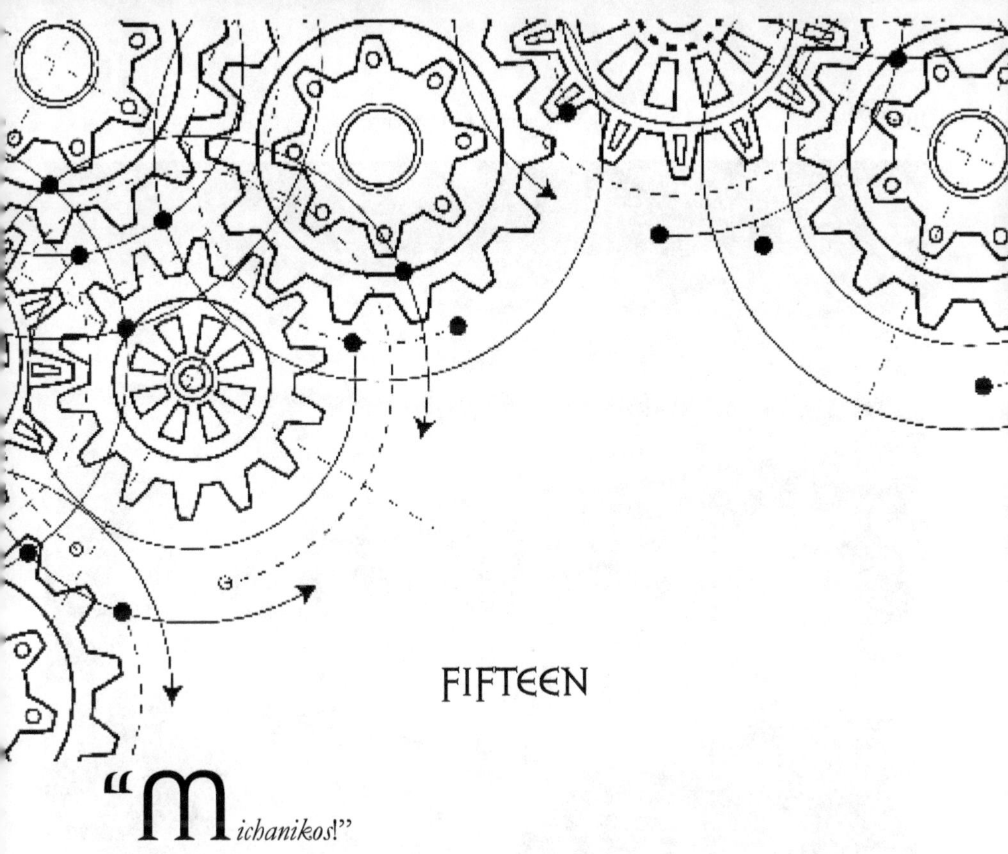

FIFTEEN

"*Michanikos!*"

Hoth the Black ran up the stairs of the Mausoleum like an antelope, dodging between absentminded scholars and runners with armfuls of scrolls. Heron cringed at each leap expecting him to knock a wizened scholar onto the marble steps, but he made it all the way up without even brushing one toga. She'd almost wished he'd bumped into one, or knocked a scroll loose, just so she could tear into him.

For the last three days, he'd been an attentive assistant, gobbling up every papyrus she'd given him and performing every task dutifully. He could even be called a model student, except for his cloying platitudes, which drove her to distraction.

Heron ground her teeth together. "You're late, Hoth. We have much work to do. Try to keep up."

Hoth smoothed his hair away from his face. "Apologies, Chief Engineer. I was so engrossed by the reading you assigned that I lost track of time."

"Then who is Mazaeus?"

Hoth smiled, letting all of his teeth shine before speaking. "*Michanikos.* Mazaeus was a Persian who served Darius, switched sides after Darius' defeat, and eventually served as satrap of Babylonia."

"*Hoth,*" she said through gritted teeth. "It is not necessary to say *Michanikos* or Chief Engineer, each time you address me." She paused with a heavy sigh. "And yes, you are correct on Mazaeus."

She'd asked the question because she kept finding Hoth in the workshop, wandering around and talking to her workers. They'd taken to him like a long, lost brother, a rich and good-looking one. Hoth kept bringing them treats during the day: spiced quail, roast dog, or pickled crocodile eggs.

She thought he was skimming his reading so he could ingratiate himself with her workers, for purposes she didn't understand, but each time she quizzed him, he was able to answer correctly.

"Follow me." Heron marched through the hallways of the Mausoleum, barely even responding to the other scholars that called out her name.

When they passed the Conservatory, one of the many lecture halls, a lilting voice reminded her of her foreman Plutarch, who'd taken to Hoth quite readily. She was not surprised, given his taste for men, especially pretty men like Hoth, but Plutarch was speaking far too freely with the sea captain these days.

"Try to keep up," she barked, only to find Hoth right behind her. Infuriatingly so.

They cut through a sunlit atrium filled with bird cages. The cacophony of squawking and chirps created a torrent of sound. Only a pair of avian scholars doted on the cages, making annoying bird sounds in response. Heron rolled her eyes at the idiocy before leaving the room behind.

When at last they came to the Halls of Alexander, Heron summoned the attendant, a balding man with patches of white-scale on his arms. Heron had listened to a lecture once that blamed the disease on adultery, but she doubted its accuracy.

"I will require full access to this hall."

"Of course," said the attendant, "you are always welcome."

"I also require that my assistant be allowed full access."

The attendant leaned to the side to see around her. His eyes widened as he took in the barbarian dressed in a ruddy ochre throw-over. Hoth had taken to brushing his hair straight and wore a simple silver necklace. Heron usually ignored her womanly needs when she gazed too long at him, but the attendant clearly didn't have that problem.

He crouched forward and whispered, "Does it read?"

Heron narrowed her eyes. "Why don't you ask it?" She stepped aside.

The attendant snapped up straight and yelled, as if Hoth was deaf, "Do. You. Read?"

Hoth smirked. "Only vowels and pointy letters."

The attendant made a little 'O' with his mouth, and then it was clear he realized Hoth was joking with him. Heron found the scene both humorous - because such assumptions infuriated her - and an annoying reminder of Hoth's behavior since he'd come to the workshop.

"Apologies." The attendant swallowed. "The great Heron, and his assistant, is always welcome in these halls."

"Good," Heron said bluntly.

Normally, she took more care with the men that ran the Great Library, for if they did not like you, you would never find what you were looking for. But today her patience had been battered like an anvil.

Heron wagged a finger at Hoth, indicating he should follow. She cut down the main aisle. Stacks of papyrus filled the shelves. The air was musty with old ink and paper, which blunted her foul mood.

When they crossed the length of the room—at least fifty steps, Hoth asked which section was for Alexander.

"All of them," she replied to his stunned silence. "This whole room, wall to wall, front to back, details the history of Alexander the Macedonian."

"There must be ten thousand scrolls in here."

Heron snorted. "Alexander was a popular man. And that's a good guess. The number is nine thousand, two hundred and forty. Estimated to the closest ten, based on the size, number, and packing of the shelves."

"Have you calculated this before?" asked Hoth in a voice that had lost its earlier simpering. He seemly genuinely interested, so she decided to give him an honest answer.

"No. I am an inventor. My mind must know numbers like a fish does water." Heron clasped her hands in front. "Where ever I go, what ever I do, I am always counting, figuring, and calculating. When I was younger it was more difficult, but through practice, it is a habit that follows me wherever I go."

Hoth nodded, clearly impressed. "So these are the scrolls we need to go through to find his heirs?"

She shook her head in the negative and received a questioning stare for it. Rather than explain, Heron opened the door not far behind her. Hoth joined her at the threshold.

"There are three more rooms, just like this one. Each one filled with a similar number of papyrus scrolls. And once we're done with those, we have a warehouse full of curiosities that he sent back to Aristotle from his travels."

The sea captain choked on the implications. "How can we even possibly get through all of this? This is madness!"

"Well, at least we agree on something. But try, we must." Heron sighed.

Hoth crossed his arms and turned back and forth a few times, truly considering the enormous task ahead of them. His patronizing grin had been reduced to a grim line. Wheels were turning behind his eyes. That he hadn't marched back out of the hall already was a good sign. She guessed that if he wasn't trying to get under her skin, he could make a good assistant.

"Twenty years," he whispered, unbelieving.

"Twenty years?"

Hoth put his hand to his mouth. "Twenty years to read every scroll in these halls."

"Did you figure that in your head?" she smirked, knowing that he was not far off in his calculations.

Hoth took her seriously for a moment, until he saw the look on her face. He raised an amused eyebrow in response. "A sea captain has to have a mind for numbers. Can't be getting lost on the big, scary sea."

Heron chortled.

"So how do I begin?"

"By telling me what information you have on Alexander. That may help us narrow down the search." She assumed he wouldn't mind her shrewdness in presenting the question under the circumstances.

Hoth shook his head. "What I know won't help here and it may not help at all." He shrugged. "But now is not the time."

Content that he was probably telling the truth, Heron asked a question. "Then we should start with what we know. You read the scrolls I gave you right?"

"Of course."

"A man cannot have heirs without a woman. Who were his women?"

Hoth thought for a moment and then answered, "His first wife was Barsine, the former wife of Memnon. Then Roxanne, the little star, who was said to be the most beautiful woman in the world at that time. Wouldn't you have liked to know her?"

Hoth winked and for a brief moment, she forgot that she was supposed to be a man. "My work is my woman now." It was her standard line and she hoped she'd delivered it well.

The slight tilt of his head suggested otherwise, but he kept going. "At the Susa weddings, he married both Sateira II and Parysatis. It was also claimed he slept with Campaspe, who he later gave to the artist Apelles in Thessaly."

"And what of the children."

"Alexander IV, birthed by Roxanne, and killed at the age of thirteen during the power struggles in the years following Alexander's death. Hercules was the second son from Barsine, later proved false and then killed for good measure."

"Is that all?" she asked, knowing the answer fully herself.

"That I know of."

"Then start there," she said. "Start with what we know. Don't linger too long in one area. Skim from place to place and see what you can learn. Don't read too long on one scroll. Look for discrepancies or for other lovers. Women that he was fond of."

"How?"

"The attendant can help you." She pointed up the rows. "Charm him like you have my workers—" Hoth smirked. "—and have him show you the tables, or *pinakes*. These subject catalogs can help you."

Hoth narrowed his brow. "And what will you be doing?"

"Consulting an old friend."

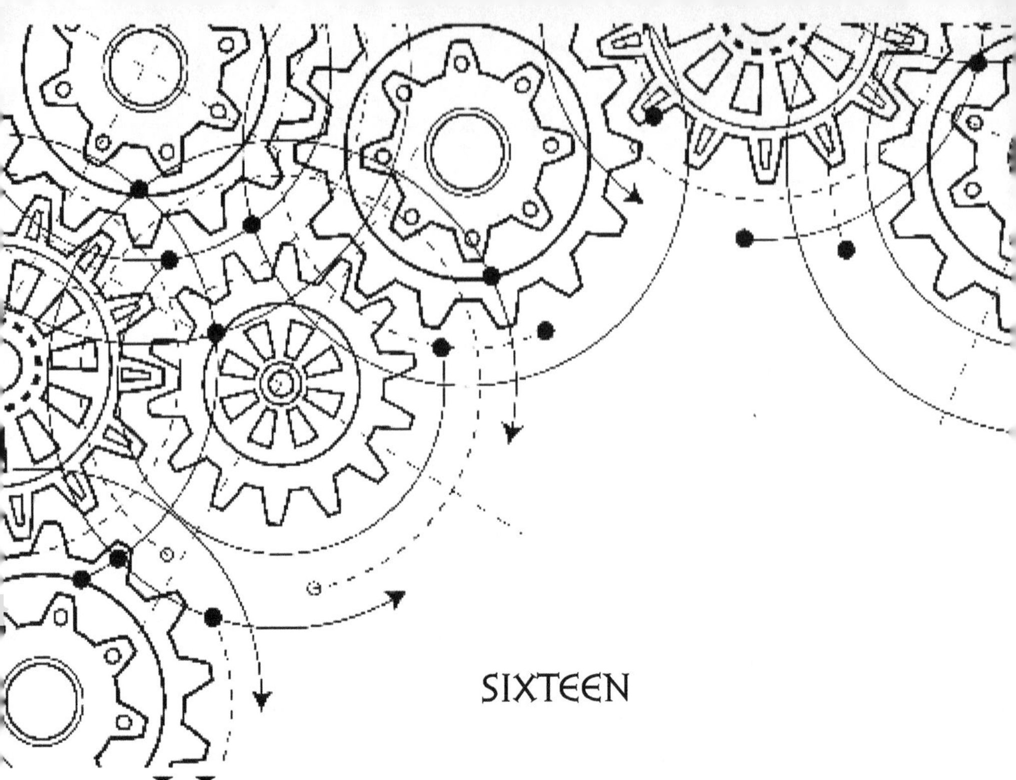

SIXTEEN

Heron did not leave the Mausoleum after she left the halls of Alexander. Instead, she went to a different part of the Library, one not known by even the longest tenured scholars.

The stairway descended and turned a couple of times, going deeper into the bowels of the Library. A long, featureless stone hallway smelled of mold, a rarity in the Library, but the scroll keepers did not pass through this location often with their drying powders.

As she neared the central chamber, her gut tensed as it did every time she came here, which was not often. In the other halls, she felt at home, almost as much as her workshop.

But in the Demetarium, named for the scholar who initially organized the Library, Heron felt every bit the imposter. Before a faded and chipped red door sat a gristled and bearded man in the dress of a scholar. Each time Heron had come to the Demetarium, this man had been at the door. Heron wondered how his replacements were chosen.

The scholar looked up from his book, set open upon the table, and gave her a toothless grin. "Heron of Alexandria."

The words came out mostly as a lisp. Heron nodded.

The scholar scribbled into the ledger and retrieved a key from a hidden pocket. In Heron's eyes, the key was unnecessary, since the old man could be knocked over with a quill and the key taken.

With the door open, Heron was ushered in. She hurried through, not wanting to let the moist tunnel air into the chamber. Once the door was closed, Heron inhaled, smelling the cool - and very book safe - dry air.

Once the door attendant had left her, Heron slumped onto a chair before a rack of scrolls. There were other things in the Demetarium besides scrolls: a papyrus sketching of the early city, the formal decree from the Ptolemies initiating the Great Library, a chunk of stone from the first dig, and other such historical curiosities.

But the scrolls were why she had come. There was nothing on them about Alexander the Macedonian. Not that would help her find the heirs. That wasn't why she was there.

Heron closed her eyes and imagined she was a hawk above the city. In her mind's eye, she saw the white stone buildings, the black tarry roofs of the workshops, the gilded temples, and flag draped parapets. In the orderly streets the people roamed, natives and foreigners alike. Alexandria was truly the greatest city in the world and the Great Library was its centerpiece.

Her eyes flashed open and in a start, she reached out and hovered her hand above a scroll. Within these rolls of papyrus were the diaries and thoughts of the city's greatest inventors. Euclid. Erasistratus. Archimedes.

Archimedes had never lived in Alexandria, his home was Syracuse, but he visited often and contributed countless works to the Library. He'd also contributed three scrolls to the Demetarium. Heron had memorized them word for word. The scrolls relayed such confidence of purpose and action that it made Heron question herself.

Archimedes never seemed to falter in his inventiveness, never questioned the purposes of his inventions. He took delight in the efficiency of his war machines, even when they killed thousands of men.

Heron had made her fair share of war machines, but hated each one. These machines should be made to work for humanity, not used as tools to enslave them. But who was she to complain when she'd profited from their use?

The failure of the now-defunct Hermes Machine only reminded her of this. Her machines were too complex for ordinary citizens of Alexandria to use, therefore they would not use them. Vestalis' devastating analysis of her machine only proved that point.

Heron wondered if her failures were because she was a woman. She did not believe it, could not believe it, otherwise she would have given up so long ago, but the doubts were there. Who else did she have to look up to? There were few great women of history and they were mostly rulers with divine power at their backs.

Because she was different, she could never get close to the other scholars in the Library. Had to use her wit and cutting intelligence to keep a safe barrier between herself and them.

Heron shook off the self pity and brought herself back to the moment. She pulled out a scroll at random and held it to her nose, inhaling the scents of old ink and papyrus. Surely these men had doubts too, different ones, doubts she could not understand just by reading their scrolls.

The edge of the papyrus had crumbled slightly. Granular chunks flecked off when she touched them. The air made her smack dry lips.

Heron set the scroll back into its cradle. The coming of the barbarian Agog had changed everything. Soon Rome would bring their massive armies and besiege the city, endangering the Great Library and its knowledge. The last battle fought in the city, the one with Caesar, had cost the

Library 200,000 scrolls. What would this one cost and would the historians blame it on her for giving the steam mechanical to the Northman?

"Will I end up dead on the end of a Roman spear like you did, Archimedes?"

She left the Demetarium and the toothless attendant scribbled in his book, smiling at her the whole time. Heron did not wonder what he wrote. It did not matter.

When she exited the tunnels, she left a different way, not wanting to pass through the headache inducing avian chamber again. But as she approached the alchemy labs she remembered why she'd chosen that previous route. Sulfurous smoke drifted out of the lab as she ducked in.

The source of the smoke was a red-faced scholar with yellowed robes and flecks of sulfurous crust around his lips. He'd clearly been trying to unplug the glass tube in his hand by sucking on it. The alchemist gave her a rotting toothed smile as she nodded.

She'd never known many alchemists to live long. They frequently worked with many dangerous chemicals. Not all were trying to turn lead into gold. Some honestly experimented with various materials of the earth, trying to decipher their secrets. The red-faced scholar was one of these.

There was another man in the lab, working near the seaward window, as far away from sulfur lips as he could get. Heron recognized him immediately. She'd seen him in the Library before, but had never thought much about him until now.

It was the man she thought of as One Eye, Titus Vestalis' slave-scholar. Knowing the merchants love of gold, she'd always assumed he was an alchemical purist, but the materials and vials he had set out before him were not of any alchemical experiments she'd ever heard of.

She'd seen him recently, she remembered. One Eye had been at the *Erusin* ceremony. The one at which Princess Shayna had died from poisoning.

One Eye had not noticed her entering the room. He was busy titrating a bluish liquid into glass dish. Heron quickly ducked out before she was seen and as she left the room, Heron thought of all the dangerous chemicals she saw arrayed before One Eye. Could it be that Vestalis was the poisoner? Sepharia had seen him wandering the outer rooms at the same time she'd seen the woman Polyxena. The connections gnawed on her brain until she gave up and decided she would have to make another visit to the Satrap.

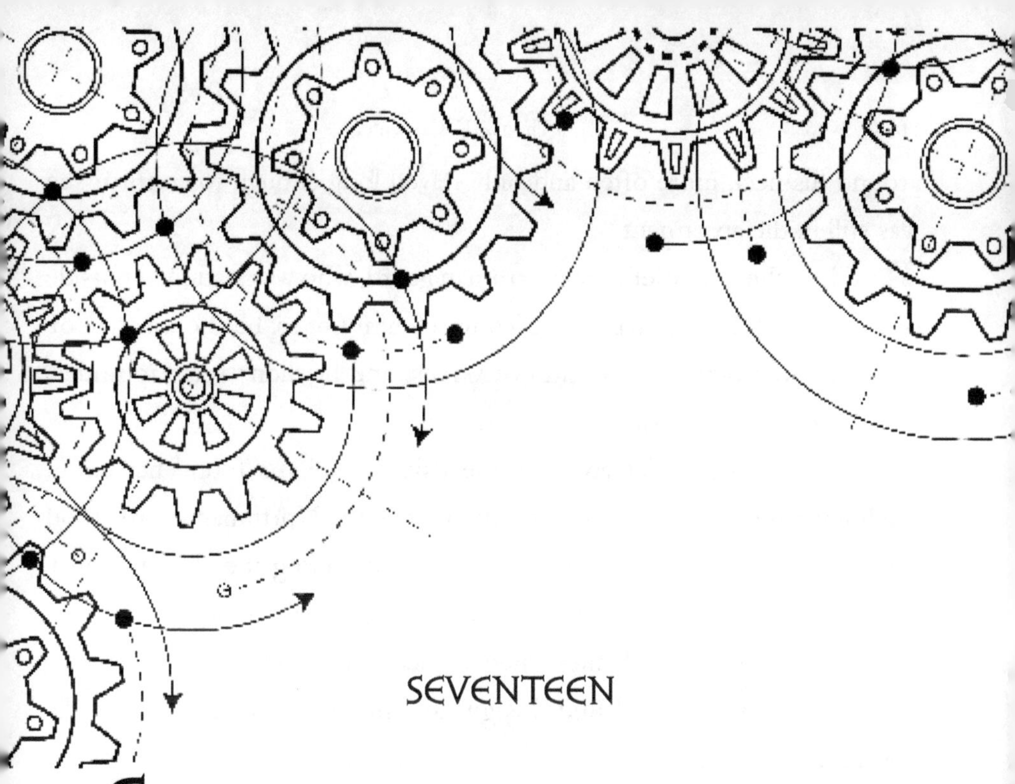

<h1 style="text-align:center">SEVENTEEN</h1>

Sepharia had been settled into the guest apartments in the Palace for three days before venturing out to explore. It seemed the Palace was full of both Baruch and Vestalis supporters, neither group she felt comfortable with.

The apartment, while lavishly furnished, did not comfort like the workshop. The shelves were filled with expensive treasures from distant lands that she was afraid to touch. Tiny jade elephants marched across the fireplace mantle. An obsidian jackal-headed statue stood sentinel on the writing desk. Sepharia didn't like the way it looked at her, so she faced it out the window.

On more than one occasion, the desire to create a tiny gear or other such delicate device welled up in her chest, but she was stuck in the Palace, so she had to curl onto the bed until the feeling passed. Her fingers itched with the memory of her tools.

Jarngard checked on her twice a day. He was anything but the laughing Northman that she'd first met. He seemed to touch the leather bag around his neck more often and only stayed long enough to confirm she was still in the apartment.

When she finally left, the Northman guard, who was stationed outside of her door, followed her. She tried to tell him not to, but he was one of the many that didn't speak Latin or Greek, and he didn't seem to understand her gestures, or didn't care.

Avoiding the busier areas of the Palace, Sepharia found herself in the library, pulling books out at random while the Northman guard stood outside. The bound books were a rarity considering the abundance of papyrus, but the Palace seemed to have many. Sepharia was reading an account of the early Ptolemies when a voice startled her.

"Of course, I would find this girl in a place of learning. A cut like her father."

Sepharia nearly dropped the book, spinning around and mumbling a greeting. An Egyptian man in tan robes and a smattering of gold jewelry stood at the entrance. It was the exile Ramses.

"Apologies." Sepharia bowed her head.

Ramses laughed and waved away her formality. "This girl has no need to apologize. It is I who should apologize for surprising her."

"My thanks again for saving me from those men. I have not forgotten that lesson," she said simply.

Ramses sighed. "I can see that."

Sepharia gripped the book with both hands. She glanced to the window.

"Has this girl's stay in the Palace been acceptable?" Ramses seemed to make an internal realization. "No. Of course not. This girl wishes to be back in her workshop, not embroiled in Palace intrigue."

"I do not want to offend," Sepharia said.

"A wise course. The hawks and the lions would readily tear her apart." Ramses strolled across the library. He had an easy smile on his face that

Sepharia found comforting despite the serious words. "And by the hawks and lions, I mean the Tanzens and Vestalis' people."

Sepharia nodded. "What will they do?"

"Right now the hawks, the Tanzens, seethe with anger, and the way this girl hides in her apartment only proves her guilt to them," said Ramses flippantly.

"Should I be seen more often?" she asked.

"Ahhh...a wise question," he said picking a book off the shelf, "but the lions would take offense by this girl's presence and her commoner birth."

"Then I cannot win, no matter which way," she concluded.

"This girl should not think of it as winning and losing." He paused and briefly examined the book he was holding. "Can a girl change a lion or hawk's nature?"

Sepharia tightly shook her head.

"Then how can a girl affect them?" Ramses challenged her with his question.

She set her book down and walked around the table. She thought best when she was moving. When the answer came, she couldn't help but smile. "By feeding them."

Ramses clapped his hands. "It makes me glad to see this girl smile."

Sepharia didn't exactly know what she should feed them with, but it gave her a thought to work upon, rather than sulking in her apartment.

"Why are you helping me?" she asked.

"This girl asks a good question. Every motive should be questioned." Ramses adjusted a wayward strand of his straight black hair. The dark markings around his eyes deepened his gaze and though he was older than Heron, he was still attractive. "What is this girl's opinion? She must be smart like her father."

A dark thought passed through her. She hoped she was smart like her pretend father, her aunt Ada, rather than her real one. Her father had been a brilliant inventor but dumb about all the important things like money and people.

"Unlike the Tanzens and Vestalis, Rome won't welcome you back if the Northmen lose the city. Your fate is tied to the Satrap..." Sepharia felt a warmth in her chest at the truth of her realization, but before Ramses could speak, another thought appeared. "—and you want something from me."

Ramses made a noise of appreciation and studied her with an amused smile. "This girl learns quickly. She might become a player yet."

Sepharia knew he was flattering her. She was a tool in this game of royals and Ramses was using her like the rest. But their alliances were in alignment, so she felt she could trust him. Agog trusted him. Ramses was constantly seen by Agog's side, giving advice on Alexandria and Egypt. The man was said to have old ties to the Ptolemaic empire, so he held much sway with the people.

"Where did you go when you were exiled?" she asked, hoping to delay whatever request he had for her.

"This girl asks a good question. Has she ever played the game Senet?"

Sepharia indicated she had not.

"The object is to get your pieces safely into the afterlife," he lectured. "But the opponent wishes to do the same, so the key tactic is to block the opponent's pieces until there is an opening."

"You went into hiding," she concluded. "Using your friends in Egypt to keep the Romans from you."

"This girl is quick."

"And now you have your opening with the Satrap."

Ramses nodded again and the moment grew tense between them. Sepharia knew she had pushed too far. Ramses cleared his throat and wandered to the window, indicating she should follow. His sandals made no noise against the marble.

At the window, which faced south, Sepharia could smell the ore reducing fires of the foundries. The wind had turned, which probably indicated possible rain, though it wasn't the time of year for it. That wouldn't come until the spring.

"Does this girl know the history of this room?"

"The Rhakotis district is my home."

Ramses nodded. "An honorable district, filled with my countrymen and most of the workshops."

Ramses proceeded across the room, his steps short and measured like a priest. When he reached the center, he extended his arms and turned in a circle, indicating the flooring. The carpet was a hand-woven treasure from the Indus Valley, far to the East near the edge of the known world. Sepharia had seen one before in the Emporium.

"This is the carpet that Cleopatra was smuggled inside to meet Caesar. Does this girl know the story?"

Sepharia nodded enthusiastically. Of course, she knew the story. Cleopatra was her favorite figure in the histories.

"Cleopatra swayed Caesar into giving her the country." Ramses pointed to the solid wooden desk against the wall. "Caesar sat there, probably composing a letter to the Senate in Rome."

Ramses moved across the room swiftly, though his face was smoothed with calmness. He stood before her and cushioned a curl of her flaxen hair with his outstretched hand. His eyes, though dark, were radiant with purpose.

"This girl is more beautiful than Cleopatra. Does she think she could do as Cleopatra did?"

She met his gaze with resolve. "She had more to offer than her beauty. She had history on her side and the millenniums of Egypt's rule. Caesar wanted the myth of the pharaohs, just like Alexander."

Sepharia flinched slightly when he squinted at her. Myth was too strong a word and she could see that he was insulted. But he let it pass unsaid.

"This girl sees with more than her eyes. She sees with her mind, too."

He was getting at something besides the impromptu history lesson. As Agog's ally, she had nothing to fear from him, but there was a message in his words. Sepharia mulled it over in her mind until the answer became obvious.

"The Satrap needs a royal bride," she said. "One with weight behind her name."

Ramses clasped his hands and wrung them, miming his concern. "I hope this girl is not insulted. After the brooch and the poisoning, the Satrap was worried."

The reason for his visit became clear. He'd been sent by Agog to remind her of her place. As the daughter of his Chief Engineer, he did not want to insult. Sepharia blushed with foolishness. She never should have made the brooch, even though she knew it was her best work.

"I understand my place." Sepharia sighed.

"This girl should understand that the Satrap believes the brooch a priceless work of art and one day he will be able to wear it, but for now, it must be a secret treasure."

The Palace had felt confining before, but now that she knew the Satrap was unhappy with her, it felt like a prison. Sepharia momentarily questioned why Heron had sent her until she remembered the scrolls she'd been tasked with reading. Heron was punishing her for interfering.

Or had Agog maneuvered for her to be in the Palace so Heron could not flee willingly should things go sour? Maybe he had heard about them preparing to leave the city when he'd been inching closer to the afterlife?

Then she remembered Ramses, who seemed to be studying her quite closely. Sepharia sighed.

"What is this favor you wish?" she asked, feeling like a wooden token on the Senet board.

Ramses' eyes alighted with purpose. "The Greek noble Polyxena."

"You know her?" Sepharia asked suspiciously.

Ramses shook his head. "That is why I need this girl's help. I do not trust this woman Polyxena."

"I don't either," she said. "I think she poisoned the Princess."

Ramses gave her a warm smile. "And if she did, then this girl's name would be cleared and the hawks would leave this girl alone."

"But why do you not trust her? Agog told Heron she was not the poisoner."

Ramses straightened his robe and looked sideways at her. "The Satrap is a busy man and cannot know all. I am his friend and I want to make sure he is safe. It is my head, too, after all."

It made sense. He was in as much danger as she was. "Even if I agree to help, I don't know where she is. I only met her once."

Ramses lifted his chin up, looking pious and priestly. Then he strolled to the open doorway. "She spends her afternoons in the Green Room waiting for an audience with the Satrap. This girl should become her friend, become trusted."

"She won't tell me that she's the poisoner."

"No, but she might let something slip that points to her. This girl is smart and should be able to make it happen."

"And how will I find you?" she asked after a time.

Ramses tapped his closed lips with a mischievous twinkle in his eyes. "This girl should put the jackal statuette in the north facing window when she wants me to visit." He paused thoughtfully. "But this girl should only call when there is something important. I cannot be seen in your presence if I am to be a helpful party should the hawks ever convince the Satrap to send you to trial."

Sepharia nodded. "I will do it."

"This girl is wise," said Ramses and he slipped out the door.

Sepharia sat in silence for a long time. Part of her felt overwhelmed by the stakes and the other part elated by the intrigue. She hoped she wasn't making another mistake like she did with the brooch. After all, even Cleopatra died in the end.

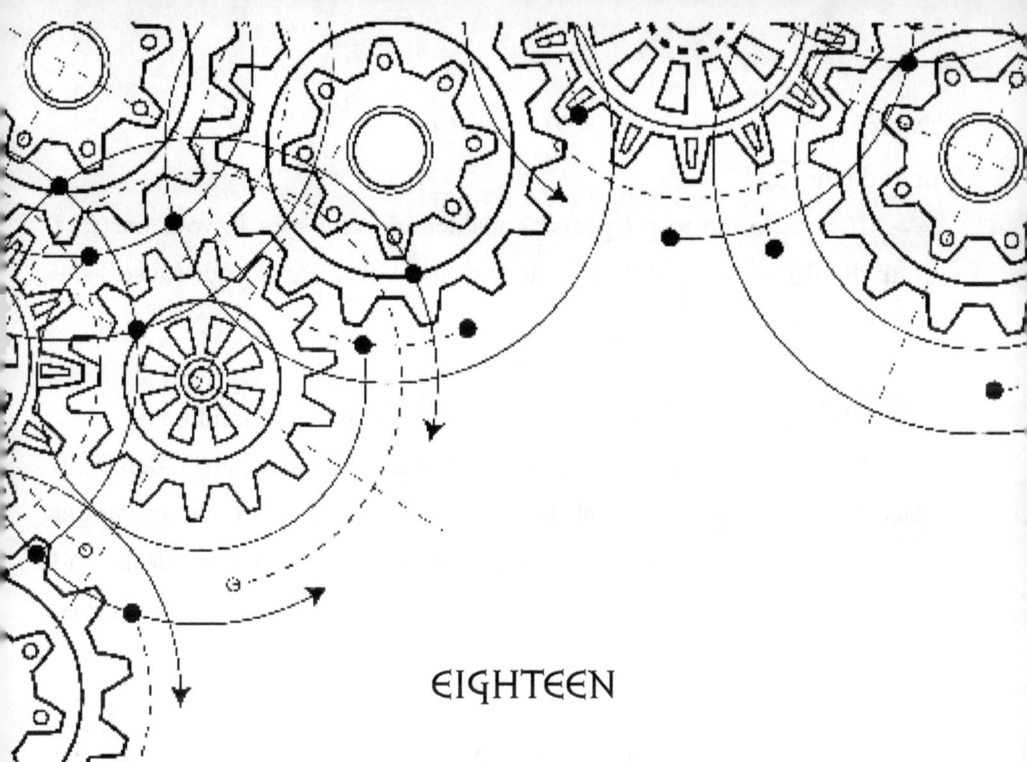

EIGHTEEN

Heron found the Satrap on the rise above the royal pier watching the ships slice through the harbor. A delegation of Armenians in woolen half-coats were walking away. Heron couldn't ascertain the result of the discussion by their sullen faces, but his silence as she stood by his side gave her an indication. Heron matched his silence and watched the setting sun cast orangish-red highlights across the water.

Heron had brought her ivory-handled cane, even though she didn't need it. She hoped it would remind him of her service. She caught a hint of movement high upon the Lighthouse near the blazing fires of the beacon. A changing of the guard, perhaps.

"Do you see, *Michanikos?*" asked Agog.

"What, Your Grace?"

Agog turned on her. "Haven't I already told you not to speak those platitudes to me."

"You have." She paused and let a smile rise to her lips. "*Your Grace.*"

Agog's bearded face twitched with amusement. "You're making me miss the north."

"If you decide to go, please consider an extra spot in your party. I think the Romans might have issue with my assistance to your cause," she said dryly.

"I think they'd scour the north for us."

"Plato have pity then, I guess we'd better make our stand here."

They watched the ships come in. A pair of Phoenician traders with black hulls zig-zagged through the water against the wind, passing under the great shadow of the Lighthouse. Men scurried about the decks and Heron could almost hear the scraping of ropes against the rigging as they tacked.

"Fewer ships," she said eventually.

Agog glanced at her briefly. "You see it, too."

"It's not hard. Usually the docks are full. Maybe half the spots are filled now. And those Phoenicians are taking long tacks rather than the short ones required when the harbor is teeming with boats."

"The Roman navy will be here in two months," he said.

"What will you do?"

"If I haven't got the support of Alexandria behind me, then it won't matter." He turned to her again. "What do you have on the heirs?"

"Nothing that hasn't been gone over by a hundred researchers before us."

"And Hoth? Is he helping?"

"An inspired researcher. He could make a name for himself in the Library if he chose."

Agog belly laughed and his whole body shook. "Hoth in scholar robes? By the gods, you jest, right?"

Heron cleared her throat. "Of course, he would never choose that. I was just pointing out that he has done well."

"How can you claim he's done well if you have nothing new on the heirs?" Agog clucked his tongue.

Heron scoffed, but kept her words clamped down.

"If you didn't come about the heirs," he continued. "Then why did you come to visit?"

Heron patted the satchel around her shoulder. "I have need of those couriers. Requests to other scholars and libraries that may have information."

"How many?"

"Twelve."

Agog glanced sideways. "I can only offer eight. The rest are carrying diplomatic efforts."

Heron scowled. "You promised me the use of twenty."

"And when you didn't use them right away, I sent them." Agog crossed his arms over his great belly. "I cannot hold them forever. I do have a city to run."

"You promised," she said. "What other parts of this deal are you going to back out on?"

"The messages will be delivered. The couriers will just make more than one stop. There are solutions if you would stop being so dramatic."

That he would lecture her on finding solutions, especially on the impossible task of the heirs, made her heart race with anger. Agog eyed her carefully, almost daring her to make a biting comment.

"Apologies, Your Grace," she said eventually. "Your solution meets my needs."

"Good, I'm glad we can get past that," he said, ignoring her sarcastic honorific. "What else did you come to see me about? Your lip twitches when you have something to say."

Heron put a hand to her lips, wondering if he was teasing her. "Yes... the, uhm, poisoner."

Agog raised an eyebrow. "If I investigated every attempt to kill me,

I'd spend all my time worrying about that rather than ruling. You shouldn't waste your time, either."

"But they killed your future wife and wrecked your alliance with the Jews."

Agog shrugged. "Tragic, yes. Shayna was quite beautiful and her father had much to offer. But it is done and maybe her absence will offer a better opportunity."

Heron couldn't believe how flippant he was about her death, and his near death, too. Then she remembered that he'd lost his real love to the Romans, and so she could forgive him, somewhat.

The reflections off the water from the setting sun blinded her, so she turned, positioning herself in front of the Satrap. The breeze tugged at her tunic and played with her short black hair.

"Vestalis' manservant," she began. "I saw him in the Library experimenting with dangerous chemicals and plants, nothing a pure alchemist would ever use."

"And?" Agog looked at her stone faced.

"He could have made the poisons that killed Shayna and nearly you."

Agog wrinkled his nose. "There are a hundred apothecaries in the city and countless other mystics and thieves who can make poison. Why should this be news?"

"But Vestalis has opportunity and motive."

Agog clucked his tongue again, and she could sense how annoyed he was at her.

"I trust Vestalis."

Heron wanted to argue, but she could see how resolute he was. Either he had other knowledge or Agog was practicing some sort of calculated trust. Either way, he clearly was not going to change his mind, no matter what she said. And truthfully, she didn't have much to go on, other than her dislike for Vestalis and One Eye's presence in the alchemy labs.

"What are you going to do then?" she asked, hoping to change the subject.

"About?"

"The city. How will you bring the nobles together before the Romans arrive?"

"I'm planning an athletic competition," he said dryly.

"A competition? That's madness."

He raised an eyebrow. "Perhaps. But it will cheer up the city and give everyone something to think about other than war."

"Is this wise? Shouldn't we be figuring out how to stop the Roman navy? If they set up a blockade, then the army can march down at leisure and take us when they want."

"On his conquest of the world, Alexander frequently staged contests to occupy his men's time. War is first waged with the mind before it is waged with the body." Agog grew even more serious. "And I expect you and Hoth to determine how to stop the Roman navy while I find us more allies."

"Should I ever bother sleeping?" she spit back.

"Only if you think you must."

"And how did you fare with the Armenians? Did you find an ally?"

He shook his head grimly.

"What madness is this that the Romans are coming and we are busy trying to find the heirs of a dead man, three centuries old, and hosting athletic games for spirits, while actual bodies cannot be found to equip with weapons we do not even have!"

"War is always mad, and perhaps it is the maddest that win." Agog gave her a dreadful smile and she knew he was being completely serious.

"Are we well met?" she asked him and he nodded. "Good, for I best hurry back to my workshop and conjure miracles from the empty air."

Heron shoved the courier satchel into his belly before marching off.

Agog called after her, and though she did not hesitate as she left him, his words put pause in her thoughts.

"Our allies must believe we will win before our enemies can realize they will lose."

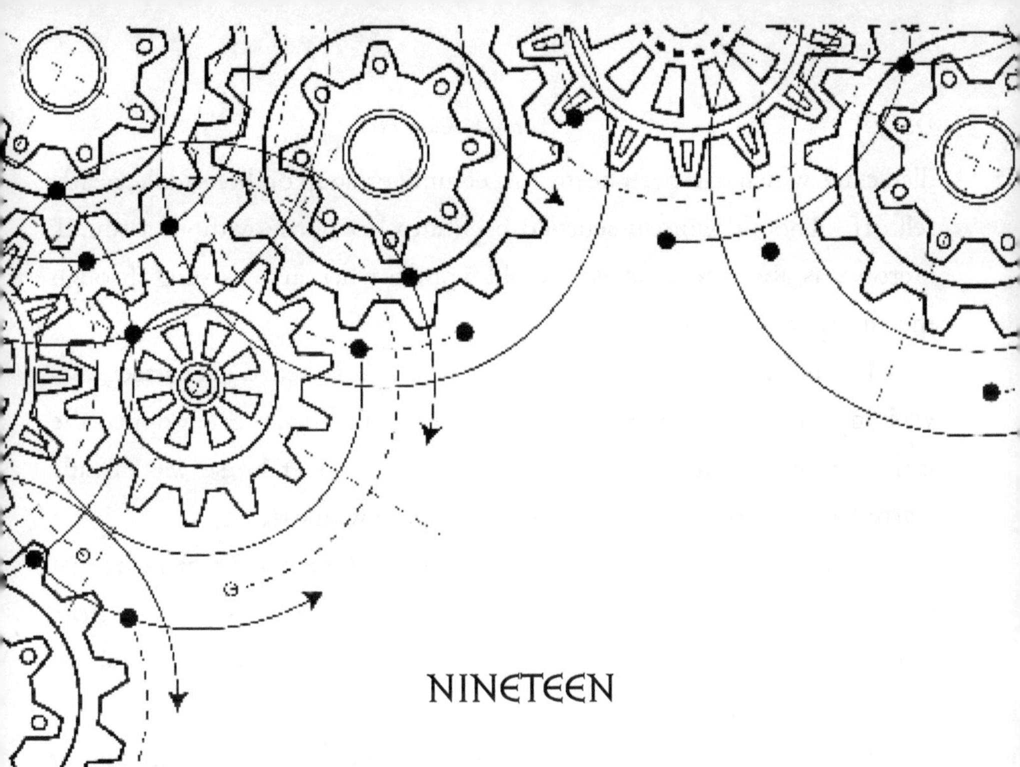

NINETEEN

Heron rode back to the Library in haste, urging her horse on with agitated snaps of the reins. She'd like to put a bit in Agog's mouth, but she knew even then he could not be tamed. Pure madness. They should be working on the strategy to defeat the Roman navy, not staging competitions.

The streets were absent of the usual teeming masses. Either everyone had returned to their homes at once, or people were leaving the city before the Romans arrived. She couldn't quite convince herself it was the first.

The light was failing and whole stretches of the street were swallowed up by shadow. Heron charged through without hesitation. The impact of each hoof beat jarred her knees, which had never truly recovered their former strength, but the pain provided a balm to her anger.

She passed a ripe sewer opening and wrinkled her nose in distaste. Her mind, occupied by the fetid stench, did not notice the old woman hobbling out of the shadows, directly into horse's path.

The horse reared up and Heron was almost thrown. The ivory-handled cane, which had been neatly tucked under a strap on her saddle, nearly fell off. The old woman scurried back into her house without a sound. Heron was about to chastise the old woman when arrows sung through the air, right over her head.

Three men on horseback appeared from a darkened side street, two wielding short bows, while the third held a sword high. She gripped the cane tightly and kicked her horse into motion. Her horse was already warm from the ride and took to a furious pace with ease.

No guards could be seen as she casted about, mentally remarking that she couldn't go half a block without running into a Roman soldier before the Northmen had come. How lightly Agog held the city became abundantly clear in that moment.

The first assassin caught up to her and she had to steer her mount away from his sword thrust. A second attempt to slash was thwarted by an unfortunate traveler who got caught between their stampeding horses. The impact of the man's body threw the assassin's horse wide and he dropped his weapon.

An arrow whistled by her head. Heron dared not glance back, lest her pace slacken or that she would run into something and be thrown.

The sword-less assassin caught up to her and captured her reins, yanking them out of her hands. His breath stunk like rotten eggs and his face was partially hidden by black markings. Heron tried tugging the reins back, but the man was stronger. Already her mount was slowing. Her back itched with the anticipation of an arrow skewering it.

Much to the assassin's surprise, Heron pulled a blade from the ivory-handled cane and shoved it into his neck. Hot blood spilled over her hands. The assassin slumped and fell over, nearly tangling in her reins. She was able to pull them back and pushed onward, stealing a glance backward.

One assassin slowed to help his fallen comrade while the other was lining her up with his bow. Her mind, despite the surging adrenaline, calculated the potential arc of the arrow and determined the best way to avoid it. Heron leaned forward in her saddle and hunched over the edge slightly, making herself as small a target as possible.

The arrow sliced across the horse, cutting her upper arm and ripping her tunic. Had she not been slumped like she had, the arrow would have taken her in the back.

Heron was able to take a different street, before the assassin could take another shot. She slowed enough to resheath the bloody knife and check on her arm. It was only a trickle of blood. She'd be fine as long as the arrow wasn't poisoned.

When she reached the Library stables, passing the guards that stood sentry at the entrance, she washed the blood off in the water trough, even rubbing water into the cut in her arm. The streets were near dark and Heron thanked her good fortune to have taken that ride during dusk, when lighting was poor.

Despite her near assassination, as she strode through the Library toward the Hall of Alexander, her hands still shaking slightly from the excitement, Heron's mind calculated the possible experiments she could perform involving the optics of different lighting. She knew the assassins had only missed because she had made herself as small as possible and that they had fired across the shadows. She wondered if the difference in accuracy mattered because of the strength of the changing luminosity or the distance of shadow between them.

When she appeared in the hall, Hoth barely looked up from his scrolls. His feet were propped on a cushioned stool. A glass decanter filled with dark purple liquid, wine she presumed, was set next to a plate of olives and fruit. Hoth munched on an apple as he read, the crisp sound of teeth sheering the skin echoed through the room.

"How's the Satrap? Busy dining and drinking with whores while we slave away at his behest, I presume?" asked Hoth, his normal biting tone infusing every word.

"Where did you get all of this?" she demanded, still hot from the ride.

Hoth glanced over his scroll and raised an eyebrow. "You said to make friends with the attendant. And I did. His name is Pykth. Unfortunate name, but charming fellow."

Once his eyes had drifted over her, his brow knotted. Heron realized that she hadn't organized herself before entering the hall. She hoped no sign of her femininity, or the tools she used to hide it, were exposed.

"How did you befriend him?" She didn't really care, but the way he had narrowed his eyes, made her want to change the subject.

"I got him a whore," said Hoth absently. "Hadn't ever been with a woman on account of the white scale." He looked up at her. "What happened to you?"

"Assassins. Three of them," she said. "Stabbed one in the neck." Heron pulled the blade half out of the cane.

Hoth tossed the precious scroll onto the table and stood up. He wore a silvery tunic and black leather belt. His hair had been meticulously brushed until it shown in the lantern light.

"What an inspired choice of stabbing location. Are all scholars this ruthless?" He grinned with aplomb.

"Though not as learned as others, I'm familiar with the body physiks as taught by Herophilus. I was concerned about getting my blade stuck in his sternum or rib cage and wanted to retain my weapon should the others follow."

"Well played, we'll make you a warrior yet." Hoth laughed, clearly mocking her. "Who were the attackers?"

Heron paused and reviewed the attack in her mind, trying to pick out important details. She remembered the man's breath vividly. It stunk worse than the sewer she'd passed.

"They'd been brought in by boat and from a distance. A man's breath usually reeks after eating nothing but dried meats and fruits for weeks," she said confidently.

"The Romans then?"

Heron shook her head. "They could have been *hired* by anyone, but they were not Romans. They didn't use short daggers like the Sicarii, so they're out. The ointments they used to hide their faces come from the east, near forests of the Black Sea. Their bows were short, strong wood, which mean they hunt in forests. Scythians maybe, but this is a useless endeavor."

"Useless?" he asked. "Do you not want to know who your attackers were?"

"Who they are is unimportant. Who paid them coin is what matters and without a live assassin to interrogate, the exercise is like measuring the circumference of the earth. Interesting, but not practical."

Hoth poured Heron a glass of wine. She drained half in one gulp and sat on a bench near the table, hiding the slight tremble in her hand. It occurred to her in that moment of respite that Agog had argued the same thing about his poisoner just that evening. But unlike him, she vowed to keep her eyes open. The identity of the poisoner was important to Sepharia's safety, no matter what his promises.

"What have you learned this week?" she asked.

"While you've been sleeping, or whoring, or whatever it is you do when you're not here? Which is almost always." Hoth took another bite of the apple and the crunch was an exclamation to his accusation.

"There are other libraries than this one," she responded. "I've been at the Serapeum and writing letters to obtain other scrolls from distant lands."

She'd also been working on the Hermes Machine, a frustrating endeavor if there ever was one, late at night when no one else was in the workshop. She'd run her powder box dry more than once. But she wasn't going to tell him, or anyone. It wasn't what she was supposed to be working on, but until she figured it out, it was like a burr in her mind.

"You didn't answer my question," she said, trying to sound irritated, though her mind was wrestling with the realization that she'd just killed a man. "What have you learned?"

"If the answer was in these scrolls, then it would have been found already. Most of this—" he waved a frustrated hand at the hall, "—deals with his exploits and battles. And reading it only reminds me that I much prefer to be the one performing the exploits and have my life recorded as such, rather than reading and cataloging it. I don't know how you scholars do it."

"I'm not a scholar," she growled. "I'm an inventor. I do not record, I create."

"Well, I'm not one either and I need to get back to my ships soon."

"Are you giving up?"

Hoth sipped his wine. The black streak in his hair framed his face on one side.

"I never give up."

"Then for the third time, what have you learned?"

Hoth smiled mockingly. "You first."

Heron pushed her anger down. She understood why Jarngard wanted to kill the man.

"The letters I sent won't bear fruit for another month or so, depending on the speed of the couriers." *Or longer*, she thought to herself, *because Agog didn't keep his end of the bargain.* "Of the Serapeum, I consulted the resident scholar on Alexander and could determine nothing new, though he did point me in another direction, though it will require a journey."

"Let me guess, the scrolls we need are in Rome and we have to get Claudius' signature to get them?"

"No, east. To Babylon."

"I thought the city was destroyed."

"First it was moved," she said. "And then it was destroyed. The old location still contains the remnants of what was once the city. The Serapeum scholar claims there're records in the old temple. He's tried to get them on more than one occasion, but the priests in charge will not agree."

"I could stand to get out of this musty hole," he spat.

"I didn't say we were going," said Heron. "Unless you've found nothing useful."

"You might decide otherwise when I explain." Hoth finished his glass and poured another, keeping his gaze centered on Heron the whole time. "After sampling the scrolls for a few days, like you requested, I got bored and turned my attention to poor Pykth. I figured he'd know where to look, being the attendant in charge. After a few days of working on him, and after a night of drinking here in the hall—" Heron did not bother reminding him that it was a place of study, not drunken revelry, since she knew he wouldn't listen, "—I got him to open up. I didn't let on to our purpose, but I did ask him if there were other documents not yet cataloged by the Library. He said he knew of one that supposedly held important revelations about Alexander the Macedonian, but hadn't yet been pried out of its owners hand."

"And who is this stingy owner?"

"A trip to Babylon will look quite agreeable after I tell you who."

Heron sighed. "Just tell me."

"They say that in battle, just like in bed, timing is everything. It might be that scholarly pursuits are just the same. You might have had this document easily a scant few weeks ago."

The answer came to her like a shot and she sat up, feeling once again like her luck was cursed.

"Baruch Tanzen."

TWENTY

Waves slapped against the hull of the hexareme, *Mars Valliant*, beating a time that would have made a row leader proud. Aulus Plautius waited on the port side for the corvus walkway to be extended to the *Rhenus*. He narrowed his eyes and watched the ship's captain and his first walk leisurely up to his flagship.

Aulus much preferred the legions. These ship captains, the centurions, were much too undisciplined like the pirates they were usually tasked with hunting.

The captain and his first found Aulus waiting with his hands clasped behind his back. They gave him the Roman salute. "For the Empire. Ave, Consul Aulus. Apologies for this interruption to the fleet's progress, but my orders were not clear in regards to the merchant ship we had captured."

Aulus did not glance to his left, where the *Rhenus* had entangled a speedy merchant ship with hooks in its sail lines. Instead, he ground his teeth and settled his cold, gray eyes on the two officers. The ship captain before him had been smiling, but that stretching of the lips slowly disappeared beneath Aulus' withering gaze.

"Your bow lines are slack and your helmsmen has the *Rhenus* riding too close." He was not an experienced sailor but he knew enough about seamanship to know the *Rhenus'* captain ran a sloppy operation.

Aulus paused and poked a stout finger into the captain's chest. "Is that a wine stain?"

The captain cleared his throat. "Yes, Consul, about that. Your orders, you see. When we captured the merchant ship, the *Olive Runner*, I realized the captain was a relation of mine and more importantly a distant cousin of a Senator by marriage."

"So instead of sinking it, you invited your relation onto the ship and have been dining him in your quarters while you wait for a ruling on the standing orders."

"Yes, Consul," the captain said, and after a moment of thought, he added, "apologies."

"Yes. Apologies. A trifle of a word for a trifle of a man," said Aulus. "Is this merchant captain a Roman?"

"No, Consul. A Greek like myself, but loyal." The ship captain bounced from foot to foot like he was standing on hot coals.

Aulus intoned his question in his most pleasant voice. He'd often found it to be more effective than yelling. "Do you know why I gave the standing order for all scout ships to sink any vessels they encountered?"

"B—Because you don't want the Alexandrian fleet to know we're coming?"

Vespasian, his legion general, approached but stayed apart. The man was slightly vain with his longer, almost un-Roman hair, a sharp contrast to Aulus' shorn cut.

Aulus turned his attention back to the *Rhenus'* ship captain. "How did you become a captain?"

"I earned my naval crown during the Batavian rebellion and when the previous captain retired, he recommended my promotion."

"I see. A river captain," said Aulus, shaking his head. "By the gods, the Alexandrians and that barbarian warlord that took the city know we're coming." Aulus thought back to the letter he found in his quarters one foggy morning three months ago. How it got there still burned him. "What they don't know is that we're a month ahead of when he expects us and that we're not coming down to blockade and wait for the army, but we're coming to wipe him out right now," spat Aulus. "Something a river captain would never know."

The *Rhenus'* ship captain and his first practically shrunk before him. Aulus thought briefly about punishing them severely and then decided against it. He would be lenient, today.

"Your actions have delayed the fleet half a day," said Aulus. "The cost of that delay in wages for the fleet is around fifty talents."

The ship captain shrunk even further and his eyes hollowed out on the spot. Fifty talents was more than the ship captain would earn in a lifetime.

"First, you will cut the lines from the merchant ship and then burn it. Second, when we attack Alexandria, you will be in the vanguard." The ship captain perked up, realizing that if he was to be in the vanguard, that he would still be a captain and more importantly, alive.

"As I expect that the Alexandrians will not be able to set forth a navy large enough to stop us, the *Rhenus* must be the first ship to reach the wall and you must be the first soldier to plant a flag on the wall earning your Battlement Crown, or you shall pay the fifty talents back to me in full."

The ship captain swallowed. "Yes, Consul."

"You may return to your ship. Be swift with your duties."

The ship captain and his first turned to leave, but then the captain hesitated. "Apologies, Consul. What should I do with the merchant crew?"

Aulus replied without delay. "Run them through and throw them overboard."

The ship captain and his first retreated back to his ship without even a sideways glance. Their earlier lazy saunter had been replaced by a rapid stiff march.

When they were gone, Aulus turned to Vespasian. "Getting soft in your old age?"

"Truth," spoke Aulus in a quiet voice. "In years past, I would have had him whipped with the flagrum and then executed, but I've learned to use these digressions to my favor. The *Rhenus* will surely be the first ship to the wall, which will spur on the others to attack with fervor."

"So you still mean to assault the city without the full support of the army?" asked his general.

"Every day that barbarian holds the city is another day the Empire is weakened. Alexandria was Rome's prized jewel and Emperor Claudius wants it back."

Vespasian raised a curious eyebrow. "He's promised the governorship to you, hasn't he?"

Aulus nodded. "He wants a true Roman in charge of the city. Flaccus allowed too much Egyptian influence into how things were run."

"And the Library?"

"I don't want to repeat Caesar's mistake," said Aulus.

"You believe he burnt it?" Vespasian goaded. "Heresy for a true Roman."

Aulus' gaze flickered over his general, which was as much a shrug as he ever allowed. "Whether he burnt it or not is unimportant. That he allowed the Library to stay in Alexandria was his mistake. When we take the city, I shall have it relocated to Rome and all its scholars put under tight control. The barbarian was able to take the city using technology of the Library's making. The Empire cannot allow this to happen again."

"Won't that diminish your governorship?"

"Alexandria is still the port for Egypt and all its gold and grain and slaves. And I'm getting old. Prestige means less these days than securing the Empire."

A piercing scream turned the two men's attention toward the *Rhenus*. The ship captain was summarily executing each of his prisoners and having them thrown over board while his men were untangling themselves from the merchant ship.

"Efficient when properly motivated," said Vespasian.

"Agreed." Aulus touched his chest absently.

"I see it's not just them. Are you still motivated by that letter?" asked Vespasian, nodding towards Aulus' gesture.

Aulus touched his chest again, feeling the folded parchment beneath his tunic. He considered Vespasian's question carefully.

"Yes."

The tint of burnt cloth caught Aulus' nose. Flames were flickering across the deck of the *Olive Runner*, while the *Rhenus* safely pulled away.

"Had you ever heard of this Hoth the Black before you found that letter in your quarters?" asked Vespasian.

Aulus shook his head, while his grey eyes watched the *Olive Runner* burn. The crackling of planks snapping cut through the sea air.

"The man is either a compatriot or rival of the barbarian warlord they call Agog," said Aulus. "Either way, he won't survive the siege."

"So you're not going to take him up on his deal?" smirked Vespasian.

"This Hoth the Black is little more than a glorified pirate. I do not treat with pirates, though I may let him believe I will, if it serves my strategy."

Aulus Plautius watched the merchant ship crumble and break into fiery pieces as they pulled away. His nose itched with the smell of burning wood, knowing its scent well from previous campaigns and previous sieges. Before the siege of Alexandria was complete, there would be more death and more burning. The only thing he needed to save was the docks, and those could be rebuilt. The rest could be smashed into rubble if it got in his way. He'd burn Alexandria if it kept it from the Northmen.

TWENTY ONE

Jarngard waited in the Palace garden for the others, spending time rolling dice across the bench. When the bone cubes whispered a certain number, he snapped his wrist, throwing the weighted dagger into the towering sycamore tree in the center of the garden.

He heard the scrape of a footfall as he was digging his knife from the tree. A litter of gashes were spread across the trunk.

"You're getting fat, Your Grace. I heard your footsteps on the marble path," said Jarngard over his shoulder.

Agog let loose a string of curses in at least four different languages. "It was purposeful, you dolt. I know your mind when you're rolling those dice. If the wrong number would have come up, I would have had a hilt sticking out of my chest."

"No faith in the gods?" Jarngard smirked.

Agog settled onto a stone bench across from Jarngard and adjusted the Suebian knot on his head. His tunic stretched across his belly. "It's no wonder that the people have no faith in us. We treat their holy symbols like toys."

Jarngard flipped the dagger into the air and deftly caught it. As he raised his arm to throw, Agog said, "If you throw it again, I'll break your arm."

The cawing of a nearby raven filled in the silence afterwards. Jarngard gave Agog a stilted grin and shoved the dagger into its sheath.

"It's a holy tree," said Agog. "Like *my* tree. And these people have been around here longer than we've been pissing in the snow up north."

"Your tree? All this Satrap and city business is running to your head." Jarngard nodded towards Agog's overflowing gut. "And to your gut."

"What gives you the right to speak to the Satrap this way," said Agog.

Jarngard couldn't tell if Agog was serious or not, but he didn't care. "By the number of times I've pulled your ass out of trouble. I think when you burned that walled village down deserves a few words, or more."

The Satrap sighed, leaning heavily on his propped arm. "A disaster, that one. The horse wasn't supposed to get spooked." He winked playfully. "But we did make out pretty well in the end."

Jarngard cupped his dice and shook them lazily a few times, just to feel the weight of them. He wanted to toss them across the marble path to see what number would appear, but not while Agog was watching. So he shoved them back into the leather pouch around his neck.

"Why did you call me here?" asked Jarngard.

"I'll explain when the others arrive."

Jarngard playfully scoffed. "Others? You mean I'm not the only one you torture with your responsibilities?"

"Heron and your favorite sea captain are coming." The Satrap's gaze speared him, clearly reminding him not to antagonize Hoth the Black. Jarngard touched the dice bag absently.

"Why not Quadi, or Grimm, or any of the others? You know I've been too busy watching Heron's daughter to do anything else."

Agog growled, and Jarngard knew he'd pushed him too far. "Your brothers tend to speak loudly when they drink. I don't know all of it, Heron has some news as well, but the fewer that know about our plans the better."

"My brothers? Aren't they yours, too, or have you renounced our barbaric ways."

When Agog clucked his tongue and rubbed his beard, Jarngard considered it likely that the Satrap might tackle him off his bench in a moment.

"I can't get them to accept us if we don't learn their customs. Have you ever stolen a sheep wearing your bear furs? No, you wear sheep skin, and creep into the pen." Agog threw his hands up. "And what do you mean you're too busy? I haven't seen you speak to Sepharia once. For all I know, Baruch could have hauled her to his torture room by now."

When the familiar voice barked out from the archway, Agog and Jarngard shared a cringe.

"Our deal was that Jarngard watches my daughter," said Heron. "If he cannot keep her safe then how can I work on the Satrap's *requests*?" The last word was infused with such venom it made even Jarngard bite back his retort.

The inventor stood beneath the stone arch, his neat black hair clipped in the Roman style. For a slight, effeminate man, he was imposing.

Agog glared in Jarngard's direction, until he threw his arms up. "I'm not a nursemaid for the girl."

"I didn't ask you to be a nursemaid, I asked you to be her protector," growled Agog.

Now they were both glaring at him, trying to make him feel guilty for avoiding Sepharia. The girl was old enough and pretty enough to be wed, which meant she didn't need to be watched. He'd seen girls younger than Sepharia strip the hide from a man using only her words.

When they continued to stare, Jarngard crossed his arms. The only thing worse than the two of them staring would be—

"If I thought nursemaid would be such a prized position, I might have fought you for it," sang Hoth from the opposite doorway.

When Heron shot Hoth a glance, he shrugged. "I got lost."

"We can still fight for the position. I'll cross blades with you anytime." Without realizing it, Jarngard found himself standing.

Hoth rolled his eyes and strolled into the garden like a peacock in his aquamarine tunic. His hair was neatly kept by a gold band. He pulled an apple out of a hidden pocket and crunched into it.

"Nessa left me. Get over it. She would have left you, too. She was *fickle*."

Jarngard barked a cutting laugh. "Ha. I'm sure she didn't want you borrowing her dresses."

A sudden noise brought them both around. Agog had slapped his hand against the stone bench. His cheeks were ripe with anger and looked more crimson than the apple Hoth was dining on.

"Hoth. Jarngard. If you don't shut your maddening drivel up, I'll kill you both myself. Half the nobles want us dead and the other half are afraid of the Romans. Let's not do their job for them."

Agog foamed with the fury Jarngard normally saw on the battlefield.

"Wodanaz." Hoth chuckled. "You're getting as fat as an ice giant down here. They might mistake you for their jarl if you ever return to the lands of the eternal night."

The simmering look that Hoth received was not as severe as it might have been in a different time. Agog had been known for his temper in younger days and in the blood lust of battle, could cut men in two with his sword.

When at last it seemed everyone had settled, Agog spoke up. "How goes the search for the heirs of Alexander?"

Heron shook his head. "We've found nothing new, as expected. The only two acknowledged heirs were killed as youths. Other children, if he had them, were born to whores and are meaningless to our cause."

The great bearded man put a heavy hand to his chin. "Then why'd you come to me? You've already told me twice before that you've found nothing."

Heron glanced at Hoth, who shrugged in response. "We've found leads on further information. Two of them. Unless you've received word from your couriers."

"You know they can't have made it back yet," said Agog, to an agreeing nod from Heron.

"The first lead is complicated and the second one might take some time." Heron grimaced. "How well are you getting along with Baruch Tanzen?"

"The man feels I betrayed him in some way, especially since I won't let him put your daughter to trial."

"For which I thank you," said Heron, bowing. "But that complicates things. Because we think Baruch may have scrolls on the subject of Alexander that might be enlightening."

"Are you sure?" asked Agog.

Heron shrugged. "It's possible. He did give me a map of Alexander's conquests for the *Erusin* ceremony. The map had details not found on other maps and it appears properly aged to be an original or close to it. And that could mean that he has more information about Alexander. Maybe he took them from the Ptolemies when they were killed."

"What do you think could be in those scrolls?" asked Agog as he sat back on his bench.

Heron steepled his fingers and paced across marble pathway. "The Alexander scholar we spoke to believed that the scrolls are a journal from his third wife, Parysatis, the daughter of Artaxeres the Third. If anyone was close enough to Alexander to know if he'd fathered any other children, it'd be her."

Agog shook his head. "That's not much to go on."

"The other lead is more promising, but will be harder to acquire," said Heron after a time.

"Harder to acquire," scoffed Hoth.

Heron rounded on him. "Quiet."

Hoth tossed the half-eaten apple into the air and caught it deftly. "Or what? You'll stab me in the neck like you did that assassin?"

Jarngard found himself standing again. By the look on the Satrap's face, he hadn't heard this bit of news, either.

"Assassin? Why are you keeping secrets?"

"Technically, it was assassins," said Hoth drolly. "Three of them. But who can count these days after reading one hundred accounts of how Alexander stormed the walls and drank endless cups of wine with his men and bedded strange women from across the known world. I'd rather be doing it than reading about it."

While Hoth rattled on, Heron marched up to Agog and put a finger into his chest. Though he only came up to the Satrap's chest, Heron didn't seem cowed by the differences in size. Of course, without the inventor, Agog could have never taken the city. Jarngard had to repress a chuckle, fearing Agog to hear him, after all, the big man didn't really need him as much as he did the inventor.

"You didn't seem to care about who poisoned you. Why would you care about a few assassins sent for me?" demanded Heron.

"I don't care about the 'who' so much, but that you've been attacked at all." Agog pointed an accusing finger at Hoth. "How did you let this happen? If I'd just wanted a scholar I would have sent Quadi, but he couldn't protect the sea from a fly."

Hoth wiggled ink-stained fingertips at Agog. "Your miracle worker had me slaving in the dark."

"Idiots, the both of you," spat Agog, indicating Hoth and Jarngard with a pointed finger. "I should have let you kill each other for that gold whoring woman of yours back in the north and save me a lot of trouble."

"Do you want to hear about the second lead or shall I return to my workshop?" asked Heron. "I could be making new machines to help us with the Romans rather than researching a centuries dead man who just happens to share a name with this city."

Agog flopped back onto the bench putting his hand to his head. "Tell me, before I hand the city back to the Romans."

"In the place that Alexander died, there was a temple raised in his name," said Heron in a level lecturing voice. "In expectation that he would one day become a god, since he had been called the son of Ammon-Zeus at the Oracle of Siwa..."

The Satrap had stopped leaning on his knee and sat up, face scrunched as he listened. Jarngard fingered the leather bag around his neck and silently scoffed at the explanation. When Agog had told him about his plan to find the heirs of Alexander, Jarngard had privately thought his captain had gone mad and the only reason he hadn't told him as much was because the inventor had agreed to do it. But as Heron continued, Jarngard found himself more interested in the story.

"...had collected detailed information about the Macedonian. The scholar that we spoke to said that the Temple of Alexander had never shared information with a single other source, no matter what the offer of gold."

"And where did he die?"

"In Babylon," said Heron.

"But that city is dead," said Agog.

"The population was moved north to Seleucia and renamed Esagila. Not all moved with the city, including the Temple of Alexander, which by the letters the scholar showed me, still exists. I should also point out that after his death, it was in Babylon that the Alexandrian Empire was divided between his generals. If there is any place that has information about Alexander that hasn't already been uncovered, it's old Babylon."

"And how will you get them to open up to you when they haven't to anyone else?" asked Agog.

"A good question," said Heron. "Which one of your Northmen can get into difficult places unseen?"

Both Agog and Jarngard looked to Hoth the Black, who held up his hands innocently. "Not me," he said. "My men need me and the Roman navy will be here in months."

"Three months," said Agog. "Vestalis' spies report that the navy was delayed by strong storms in the seas around the strait. You can go with Heron."

"But is he the right thief?" asked Heron.

"When a man sleeps with as many women as he does, he learns to sneak out of houses and villages quite well," said Agog.

"You wound me," said Hoth. "I don't have to sneak in. They invite me."

"I said 'out' of those houses. Eventually the husbands come home."

Jarngard chuckled. "I've caught him sneaking out of the occasional barn, too."

"So he can sneak through barn doors. But the temple is rumored to be an impenetrable maze designed to foil thieves." Heron glanced almost disgustedly in Hoth's direction. Clearly the inventor didn't want to take him.

"Hoth still," said Agog. "The man could dance his ship through a maze in the fog if he had to. I suspect he's been fucking Poseidon's daughters for this gift."

Hoth put on a mysterious grin and shrugged.

"Fine. I'll take him and Punt, too, in case we run into trouble. A loaded steam chariot should get us there and back in under a month, assuming everything goes well."

Jarngard could sense that Heron had some other plans about the trip by the way the inventor's inner wheels seemed to be turning.

"What about me, Your Grace?" asked Jarngard. "Shall I ready myself for work in the kitchens? Feed you at night?"

"Finally," said Hoth, "a job worthy of your skills. Maybe you should shake your little bag for some babies to amuse them."

Jarngard showed his teeth while stroking the hilt of his dagger. If it weren't for Agog, he might have killed the man already.

Then Jarngard noticed Agog staring at him with an equally amused grin, almost too amused. One that made his backside pucker up.

"Don't worry, my friend. You have much to do while they go visit Babylon," said Agog.

"Does it involve cold beer and warm wenches?" asked Jarngard dryly.

When Agog's eyes lit up, he knew he was in trouble. "Why yes, beer and wenches in droves. You're going to enter the Alexandrian games I'm hosting."

"And why would I do that?" he asked.

"Because during the games, I'm going to make a wager with Baruch Tanzen. You win, I get the scrolls on Alexander. He wins, he can put Sepharia to trial."

"I forbid it!" Heron looked ready to burst into flames.

"I'm your Satrap. You can't forbid it," said Agog. "And don't worry. I've never seen Jarngard lose a wrestling match before."

"But what if he does?"

The look the inventor gave Jarngard, put a stone in his belly. He hadn't wrestled in years, only advised his cousins from time to time, but he'd never lost before.

Agog stood up, towering over Heron. "Even if he does, I still must agree to the final judgment. And since I'm one of your coconspirators, I think we know how I'll judge."

The famed inventor wrestled internally with the issue until after coming to a conclusion, sighed regretfully. "Agreed." Then he pointed a finger up at the Satrap. "But if he loses, or something goes wrong, I'll arm the Romans with my war machines and help siege the city myself."

"Then we are agreed," said Agog as he walked toward the archway, dusting his hands off. "Leave as soon as you can and without being seen. We can't let any assassins know you're leaving the city."

Heron left right after Agog, and before Jarngard could leave, he heard a rough whisper turning him around. Hoth the Black stood on the far side of the room with a curved blade in his hand, pointing at Jarngard.

"If you ever want to cross blades with me," said Hoth. "I can make a special arrangement for you."

Jarngard took a step back, as if he was turning to leave, and in one fluid motion, spun, and threw his knife at Hoth. The blade stuck into the sycamore tree near Hoth's head, exactly where he'd meant to put it. To his credit, Hoth didn't flinch and stared back with a forced grin. Jarngard left, leaving his dagger in the tree.

TWENTY TWO

The evening bells rung softly in the distance like announcements for a dream. Sepharia stepped quietly through the Temple Room, trying not to disturb the few practitioners standing near their miniature altars. Incense was thick and created a light haze in the upper portion of the room. The few lanterns flickered like eyes in the mist.

The room had been created to allow the Ptolemies, or other visitors to the Palace, an opportunity to sacrifice to their gods without having to descend into the city. The black and gold inlaid marble made the room a cultured tomb.

Sepharia stopped at a small shrine dedicated to Artemis and threw a ha'penny on the altar and lit a stick of incense in the nearby copper brazier. Heron would frown disapprovingly if she saw Sepharia in the Temple Room. Despite the years of working for the Temples, making miracles, Heron had never spoken positively of their influence.

Sepharia saw them more as a way to signal your desires to yourself and the wider world. She spied a doe-eyed noble girl around her age in a light blue chiton hovering near the shrine for Aphrodite. A noble boy could know her heart just by seeing her in front of the shrine.

Near the back of the room, an old man in a toga, wavered before a tall shrine with delicate colonnades carved into the stone. She knew the Roman shrines by their towering stone importance. Sepharia had heard that Governor Flaccus frequented his Roman gods. The shrine was Saturn—a god of agriculture and time.

Content to take her time, Sepharia circled the room, observing the other temple goers. When her eyes laid upon the obsidian black altar tucked into a cubby, she shuddered uncontrollably. Etched upon the front was a shedu—a winged bull man. She knew an altar of Nanna when she saw one, since she'd been tied to one by the Cult of Ur, just this year. Thankfully, no one attended it. Next time she saw Agog, she would warn him about the shrine.

But the Cult of Ur was not why she had come to the Temple Room. For days, Sepharia had been looking in vain for Polyxena, so she could prove the woman had poisoned the Satrap and his future bride.

She had not found her in the Green Room as Ramses had suggested. A chance inquiry with a guard revealed that she'd been seen some evenings in the Temple Room. This was the third day Sepharia had visited with no sighting of the Macedonian.

After a full circuit, around the various columns and past the many shrines and cubbies, Sepharia paused at the entrance. The room was dim and hard to see, and she was certain that she'd visited every corner of the room, but once again, she hadn't found Polyxena.

Of course, she hadn't seen the Sumerian shrine to Nanna and she'd been here twice before. So Sepharia continued around for another loop, taking care to check every nook and cubby. Halfway around, she found an area that she hadn't seen before. A pair of columns and the massive shrine to the Roman god Mars crowded out a small shrine that curled around the backside.

Sepharia avoided the Palace guard lighting a stick at the Mars shrine. Standing behind the columns, wearing a dark chiton that blended with the soot covered cubby, Sepharia found Polyxena. The woman, wearing the same crimson cloak she'd seen her in during the *Erusin* ceremony, was leaning into a niche in the wall and seemed to be running her hand over an altar shaped like a coiled snake.

"Sepharia," she said, speaking in warm regal tones. "Are you a fellow worshiper of Aite?"

Sepharia opened her mouth to lie and say she was, but the way Polyxena looked at her kept her hewed to the truth. "I...am not. I was just looking...at the shrines. I'm studying the scrollwork on the altars and columns for ideas."

The woman clapped her hands softly, barely making a sound. "How wonderful. You should take a lesson from Aite." Polyxena stepped aside revealing an empty alcove. Her eyes twinkled with mirth and Sepharia was glad for the dim light so she could not see the difference in their color which had made her dizzy last time.

"It, it's empty? I thought I saw..."

"Sometimes even when nothing is there, something is there." Polyxena winked. "Aite is a sly teacher and a fitting goddess for a Macedonian woman."

Sepharia put her hand in the niche and patted around to find a clue of where the altar had gone. There might have been an edge along the back, but she couldn't be for certain.

"A wise girl not to trust your eyes. They can be deceiving." Polyxena hooked her arm around Sepharia's and pulled her towards the exit. "One shouldn't linger at such an auspicious goddess."

Sepharia was familiar with the miracles her father made, but those required preparation. Polyxena had made the snake altar disappear as simply as snapping her fingers and without warning.

"I've been hoping to see you again," said Polyxena. "I meant it when I said that we Macedonian women should stick together.

"I would like that," said Sepharia hesitantly, trying to think of a reason why. She needed to get close to the woman. "I...I've been very lonely in the Palace."

"You have?" Polyxena patted her arm. "You should have come to me sooner. I know the Palace is a foreign country to you, having spent your time in the famous Heron's workshop, but I could teach you. Show you what weapons a woman has at her disposal."

Polyxena's face wrinkled in thought. "Of course, girl. You've had no mother to show you these things. No wonder you spend your time making beautiful jewelry. Your father cannot understand you, nor teach you."

Despite the fact that Heron was actually a woman, Sepharia agreed with Polyxena. Heron had always had to act as a man and so had rarely given her the comfort a mother might. Her real mother had died young, so she knew little about her.

"I would like that." Sepharia smiled and it was not a lie. In truth, she liked Polyxena, and knew she could learn much from the woman. But she also suspected her of being the poisoner, having seen her away from the party giving dubious directions to her servant.

"Good." Polyxena patted her hand again. "Tomorrow I will fetch you and together we will stroll the halls and I will introduce you to the other petitioners in the Palace. Your lessons will begin then."

A loud crack overhead startled Sepharia, while Polyxena barely flinched. Then the air was filled with the sound of tiny drumming.

"What an odd time for a rainstorm," mused Polyxena, staring up at the painted ceiling. "Maybe the gods are planning mischief on this night."

They strolled a bit further and Sepharia realized her hands were shaking slightly. She hoped Polyxena hadn't noticed.

Sepharia politely cleared her throat. "May I ask what you are here to petition the Satrap about?"

"You may ask, but it is between me and the Satrap. And I am content to wait, though I hope he answers me before the Romans arrive." Polyxena drifted away, the knowing gaze making Sepharia feel like a young child.

The walk back to her room was filled with conflicted thoughts about Polyxena. Sepharia desperately wanted to like Polyxena, even though it was probably unwise. But she'd spent her life sequestered in the workshop and her first tastes of Palace intrigue had met with disaster. She needed a confidant, a teacher. Someone to help her survive the world of the nobles, even if it might be the person who caused the trouble in the first place.

So Sepharia promised herself she would be careful. She would learn from Polyxena, but also use that time to find out if she was the poisoner. It might just be that her life would depend it.

Entering her apartment, Sepharia was surprised to find Ramses and two female slave-attendants. Colored rolls of dressing cloth lie in a heap on the couch. The Egyptian exile looked dressed for a party with black eye-makeup and gold jewelry.

"Where has this girl been?" asked Ramses.

"Just. I..."

The slave women captured her gently and brought her to the center of the room and began to undress her. When Sepharia protested, Ramses stayed them.

"Apologies. I expressed my impatience to them while this girl was missing and they followed the whims of my desire."

"I don't understand."

Ramses tilted his head. "Was my message not received?"

"No. I haven't been in my apartment all day."

"Pity. Pity," he said. "But we can hurry."

"Hurry to what?" The slave women looked ready to continue to undress her with their hands hovering just inches away.

"Dinner with Baruch Tanzen," said Ramses. "I have convinced him of your innocence but he wishes to speak to you himself."

"What? I cannot. Does Heron know?"

Ramses bowed his head in apology. "I could not reach your father, but the Satrap agreed to the dinner."

Sepharia's stomach squeezed into a knot. She hadn't eaten all afternoon and the thought of eating with Baruch Tanzen made her nauseous.

The exile sidled up close and put a comforting arm around her shoulder. Lines etched his face in concern. "This girl should not despair. I will be at her side. This girl will only have to answer his questions and if he is satisfied, he will withdraw his complaint."

Despite her innocence, Sepharia was worried about speaking with Baruch. She wished Heron knew about this. She doubted her father would have allowed this, but the Satrap wouldn't make her go if it wasn't safe.

"I will go," she told him, trusting she was in capable hands.

Ramses nodded to the slaves. "Ready her for the dinner." A smile. "This girl must look her best."

TWENTY THREE

The hot Alexandrian summer day turned to an evening storm. Heron splashed through rivulets of water streaming from the building tops. The city struggled to hold back the torrential rains.

Heron had left Punt and Hoth with the modified steam chariot near the stables and made her way to the Palace alone. The grounds should be safe, she argued with Hoth, who'd wanted to come with her. She'd taken the ivory-handled cane as a weapon to placate Hoth's concerns. She didn't want him along in case they encountered Jarngard. The animosity between the two during their last meeting had been like swimming in unlit Greek fire.

She examined her tunic, soaked through and clinging to her form. The fabric had been chosen for desert sun, not pouring rain. Ducking under a pavilion, she adjusted the fake male genetalia. The leather straps had slipped down, loosened by the rain and running.

"Halt! In the name of the Satrap!" The voice was highly accented Greek. A Northman, she thought.

A guard appeared in the darkness. A flash of lightning scratched across the sky behind him.

"It is I, Heron the Maker."

The guard, clearly a Northman with stringy long blond hair and wide muscular shoulders, ran up with his hand on his hilt, and paused, waiting for the next lightning flash to view her face.

"Apologies, *Michanikos*. Practicing your defiance of the gods by running through this storm?"

Heron recognized the man by his facial pock marks. One of Agog's lieutenants. "You are Agnar."

Agnar answered something long and rolling in his native language. Almost a dirge or song. When he was finished, he bowed. "Yes, I am Agnar."

"I've come to visit my daughter. The storm caught me quite unawares."

"I think the gods are testing us. I can hear Donar up there throwing his hammer." Agnar grinned wildly and then he turned grim. "But be careful. I have seen strange shapes this night in the storm."

"Then run with me to the Palace."

Heron knew she would pay for the run with chaffing around her thighs, but the storm was showing no signs of abating and they needed to begin their journey to Babylon at once. Thankfully, they were able to skirt the edges of buildings and cut through long covered walkways to reach the Palace safely.

When they parted, she spoke a phrase in his language that Jarngard had taught her. The words tripped awkwardly over her tongue, but he understood and responded in kind before he returned to the darkness. The phrase meant: *may your sword always be sharp and you father many strong children.*

The cold marble halls of the Palace chilled her. Heron left a trail of dripping water behind. Sounds of other people echoed from archways, but she never saw them. She expected to see more people in the Palace, because they were trapped by the storm, but it was empty instead.

She found Sepharia's apartment easily enough. No guards outside. No Jarngard, particularly. She would have to speak to Agog about that. The man was not living up to his duties. She knew it was pride. Watching Sepharia was beneath the proud warrior. She believed Hoth only tolerated their scholarly pursuits because he had a curious mind, though he made her pay with his constant barbs and posturing. Vain as a peacock, that one.

Sepharia was no where to be found. Rolls of colored cloth lay strewn across the floor and the luxurious couches. Heron poked a pile of delicate sandals with her cane. At least Agog had given Sepharia a comfortable space to be sequestered in.

For herself, Heron knew the stately quiet and polished elegance of the Palace was no match for the bustle and clanging of the workshop. When Punt stoked the hearth fires, and orange flame came licking out like a mythical dragon, Heron would inhale deep and enjoy the smells of her labor. Nothing filled her with pride more than seeing a host of craftsmen crawling over scaffolding like ants, bringing to life the very creations she sketched on a papyrus. If anything was magic, it was that—how a group of men and one woman could transform the elements of the soil into working mechanical wonders!

Of Sepharia's thoughts, she did not know. Heron fingered the jars of pigment on the table and eyed the litterings of leftover cloth. It appeared that her daughter had been readied for some party. Agog was treating her well, or maybe it had been the exile Ramses? Probably the later, since that seemed more his realm.

Was this the life that Sepharia preferred? Heron had allowed her to join the *Erusin* ceremony, hoping the practiced dishonesty of the nobles would turn her back to the workshop, but it had backfired. Heron sighed.

Before she left, Heron scribbled a note and left it on the writing desk.

The note was coded by a cipher that Heron had designed long ago. During her instruction of the younger Sepharia, to get the girl to take more interest in mathematics, she would write the daily lessons in code. Sepharia would have to work through the problem to solve the code before she could begin her lessons.

A crimson cloak, acquired from Sepharia's room, worked as a shield against the rain on her journey back as she wrapped it around her head and shoulders. Not wanting to be delayed any longer, Heron kept to the expansive dark patches between the occasional lantern.

She was passing through the Procession of the Gods, a wide space at least one stadium long between the main Palace and the Great Theater. Statues of the gods from various pantheons were littered across the grounds. Not far from her was the Soma of Alexander, the burial place of the great conqueror. His body was entombed into the ground and occasionally visited by kings. Heron vowed to visit the tomb on her return, not for information, but inspiration.

Passing behind the statue of Hermes, Heron ran right into a man hiding in the shadows. He turned, brandishing a weapon.

Lightning flashed, but Heron was too busy scrambling for her hidden blade to see the man's face. He spoke, and in her haste, she did not recognize the word.

She could not understand the assassin's slowness, maybe he was as startled as her, but when the man lunged forward with his weapon, she responded with her own. The hilt sunk deep and she pulled it free. He collapsed and dropped his weapon.

After another lightning flash, she realized it was not a weapon but a papyrus scroll. Heron quickly snatched it out of a puddle and tucked it under her tunic. Then she rolled the man over on his back. He was oddly blotched and invariably ugly. He was also dead.

Heron did not want to be found with the dead man, but the nature of the unexpected meeting left her curious. She patted him down for clues, while his open mouthed stare collected rain.

Movement near a distant lantern startled Heron, so she fled. Reaching the steam chariot, she said nothing to the others as she climbed on. Her hands trembled as she wiped the rain from her face.

"I've been keeping the fires stoked," said Punt. "Shall we make for the Moon Gate or wait out the rain?"

Hoth rapped his knuckles against the barge wall. "Let us wait. The gods may strike us down if we venture into this madness. I've seen a man roasted alive when hit by one of Donar's bolts."

Heron believed him. She'd seen the sky fire strike the ground before during heavy storms, but waiting could be more dangerous to their goals.

"The rain will make a good cover for our leaving. We're trying not to be seen, remember," she countered.

"Fine," growled Hoth, "have it your way. Get us killed before we even get out of Alexandria." Hoth climbed under the tarp that protected the back side of the craft, stomping his feet in protest repeatedly like a petulant child.

The steam chariot was larger than the war mechanicals she'd made, but smaller than the transport barge. The hardest part had been fitting both fuel and her remade Hermes machine on it for the journey.

As they traveled through the city, the rain seemed to let up and by the time they reached the Moon Gate, it was a faint drizzle. Caravans, delayed from leaving by the downpour, were lined up and readying to make their journey to far-off lands.

The gates were open and they passed through quickly, but when Heron looked back, she saw a familiar face speaking to a caravan driver. The man's soldier physique and shorn head was unmistakable. Additionally, she saw his merchant house markings on the caravan—black wheel on an ochre background. And as they left the city of Alexandria, to eventually head east toward the ancient fallen city of Babylon, the merchant Titus Claudius Vestalis watched them go with his cold, gray eyes.

TWENTY FOUR

Sepharia followed the exile Ramses through the quiet halls while the storm raged outside. She was once again struck by his solemnness, his almost priestly demeanor, and wondered if he would be a stern enough ally to help her with Baruch Tanzen.

She knew about Baruch. Everyone in Alexandria who had been there for any length of time knew about Baruch. While Jews prospered in Alexandria, there was always the threat of exile. Baruch, a man who considered himself the ethnarch of his people, always kept himself close to whomever ruled the city. When the Roman governor Flaccus had been in charge, Baruch had been seen at his side during chariot events or wrestling matches. The Jewish leader was known as a flexible man, but also quick to strike at his enemies when the opportunity arose.

There was a story commonly told, enough that even Sepharia had heard it from one of the craftsmen in the workshop. When a rival in the city had wronged Baruch Tanzen, the details of the supposed crime not offered widely, he had struck back with sinister vengeance.

Under the guise of a celebration for the governor's chariot winning the Grand Melee, an invitation that could not be refused, the rival came to Baruch's estate. The Jewish leader had one of the largest manors in the city, set right near the royal pier, and almost running up to the Temple of Artemis.

The gathering of nobles was a joyous affair, and they ate olives and stuffed figs, and drank liberally of spiced and sugared wines. It was said that his rival drank neither more nor less than the other nobles, yet he acted the fool, stumbling and speaking strangely to the other guests. When at last, the rival fell into Governor Flaccus and spilled his wine across the governor's toga, guards snatched the rival up and carried him away and no one ever saw him again.

The story teller would often remark that it could have been bad luck, or a drinking problem that had done the rival in. Even a bit of spite from a petty god, or maybe punishment for some unseen hubris. But most believed it had been Baruch Tanzen who had arranged for some drug to be put into the rival's drink, or that maybe he had been tripped into the governor. Or both.

Sepharia had thought it a good story when she heard it. The common folk enjoyed tales of the nobles' backstabbing and subterfuge. It was a way to believe that the nobles' lives were actually worse, despite the fancier clothing and richer foods. A simple Alexandrian lived a plainer, duller life, but one with less worry.

The story gnawed at her thoughts during the covered chariot ride to Baruch's estate. The exile Ramses seemed clever enough and Agog trusted him, but he was no match for Baruch. Sepharia vowed to be careful with what she ate.

The chariot disembarked under a stone pavilion, wrapped in grape vines. Fallen, withered grapes littered the ground, and the pungent aroma tickled her nose. Bare-chested slaves of both sexes helped them out and ushered them into the domicile.

Sepharia stepped tentatively, the slaves had wrapped her legs tightly, more than she was used to. Of course, she preferred the man-style tunic when she worked in the workshop. The chitons and togas did not allow her to move freely when she worked. This was a different kind of work, delicate like her jewelry, but with much more at stake. But with her jewelry, she could always melt down an error and start over.

Suddenly, Ramses' dark, painted eyes were in her face. The Egyptian cut of his hair framed his features like a neat box. He whispered through unmoving lips. "Careful, careful, this girl should be very careful. Be polite and be honest, and do not refuse anything he offers. Anything."

Words choked in her throat. Do not refuse anything he offers? Had he not heard the stories?

Arm around arm, Sepharia walked into Baruch Tanzen's domicile, while her stomach churned in anguish. Ramses had probably been absent from the city when that story had occurred. He didn't truly know the danger they were in. Well, her mostly, but if he was seen as her ally, anything could happen.

Baruch strode toward them as slaves wiped water and street mud from their sandals. His neatly trimmed beard, covering only the bottom half of his face, gave him an almost permanent frown.

"Ave, Ramses," said Baruch in what could be called a pleasant tone, "my thanks for attending this gathering. The others wait in the main hall."

"When the great Baruch Tanzen calls, this humble man must answer." Ramses bowed low, a feat given the tight, pharaoh-like wrapping he wore. "Your house is a feast for the eyes."

Sepharia took only a furtive glance, not wanting to be seen avoiding his gaze, but even that quick look was impressive. The white stone walls were carved exquisitely at the corners and scrollwork lined the ceiling, while flowers gathered in niches, spilling out their vines and colorful petals.

Voices resonated from behind Baruch, the ebb and flow of a party that in different circumstances, Sepharia would have been thrilled to attend. When Baruch brought his gaze upon her, she tried not to shrivel. She had nothing to worry about, she told herself. She wasn't the poisoner; hadn't killed Shayna.

"The Maker's daughter," said Baruch.

That he didn't name her turned the churn in her stomach into a whirlpool. Sepharia gathered the fabric around her hips and bowed, as deep as the chiton would allow.

"Ave, good Baruch Tanzen. I am honored to be welcomed into your house." Sepharia hoped the words were formal enough. Ramses had given her no direction.

Baruch studied her like a hawk watching a mouse. "You are not welcome in my house, but here you are. I will speak with you later."

He returned to the party as quick as he'd come and Sepharia realized she was holding her breath.

"And so," said Ramses. "It wasn't so bad. This girl did well."

After giving Baruch plenty of time to attend to other guests, Ramses led her into the party, quickly finding a quiet corner to stay out of the way.

"This girl looks pale and worried," he whispered through gritted teeth. He was trying to speak to her without being seen to. "Smile and be happy or others will presume guilt."

Sepharia curled her lips into a smile, but it felt like a grimace. He gave her a sideways glance.

"It will do, I guess."

His words were not comforting.

"Maybe if I ate something," she offered. "I'd been busy all afternoon."

Ramses sighed. "Wait here. I will go and find the kitchen. As he said, you are not welcome here, so do not take food or drink from the slaves."

After he left, she mumbled, "Take what he offers, don't take his food or drink. Which one is it?"

She felt bad for saying the words. Ramses was clearly trying to help. And for a man of his position to fetch her food was touching. She vowed to make him a beautiful trinket for his outfit when she returned to the workshop. Or maybe she would have a few tools and some raw gold sent so she could start work immediately. Throwing herself into her craft would be a good way to erase her constant unease in the Palace.

Suddenly, Sepharia realized there was someone standing behind her, quite near, in fact. When she smelled the lilacs she knew who it was. Polyxena always wore the lilac perfume.

The petite Macedonian was looking up at her when she turned. Her expression was one of concern, which made Sepharia feel even worse, if that was possible.

"Is this wise for you to be here?"

"I...I don't know," she responded honestly. "I'm here with the exile Ramses."

Her eyes flickered in response to his name. She glanced around quickly before speaking. "I would not trust that one."

Sepharia almost said that she could say the same about her, but she was supposed to be getting closer to Polyxena.

"I will keep my eyes open."

A slave dropped a platter and the noise startled Sepharia, making her jump.

"I'm sure it's difficult to be here. You're a Macedonian, you'll get through it."

"Yes," said Sepharia. "My nerves are a little touchy."

She didn't know how the nobles did it. It was Polyxena she didn't trust, but she had to lie to hide the truth.

Polyxena considered her for a long moment and then after coming to an internal conclusion, shook her head. "I don't think you should be here." She gripped Sepharia's arm with two hands. "If I were you, I would leave now. This Ramses is probably luring you into a trap."

"I can't," she said, trying to think of a reason she had to stay. "Baruch has already seen me. He expects to talk to me later."

Polyxena made a frown that would have soured milk. "A minor insult compared to this trap. Did your father agree to this meeting?"

The room grew warm and Sepharia suddenly had visions of Baruch chopping her head off in the courtyard to cheers of the guests.

"No," she said, quite surprised at the unease in her own voice. "But the Satrap agreed to it."

Polyxena squeezed Sepharia's arm until it hurt, but she dared not pull away.

"Did the Satrap tell you this or did Ramses?"

This last question gave her pause. Had Ramses tricked her by saying that the Satrap had agreed? She had not seen the barbarian at the party and now that she looked around, she didn't see any Northmen. Was this a party of conspirators against the Satrap? Was she their reward, their vengeance? Why had she come?

Sepharia took a deep steadying breath and looked deep into Polyxena's eyes. Was it the Macedonian woman trying to trick her, instead? Her gut told her to trust Polyxena, despite thinking she was the poisoner. Of course, that was the whole point. A woman like Polyxena would know how to get past her defenses, calling her '*a fellow Macedonian*' and '*we Macedonians need to stick together*'. Suddenly, Polyxena's eyes widened and she released Sepharia's arm.

"Get away from her, you viper," Ramses said as quietly as he could— though nearby party guests turned towards them, clearly hearing his words.

Ramses strided toward them with a glass of wine and a handkerchief full of figs.

Sepharia balked, caught between the two. Part of her wanted to flee the party, but the other part remembered that she'd asked for this. As much as she didn't want to meet with Baruch, she did trust Ramses. In a strange way, trusted them both, but for different reasons.

When it was clear that Sepharia wasn't going to leave the party, Polyxena left quietly under the murderous glare from Ramses.

Once Polyxena left, Ramses' face returned to its earlier pleasant state. He handed her the figs and wine, the latter of which she took only tentative sips, knowing her wits needed to be with her for Baruch.

A thought crossed her mind as she was munching on the figs. "Why did you run her off if you want me to get close to her?" The answer appeared as quickly as the words had left her mouth and he seemed to be waiting for her to come to that conclusion. "Wait. You want her to trust me more, maybe not trust, that's not right, but desire to get close to me."

"Something like that." His eyes twinkled and for the first time, she realized that maybe she was in good hands. Or if Polyxena had been right, she was in devious hands. Either way, she'd made her choice and she needed to go through with it.

"Eat quickly," he said. "They will come for you soon."

Sepharia stuffed the figs into her mouth in as much of a dignified manner as she could manage. The other guests were laughing and nibbling on their rich foods. Her figs had been only slightly spiced, but delicious.

When the man-slave came for her, Ramses whispered and he was so close, his breath tickled her ear.

"This girl should be honest, but very careful."

As she followed the slave away from the party, she realized that Ramses was not coming with her. He nodded reassuringly in her direction when she looked back.

The arched hallway she passed through was lined with tiled frescos, glorying past Roman battles. The images of glorious slaughter for the Empire were not reassuring.

When they reached an engraved wooden door, the slave opened it and beckoned her through. Sepharia took a deep breath and entered the room.

She only had enough time to register that the room was a place of curiosities before the door closed behind her. Standing on the far side of the room waited Baruch Tanzen, looking as grim as a headsman.

He strode towards her with two glasses in his hand, quickly passing one to her. At first she flinched, not wanting to take it, but his stern eyes demanded her obedience, coupled with Ramses' advice outside.

"Drink, girl."

Sepharia gave it a cautious sip, not wanting to ingest too much should it be drugged. The wine was spiced and not unpleasantly so, and her thirst from gulping down the figs made her want to take a larger drink, but she only let the wine moisten her lips and tongue.

Baruch watched the whole time, not lifting his cup even one finger while she mimed at drinking. Intimidated by his withering gaze, she glanced around the room, trying to distract herself.

The momentary distraction did nothing for her fears as she realized he kept a number of gruesome implements on his walls. A strange wicker clamshell with tiny spikes along its inside looked like a torture device dreamed up in the Far East. Long handled spears with brightly colored tassels rested on hooks across the upper walls. A basket full of eerie looking screws was positioned in the corner. A chipped, ancient looking blade took a position of prominence on the back wall.

"Alexander the Macedonian's sword when he crossed the Indus river."

Baruch walked away from her to gaze upon the sword. She was glad for the respite from his stare.

"Do you know why he conquered the known world?"

Sepharia waited quietly, she knew it wasn't her place to speak. Quiet as a mouse, she decided. For even mice can live in houses with cats, if they are careful.

"Because he could," Baruch said. "And because if he stopped, he knew his enemies would take that as a sign of weakness. As long as we are moving forward, battling with our arms and our wits, we have a chance."

Sepharia took time to take cautious glances around the room. There was a shelf of ancient looking scrolls along the back wall. Large, ornate boxes were set at the corners. Full of more curiosities, she guessed. The room was at the rear of the house and near the back wall. It had stopped raining and she could see the eye of the Lighthouse beaming into the dark.

"I loved my daughter dearly." Baruch turned on her. "Did you poison her?"

Sepharia shook her head, not daring to speak. When he moved near, it was like the whole world had become Baruch Tanzen. He stared at her like he could see into her soul.

"Did you give that trinket to the Satrap because you wanted to catch his eye?"

She hesitated. Be careful, Ramses had said. Her gut wanted to give the honest answer, that she had wanted to catch his eye. But then she thought of Polyxena. No, she would not give him the truth.

So she shook her head again and added for good measure: "I'm only a jeweler, at best. My job is to make my betters beautiful."

Baruch pursed his lips together. Sepharia kept her back straight and tall, but her face slack with emptiness. *I'm only a mouse*, she thought. *Just squeaking quietly in your walls.*

He cleared his throat and she jumped a little inside. "A girl like you could never be the poisoner. You may be your father's daughter, but you aren't clever like him. A failure of your femininity."

He called his man-servant and instructed him to take her back to the Palace. Sepharia stayed quiet and stone-faced the whole way until she reached her apartment, and then she broke into the widest smile her face could hold.

TWENTY FIVE

Punt took his turn in the back of the steam chariot under the make-shift canopy as they made their way to Old Babylon. Hoth steered the vehicle, his whitish hair snapping in the wind, while Heron stayed in back, occasionally feeding the steam mechanical, and tinkering with the Hermes machine.

They'd passed Memphis three days ago. The stark white pyramids were blinding in the high sun, but it didn't stop Heron from gazing at them until they were out of sight. Punt had watched Master Heron more than the pyramids at that moment. It seemed the inventor fell into a melancholy state after that, always adjusting levers and gears in the mechanical workings of the machine, never quite seeming satisfied.

Without his tools and fires to busy him, Punt passed his time with stories from Hoth. The tall Northman had rarely come to the foundry, preferring to stay in the workshop with the numerous craftsman, so Punt hadn't heard his stories yet. Punt would have preferred to stay in his foundry rather than make the journey to Old Babylon, but he also wanted to keep Master Heron safe. During one evening, while Heron rested, Hoth explained that assassins had attacked Heron twice already. Punt kept the warhammer he'd brought on the journey tucked under the sleeping rolls.

Early in the trip, Heron had explained the route that would take them past Jerusalem, Damascus, Thapsacus, and then down the Euphrates to Old Babylon. An arcing path that kept them near cities and good roads, though at one point near Jerusalem, Heron and Hoth had debated taking an old trading road that cut across the Arabian desert. It would have cut ten days off their journey, there and back, but Hoth didn't want to risk getting stranded in the sand despite Heron's assurances of navigation with the Hermes machine. Punt didn't offer his opinion since every day was the furthest he'd ever been from Alexandria.

Somewhere near Damascus, the steam chariot rattled over the road, rapidly overtaking a huge caravan loaded down with chained slaves. Men on horseback in flowing robes took defensive positions around the caravan—a typical reaction to the sudden appearance of the steam chariot.

"While this damned machine threatens to shake my teeth from my head, at least I don't have to smell horse and human shit for weeks on end," Hoth shouted into the wind, as his hair swirled around his face.

"I'm pleased my invention could cater to your needs," said Heron, who was adding blackish fuel to the mechanical. "Though I suppose you could do me the same favor with your perfumes? I didn't realize a sea captain needed such amenities."

Hoth deflected the barb with a rolling laughter. "One never knows when we'll encounter a wagon full of young virgins. I'd hate to be unready if the gods gifted us so."

The steam chariot passed the horse-drawn wagons. Dust plumed behind them. The guards matched the pace of the steam chariot briefly. Their unbelieving gazes were the same as the others they'd passed. A few made signs to the gods.

Punt could only imagine that they thought the steam chariot was a vehicle stolen from the gods, or was drawn by invisible horses, as some had suggested after Heron's first fateful test.

This vehicle was much larger than that first one. They kept the curved bronze shield at the front to deflect the wind and added another set of wheels to stabilize the steering. Punt had specially casted the steering mechanism to withstand the long journey.

The platform had been extended and another set of wheels set in the middle for stabilization. The back half housed the steam mechanical, along with a wagon sized load of fuel. In the middle, and comprising part of their sun shield, squatted the Hermes machine. It was smaller than the original version, and packed with seals to keep sand and dirt out, though Heron cleaned it every morning with a brush.

Whenever they stopped, Heron used the machine to calculate their position. The little chariot on top was never where Heron wanted it to be, and the inventor would scribble notes in a little book. Occasionally, Punt caught the inventor staring at the Hermes machine with what appeared to be great disappointment, though it was hard to tell, since Heron's moods nearly all looked the same.

"Oh great Heron, can we stop at this village I see in the distance?" asked the sea captain. "I would dearly love to spend a night in a warm bed rather than this cold wood platform or the flea-ridden dust that surrounds this road. It seems the slaves that pass this way keep forgetting to take their pests with them."

"I assumed you were well acquainted with fleas on your ship," Heron said dryly. "Or do you keep them at bay with your perfumes."

"I take great offense to that, o' Maker of Makers," grinned Hoth. "I instruct the fleas on my ship to infest the rowers and stay away from the officer quarters. These fleas are much too uncultured."

For the last day, Hoth and Heron had been going on like this. Punt stayed out of it, except to chuckle quietly when Hoth said something particularly amusing, though he was careful not to let Heron see him.

"We must press on," said Heron. "Titus Vestalis clearly saw us leave Alexandria and he could have assassins on their way. Since they're most likely on horseback, if we ride through the night again, we can extend our lead."

Hoth seemed to consider Heron's words, but only for a moment. "I'd rather have a bath and a good night's sleep and face these assassins head on and without a single flea infesting my head." Hoth dug a finger into his tangled hair.

"Another reason I think we should have taken the Arabian road," said Heron. "They wouldn't have dared follow us and we could get to Old Babylon and back in plenty of time to prepare our strategy against the Roman navy."

"Strategy?" said Hoth incredulously. "If by strategy you mean slaughter, then by all means. We need ships to oppose them and I only have twenty. They could bring many hundreds if they wished to properly crush us."

"An impossible task, I'm sure, but a solution lies within us if we just think," said Heron, but Punt wasn't sure that the inventor believed his own words.

"Then I would hope the gods could bless us with a great fog and I could attack the fleet like a stingy pirate," said Hoth.

Heron retorted with a biting laugh, pulling more fuel out for the mechanical. "The gods are as fickle as a certain sea captain I know and fog is no place for a ship."

"Compliment accepted." Hoth bowed, while keeping the steam chariot moving forward. Then he looked sadly to the north. "Ahh...town, whose name I do not know. How I will miss your warm baths and flea-less beds."

Heron unrolled a map that had been shoved into a box. The inventor squinted at the town that was surrounded by a wooden palisade. "Miter, I think, unless we've passed it already."

"The *Michanikos* must be mad to put name to my desire," sung Hoth from the front of the chariot. "I would have rather this town pass by unnamed, like a beautiful woman in the street, than know the word that would call her to me. Oh, Miter, how I wish I could lay my flesh in your warmth!"

The steam chariot weaved as Hoth made his proclamation. Heron stared momentarily and quickly rolled the map up, jamming it uncharacteristically into the box.

"Good blacksmith," called Hoth, "would you come up to the quarter deck and entertain a certain sea captain with a few stories to pass the time."

Punt glanced back, but the inventor had his face buried in a water-stained scroll that he'd been consulting from time to time. The scroll seemed to cause as much facial tension as the Hermes machine, so Punt decided it might be best to keep Hoth the Black busy. The steam chariot shifted and wobbled as he made his way up and more than once, Punt thought he might fall, but eventually he grabbed the front shield.

Hoth gripped Punt by the shoulder. "Apologies, the dirt seas sail rough and my linemen have set the sheets at cross-purposes, leaving us to rattle on like thunder."

Punt didn't know what Hoth was talking about, but he kept quiet and let the sea captain speak, especially since his eyes were wild and not at all sane looking.

"Stories, Punt, tell me a story. I'll share one of mine if it pleases you."

Punt cleared his throat and wiped the sweat from his bald head. "I'm a blacksmith not a taleteller. I have no tales."

The sea captain eyed him suspiciously, weaving slightly as he did so, and then he lowered his voice. "I think you have more than a few words in you. Tell me why our illustrious Maker and the Merchant of Alexandria hate each other."

As he spoke, Hoth seemed to straighten up and his eyes grew clear. Either the former near-drunken behavior had been an act or he'd snapped out of it.

"The details are Master Heron's—" Hoth frowned until Punt continued, "—but, I know the basic story."

The chariot jumped as it hit a rock, causing Punt to bite his tongue enough to bring the taste of coppery blood. Hoth stood straight and poured his attention back into driving. Heron glared up at them both, so Punt stood next to the sea captain.

"The Magistrate of the Rhakotis district, a man whose name I do not know, had a problem that he could not solve and he came to Heron for advice."

Hoth held his hand up. "Explain this word Magistrate. Though I have studied Greek, I'm not as familiar with the Latin words."

The blacksmith cleared his throat again. He wasn't the right one to be explaining these things, but it was best not to bother Heron when he was working.

"They can be many things, depending on the assignment." Punt paused, searching his mind for the right words. "For this man, he is the judge and executive of the district."

"And Vestalis is of the Rhakotis district?" asked Hoth.

Punt shook his head. "No, but there was a favor...and—"

"Don't worry. It's enough to know that Vestalis is not of the district."

Punt took a breath, glad to not have to explain what even he didn't understand. Ask him how much coal to add to a bath of iron to get the proper flexibility during forging and he could rattle off facts and figures like breathing. But the workings of the former Empire made him wish they'd asked Plutarch to come.

When he couldn't think of a way to properly explain the rest, he let the words tumble out of his mouth like rocks down a ravine. "There was a dead man and something with a crown, and in the end, Vestalis lost gold and reputation on the deal."

The sea captain kept a blank face for a couple of breaths and then leaned back his head and gave a great belly laugh that made his hair dance in the wind. If Punt hadn't seen his earlier sane face before, he might have thought the sea captain quite mad.

Eventually the laughter subsided, and Hoth patted him on the back and squeezed his shoulder familiarly. "You're quite right, Punt. You're quite right. You are not a taleteller, as you say."

After a time, a question formed in Punt's mind, and since the sea captain had proposed a trade of stories, Punt asked it without much thought.

"How did you get the name Hoth the Black?"

The sideways glance he received told Punt that it might have been a question better left unasked. Punt wiped another stream of sweat from his head and decided to return to the sun shield for rest.

But Hoth grabbed his arm and the wild look in his eye told Punt that the earlier Hoth had returned.

"The tale's not one for me to tell," Hoth started, more seriously than Punt expected, "though a trade's a trade, and you held up your end of the bargain."

The sea captain leaned in real close and Punt hunched down, even though Hoth was a good two hands taller. The narrowed gaze suggested to Punt that the sea captain was deciding whether or not to go through with his story. A smile slowly rose to Hoth's lips like a rolling boil in a bucket of quench water.

"There was a woman and something about a spear, and in the end, I lost much and a friend on the deal."

Hoth began a great cackling laugh and left the steering rod untended.

The steam chariot shifted to the right, headed towards an old stone wall, long ago crumbled until only a few head-sized rocks remained.

The sea captain weaved drunkenly back to the sun shade, and Punt stared, expecting the Northman to lunge back and take control of the chariot. But when Hoth crawled under the shade, Punt grabbed the steering rod and pointed the chariot away from the wall.

After he'd stabilized the chariot, Punt glanced backwards. Heron hadn't even noticed that the steam chariot had nearly been wrecked by Hoth's carelessness and Hoth himself was curled under the canopy as if he was asleep.

Punt had hoped to catch a nap himself, as he'd just finished his turn steering the steam chariot, and though he was used to the heat of the foundry, the searing sun in the cloudless blue sky was all together different. Punt wiped away the sweat from his bald head for what seemed like the thousandth time and tried not to think about how much he missed his foundry.

TWENTY SIX

The rooms in Polyxena's apartment were much larger than Sepharia's, though further away from the main Palace. Sepharia sipped gingerly at her goblet of sweet red wine and tried to pay attention to the chattering of the ladies around her.

When Sepharia had come to visit Polyxena, she'd thought that it would be the two of them alone at first and then maybe a walk through the halls, relying on chance encounter for their introductions. Sepharia had worn her loosest chiton for that reason. It was as much a toga as a chiton, and very plain. The colorful chitons, silken cloaks, and ample jewelry the ladies wore made Sepharia want to hustle back to her apartment and change, but Polyxena forbade it, explaining that she'd dressed perfectly.

Bani, the Cushite woman next to her on the couch was telling a story about a drunken Northman who she'd lured to her bed. The woman had dark skin, even darker than the Bantu people Sepharia often saw at the market, almost as dark as a scarab's back, and a colorful headscarf that didn't seem to match her coppery Roman chiton.

"He stunk like a dog and spilled ale over my bed, but he made for a skillful lover once the clothes came off," said Bani.

The woman was a princess from the lands far to the south and had been sent to curry favor with the Roman governor. The change in ownership of Alexandria did not change her duties. Agog had not seen her yet, but she was not dissuaded. Polyxena, who was sitting next to Sepharia, had whispered this after the introductions.

"If by skillful you mean he didn't pass out before he finished," said the Spartan woman with a long braid.

The women burst into laughter while Sepharia drank her wine. It was said the Spartan women fought along side their men, and Sepharia could believe it. The woman had square shoulders and a jagged scar on her forearm.

Polyxena put a hand on Sepharia's leg and squeezed. "Have you ever been with a man?"

Sepharia could have crawled into her goblet. The six women around the sitting area watched her intently for an answer. She shook her head rather than speak. They cooed when she did, and Polyxena patted her leg.

"Well, I could find you one if you were interested," said Polyxena. "A woman shouldn't go into battle without having tested her weapon."

The other women laughed gently, though it felt like knives to Sepharia.

"Battle?" asked Sepharia.

"A man and his sword only think about one thing—where to stick it. And though a man professes all the legal power over us women, it's we that rule when their minds fall to sex," said Polyxena. "But you have to know how to use it."

"I had no idea," Sepharia said softly.

"Of course not, girl. Without a mother to teach you, how could you?"

"And what do you get with it?" asked Sepharia, taking another long drink from the wine glass.

Polyxena's eyes twinkled with mirth. "Gold. Power. Whatever you want. How do you think Cleopatra convinced Caesar to side with her? It wasn't just her beauty."

"I always thought it was her wit."

"Wit matters, girl. But not as much as the place between your legs." Polyxena nodded toward the Cushite woman. "Bani didn't just invite the Northman to her bed so he could make a mess of it. She's trying to get an audience with the Satrap and the Northmen are his personal guards."

Bani laughed. "What have you been doing in that workshop all this time, girl?"

"Making jewelry."

The women appraised her with their eyes and Sepharia couldn't tell if it was curiosity or judgment or pity. The attention and the wine she'd been liberally drinking suddenly made her head spin.

"Apologies," she stumbled to her feet, spilling wine into the middle of them. "I feel unwell."

Sepharia tried to run out of the room, but remembered she wasn't in her apartment. She could hear the women talking about her, but not the specifics. Her heartbeat thundered in her ears and the room made a long slow spin around her head.

Suddenly, Polyxena was there, taking the wine glass out of her hand and leading her into the bedroom.

"I've made a fool of myself," said Sepharia, holding the spinning at bay by closing her eyes and steadying herself.

"No, girl. We all remember the time before we'd been with a man. Frightened of it, every one of us. That's why you've got to get over your fear. I can arrange a gentle lover for you."

Sepharia pushed Polyxena away and stumbled to the edge of the bed to grab a hold of the carved wooden post. Opening her eyes momentarily she realized the post was quite phallic.

Polyxena's gentle hand pulled her around. The Macedonian woman had a soft smile on her lips. She caressed Sepharia's shoulder.

"In Macedonia, I was a member of a secret *thiasoi*, a learning place for women made illegal by the Romans. I was taught love making by another woman. I could do the same for you?"

Her hypnotic gaze made Sepharia almost want to say yes, only to take the shame away. She heard the other women still giggling in the other room.

She was supposed to be spying on Polyxena, not becoming indebted to her. Though, a part of her deep inside recognized it would be a way to gain the Macedonian woman's irrevocable trust. But Sepharia didn't trust herself after so much wine. Now she knew why Heron rarely touched it, instead relying on that violet powder she was always sniffing when the work came faster than she could deal with it.

"I'm so thirsty," she said instead of answering Polyxena's question. It seemed safer that way.

Polyxena cupped her chin and smiled a patient smile. Not condescending - just serene and maybe a little bit sad. "Wait here."

As soon as she left, Sepharia took a step back. Something hard hit her in the back of the knee and she plopped onto her bottom. The wooden chest beneath her knocked from the inside. There was something moving in it.

Sepharia hesitated to stand up, fearing that if she did, whatever was inside would come springing out. Her mind, suddenly sober from the jolting fear, wondered what could be in there? It had to be living, or maybe something had fallen when she bumped into it.

Carefully crouching next to it, Sepharia put her ear to the box. She could feel soft movement. A rope being uncoiled. Multiple ropes.

Then she remembered Polyxena's brooch. The one she'd seen her in their first meeting—the day of the *Erusin* ceremony. The Vergina Sun had been paired with snakes. Sepharia was sure the creature or creatures in the box were snakes.

The surety that Polyxena was the poisoner came back doubly. And when her eyes fell upon the glass jars filled with roots and leaves and other herbological materials, fear quivered in her heart like a baby rabbit. Sepharia was familiar enough with the plants of Alexandria and not one of them was recognizable.

She heard the scuff of sandals. Polyxena stood at the door with a clear tumbler of water in her hands. The petite woman held the glass like an offering. Her eyes flickered to the shelf of plants and back to Sepharia. Was it concern she'd seen in Polyxena's eyes?

"It seems even the thought of water has brought you around," said Polyxena almost coolly. "But here is the real thing if you still need it."

Sepharia let the previous dizziness claim her a little bit, just for show. "Apologies, Polyxena, I drank too much wine. I should go back and lie down and rest."

"Are you sure?"

Sepharia could tell Polyxena didn't believe her.

"I must go."

Sepharia rushed past the Macedonian woman who still held the glass of water. There was no way that Polyxena could stop her. Especially with her guests and Sepharia's position as Heron's daughter.

She felt the hot gazes of the women as she left. She knew her sudden departure would be rudely taken, but there was no other way around it. Not only did Polyxena keep a chest full of snakes, but she had other exotic plants, any one of which could be poisonous.

When she reached her apartment, the wine had fled from her mind. She turned the ebony jackal statuette in the window and prepared to throw herself onto the plush couch when she heard the clearing of a throat.

The exile Ramses stood in the doorway with his hands clasped behind his back, his dark coppery eyes looking on with faint amusement.

"How did this girl fare in the den of Polyxena?"

Sepharia paused, still recovering from his sudden appearance. "How did you come so fast? I just turned the statuette."

Ramses pursed his lips. "While I would love to claim secret powers of eternal observation, the truth is that I was wandering nearby when I saw the door open."

Sepharia found a comfortable spot on the couch and poured herself a glass of water. Ramses stayed in the doorway, silently waiting for her explanation.

"I think she's the poisoner," she said eventually.

"This girl has claimed this before." His eyebrow raised slightly, clearly he knew she had more to say.

"I found proof," she said and then added, "maybe."

"And this proof?" he asked expectantly.

The words tumbled out of her mouth almost faster than she could move her tongue. "She keeps snakes in a chest and has poisonous plants right on her dresser."

Ramses had appeared ready to walk into the room to hear more, but he narrowed his eyes instead. He sighed.

"This girl should do better than this. A noisy chest and a plant-thing is not proof. Bring me a snake or a poisonous plant and I might be able to convince the Satrap." And then he smiled, a deep smile that pulled his lips wide. "And if this girl can do that, maybe the Satrap will be eternally thankful."

The exile Ramses promptly turned and left, leaving her in the company of her thoughts. Her thoughts were numerous, but none of them pleasant. She wished Heron was here, so she could seek her advice, but her note had said she was headed to Old Babylon in search of truths. Sepharia would just have to figure it out for herself.

TWENTY SEVEN

Heron was loading fuel into the steam mechanical when the assassins attacked. The hesitant light of morning shaded the eastern sky with oranges and pinks. Heron was placing charred wood into the stoking fire when Punt shouted the alarm.

Heron was glad she'd kept the coals burning and the water warm during the night. Once the last bags were hastily thrown on and the drive engaged, the steam chariot lurched forward.

Tearing through a field of tall grass and stumpy trees were five men on horseback. Even from a distance, Heron recognized the curvature of the assassin's short bows. These were the same men that had attacked her in Alexandria. Or at least two of them. Probably the other three had set an ambush at a different location and it'd just been chance that had taken her by the first.

Punt steered the vehicle while Heron shoveled more fuel into the fire and pumped the bellows, desperate to increase the churning of the mechanical. Pistons clacked as they ramped up, torquing the wheels, and forcing Heron to momentarily pray to the gods that the gearing wouldn't snap. She regretted her words the moment after they left her lips.

Hoth stood on the back of the steam chariot with his blade out, taunting the assassins, as the chariot rumbled back onto the hard-packed dirt road. His insults were inventive and those were only the ones in the languages Heron knew.

"Get down, you fool. You make for an inviting target," seethed Heron.

"Anger makes for a poor aim," he shouted over his shoulder, while his hair swirled around his face. "A tight arm is worth a length of error."

The five men following had stopped gaining and were slowly falling back. Hoth turned and bowed with great embellishment. "My cutting wit has saved the day again."

Out of the corner of her eye, an assassin loosed an arrow and before she could shout a warning it appeared to hit Hoth and he crumbled over. Heron scrambled to the back of the chariot, which required skirting the edge of the Hermes Machine, no easy feat with the constant jarring and shaking.

She moved to pull him to safety, as the other assassins loosed their bows.

"Evade!"

Punt pulled hard on the steering rod and Heron had to jam her foot into the wagon wall not to get thrown off the back along with Hoth.

The arrows landed harmlessly in the dirt and the steam chariot pulled further away. The mounted assassins stopped and stared like birds of prey in a high tree.

As Heron moved to turn Hoth over, she heard laughing. She was expecting to find him dead or at least mortally wounded, but instead he smiled up at her with faint madness.

"Saved by the famous *Michanikos*. I am in your eternal debt," Hoth snickered.

Heron growled, too angry to speak, until she noticed the crimson drops on the wood. "Your arm is bleeding, you dung beetle."

"A lucky shot, no matter."

"You should clean it," she said. "It could have been poisoned."

"Yours weren't poisoned." Hoth shrugged and proceeded to climb back around to the sun-shade. Heron stopped halfway to check on the fuel. The bin was nearly empty but she calculated they weren't far from Old Babylon, having passed Thapsacus a few days ago.

The Euphrates river had curved away from them before they camped—a mistake Heron didn't plan on repeating. She wished she'd stayed resolute against the sea captain's constant complaining about the eternal rattling in his brain. She'd decided one night wouldn't hurt, but now she knew the truth of her decision.

Hopefully, they'd find more fuel in Old Babylon. She'd used the black rocks they burned in the melting furnace. If the old city still housed a foundry, it would give them the fuel they would need for the return trip. Otherwise, they'd have to use gathered wood or oils and Heron figured it would slow their chariot by a third.

While Heron loaded more fuel, getting the steam generator glowing hot, Hoth sat under the shade and whistled the same tune he'd been whistling for five days.

"Can you find a different song?" she tried to ask as nicely as possible.

"We should have stopped and fought them. I could have taken them, you know."

She knew the man was boastful, but this was dangerous bravado. Heron scoffed and threw a few more chunks into the hissing fire.

"We might have to when we stop in the city," she said. "Better we do it prepared rather than during an ambush."

Hoth uncharacteristically cast a disapproving gaze in her direction.

"We might be headed back already with our prize had you not brought that hunk of metal with us. Or maybe you could have replaced it with one of your remarkable arrow launchers."

"It's called a cheirobalistra and I told you before," she spat back, "if the Hermes Machine works, then I can sell it - and many like it - for gold to help fund the war. Soldiers don't grow on trees."

"Then why not make soldiers? You seem to be quite skilled with these machines. Make us an army of metal soldiers, unkillable except by volcano!" His mocking tone set her teeth on edge. "Better than that over-complicated farce."

"If it were only that easy," she grumbled.

"Even if it works, no one will buy it. You're like a woman with that machine, always overcomplicating things."

The last barb stung and Heron found herself jawing at the air. When she was finally able to gather her wits, she flung her words at him as venomously as possible.

"You only blame me to hide your guilt. Crying like—" A pause. "—a child. If we hadn't stopped to rest for a night because of your incessant whining, they would have never caught us."

His jocular, sparing mood turned dark. He stood and pointed a bony finger in her direction. "Then let madness overtake me while you pour your face into that worn-out scroll of yours, or tinker with that machine, or scribble notes in your little book. Keeping secrets while I waste away in my head. I'm a sea captain, not a passenger, not even a sneak, though I've been sold off as one by the so-called Satrap. Let madness overtake me as you stare into the distance, calculating things that no sane man would understand. The gods are more knowable than you—statuelike, impene-trable, just like your metal creations!"

Heron was more than a little surprised when the sea captain's knees gave way and he fell forward, barely catching himself on the pole that held up the sun-shade. He had a cold, paleness that shot fear through her heart.

"You *are* poisoned!"

Hoth blinked, coming to that conclusion himself. "It seems I am. Fetch me that arrow, if it's still with us."

Heron scurried to the back and found it lodged in the chariot planking. She wrestled it out and presented it to Hoth, who was washing his wound with water. Punt watched them from the steering area.

The sea captain took the arrow and examined it by sniffing the jagged bone tip and caressing the stunted brown fletching, while Heron cleaned his wound. A bead of sweat formed across Hoth's forehead and his movements seemed listless and slow.

"You were near the mark on your earlier guess," said Hoth. "These were Sarmatians assassins, an off-shoot of the Scythian tribes north of the Black Sea."

"How do you know?" The flesh encircling the wound had a crimson stain that seemed to grow as she watched.

"They wear dragon armor and worship reptiles," said Hoth, his voice growing weaker with each word. "I could see the overlapping scales beneath the black robes as they rode."

"There are no dragons," Heron said absently.

"The arrows are Sarmatians making as well. Which means the poison comes from a small reptile."

His eyes grew glassy and spit formed on his lips as tiny connected bubbles.

"Is it fatal?"

Hoth coughed, trying to focus on Heron. "Why didn't the poison affect you? Or did they fire one without?"

"It doesn't matter. What matters is if it's fatal and if there is an antidote."

He nodded.

"Fatal or an antidote? Which one?" she cajoled him. "I must be mad to say this, but don't stop talking."

Hoth forced his lips into a grin.

"Fatal," he whispered, "and yes."

"Then what is it?" she asked frantically. "I'd rather you not take your secrets and your sneaking skills into the grave."

"Dragon's wings. Not the balls, soft flesh under the..." She could barely hear his whispers over the clanking of the steam mechanical and the end of his sentence trailed into nothing.

"I've never heard of such a plant," she said.

Hoth the Black shook his head, almost imperceptibly, and then he closed his eyes and fell limply onto the planking. She put her cheek to his mouth and felt the faint heat of breath. He lived—for now.

Heron yelled to the front. "Have you heard of a plant called Dragon's Wings?"

She realized she'd made a leap when she'd decided it was a plant, but almost every antidote she'd ever heard of had been a plant of some sort. Punt shook his head and she pounded her fist into the wood near Hoth's head, breaking the skin around her knuckles.

Then she set to wracking her brain for every bit of herbological knowledge she'd ever learned in the Great Library. She hadn't attended many lectures since she was inclined to the mechanical, but when her mind was stuck on a particularly thorny problem, she liked to break it loose by focusing on other topics.

Given the Sarmatians predilection towards dragons and reptiles, she assumed the name was particular to their region and she would know it under a different name. Wings suggested a wide leaf and the balls were a berry?

Heron glanced down to see Hoth's arm enflamed with crimson and the wound crusty with pus. His chest didn't seemed to be moving at all.

"Tree, not plant," she murmured to herself. "Wide leaves with round fruit."

The lectures were like paintings in her mind and she ran down the hallways, trying to remember a lecture on the trees of the eastern lands or the Black Sea. The tree with the biggest leaves she knew of was the chinar, or the tree of Hippocrates, and she'd seen some on their route.

Deciding that any trees not native to the area wouldn't matter since she couldn't harvest their tree-flesh, she instructed Punt to look out for chinar trees. He found one not long after, and when he couldn't slow the chariot enough, Heron jumped off and rolled, careful not to impale herself with the dagger clenched in her fist. Swollen knees screamed at the impact - still never quite recovered - but she didn't have time for old injuries and kept moving despite the limp.

The bark peeled off easily and she scraped the white pulpy wood into a cup. When the cup was half-full with shavings, Heron scrambled after the chariot, which was circling around the tree as slow as Punt could make it go. Eventually, she scrambled on and began preparing what she hoped was the antidote.

She split the scrapings into two piles, one in a cup and one in a pile. She took the cup and carefully opened a valve on the steam mechanical to release steaming water, while slightly burning her fingers with spray. The water was rancid, but it would have to do. She set it aside to cool.

The other portion, she smashed with her dagger hilt in a second cup, tipping drips of hot water into it to create a mash. A pungent aroma erupted straight away and Heron turned away to cough.

She applied the paste to his arm until it dried into a lump. The cup of wood tea, she dripped into his mouth. He didn't reflexively drink, so she massaged his throat so he would swallow.

Then she perched over him, carefully watching for signs of improvement. Her knees ached as the chariot rattled, but she focused on him like an optic.

After a few minutes, it seemed the angry flesh around his wound had stopped spreading. When she put her cheek to his mouth, she felt faint breath.

Heron boiled a second cup of wood tea with the remnants. She didn't have to massage his throat the second time. Content she'd done all she could do, Heron positioned Hoth under the sun-shade, repacked the mash around his arm, and waited.

The sun climbed high into the sky before Hoth opened his eyes again. By then, she'd collected more chinar pulp, but hadn't given it to him in case the antidote was poisonous in larger doses. Her herb lore was weak and the writings of Herodotus didn't address poisons. The wound had stopped pulsing and the crimson flesh turned pinkish and was only the width of a hand.

Heron gave him water when he could sit up. His wounded arm stayed limp at his side and he grimaced when he moved.

"Apologies for my hubris," he said soberly. "The gods are quick to punish in these lands."

"The gods don't care about your hubris. But waving your arms around within bow range is madness." A little more anger than she wanted leaked into her words, but Hoth didn't seem to react. In fact, he seemed apologetic, a state she didn't expect him to stay in long.

"If it wasn't for your usefulness, I might have let you die as cruel justice."

A faint smile rose to his lips, though it seemed to pain him. "You would have missed my clever banter and my scholarly ways."

"A scholar?" she scoffed. "Scholars don't bribe the attendants with whores for their secrets."

"Maybe they should more often," he said after a labored breath. "I'm tired."

Heron narrowed her eyes. "You'll rest in a bit, but first, out with your secrets. I want this story of yours before we reach Old Babylon."

"Secrets for secrets. I want to know what's on that dingy scroll you keep looking at."

"Agreed, though you'll be disappointed."

Hoth coughed and the effort made him wince and hold his arm. Heron didn't think he'd be crossing swords with the assassins any time soon.

"That's not all I ask," he said with much effort. "I want a ship powered by your steam mechanicals."

"Impossible," she said. "There are no wheels to turn."

"Then stroke the oars or make a great wind. Don't deny me my miracle."

Heron sighed. All they ever wanted was her miracles. Always for their ends, rather than to make lives better. When will it ever end, she thought. "I will try. That's all I can do."

"Agreed."

She pulled out a fig and stripped off a sliver with her knife and handed it to Hoth. He sucked on it for a while before swallowing gingerly. She repeated the gesture until he'd eaten a couple of figs and sipped a draft of water.

"Now, your story," she said, "before the sun sets and I take my turn at the steering. And no embellishments like before. You're too weak for overflowing words."

When he grinned, hair sweatily plastered to his face, she knew he'd recover, though she hoped it'd be fast enough for their task. He'd need strength in the temple.

"Before I was the captain of the *Cloud Giant*," he began quietly, "I rode the plains east of the cold seas. My brothers and I had many fine adventures and one of these took me far from the oceans to the lands of the dragon people—the Sarmatians. Since you restrict me, I will not tell you about the woman made of gold that we rescued or the dragon fire we saw in the skies one cold night. Instead, I'll tell you the story told to me by one of their women while waiting out a snow storm in our elk-hide yurt. I had told her a tale from the *Alexandrian Romance*, and in all lands it's the same, a tale begets a tale. She proceeded to tell me a story about Alexander that I had never heard before, yet it struck me as truth."

Hoth the Black paused to take a long drink and then a few heavy breaths, as if his chest was made of iron, and then continued: "The tale is one about the Amazons and their Queen Thalestris, who slept with Alexander during his Scythian campaign. After thirteen nights in bed, the Queen left, and took her entourage of three-hundred Amazon warrior women with her back to the steppes. The Sarmatians claimed to be an offshoot of the Amazons, though they did not claim to have Alexander's blood, this being the point that made me believe her tale. In my travels, I've always found that the grand events people tell about others, tend to be more true than the grand tales about themselves."

A painful wracking cough claimed Hoth and once he recovered, he spoke again, this time more weakly. "When Queen Thalestris returned to her lands, she did with child in her belly, Alexander's child, one they called Alexander in his name and she birthed him and raised him. The Sarmatians knew the Amazonian tribe until the Amazonians dwindled and headed west toward civilized lands. It was said the Amazonians kept trinkets given to them by Alexander the Macedonian as proof of their link to him and this is why the woman believed the tale as true, because her grandmother had seen these trinkets, though she did not say what they were. She guessed they were personal effects with markings immediately recognizable by those with the proper knowledge."

Once Hoth was finished, Heron ruminated on his tale. "You're right," she said regretfully, "it doesn't matter. There's not a shred of information that we can use to find the heirs of Alexander.

Hoth shrugged. "I said as much. Now tell me about the scroll before I rest again."

"Better to show you than explain." She retrieved the water-stained scroll and unrolled it for him. His eyes went wide in curiosity and then narrowed with confusion.

"What madness is that? It's filled with numbers and half of them are smudged."

"When I killed that man in the rain, on the day we left Alexandria," she explained. "I thought he was an assassin. Instead, I think he was a messenger, and I, in my surprise and fear, killed him. But his message is hidden by a cipher."

"A cipher?"

"A code. A way to pass messages without being read."

Hoth made a noise that meant he had heard of such things.

"I might unravel its secrets except that when he dropped it, the rain water ruined part of the message and part of the cipher." She sighed. "I have studied this scroll for days trying reveal its secrets, but I have nothing for my efforts, even though the cipher seems tantalizingly familiar."

Heron fell back into a quiet state along with Hoth the Black. Now that their secrets were told, they had no more impetus to speak. With the sun drifting behind the western horizon, Heron lit the lanterns and added a few handfuls of fuel to the steam mechanical.

When she took Punt's place at the steering, relieving him to curl beneath the shade and begin snoring within breaths of laying down, she found herself utterly alone. And though the lantern cast its gaze forward so she could steer around obstacles left in the faded trade road, it did not silence the multitude of stars painted across the deep, dark sky. Normally, such grandeur and space would reveal previously veiled roads for her imagination, and she would race along them like chariots, but the day's events had drained her, and the night, though fresh with the cool scents of the nearby Euphrates, claimed her thoughts as she piloted the steam chariot toward the mysteries in Old Babylon.

TWENTY EIGHT

As the days rolled on and the heats of summer ended, talk of the Roman navy set fire to the city, reaching even Sepharia's ears in the Palace. Talk amongst Polyxena and her friends had even descended into worries about the Romans and what they would do if they took the city.

The docks were as empty as Sepharia had ever seen them, which struck Polyxena as odd because it was still nearly two months until the navy would reach them, which was plenty of time for merchants to do their business and leave. Bani the Cushite suggested that the merchants were not wanting to be seen supporting Alexandria and the Satrap, since it was well known that the city was ripe with Roman spies. The women all agreed with her wisdom, though Sepharia only did with her lips so she didn't upset her fragile acceptance.

With the awkwardness of the first visit behind her, Sepharia found she quite enjoyed Polyxena's friends. She mostly kept her mouth shut and ears open, which was probably fine by the women, since the only thing Sepharia really knew about was the inner workings of the workshop. The women, however, dissected the political intrigue of the moment with un-canny accuracy.

Through Polyxena's friends, Sepharia heard that Baruch Tanzen still harbored enmity toward her despite his statement at the party. The women were supportive, pledging their friendship and support to Sepharia should it ever come to trial, which she found touching.

Most of the time she spent in Polyxena's apartment, she forgot she was supposed to be spying for the exile Ramses. She did occasionally re-port to him, giving him bits of information - but not all - that she thought could be useful. Even though she still believed Polyxena was the poisoner, she didn't like spying on her.

Of the snakes and poisonous herbs, Sepharia saw nothing. The chest in Polyxena's room had been removed upon the next visit and the shelf of plants were gone. She never saw the Vergina Sun brooch again, either. In-stead, Polyxena often wore silver necklaces or emerald rings, distinguishing herself from the gold and opals of the other women.

Sepharia was sitting on the short wall above the royal pier watching the anti-siege preparations when Jarngard found her. The location on the hill gave her a complete view of the new constructions all the way to the Moon Gate on the west wall.

A black smog hovered over the city, as the workshops had been work-ing day and night, churning out defenses. Skeletal-looking catapults lined the walls of the dock district. Wagons filled with rock were being hauled into the city and unceremoniously dumped into scattered piles. Sepharia often heard shouts from soldiers drilling in the city streets, preparing for urban warfare.

The army was mostly Egyptians, led by Northmen captains, though she saw some bronze-skinned men in charge, as well. She also noticed the mercenary groups, mostly lounging in cafés or open areas, as they were only paid to fight, not to prepare defenses.

"Not drinking wine with your new friends?" said Jarngard as he strode toward her with a handful of figs.

He was ruggedly handsome, different than the sea captain, but pleasant to look at, just the same. His nose was broken, just so, and his smile made her wonder what sort of places he'd seen. Sepharia smiled sweetly as he took a spot right next to her on the wall.

"I drink water mostly, safer that way."

"Cryptic like your father, I see. Never an easy answer."

Sepharia gently bit her lower lip and gazed up at him, practicing what the women had taught her. When he looked down, he did a double take and then quickly looked away. She smiled inside, knowing that it'd worked.

He offered her a fig and when she refused he said, "Stolen from your room when I found it empty."

"But I locked it?.

He shrugged, which meant to her he'd picked the lock or gained entry in some other way. She'd have to be more careful if it were that easy.

After a time she asked, "Have you word of my father?" Jarngard raised an eyebrow, so she continued, "He left me a note to their purpose, coded, of course."

Jarngard absently touched the leather bag around his neck as he gazed with his cold blue eyes into the harbor. A trio of war-vessels with black rams fitted to their prows performed maneuvers in the waters between the Lighthouse and the Palace pier. Even Sepharia knew the only way the Alexandrian navy was going to survive was to fight in the tight confines of the harbor, much as Caesar had done.

"They should arrive in Old Babylon soon. If their errands go quickly, they should be back with enough time to prepare our strategy against the Romans," said Jarngard. "And maybe they will have figured out a way to defeat them."

"Doesn't the Satrap have a plan?" she asked.

Jarngard appeared amused, as if he had just come to the realization that he was having a discussion of war with a young woman.

"He always has a plan, but even he doesn't think it's a good one. He spends too much time on city politics and gathering resources for war." He paused and nodded toward the Rhakotis district. "They've had two more steam mechanical explosions, none as bad as Nektam's, but Agog's had to dole out funds to pay for repairs or the workshops would go on strike."

"He should remove the protections my father put on them," she said. "That's why they're failing."

Jarngard nodded in agreement, his pale blond hair falling into his eyes. "He won't listen. He's too afraid the Romans will steal the technology and take the city with steam mechanicals of their own."

"You're not here to ask my opinion about the war, so what do you want?"

Jarngard chuckled. "Perceptive like your father."

"I've seen the Satrap more than I have you, and you're supposed to be my guardian."

"Better not to be seen watching," he said. "And the Egyptian exile has better spies than me."

Sepharia suppressed a grin and asked a question before he could, "Are you here about Polyxena?"

A strange look passed across his face, not concern, but maybe surprise.

"No, not that one. I came about Baruch Tanzen."

A cold shiver went through her midsection. "He doesn't want the trial, does he?"

"Freya's frigid tits, no. Agog wouldn't let him. I came because I heard you've been in his house and particularly—in his Alexandrian study."

"You heard?" she said sarcastically. "You mean Ramses told you."

He shrugged. "Well, have you?"

"For a little while. Why?"

Jarngard glanced around briefly before he spoke again. He was evidently concerned about being overheard, but no one was within a stone's throw of them. "Before he left, your father said there was a scroll that Baruch had that might enlighten us on the heirs."

Sepharia's stomach tightened. "And because he thinks I murdered his daughter, he won't give up the scroll."

He tried to give her a reassuring smile. "The brooch was expertly made..."

"—but I should have never given it to him at the ceremony."

"Lessons learned," he said. "I've made my share of mistakes, and so has the Satrap. He accidentally burned down a village when we were younger. Your father seems to revel in his mistakes. As long as you survive it..." He shrugged, seeming to indicate where the logic should take her.

"So what do you need to know?" she asked, and then after a moment, in an untrusting tone. "And why?"

"I want to steal it."

"Is that a good idea?"

"The Satrap intends for me to wrestle one of Baruch's men at the games. If I win, he gets the scroll." Then he lowered his voice almost to a mumble. "If he wins, Baruch gets to put you on trial."

Sepharia jumped off the short wall. "Why was I not told?"

"Better that you didn't know."

"So when he talked to me at his house, that was just a farce?"

Jarngard's eyes were hard with purpose, they made her think of hard ice. "It seems that way. You may just be a way for Baruch to get back at your father, he doesn't seem to like him for some reason. Or maybe it's just a political play."

"Political? His daughter died!" She was aghast with outrage.

His eyes flickered with amusement. "You've lived a sheltered life in the workshop with a father that protects and cares for you. Don't forget most girls are sold to husbands by your age. That you're even here at the Palace is a testament to your father."

Sepharia flopped back down on the wall. In perspective, it made sense, especially given the scrolls she'd read.

"In his eyes, Shayna's gone to him, and now he's just trying to regain the power that he lost when she died. She was just a stone on the board like you and I."

"So don't you think you can win?" she asked quietly.

Jarngard cracked his neck with a practiced tilt of the head. "They call my opponent Little Hercules. His arms are as big as my legs and he wrestles crocodiles at the Temple of Sobek for show."

"So you can't beat him." She sighed regretfully.

"I didn't say that." His voice bristled with pride. "I just haven't wrestled in years."

"Have you been practicing?"

He shook his head and her stomach tightened even further. Sepharia didn't know what wrestlers should look like, but Jarngard didn't match her expectation. He was tall and lean and not as muscular as most. It sounded like Little Hercules was the perfect build.

"I can beat him," he said eventually. "But I don't like to leave things to chance."

"Chance? Isn't that why you're always rolling those dice? Asking the gods what you should do next?"

A sly grin tugged at his lips and Sepharia suspected there was more to his dice than what he let on. He shrugged to let her know he wouldn't answer.

"Are you sure you can beat him? You said he wrestles crocodiles. That sounds crazy."

"Wrestling crocodiles and wrestling men are two completely different things."

"But you're not leaving things to chance?"

"No." He winked and she grew heady and flush. "I plan on stealing the scroll and I need to know the layout and the best way to get in."

She closed her eyes and reimagined herself back in the room. "There's a wall nearby and a convenient window. Shouldn't be too hard to get in. And the scrolls are on a rack against the wall."

"Can you show me the location if I took you there?" he asked.

She opened her eyes and her face grew flush as she realized how close he was standing to her. He smelled like he'd been eating mint. "Yes. When do you want me to show you?"

"Tonight," he replied. "I have to leave the city for a few days and I want to get the scroll before I leave. There's good cloud cover and the moon is full tonight. I'll get you when I'm ready. Wear dark, loose clothing."

Jarngard left and her heart raced with thoughts of the evening's adventure and she wondered if this was how Cleopatra felt before she was smuggled into Caesar's room in a carpet. Sepharia just hoped she didn't end up like Cleopatra did, letting an asp bite her to escape Roman vengeance.

TWENTY NINE

The path curved away from the Euphrates as they neared the ancient walls of Old Babylon. In healthier times, the river snaked through the city, contained by high embankments. Heron knew well the story of Cyrus the Great, in which the Persian king had taken the city by diverting the river and marching his army under the water gate rather than assaulting the impenetrable western or eastern gates.

Herodotus chronicled that the city was so immense, most of its residents were unaware the Persians had captured their city. Heron believed it, seeing mounds of rock, melted away by the rivers when they rose during the rainy season, far from what she assumed was the city proper.

They came upon an old mud covered man beating reeds in the water of the river's tributary. Light wrinkled across the surface as he thrashed it like an unruly child. When at last he noticed them, he smiled with black teeth and crocodile eyes. The man started to climb the bank, so Heron urged Punt to steer away.

"The mud people are diseased, and some scholars say they are cannibals," she told them.

"A quick sword thrust will cure any ailment," Hoth quipped.

"I wouldn't dare to get that close," she replied.

They made their way slowly, partially because the road was less sure as the frequent floods had washed away sections, leaving gutters and ghostly imprints of giant wagon wheels. Driving the steam chariot into a wash out would put an end to their journey. They'd also used up their black rock fuel and scavenged wood in the forest, which burned cooler and with more smoke. Her clothes reeked of forest fire while the steam chariot puttered along listlessly.

Punt slapped away an insect. They'd been feasting on his uncovered head and he had tiny blotches up and down his neck. Each slap jerked the chariot as if the two were connected.

"Steer straight, helmsmen," Hoth called to the front.

Punt grumbled and slapped another fly and glared angrily at the scrubby swamp.

As they neared what they assumed to be the city, more mud people were seen in and out of the reedy blue-green waters. Algae climbed seductively up water-logged trees. Black teeth seemed to be the norm, though they saw few smiles, or what could be passed as smiles.

One mud man was gnawing on a handful of mud like a haunch of delicious chicken when Heron called out: "Where is the city gate? Is it up ahead?"

The mud man cackled and replied in a guttural language that shot flecks of mud from his lips far and wide.

"Did you understand any of that?" she asked Hoth.

Hoth spoke, amusement tingeing his still weak voice, "Which god owns Babylon?"

"Bel-Marduk the Sun God," she said.

"He told us that if we enter his city, this Marduk god will fuck us with thunderbolts."

The steam chariot wobbled as Punt steered it over an upthrust stone. Heron grabbed the railing reflexively.

"You're more a scholar than I thought, Hoth the Black. What language did he speak?" she asked honestly.

He shrugged and spit over the side. He'd been hiding under the sunshade since his near death. His already pale skin was still washed with green.

"By the cold winds of the North, I wouldn't know. But that's always what mud scrubbers like him think. Otherwise, why would they root around in a swamp and eat mud?" Hoth left a smirk on his face and leaned back into the nest of blankets and crossed his arms.

"I guess that means you're recovered enough to help us on the next round of wood gathering," she remarked.

Hoth made exaggerated groaning noises that almost made Heron smile.

Punt said in his rumbling voice, "The gate's ahead."

Immense mounds of earth and broken stone blocked their view. Probably, they had once been lookout towers or out-buildings of some kind when the city had been prosperous. But their gaze was quickly captured by the sights beyond the mound.

Rounding the slow curve of the path, the enormous gate slowly appeared. All during the journey, Heron had been thinking of Old Babylon as a brief stop, like visiting the Great Library and consulting a few scrolls. Little had she considered the arc of history contained within the fallen city, but that history came rushing back upon viewing its western entry.

The gate was still a few stadia away from them, yet it seemed to lean over them in colossal fashion. It was said during the city's glory, that it had been the world's capitol, that the city gates and walls were impregnable, and only Cyrus the Great's ingenuity had overcome its height.

Here within the tired walls, shaved of their scrollwork and plucked of their golden baubles, was over two millennium of history. Seeing the triumphant gate in its decline, still reaching the height of the lower level of the Great Lighthouse, made her appreciate the wonders of the ancients.

The open archway curved away from them, yet she could not see the other side, the walls were so thick. Even the normally muted Punt murmured affections to the gods. Hoth rose to his feet, not capable of lounging while they rode toward the entrance to Old Babylon.

Heron had felt this way when she'd seen the pyramids, though she'd been so far away, she hadn't been fully able to appreciate the scale. And part of her recalled this sense of wonder when her ship had first arrived in the port of Alexandria under the watchful gaze of the Lighthouse.

And though long decayed, she wished to visit the Hanging Gardens and understand their mysteries. The writings of Archimedes suggested his famous screw had been conceived while dreaming of the gardens.

Amazement at the vastness of scale was quickly replaced with a cool dread as she realized they would have to find the Temple of Alexander within its walls. A putrid gray jennet pulled a rickety wagon through the gate ahead of them, led by a rag-wrapped man.

Punt steered around him and into the city, while the man barely acknowledged them. The gate was more a tunnel and the underside was pock-marked and mold ridden.

"There's something odd about these mud people," said Hoth coolly. "They don't react to the steam chariot. Either the mud and disease has rotted their brains, or they've seen such mysteries before."

Heron frowned as Punt made a sign toward the gods. "I doubt they have seen a steam chariot before, but the world is full of strange things."

The wide avenue shot straight through the city, though they couldn't see too far since the ground rose upward, but off to the east, a great vine covered ziggurat scraped the sky. When Hoth gave her a look, she responded, "Maybe the Temple of Bel-Marduk, but not Alexander. We're looking for a small temple."

"Do we ride in search of it? Or hide the steam chariot and go on foot?" he asked.

"In the histories, it was said Babylon was over a hundred stadia at its width and length, but I never dared believe it," she said. "Now that I have witnessed it with my own eyes, I think the estimates may have been too small. This city dwarfs Alexandria even if we included the island of Pharos and all the shanty towns surrounding the city."

"It is of a scale I have never imagined," Hoth agreed, the amazement still filling his voice.

"So I think we go in the steam chariot if we want to get back to Alexandria before the Romans arrive," she said.

Hoth peeked into the fuel bin. "We're down to twigs and brush at the bottom. Maybe half a day, if we're lucky."

Heron stretched her arm out, indicating a few lazy blotches of black smoke hovering over distant parts of the city. "A workshop or foundry of some kind, I imagine. If the wind was blowing this way I might know by the iron."

A heavy sniff came from the blacksmith. "Foundry fires, I can smell the ore."

"Good," said Heron. "Then we can visit them and purchase more coal. Let's head toward the smoke."

"How will we speak to them? Do they all grunt like the mud people outside?" asked Hoth.

Heron shook her head emphatically. "This city was once a beacon of Hellenic culture. There will be those who speak our languages. The temple, at least. And I've seen others spying on us from side streets without the covering of mud on them."

Hoth soured and crossed his arms. "The Sarmatian assassins will find us easily here."

"More reason to get to our business and leave. Every fallen building is an excellent spot to stage an ambush."

Hoth flexed his shoulder as if remembering that he may have to swing a sword at some point. The steam chariot carried them through the streets, and either by design or chance, few residents could be seen, except at a distance. Deeper into the city, they found pockets of people keeping the entropy at bay, enough that the walls weren't completely falling down. Women beat dust clouds from shoddy rugs and arm-carried their children inside when the chariot rumbled into view.

They doubled back a couple of times on their search for the smithy. Hoth kept glancing worriedly at the steam mechanical as he scraped twigs and black dust from the bin. Punt found the shop as the chariot struggled to keep its pistons working and the clanging had been reduced to a tired old woman beating pots together.

Heron knew they'd found the right place when she saw the strong timbers and iron supports holding the stone roof. Blasts of sparks could be seen from the back of the shop near a chimney that climbed from the top of the building and spit black smoke into the sky.

The steam chariot wouldn't go much further, so Heron instructed Punt to hide it behind a crumbled building not far from the shop. The three of them waited at the edge of the open-walled shop for the smithy to notice them. Tools and other implements hung from hooks in the rafters of the stone-roofed building. Punt gave an appraising nod toward the wares on display, high praise from the master blacksmith.

After a time, when the sound of metal on metal stopped ringing, the blacksmith appeared, ducking through the far door to his foundry. From his height, Heron immediately guessed the reason for the style of his building construction. He was too tall to fit in the stone buildings the other residents used.

The blacksmith made a motion of what Heron assumed to be a greeting and set his hammer on a bench. His dark skin had even darker rings around his eyes, making the whites stand out. He said something and when they shook their heads, he tried again, "Greeks?"

His accent was thick like a mouth full of stones, but Heron understood him.

"I am Heron of Alexandria, and yes, a Greek, but not my companions."

She momentarily worried about giving the blacksmith her name, but decided the assassins knew who they were and the steam chariot was unmistakable.

"I am Tuath." He jammed his thumb into his chest.

Heron pointed to her companions. "Punt, my blacksmith—" Tuath's eyes widened. "—and Hoth the Northman."

Tuath grinned and nodded his head vigorously. "You come to see Tuath swing hammer? I am Babylon's greatest smithy."

"I'm certain you are, but we are here for a different task. Have you heard of the Temple of Alexander?"

Tuath ducked into the street and wandered to the middle, serious thoughts posed on his face. He turned once or twice and then indicated a direction deeper into the city with an outstretched arm. The direction was near the great ziggurat.

"Maybe that way," he said. "Once I fix gear for them, but they did not pay me. Temple guards put a sword to my neck and then take."

Tuath spit into the dust and made a gesture in the direction he'd already indicated. Heron smiled, knowing he could be a willing ally. Fortune favored them for once, though talk of guards bothered her, she had hoped for a simple theft.

"Maybe we can avenge you when we visit them." She paused before asking a question: "Can we purchase fuel from you? Do you burn the black rock for your fires?"

The sun forced Tuath to squint, but even then, his eyes were still wide circles. "I know this Alexandria is far away. You not need black rock for Punt. Why need?"

"Punt would you show our new friend the steam chariot and discuss the terms of purchase? Hoth and I will discuss plans while we wait."

Punt nodded and led the impossibly tall Tuath around the corner.

"Where does that man come from?" asked Hoth. "I've never seen such a color of skin."

"Beyond the Indus river, I gather. Far to the east."

"And tall." Hoth shook his head. "A proper smith is short and broad-chested like Punt, not tall and lanky like this Tuath."

"And a proper sea captain shouldn't smell like a prostitute," she remarked dryly.

He seemed to take amusement with her words. "What next, O' Great Inventor?"

"We leave the steam chariot here with Tuath and scout this temple on foot."

"Is that wise? Do we trust this man?"

Heron shrugged. "As much as we can trust anyone. I would leave Punt with the chariot but I think it's best we stay together."

Exclamations of wonder in an unknown language made them both turn around.

"I gather Punt has shown him the steam chariot."

"It's good to see my work can still inspire."

"And you accuse me of hubris," muttered Hoth.

Heron trained her gaze on the sea captain. "I hope to gain an ally, not thumb my nose at the disinterested gods," she said, though privately, she still enjoyed a shiver of pride.

"So you believe in them now?"

"It doesn't matter, though I should wonder if your presence is proof of their continuing desire to curse me."

Hoth made a pained face and put his hand over his heart. "You wound me, *Michanikos*. I am but a simple seaman."

"Plato have pity," she scoffed. "I often wonder whose side you are on. I'm sure Jarngard wonders the same."

Hoth's playful demeanor quickly soured. "The Satrap trusts me. You should do the same."

Heron released a tired sigh. The trip had worn her patience thin and she still had the return journey ahead. The fair Northman studied her and she was once again annoyed by his casual ambience.

The fake genetalia she used to hide her female urination chaffed her legs and her teeth were sore from rattling. Additionally, the Hermes machine, while she had used it during their journey, was no simpler than organizing a thousand mud people to sing the *Alexandrian Romances*.

"Apologies," she muttered. "I prefer the bustling and sooty comfort of my workshop to the fresh air of this ancient dead city. I'd rather we were back in Alexandria than on this foolish quest."

Hoth the Black murmured and Heron took it as acceptance of her apology, or at least agreement that their task had not been well thought.

Punt and Tuath entered the smithy and Heron overheard him discussing the fuel. Two black broad-winged birds drifted over the street. Caws floated down in the silence between them.

"Why did you take Jarngard's wife?" she asked suddenly, the words out of her mouth before she could make weight of them.

His gaze darkened and his lips twitched. Some deeper emotion was leaden beyond his eyes. It might have been sorrow, but Heron was no judge of people. Punt's heavy footsteps could be heard approaching them.

"As you've said many times before," Hoth the Black said directly to her in an unyielding voice, "I smell like a whore and I sleep with them."

"Do we have fuel?" asked Heron, without breaking the locked gaze with Hoth.

"All the fuel we want," grumbled Punt. "But there's a problem."

"Don't keep us waiting, good Punt," she sighed, looking away. "We're no strangers to disappointment."

"Tuath is out of fuel and he needs to make the journey to get more. I offered to help."

"And how long will this take?" she asked, knowing she would not like the answer.

"Two days, there and back. We have to go to a place east of the city."

"Two days," said Heron, shaking her head. "The Sarmatian assassins will enter the city in a day at worst, even if they didn't push their horses hard. I hoped to get fuel and the scrolls and be gone by sunrise. Are there any other smiths we can visit?"

"Tuath said the others do not use the good fuel. Only wood and brush, which does not burn hot enough for iron. Those are makers of bronze and fixers at best."

"We need the black fuel if we're going to get back in time," warned Hoth.

Heron nodded. "Head out immediately then, Punt. Even if he's not ready."

At her words, Tuath appeared in the doorway with a scraggly looking donkey and began hooking him to a wagon.

"Settled then," she said. "We'll see you in two days around nightfall. Hopefully, we have the scrolls by then. We'll do our best to hide the steam chariot before we set out for the Temple of Alexander."

Punt left, ambling after the long-striding Tuath. A wry, sarcastic smile appeared on the sea captain's lips.

"Ready for more disappointment?"

Heron nodded.

"If there are gods, then they are forever testing me."

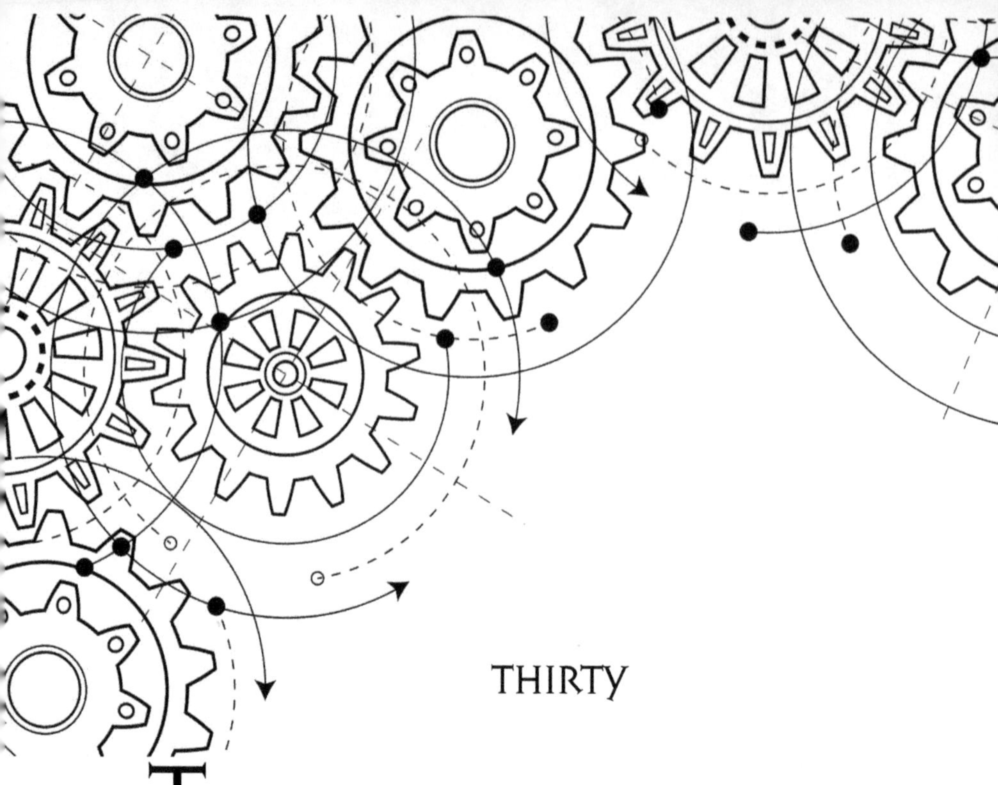

THIRTY

The night was chill. A cold wind had come down from the north, bringing fog upon the harbor. Sepharia rubbed her hands together and silently wished for warmer clothes. She'd sewn together a black tunic that hung down to her knees, but the fabric was thin and the wind broke right through.

A soft bird whistle alerted her to Jarngard's presence. The cloud cover was patchy and stray beams of moonlight illuminated random portions of the noble district. Jarngard had been scouting the wall near Baruch's estate. When he went over, she would stay outside and watch for guards.

He waved her on, and she ran across the empty space between the buildings, feeling the crisp air against her thighs. On the royal pier, they could have approached a building with relative ease, not worrying much about the guards, since they were Northmen or loyal Alexandrians. The noble district kept their true loyalties close, hiring foreign guards and mercenaries.

"I found no tracks around the outside of his wall," Jarngard whispered, and even in the near darkness, his cold blue eyes caught the faint light. "So you'll be safe as long as you stay there."

As they moved to the hiding location, Sepharia admired the supple grace of the Northman. A few years ago, there'd been a panther in the Library zoo, captured in the deep jungles to the south. Jarngard reminded her of it.

The estate wall was nearly her height, but she could pull herself up to the edge if she wedged a toe into the gap between the stones. Arms draped over the side, ignoring the rough scratching against her chest, she explained the layout of the Alexander room to Jarngard. They had to slide down once when an estate guard wandered around the corner, but the guard looked disinterested and probably wouldn't have noticed them even if they'd been crouched in the middle of the yard.

"When I go over, you stay here and watch. When I come back out, I won't be able to see around the corner, so you'll have to give me a sign when it's safe to move."

"How long will you be?"

He shrugged. "Depends on how long it takes me to find this scroll. It's supposedly an account from his third wife, Parysatis. My Greek is poor, so I memorized her name."

Leading up to this moment, Sepharia's heart had been jumping around in her chest. The thrill of sneaking through the noble district made her lightheaded, and on more than one occasion, she thought back to Cleopatra in her carpet and wondered if she had felt the same.

But now that they stood at the estate wall, doubt crept into her limbs. The earlier giddiness now felt like dread.

"Are you certain this plan is better than wrestling that man?" she blurted out louder than intended.

He raised an eyebrow as he was adjusting the bag on his hip. "Afraid the gods won't look kindly on our theft?"

"Not that," she said. "Even if you steal the scroll, won't you still have to wrestle Little Hercules? Won't that put me back to where I started? In danger of going to trial?"

He put a callused hand on her shoulder. "If we are successful tonight, then I will feign an injury and cancel the match."

"But won't he notice the scroll is missing?"

"I have a pair of *charakitai* waiting this evening for me. I will have it copied and returned by morning. Returning the scroll will be much simpler than finding it."

Jarngard leaned forward until his face was only a finger-length away. His hot breath washed over her, and it was not entirely unpleasant.

"My stomach has stones the size of an elephant's balls in it right now," he said. "This worry you carry with you is good. It makes your senses sharper, and your mind quicker. Just remember to breathe and we'll have the scroll shortly."

Sepharia wanted to open her mouth to protest. To say that this scroll wasn't that important. That the search for the heirs was a foolish idea. That they would get caught. But she didn't, and Jarngard slid over the wall like silk.

A wide cloud had passed between the moon, so the estate grounds had turned to ink. She couldn't see him again until he appeared at the window. He crawled through the opening after unlatching the glass.

Sepharia wondered what he would do about reading the scrolls in the dark room when a faint light appeared. It must have been a thieves' lamp that he had in his bag. Soon after, the light disappeared.

The wait was long. Her arms grew numb and tingly from gripping the top of the wall. She had to hop down occasionally and shake out her limbs, but she didn't like doing it for long, afraid a guard might wander past when she wasn't watching.

When a guard did pass, there was no sign of Jarngard. The fear in her chest rose and fell like the tides. In the darkness, her mind wandered, and her focus faded until she barely noticed the Northman sliding out the window with a scroll in hand.

Her heartbeat blasted her eardrums, and her stomach tried to climb out of her chest. Then she saw the guard.

Jarngard was still leaning out of the window, trying to pull it closed and relatch it. He couldn't see the guard about to turn the corner.

The moon decided to make an appearance and the grounds of the estate were bathed in cool luminance. Sepharia grabbed a chunk of stone at the base of the wall and threw it high over the guard's head.

The rock sailed through the air and out of sight...

Thunk.

The guard turned his head toward the sound, only steps away from the corner. Jarngard heard the man and dropped the scroll inside the room. He was crouched at the base of the building with a dagger in hand.

Instead of rushing across the expanse between the building and the wall, Jarngard slipped around the corner, further away from discovery. Back from investigating the noise, the guard, with his hand firmly on his short sword, was more alert. Sepharia held onto the top of the wall by her fingertips, trying to watch while not being seen. She jammed a toe into a hole near the base.

As soon as the guard found the open window, she cringed. He glanced back and forth, clearly considering what to do, before jogging back around the way he'd come.

Sepharia didn't think long about it before she found herself hopping over the wall and running across the grounds, dark tunic slapping against her thighs. She knew she didn't have long before the guard would return with others, or investigate the room, but she thought it was enough time to get the scroll.

She hit the wall and scrambled into the window as her heart thudded in her ears. Her fingertips searched around for the scroll and at first she wasn't sure it was inside the room. She caught the edge of it and then lunged back in to grab it like a fish-catcher on the Nile.

With the scroll in hand, she slipped out the window, caught a toe on the wall and tumbled to the ground. A cloud passed over the moon and the grounds were bathed in darkness again.

Sepharia silently said a prayer for her good luck. It would only be a short sprint and then a brief climb over the wall and she would be safe. How they would get the scroll back in would be another issue, but the shelf of papyrus was packed thick, so it was doubtful Baruch would easily know that one was missing. There were other more valuable items in the Alexander room that would surely be thought the target—like Alexander's sword.

She climbed to her feet and scanned to the right, ready to run. A bird whistled in the distance. She paused.

Pushing off into a run, she noticed the fiery beam of the Lighthouse shining to the north. Her senses overloaded her with information: heart pounding, the smell of bakeries preparing for the next day, the stinging of sweat on her scratched underarm.

All those senses overwhelmed until she felt the firm hand grab her by the shoulder, tumbling her to the ground, then the feeling of hitting the earth was the only thing she knew. Lying on her back, she looked up, and for a brief moment, she thought it was Jarngard standing over her. But then she saw the leather chestplate and the short sword gleaming in the faint moonlight and heard the estate waking with shouts and lanterns spraying their light against the walls and men appearing.

The chill wind that had been blowing from the north could not quench the heat burning in her face. As the lantern lights blinded her and men pulled her roughly to her feet, Sepharia choked back the words in her throat.

And then in the darkness, a man appeared, and she knew who he was by his rigid shoulders—Baruch Tanzen. The light cast across his back, so she could not see his face clearly but she knew it was grim. He snatched the scroll out of her hand and briefly examined it. She could only close her eyes until she felt his gaze upon her again. Then a guard with a lantern moved up and Sepharia shrunk away from the light as if it were fire. As Baruch Tanzen stood before her, face notched in quiet fury, Sepharia silently prayed she would live the night.

THIRTY ONE

The Temple of Alexander was not a temple like any she'd ever seen before. There were no wide gates welcoming its followers. Fires did not burn brightly, beckoning men with coin like moths. There was barely even a building, though meticulously kept it was, with white stone scrubbed clean of dirt and vines.

And it was small, at least the part she could see. Matching columns with extensive scrollwork set at each corner lifted the roof high into the air. A marble statue of Alexander riding Bucephalas, hooves raised triumphantly, sat proudly in the middle of the temple.

Braziers rested at each corner, sending out a cool orangish glow that warmed the statue's colors, but did not even flicker against it. Of course, it was still day and the sun held court in the sky, but even the lowliest Alexandrian temples burned great fires to draw crowds.

But that was bustling Alexandria and this was Old Babylon—mostly dead beneath the yearly floods of the Euphrates and the Tigris and the rot of untended entropy. There was little coin here to succor with guile and manufactured magic. Instead, there was an archway going into the ground beneath the temple and etched into the stone above the archway was the phrase in Greek: "To the Strongest."

Heron knew this phrase. It'd been uttered by Alexander the Macedonian on his death bed when asked by his generals which one of them would succeed him. An ending that had allowed his duplicitous generals to split his empire into four parts and then battle each other for centuries.

The clicking of stone made Heron reach for her dagger. Hoth appeared from the corner, returning after his scouting trip around the temple. Their hiding place was perched on top of an old building, not yet fallen, and Heron didn't feel entirely safe on it. She'd climbed the trellis of vines on the backside, her sore knees aching on the climb. Their vantage point gave them a clear view of the temple and the surrounding area. They could even see the peak of the Bel-Marduk ziggurat.

"No other entrances on the other sides. Just that cursed hole in the ground."

When they'd first spied it, Heron had suggested that they go in, but Hoth clearly distrusted it and said as much.

"Then you go in. An acolyte entered while you were gone. He was carrying a bucket of water," she said.

"So it's not deserted. I could have told you that by the way the place gleams like a virgin in this rotten city."

"Afraid of the dark? Is that why they name you the Black?"

Hoth scowled. "I just thought this rumored maze would be above ground. There best not be any minotaurs in there."

"Doubtful, but if there are, you can put those blades to good use," she said, nodding toward the pair of curved blades at his hips.

"Remind me when we return to tell Wodanaz he can leave me out of future scholarly adventures."

"Why, Hoth," she tried to say without smiling, "are you afraid you might dirty your linens in there, or maybe your perfumes will call the horned beast upon you?"

Hoth replied with particular emphasis on the last word. "You go in there, scholar."

"Then why did I bring you? You're supposed to be the sneak."

Hoth froze suddenly and her first instinct was to reach for her dagger. His gaze fell across her shoulder, so she turned slowly.

"What do you see?" she whispered.

"Upon the ziggurat. Third level from the top."

It took her many heartbeats to locate the man, but when she did her heart ran cold. Though he was difficult to see against the ivy and stone, once she'd found him, she kept her gaze locked on.

"Is it?"

"Yes," he responded grimly. "It seems our Sarmatian friends have found us."

The assassin on the ziggurat raised his arm in their direction. Heron caught a glimpse of another dark shape leaping from a distant building.

"Maybe you'll be coming with me, after all," said Hoth with a smirk.

Heron sighed, knowing he was right. She'd be no match for the assassins out in the open. Even if she tried to hide, they would surely find her. Hoth had told her stories about the Sarmatians tracking mountain lions through the forest for days as practice.

"Quickly, then."

Heron followed him to the entrance. No one jumped out to stop them as they approached.

"Keep your blades ready," she told him.

"I see that grin has disappeared."

Heron ignored him and pushed him in the back. "To the strongest," she muttered as she passed beneath Alexander's last words.

The tunnel quickly plunged into the ground and Heron had to lean back and hold her hand against the wall not to fall forward. Hoth kept glancing around in searching patterns.

After a long descent, at least one stadium, the tunnel leveled out and Heron realized that the light had not dimmed. Holes in the ceiling seemed to be bringing the light in, though she did not understand how.

"I see it, as well." Hoth pulled something from beneath his tunic and examined it momentarily before putting it back. He made a satisfactory noise before continuing on.

"Maybe this won't be so bad. Those holes bring light from the sun," he said.

Heron wrinkled her nose. She was familiar with optics and knew no way to tell one light from another. "How can you tell?"

"By magic," he said and the amused tone in his voice made her scowl silently.

"They probably use mirrors."

"Probably..."

As his voice trailed off, Heron stopped staring at the ceiling and looked down. The walls had stopped being blank stone and were now covered in colorful murals. On her right, there was a painting of a woman giving birth. Surrounding the woman was a host of royally dressed men, some with swords and others with cups. Standing to the side was a tall woman with a faint nimbus around her. The woman held a serpent and wore a bronze helm.

Heron ran her fingertips over the painting, feeling the thickness and the texture. "This is Alexander's birth." She pointed to the woman on the side. "And that is Athena."

She turned and was not surprised when she found a great temple on fire, painted on the opposite wall. The temple scraped the clouds, and based on the size of the tiny people drawn around its base, it would dwarf even the Lighthouse.

"The burning of the Temple of Athena. It happened the day Alexander was born and they said it was because Athena had left it to attend to his birth."

Hoth glanced down the hall. "More paintings ahead. It appears we are going to receive an education in Alexander the Macedonian."

"I suspect it will be more than that," she said. "The epitaph 'to the strongest' seemed as much a warning."

"And I, as well." Hoth chuckled lightly. "I worry we may have to battle a fearsome acolyte with a bucket of water. Oh, how my legs tremble."

"Quiet, fool. They're probably listening to us right now. Temples enjoy spying on those that they purport to serve."

Hoth crossed his arms, looking in his own right like a man waiting to be painted. "Then where is our water bearer? He splashed his way to the entrance, yet I do not see a single drop here."

Heron silently cursed herself that she did not see that as well. She decided she'd been too long away from the workshop. "Every temple has a secret entrance or two for the initiated. Either by secret lever or attended guardian."

"Then let us find it and make our way to..." Hoth paused, momentarily confused, "...to whatever it is we're hoping to find here."

Heron felt his concerns keenly. She'd harbored thoughts that their journey was a fool's errand, but kept them to herself. They were hoping to find secret knowledge, but the temple could be nothing more than an empty stone maze.

"We know the temple has many guards, based on Tuath's experience. Trying to go that way will only anger them. Let us instead accept this challenge and navigate the maze together."

Hoth playfully rapped his knuckles against the stone. "They must have hired a blind minotaur to design this one. A straight tunnel is hardly a maze."

Heron pushed him forward, repressing a grin as to not encourage him. His glib tongue would earn them trouble eventually.

After passing a few paintings, illustrating the important events of Alexander's young life, including his tutelage under Aristotle, and the taming of Bucephalas, they came upon a split in the tunnel.

Upon the wall was a young Alexander, but one who was king of Macedonia, by the crown on his head. To his right and left were two soldiers and behind each, in smaller detail, were armies.

"A choice, it seems," said Hoth the Black, glancing down each tunnel. "Do you know these men?"

She nodded. "Attalus and Parmenion. His father Phillip's generals, and then his after the father was murdered. He had to choose one or the other or let his army be led by rivals."

"Ahh..." said Hoth. "To the right, Parmenion was known for the scar along his jaw."

Heron made an approving noise. "It seems you were reading those scrolls after all."

"Well I had to do something to put me to sleep each night."

They took the right passage together and no sooner had they taken three steps past the turn, a wall slid down and blocked the way behind them.

"Lucky guesses are out, it seems," said Hoth before continuing to the next set of paintings.

They were presented with a few more splits and matching paintings, but combined, their knowledge of Alexander kept them firmly on the right path. A growing unease filled Heron the further they went. Hoth seemed to be taking the journey lightly, whistling as they walked with only one hand on his blade. He had a quip for each painting, whispered quietly so only she could hear, but it worried her just the same.

When a room opened up before them, they slowed. Light reflected in and gave the space a warm glow. Heron thought it must mean the sun was setting and hoped they would not soon be in darkness. They would have no chance of navigating the maze then.

But she quickly banished those thoughts as she examined the new puzzle. The passage ended in a room without an exit, and a wagon hitch stuck out the far wall. Upon the yoke of the wagon was a knot of rough bark rope, bound so tight she could almost hear it crackling.

"The Gordian knot," said Hoth.

"And whoever could undo it was said to rule all of Asia," said Heron, "which is why Alexander stopped in the town it was housed. He always made a point to prove the gods favored him."

Hoth loosed a blade from its sheath. "Well, this should be an easy one." The sea captain moved forward, measuring the knot of rope with his sword.

"Wait," said Heron, "there are two stories about how he solved this puzzle."

"Two?"

She remembered discussing the very same story with Agog back in Alexandria. "Yes, two. In one, he cuts the knot as you are preparing to do. In the other, he pulls the lynchpin on the yoke out and that allows him to loosen the knot from the hitch."

Hoth pointed back the way they'd come with his sword. "That etching said, 'to the strongest' and I think cutting it would be quite fitting."

Heron nodded slightly, almost agreeing with him. "A literal translation, but I always thought cutting it sounded like cheating. Alexander was always careful to perform the rituals in the proper way and treated priests and soothsayers with reverence. I never truly believed he would just cut the rope."

The room was rather small and barely big enough for the two of them. Hoth sheathed his blade, walked out of the room and indicated with a flourish that she should go. "You're the scholar and the clever one. I'm just a sneak." Hoth crossed his arms.

Heron wasn't completely sure she was right, but Hoth's almost childish reaction gave her no choice but to forge ahead. She sighed and began examining the knot to make sure she wasn't missing anything.

The rough bark made the rope nearly impossible to loosen in its current form and the fading light spurred her to action, so she decided to yank the linchpin and see what happened. Heron glanced behind her. Hoth was staring at the floor. She gripped the pin with her fingers and tugged.

The moment the pin slipped from the yoke, a hand grabbed her tunic and yanked. Flying backwards, she was vaguely aware that the floor had fallen from beneath her. Once she landed in the hallway, toppled on top of Hoth, she blushed with failure.

Heron scrambled to her feet, careful not to fall into the pit. She leaned forward and though the pit was dark, she could tell it went down a long ways.

"Apologies," she muttered, not quite knowing what else to say.

As she dusted herself off, the trapdoor on the pit slowly closed until the room looked the same as before.

"I guess we should try your way now," she said, still reeling from her near death. As Hoth moved in, she stepped outside, just in case his idea was wrong, too.

Her concern didn't last long, as he struck the knot with speed and force. The ropes fell away and the right wall slid into the ceiling revealing the way forward.

Moving together, Heron barely examined the next set of paintings, mentally coming to grips with her failure.

"I think three sighs in a row is enough. Or are you going for a record?" Even in the dimly lit hallway she detected his concern.

"I overcomplicated it when the answer was simple," she said. "Just like the Hermes machine or my newest steam mechanical designs. Clever to a fault."

"Sometimes clever can be good and it seems you've survived quite nicely in Alexandria with a fist full of clever." Then he glanced at the fading light. "But for now, we need to pay attention, otherwise I'm afraid we'll be finishing this maze in the dark."

Heron nodded and they continued. The passages took them left and right and sometimes split. Hoth was cheerful and she decided it was because he had been right, which shouldn't bother her, but she knew it did. It wasn't that she had failed. Failure was the only real key to learning. She wondered if she was trying too hard to impress the memories of the great inventors before her like Archimedes. Though she had done so much, it felt trivial to what they had accomplished, and never truly matched what she thought she could do. Her time making miracles for the temples seemed wasted and besides the steam mechanical, nothing she'd done recently had helped turn Alexandria into a City of Wonders as she truly desired.

"Another battle won," he said after passing the siege of Tyre, "I wonder if he'll win the next one?"

"Of course he won the next one. He won every battle," she said dryly.

Hoth was leaning his head back to speak over his shoulder when he suddenly reversed direction and lunged forward. He moved so fast she didn't even realize he'd pulled his saber out and struck something white that had flashed across the tunnel.

With her eyes trained to the movement, Heron caught the second one, a spear thrust through a hole in the wall. Hoth chopped the head off the second as easily as the first.

"To my back," he called, "and pull your dagger."

Heron did as he commanded, knowing he was her superior in battle. She kept close as he attacked each spear thrust, sometimes stepping back into her, but she was watching closely and moved with him. Once they were through the hallway and no more spears came at them, Heron realized the walls were painted with Macedonian shields.

"The Foot Companions battle formation," she said.

Hoth nodded. "And those were sarrisa spears, if I know my weapons. Designed to keep the enemy at bay with their length."

"Thankfully not as effective in a short hallway," she said. "Your keen eye saved us, Hoth the Black."

"A simple feat, let us hope they do not make it more challenging."

His earlier quips disappeared, as he was clearly taking the maze more seriously, and the same for her. She dismissed her brooding and focused on the tunnel. As they moved, they studied the paintings and discussed possible challenges ahead.

Heron found herself moved with pride by the painting of the founding of Alexandria, though it did add to her underlying feeling of inferiority. Alexander himself had laid out the city using grain, but when ravens ate the seeds, his companions were worried about the sign. Skillfully, his interpreter of omens gave a favorable reading: that it meant Alexandria would feed the world.

Heron smiled, knowing the 'reading' to be great propaganda, and Alexander never shied away from letting it be known he was favored by the gods. Alexander had used the Oracle of Siwa to further his godhood, the painting of which Heron now found herself before.

The tunnel split again and on the wall was a colorful scene showing Alexander approaching the temple of Ammon-Zeus high upon the rock in Siwa. Heron knew this place well as she had visited it and asked her own question, but for different reasons.

In the painting, the doorway was open and the walls of the adytum, or inner sanctum, could clearly be seen. Gods marched along those walls and Heron remembered the altar in the back of the picture that had clued her into the Cult of Ur.

"What is the choice here?" asked Hoth, scratching his head. "There is nothing to his left or right to indicate which way we should go."

Heron stared at the painting, and deep in her gut, she knew there was something wrong, but she couldn't quite place it.

"Have we gone down the wrong path?" he asked.

"This is the correct place. This is the temple as I remember it, but something is off." She rubbed the cold stone with her fingertips, finding herself tracing the adytum. Trusting the instincts of her fingers, she studied the tiny painted walls. Reviewing the scene in her mind, she realized the difference.

"The right wall is not the real painting from the temple. It should show King Amasis, who founded the temple. Instead, it is a list of Egyptian gods that were never on either wall."

"Are you sure?"

She nodded. "We go left. That way is the correct way."

Heron grabbed him by the arm and marched confidently down the left tunnel. When the wall slid behind them, Hoth shrugged and they continued.

After Alexander had left the Oracle of Siwa, he'd marched across the desert using a string of oases to cut time from his journey. It was dangerous, but bold—typical Alexander. One of the paintings depicted an arched stone structure and a cave in the cliff wall, beneath which his men swam in the oasis and washed the dirt from their skin while Alexander, who never appeared satisfied, looked on.

Just like they had when setting off for Old Babylon, Alexander passed through Memphis and the pyramids and headed north. After Damascus, Heron found herself hurrying, constantly checking the light coming in from above. They hadn't bothered to bring a lantern from the steam mechanical and the assassins' appearance had forced them to head into the tunnel.

At the third split since the Oracle of Siwa, they found themselves flummoxed by a painting of the crossing of the Euphrates. Heron knew that Alexander had crossed at a different location than Darius the Great had expected. Neither she nor Hoth could remember if he'd gone upriver to the northeast or downriver to the south.

Heron drummed her fingers on the painting as she stared at it. "I want to say that he went northeast to Nineveh, but my memory of this portion of his journey is thin." She glanced at the opening. "And even if we guess correctly, we don't even know which direction is the northeast!"

Hoth smirked with the grin of a hidden secret. "If you say it is northeast, I can sooth it."

"No one can do that," she said. "We're far beneath the ground and only these holes give us any light."

"Tell me the direction and I will take us that way safely."

Heron shook her head, knowing time was growing short. "It had to be northeast. I think he crossed the Tigris before reaching Babylon, which meant he had to go around from the north."

Heron shrugged to show it was more than a guess but not quite the remembered truth. Hoth positioned himself directly beneath the nearest hole in the ceiling and pulled out a chain from beneath his tunic. Hanging on the chain was a chunk of bluish-violet gemstone. Hoth examined the stone while holding it in the light from the ceiling. After a few moments, he pointed to the left passage.

"What sort of madness is this?" she asked.

"We call it cordierite in the North, or water-sapphire," he explained. "Most know it only as a valuable gem, but it can also tell the position of the sun, even in a dense fog, or deep beneath the ground, it seems."

"Magic from the north." She shook her head and together they took the left passage and the stone wall closed behind them.

"So the *Michanikos* believes in magic now?"

Heron shrugged. "It could have been a guess for all I can tell, but it seems we took the right path. It's not like we have much time before it grows dark."

The sea captain seemed annoyed by her casual dismissal. "It works by reflecting the light in some way, even through the fog. The slanting of the light through the stone tells me the direction of the sun."

It sounded plausible enough, though she would prefer to examine it herself at length. Her continued silence was interpreted as more disagreement and Hoth kept explaining.

"With the water-sapphire, I take my advantage in the fogs, winning battles when the odds are against me," he boasted.

"Will this magic rock help you with the Roman navy?"

"Two to one odds, maybe. Twenty to one, never," he said, and then added after a pause. "Have you ever heard of the stones that like metal?"

Heron nodded. "There's one in the Curiosity Rooms. They call it magnetite. What of it?"

"I met a trader from the lands far east of the Indus and he said they used it to find true north, but he never said how."

The conversation ended when they came upon another room with a painting. Before them was the Battle of Gaugamela, where Alexander defeated the Great King of the Persians—Darius. Instead of the familiar visage of Alexander, the wall was painted with battle formations. In the middle of the wall was a lever that could be moved to the left or right, to choose the correct formation she assumed.

Heron sighed. "What do you see? These mean nothing to me. The *Alexandrian Romances* tell a story, not instruct tactics."

The sea captain brushed his hair away from his face with a free hand and touched the painting as he studied it. He still smelled faintly of perfume and that annoyed Heron for some reason.

"Alexander was outnumbered, but had already beaten Darius once on the plains of Issus," he said. "The formation on the left fits with his usual tactics, clever and well organized but deliberate. The formation on the right is nothing I've seen before and bold and reckless."

Hoth backed up until he stood next to her, shaking his head the whole time. "I know not which he chose."

"Give counsel, the light fades."

He glanced up before answering. "If I had to, and I must, I would say the left." He said the words, but Heron could hear doubt in his voice.

"That would seem to be the choice," she said with a thoughtful hand on her chin.

Hoth walked forward until Heron grabbed his arm in haste. "Wait. Are we making the same mistake I made at the Gordian knot? To be too clever when boldness is necessary?"

"Alexander was known for doing things no one expected. But I still say it's the left."

Her gut churned with worry. Was she second guessing the decision because of her earlier failure, or because she was right?

"Could you pull the lever and jump out of the way if you're wrong?" she asked.

Hoth studied the floor and the ceiling in the hallway. "It seems they've prepared for that. The whole floor falls away this time and there's a wall in the ceiling at the entrance. It could be that it closes when tried. We might only get one choice. Which one is it?"

Bold. Bold. Bold. She knew she needed to be bolder. But should her decision here be the same? Bold meant uncomplicated, and sometimes simple was best. Her recent failures were proof enough of that. But bold action sometimes resulted in spectacular failures.

"To the right," she said finally. "We shall throw ourselves into the breach."

Hoth put his hand on the lever. "Together then?"

She grabbed the lever with him. "Together."

"I'll see you on the other side, either way."

They pulled it together and the floor fell from beneath them, eliciting simultaneous noises of surprise. She expected a deep pit, but instead she almost immediately hit a stone chute that threw her forward when her heels hit, sending jolts of pain through her knees.

Heron tumbled head over heels, crashing into walls as she flew down the slope. Her vision was filled with spots from the impact. Hoth was right behind her, his scabbard punching her in the side more than once.

Then battered and bruised, the slope kicked them out into a large room with flickering torches and many robed men. Swords were thrust into faces. Rough hands quickly disarmed them, not that she could have put up much of a fight. She felt like she'd been put in a stone box and shaken vigorously.

On her hands and knees with Hoth at her side, she looked up to see a gray-bearded priest in crimson robes and a wicked blade in his hand. His expressionless eyes matched his taut lips, barely seen through the wispy, unkempt hairs around his mouth. As he approached, it was all she could do not to think about her near death from the cult of Ur.

THIRTY TWO

Religions were like wines and each one tasted different. Some were sour with nose-pinched duty, or others tart with age, while the most popular were sweet with honey and full of delirious dreams. Though she'd never believed in their gods, Heron had sampled their wares through her dealings with the temples and seen their effects on the true believers.

But she'd never feared them. The Temple of Nekhbet had sorely vexed her with its ceremonial rigor and even threatened her in the end after the disaster, but dead rats thrown over the courtyard wall hardly inspired fear. Disgust and loathing, maybe, but not fear.

The cult of Ur had been entirely different, and there her thoughts of wine and religion diverged. Wine had some inherent value to the masses. Sweet, sour, or tart—it was a matter of taste. The temples offered their particular flavor and potential believers could join, or find another. But the wine of Ur had been buried in the dark and turned to vinegar and poison.

Head still swimming from her tumble, she barely resisted as they stood her up. Disarmed and shaken, she posed no challenge and so the guards around the priest sheathed their swords and took a step backwards, but kept their ring around them.

Blinking twice, she cleared her vision and for the first time truly saw where she was standing. The room was a cathedral beneath the earth. Pillars rose to a high ceiling that collected smoke and darkness. There were paintings on every wall and between them, suits of armor and other implements of war. Heron was finally able to look past the high-priest, who had put away his curved dagger, and see the statue behind him.

There, upon a raised dais inscripted with Greek lettering, was a transcendent Alexander the Macedonian, wielding a lightning bolt like his supposed father Zeus, and sporting ram horns like the Egyptian god, Ammon. Heron resisted a heavy sigh, because though they were not standing in the ancient cult of Ur, the temple of Alexander had tried to kill them in the maze.

"Are you recovered, Heron of Alexandria and Hoth the Northman?" The high-priest's voice was calm and wise, unlike what she had imagined when she was kneeling before him. His Greek was understandable, though accented oddly.

"Well enough," said Heron cautiously.

The high-priest waved the guards away and motioned for Heron and Hoth to follow. "Apologies for your rough entrance, we had visitors who had no interest in following the god-man Alexander and before we can purge them from the temple, we had to bring you here."

"So the maze continued?"

He nodded solemnly. "Until Alexander's death and resurrection."

They stopped beneath the great statue of Alexander the god-man. Beneath their feet was a painting of a woman. The high-priest noticed them staring downward.

"The cursed Roxanne. Wife, mother to his son, and stealer of godhood," muttered the high-priest with tired venom.

Hoth looked to her for explanation and she remembered a story she'd read about Alexander's last days. "When he was dying, he tried to sneak out of his tent to throw himself into the river, so they would—" Heron paused when she realized the high-priest's eyes were upon her. The word on her lips was *think*, but she quickly changed it. "—*know* he had become a god."

The high-priest gave her a knowing smile, but beneath it, she could see danger, too. "You know the story well. Which is why you came furthest through the maze."

"What will you do to the unwanted visitors?"

"Make an example of one and turn the rest back into the city. Not all paths in the maze lead here."

She shared a glance with Hoth. It would be better if they killed the Sarmatian assassins.

Hoth spoke up, asking a question using a slightly less reverent tone that she would have liked. "What is your name, priest?"

"Forgive me," said the high-priest, touching a fist to his forehead. "I am Derdas, the high priest of Alexander. Fifteenth of my line."

"Why do you keep the maze, Derdas?" Hoth questioned. The Northman was getting at something, but what, Heron couldn't determine.

Derdas smiled, though his eyes did not. "He who completes the maze is heir to the god-man Alexander."

Hoth looked to her with a slight smirk on his lips, but the high priest caught it as well, and she didn't like his almost imperceptible frown.

But Heron understood the implications. Derdas hadn't wanted them to complete it. Maybe in doing so, it took away his power, or something worse. So he'd used the excuse of the assassins to bring them to the temple. It also gave them some manner of protections. They hadn't failed the maze as she first thought and the high priest couldn't kill them now, or so she hoped.

Hoth turned to her, but his eyes glanced to the left. "What an amusing word to use—heir. It just so happens that is what we seek."

Heron feigned at wiping pebbles from her knee and glanced sideways in the direction Hoth indicated. At first she only saw the rows of papyrus stacked upon a high shelf, but then she noticed the painting of Queen Thalestris of the Amazons. The proud warrior-woman was marching past a great lake and the front of her armor bulged with child, while her amazons followed, spears pointed skyward.

"But the maze itself should have told you what you wanted to know," said Derdas. "There is no physical heir, only the strongest may take up his legacy."

The high priest pointed a wrinkled arm at the inscription on the base of the great statue. "That is Alexander's last wish as a man, and who can accomplish it, will be his true heir. These instructions were given to Craterus before his death."

Heron read the inscription out loud:

"Build a pyramid for my beloved father, Phillip, to match the greatest of Egypt. Erect great temples in Delos, Delphi, Dodona, Dium, Amphipolis, and the greatest of all temples to Athena in Troy. Conquest of the Mediterranean Basin and all of Arabia. Circumnavigation of Africa. Bring the populations of East and West together as one people."

"Madness," Hoth muttered.

"Not madness, prophecy. The will of a god and whoever brings it to fruition will become one in his image," said Derdas solemnly.

"But what of Queen Thalestris?" Heron indicated the painting. "Did she not have his child and raise an heir?"

"It was a good match as the Queen was as much a warrior as he, but the line ended after a few generations with the warrior-maiden Andromeda. It may have been the hubris of that name that doomed the child."

The news took her in the gut and her head, already dizzy from the earlier tumble, grew faint. The thick smoke from the oily lanterns caught in her throat. She had to push back a wave of nausea before she could speak again.

"Are there no other lines? The son Hercules by Barsine? Another woman? How could the greatest man of his time leave nothing behind?"

His tangled beard hid his lips, so Heron could not determine the nature of his smile. If anything, it was kin to the wise smirk of a scholar imparting closely held wisdom to an ever-questioning pupil.

"The god-man Alexander changed the world for us. Is that not enough? His conquest of the world brought the east and west together. Forged alliances and trading partners where there were none. His vision married Greek democracy with Persian mathematics. Your Great Library wouldn't exist without him, or your city."

The high-priest finished and she had to bury her anger. Not at Derdas, but at herself. His words were wisdom she knew too well and her earlier outburst had been pure frustration. She deserved his lecture.

"Apologies, high priest Derdas," she said. "We have come far in hopes to find new knowledge and going back empty handed makes for a heavy load."

"But did you not gain knowledge about the Queen? I think the maze instructive."

Heron bowed, feeling foolish. Knowing there was no heir was still knowledge. She doubted Agog would like the answer: "to the strongest" but that's what she would give him.

"High priest, can we trouble you for one more favor."

He indicated she should continue by the slight inclination of his head.

"Our horses are on the other side of the city near the blacksmith Tuath. Is there a way to reach them without being seen?"

Derdas raised an eyebrow. "You wish to avoid the men in the maze."

"Apologies," she said. "It wasn't our intention to lead them to the temple. They're here because of some political disagreements in Alexandria."

Heron feared to get into the details of the assassins, but it did not seem to matter to Derdas. In fact, he seemed delighted by his tone.

"No need. A little excitement has been good for the temple. We only get the occasional brave soul wishing to enter the maze, and few get far enough to make it worth even readying the hall of spears. Your efforts here will be the talk of the temple for years to come. The clearing of the maze and its resetting will take some time, but in the morning, I can spare a guide to take you through our tunnels to a location past the ziggurat of Bel-Marduk."

Heron bowed. "Your kindness is well received."

"I shall have the acolytes make you a cot in a chamber near the sleep hall. Then you can be rested and ready to return to Alexandria on the morrow."

Heron thanked the high priest again, though she suspected he couldn't wait to get rid of them. They were led to a room and given fresh water and the best meal they'd had in weeks: honeyed dates, roast chicken, and a steamed purple root she didn't know the name for that melted in her mouth.

With guards posted outside of their room, further exploration of the temple was out of the question, so Heron and Hoth settled on their cots and tried to sleep. At first, Heron slept soundly, but deep in the night, she awoke, her mind going back to the inscription on the great statue. Most historians of her age viewed Alexander the Macedonian as a warlord or a great general, the greatest of generals. But the Greek words on the stat-ue reminded her that he'd also, in a short time, built an empire that had changed the world for centuries after his death.

While she had no want to conquer, she felt a kinship with his desire to change the world. It was after all, what she wanted for Alexandria; to be a beacon for the world through her inventions. If she could show the world a true City of Wonders, they might cast off the yoke of slavery, and through the learnings and inventions of the Great Library, give man the powers of the gods and chart their own destiny. These thoughts occupied her mind through the night, until at last, she fell asleep, and dreamt of great machines that carried cities on their backs.

THIRTY THREE

Agog woke to the sounds of shouting and he was in no mood to have been woken. The stone was cold, leeching the warmth from his feet as he pulled a silken tunic over his head, right before a servant entered the room.

"Baruch Tanzen demands to see you," said the wide-eyed servant.

"Demands? Hrmph. What in the gods does that man want at this time of night?" asked the big Northman. "Forget I asked you. Fetch me that bowl. He can wait until I'm washed."

Agog shoved his face into the cool water, slapping his wet hair away from his eyes. The coarse black hair on his arm raised slightly, and his flesh tingled with what could have been called a shiver, for him.

"Curse this land of endless summer," he said to the servant waiting nervously by. "I've bathed in holes cut into the ice in the dead of winter and now I feel chill from a bowl of water."

There was shouting and the clatter of brass trays. His door guards must be preventing Baruch from marching down the hallway, he assumed from the tone of the argument.

"Lead on, boy," said Agog. "I best get this over with so I can go back to sleep."

Halfway down the hall, he realized he'd forgotten his belt. Even after half a year in the southern city, he still wasn't used to the way the clothes hung on him.

"Satrap!" shouted Baruch, his cheeks blotched with anger. "I have been grieved."

A thin-armed Egyptian Palace soldier in leathers held Baruch back, glancing nervously at the mercenaries standing in the archway. Matching crimson breastplates and gem studded shortblades told the Satrap everything he needed to know about their fighting prowess. Mercenaries like them specialized in protecting rich nobles from non-existent foes.

Rounding the corner, he found the source of the clatter. A servant had brought food and drink for Baruch, but clearly he'd knocked the tray away.

"Can't this wait until the morning, good Baruch? I have early meetings with the grain merchants, they feel the grain tax is too burdensome, despite it being less than what they paid the Romans," said Agog, finishing with a good-natured smile.

When Baruch's eyes bulged with feverish anger, Agog knew it was no ordinary problem. Baruch actually choked before he could speak again.

"That little thieving cur." Spit frothed on his lips. "I caught her on my property!"

The beginnings of a headache formed at spot right above Agog's eyes. "If I am to be woken every time there is a robbery in Alexandria, I doubt I will ever sleep again. Good Baruch, cannot this wait until morning?"

Agog wanted nothing more than to crawl back into bed, but he needed the Jewish Exilarch. The nobles were a fractured lot, and the man seemed to hold sway with them.

"The miracle worker's daughter," said Baruch, spit flinging from his lips. "That filthy cur, I caught her stealing from me, the very scroll we wager on! This proves her guilt! She killed my daughter and now she seeks to hide her crime! Heron must be behind this, trying to find place for her up-jumped daughter. I want that man brought to the Palace, so he can watch me flay the skin from that girl!"

"By the gods, Baruch, hold yourself," said Agog, searching for a reason why Sepharia would do such a foolish thing. "Are you sure you have the way of it?"

"Do you think me a fool, Satrap? I found her with the scroll in her hand."

Agog turned away, pushing his hand though his damp hair. The mercenaries lounged against the wall, dangerous smirks on their faces. He could see they knew what kind of man he was, as well. What had he gotten himself into by allying himself with this man? And more importantly, who had gotten Sepharia into this trouble? He knew she couldn't have come up with this foolish plan on her own.

He was about to say something, when he saw Jarngard lurking in the room beyond the archway. Curse his friend for dragging the girl into his mischief. Jarngard made some incomprehensible motion, trying to convey a message, but Agog ignored him.

"If the girl is guilty, then I shall punish her," said Agog. "I'll send my men over and collect her."

"*I'll* punish the girl," blustered Baruch. "It's the father I want. He's the one that put her up to this. I'll be taking the girl's hands off myself when I return, but the father should be hung. That is the grievance I bring to you."

Agog tried not to tear the hair from his head. It seemed all his plans were quickly spiraling out of control. "You will not exact your punishment on the girl. Only I, the Satrap, lest you forget, can do that. And while I do not understand the foolishness propagating this night, I can assure you the father was not involved. Some other idiot—" At that, he glanced up to Jarngard still lurking in the other room. "—must have put her up to it."

Baruch thinned his eyes. "What is the importance of this scroll that you wish to obtain it? If you weren't my Satrap, I might have reason to believe you were behind it."

Agog bit back his first words. That the man felt free enough to accuse him of conspiracy, showed how tenuous his hold on the city was.

"Let us not do the Roman's job for them." Agog made a fist, cracking his knuckles with a squeeze. "This scroll has importance, though I do not wish to divulge my purpose. But I can only assume someone wished to gain my favor by obtaining it."

The reason for the theft was apparent to Agog, Jarngard was trying to avoid his match, but why he involved Sepharia was beyond him.

"Is it not obvious? The girl and her father. How can you be so thick?" accused Baruch.

When Agog moved, so blindingly quick Baruch barely had time to startle, the mercenaries nearly fell over themselves reaching for weapons. The Alexandrian soldiers pulled their steel moments after. Agog's fingers were stretched wide around Baruch's neck, but did not touch.

"Let us not forget that when the Romans come, it is your neck on the block, too. So forgive me if my attention is not focused on petty thievery, however infuriating it is to you." Agog paused and caught his breath, he really did need to get back in fighting shape. "However, your grievance is real and the girl is clearly guilty. So I will send my men to your house to retrieve her and bring her back to my holding cells. Once we understand the facts, we will give her the proper punish—"

"—I want her punished now!"

Agog blew a breath out his nostrils. "I will have her whipped, and put on rations, until a trial can be convened. And until then, I hope our deal on the match still stands."

"I will not wager her punishment for both crimes on the match," said Baruch.

"Understood and agreed. The match is for Shayna's death. May the gods guide these two champions to the truth by their efforts. The crime of theft, since it is known, will be dealt with afterwards."

"I want to see her whipped," said Baruch.

I'm sure you do, thought Agog, knowing the stories about the man and his dungeons.

"There is my man Jarngard. He will bring her back, along with your men, and I will whip her myself. I assure you, she will feel my punishment," said Agog.

The sheepish Jarngard pushed through the mercenaries. The guilt on his face was plain to Agog and he hoped Baruch wouldn't notice.

"The support of the noble district will falter without my enthusiastic encouragement," said Baruch, crossing his arms.

"Hrmph." Agog rubbed his chin. "Name your compensation, I wish to be done with this."

The secret smile on Baruch's lips told Agog that he'd been angling toward this result the whole time.

"Name me your Alabarch," said Baruch. "You'll find no better customs collector."

"That position has already been promised," said Agog. "Name another price."

Baruch paled and his smile faltered, eyes crinkling at the corners as he considered who might have beaten him to the prized position.

"Grain transport contracts," said Baruch finally, eyes hardened with purpose.

Alexandria was a very rich city, but he could only divide its spoils so many ways. He'd promised the contracts to the Phoenician trading group, but he could see the resoluteness of the Jewish Exilarch. They would just have to accept his apologies, and maybe they would go back to Rome's waiting arms.

"Done," said Agog. "Now fetch the girl so I can return to my bed."

After Jarngard left with the mercenaries, Agog moved to his room to finish dressing. By the time Jarngard would return, Agog knew a crowd would be assembled, even at this time of night, to watch Sepharia's whipping.

Agog shook his head as he wound the belt around his midsection. The price for the girl's safety was too high. He needed the Phoenicians, but he needed Baruch too, just like he needed Heron and his wondrous machines. He sighed. Taking the city was easier than holding it, and he knew things were only going to get worse.

THIRTY FOUR

The dust of the ancient road plumed behind them. Wheels rattled across grooves and bounced over tufts of grass. Though she had wished to see the ruins of the Hanging Gardens for clues to its engineering marvel, she was not sad to leave Old Babylon. She was not a historian, nor did she trust the temple of Alexander, and her visit had been nearly fruitless.

The high priest Derdas had given her a thin wood-bound book with crumbling parchment between that smelled faintly of rat urine. Upon its sheets were the known heirs of Alexander, including the line of Queen Thalestris that ended with the warrior-maiden Andromeda. The poorly kept state of the book and how easily he'd given it up was further proof there was no heir.

When they reached the smithy, they found Punt returned from his errand. After an apology, one which Heron dismissed, Punt showed them the load of charcoal that only filled the bin three-quarters full. Along with the quality of the fuel, the quantity ensured they would need to use harvested wood on the return journey. Heron argued to take the Arabian desert road back, but the way was perilous and both Hoth and Punt disagreed until she relented. She thanked Tuath for his help and invited him to her workshop should he ever come to Alexandria.

On the steam chariot, Heron studied the coded papyrus she'd taken from the dead messenger. The message was hidden by a substitution cipher. The cipher was a familiar mathematical number, but she couldn't determine which. She conjured numbers to her mind and compared them to the scroll. Neither the numbers of the circle or the golden ratio seemed to fit, but she only knew a handful of digits and if they were taking their cipher from deep past the decimal point, she wouldn't be able to uncover the message without tables from the Great Library.

Before midday, Hoth spotted the Sarmatian assassins riding hard behind them. She put away the coded message and focused on squeezing speed from the steam mechanical. The Babylonian fuel didn't burn as hot, so the pistons churned listlessly.

"They have extra horses," shouted Punt over the wind noise. He was standing on the back of the chariot and squinting into the sun.

"We should take the old Arabian trading road," she told them once Punt joined them at the front.

Hoth steered the steam chariot. His blond hair whipped in the wind. The black streak had faded and now only appeared to be a sooty gray.

"If we run out of fuel in the desert, we are dead men. Nor do we have the water. Not that we could stop with these Sarmatians following us."

"Following? They're gaining by the turn of the wheel and with extra horses, they can ride longer. They might even catch us by late day." Heron glanced back, trying to judge if she'd guessed correctly.

"We might go faster without this junk on board."

"No," she replied quickly. "I can't leave it behind. It's too valuable."

"Good, then," said Hoth. "They might stop and pick through the leavings rather than pursue us."

The sea captain turned as he spoke to her. The steam chariot hit something in the road and the whole vehicle jumped. Wheels slammed back onto the road, knocking over their neatly kept belongings. Punt and Heron grabbed for railings.

"Pilot your ship, sea captain," she said and returned to the steam mechanical.

Punt joined her. He looked like he'd swallowed a butterfly.

"What is it, good Punt? Did you come to tell me you agree with him?"

Punt sheepishly nodded.

She studied the concern in his gaze. "I suppose he might be right," she said after a time. "But for now we keep it. They haven't caught us yet."

Punt frowned and Heron followed his gaze to their pursuers. "Their number was five, wasn't it?"

"Agreed. But now there are only three. And extra horses," she replied.

"Maybe they've turned to get supplies, or given up."

"Doubtful," said Heron. "Keep your guard."

Heron tended the steam mechanical and Punt watched from the rear with his warhammer in hand. The attack came not long after.

The road climbed into hills along the western edge of the Euphrates. Wretched wheel-shattering rocks pock-marked the path and Hoth steered carefully. Cresting each ridge, they lost sight of the Sarmatians, which kept them focused on road behind rather than the road ahead.

A curve and gentle cliff provided the ambush point. Heron didn't see them until the first man leapt onto the steam chariot. A sudden steering maneuver forced the assassin to grab the railing. His blade kissed across her chest and the tunic blossomed red.

The sword swooshed past her head. She was only dimly aware that the second assassin had boarded. Steel clanged and men grunted. Punt fought with the might of Hephaestus. She reached for an axe, but the assassin, wearing scaled leather armor and a dragon mask, kicked her in the chest.

The air fled her lungs and she thought she heard something crack. The Sarmatian assassin raised his sword high. The rattling of the chariot grew in tempo and he could barely keep his balance. She raised her arms in vain, hoping to ward off the strike.

The assassin stiffened, and appeared to vomit. A bloody blade appeared in the middle of his stomach. Hoth was standing behind him. Trees on the side of the road came rushing toward the chariot.

Hoth scrambled back and yanked the steerage. The chariot bumped across the ground until it met the road. Punt appeared by her side. His eyes were white with concern.

Heron pushed away his hands as he tried ripping away her tunic to get to the wound.

"You'll bleed to death." His eyes searched her as if she'd grown a horn in the middle of her head.

"I can fix it," she said, "just give me the needle and thread."

The normally reserved Punt did not defer to her command. He half-shook his head like a horse flicking off a biting fly. She pushed away his hands. Her arms were dripping in blood.

"It's down to the bone," he growled. "I'll knock you out if that's what it takes."

Heron relented. The broad-shouldered blacksmith set to fussing over her wound like a concerned mother. The tunic fell away from the knife, revealing the bindings.

Her chest bindings were known by Punt and Plutarch, but she had always deflected their questions by claiming she was really an automata in disguise. Putting her chin to chest, the white of her bone could be seen through the cut.

"Hoth!" Punt barked. "Steer this chariot gently or I'll sew your hands to the steerage!"

Heron wanted to smile at the way Punt was caring for her, but she was in too much pain. Even looking down at the wound stretched the chest muscle, which dotted her eyes with agony. Another part of her wanted to fend him off to keep her secret, but her arms were weak with blood loss.

Punt slipped the tip of the knife under the binding. The blade was cool against the warm flesh. When he split the tightly wound cloth and her smallish breasts sprung out, Heron expected surprise, but the look on his face was more than that. Punt pulled up and away, nearly dropping the knife. The worse part was the emotion she most keenly detected—betrayal.

But as a dutiful worker, Punt swallowed whatever thoughts were going through his head, and got to work, pouring water on the wound to clean it before sewing it up. He finished the job without comment, though she could see his hesitations each time he had to rest his arm on her breast.

"A fresh tunic," she said through the pain. "Please."

She kept her arm over her chest while he retrieved it. Her arms and chest were still bloody. The new tunic was quickly stained, but the loss of her secret hurt more than the wound. Suddenly she didn't feel like the person in charge anymore. Too often she'd heard the men talk about their women and how they viewed them. She thought Punt was different, but the look of betrayal was unmistakable.

Before Punt could retreat to the back of the chariot to feed the fire, Heron called out weakly, "Punt, please."

The bald blacksmith glanced behind them grimly. "They're catching up. The chariot is too heavy."

He said it without a trace of concern as if what he was implying was as simple as throwing a few rocks from the vehicle. It made her realize that she might have just lost her blacksmith and her friend. And maybe more than that if he told anyone else.

She said it again, the words straining through her teeth. "Please, come here."

Punt ambled over, not meeting her gaze.

"You cannot tell anyone," she whispered. "They'll have me killed."

Punt shrugged. "We'll probably die anyway if we can't escape them."

"Fine," she said. "Throw the Hermes machine over. I'll make a new one."

Punt nodded and after adding more charcoal, got right to work on removing the machine. The box tumbled off and shattered into pieces. The center gear mechanism broke loose and rolled down the hill, flashing randomly as the sunlight hit it, until it lost momentum and fell over.

A wracking cough overtook Heron and she doubled over in agony. The stitches weren't even half of the pain. It appeared a few ribs had been broken when the assassin had kicked her. Suddenly it felt like she was breathing through a straw.

When Punt took over at the helm, Heron waved Hoth over, careful to keep her arm over her exposed chest. It hurt to hunch, but the alternative was worse.

"How far behind are they?" she wheezed out.

Hoth pulled his hair away from his face and quickly surveyed her. "You look terrible, man."

She let him know she wasn't in the mood with a hand motion. He checked the road.

"Keeping pace. We won't outrun them and we won't be able to stop."

"We have to take the Arabian road. That will get us back."

"You won't survive the sun and we don't have the water. Remember, we can't stop at an oasis," he said.

Another round of coughing delayed their conversation. Heron wiped her mouth only to find blood.

"Are you poisoned?"

She shook her head, too tired from coughing to speak.

"Well, that's good," he said.

After a time she was able to speak again. It came out barely above a whisper. "The Arabian road. We must take it."

Hoth the Black nodded and patted her gently on the shoulder. "Save your strength, then. You're going to need it. I'll tell Punt."

When Hoth told Punt, she saw the way he glanced back at her, looking like he wanted to disagree. Heron fell back into the blankets. The constant rattling made her want to cough, but she resisted as well as she could.

Not long after, the chariot bumped over the edge of the road, headed toward the Arabian desert. Either path would get them killed, but the opportunity to get back to Alexandria faster, despite the dangers, made her glad they picked it. But then, even getting back would be no salvation. All the power and influence she'd gained from her reputation as the *Michanikos* would be for nothing if she was exposed as a woman. But even that didn't hurt as much as thinking that Punt had been her friend.

Heron pulled the blanket up to her chest and tried to close her eyes. But visions of her workshop being torn down, brick by brick, and her writings being burned danced in her head, and kept her from sleeping. It was going to be a long journey home.

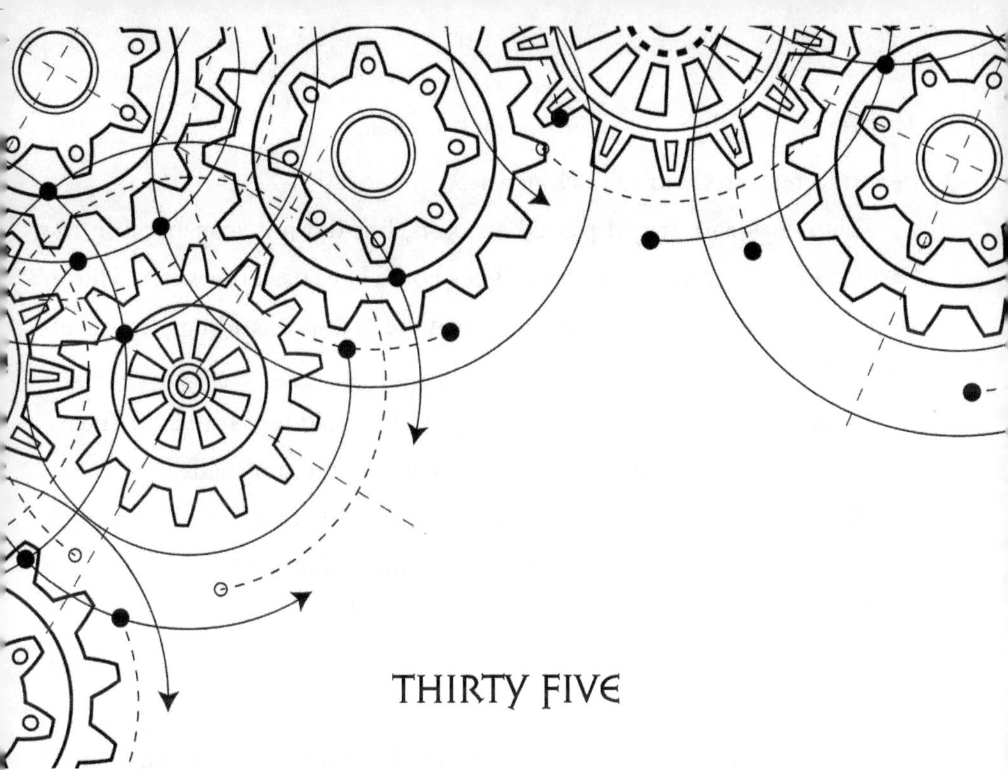

THIRTY FIVE

Heron swatted at the flying bug. She was too weak to swing with any force so her hand just fell against her arm. It didn't matter, anyway. Even if she'd killed it, there were a hundred more swarming around her mouth.

Even the gritty sand constantly grinding against her teeth was better than the bugs. Their tiny pinprick bites made sleeping impossible.

The wound beneath her breast was covered in a blanket of the tiny creatures, shifting around like pepper on a shaken pan, which only made her want to itch, but she knew once she started, she'd never stop and the wound would open right back up. Punt threatened to tie her down if he had to fix the wound again and the feverish look in his eyes told her that he meant it.

Summoning a reserve of energy – a reserve that was almost empty – Heron climbed the pile of blankets so she could see their location. The sand dunes had flattened out, so the whitish hills rolled into the distance like an infinite sea. The old road was mercifully flat, but the dunes had begun to reclaim them for lack of use.

Two days ago, they'd passed an oasis, but did not stop because the Sarmatians had been within sight. They could have used the water. Heron sipped at the water pouch, washing down the ever-present bugs, but reveling in the wet relief.

Squinting through the bright sunlight, she could see Hoth at the helm. Punt was behind her, snoring under the edge of the sun shade.

Robes billowed around the sea captain's body as he tried to protect himself from the sun. His face was puffy and red the last time she'd seen it. Mostly, the two men took turns driving and sleeping and keeping the fire going. Running the chariot was a three man job and now there were only two.

Heron grimaced at her own thoughts. *Three men*, she thought, *it'd never been three men. Just two men and a woman in disguise.* She'd been so long in their world she'd forgotten what it was like to be a woman.

But lying under the sun shade had given her ample time to remember. When her twin had been alive, and they'd been living in Macedonia, she'd always had to hide her learnedness. And while Sunny went out drinking and gambling after his day in the workshop was done, she spent her time studying the scrolls and books he'd brought home. She couldn't control how the men treated her (like something little more than a slave) but she could make the machines do what she wanted.

A self-trimming lamp had been her first real creation. She'd left the design on his desk and in the morning her twin put his craftsmen to work building it. When she held it in her hands, stroking its coppery brilliance, she knew what she wanted to do with her life, even if she had to do it in secret. Though at the time, she never imagined that she would have to steal her twin's identity to make that happen.

Swaddled in blankets and still shivering despite the heat, Heron crawled to the mechanical to feed more fuel in. Each movement with her right arm brought the sense of a knife being pressed under her breast, but she kept crawling. Even with the bugs and the sand and the injuries, Heron could tell the chariot was slowing.

She pulled herself erect using the side of the fuel bin and the emptiness of it made her grimace. But she carefully grabbed the scooper and added fuel to mechanical without tearing her chest open again.

Tiny black dots followed after them and a brief shake of the head told her they were real and not spots from sun blindness taking hold. She squinted but they didn't come into focus. If she'd known they were going to take the old trade road across the desert, she would have brought the darkened glasses they used in the foundry to protect their eyes.

Heron hobbled to the front and leaned against the bronze guarding that protected the helmsmen from the wind. Hoth glanced at her from beneath his shroud with haggard eyes. The sea captain didn't look like he'd be visiting temple prostitutes anytime soon.

"Riders," she said, wiping bugs from her mouth.

Hoth nodded and tried to speak, but his throat was too dry. Heron eventually retrieved the water pouch and he took a cautious sip before speaking again.

"Appeared after sunrise. Riding hard now. Catch us soon."

The look in his eyes told her they would have to make their stand before the day was done. She just hoped the Sarmatian assassins were in as bad as shape as they were.

"Location?"

The movement beneath his robes appeared to be a shrug. "The road split during the night and I took one." His voice was slightly more lubricated now but still rough.

Eventually the Sarmatians were more than tiny black dots and Heron woke Punt. The gruff blacksmith initially smiled at her as he rubbed his eyes and sat up, but then memory took hold and his face soured. Heron wasn't about to apologize for being a woman, but she wanted to say something to bring back the Punt she loved like a brother.

The blacksmith shouldered past, her good arm at least, and began stoking the fires while keeping his hammer at the ready. Heron gave them the remnants of their food and water. They needed strength now and if they won, they could take the assassin's supplies for the final leg of the journey.

There were five assassins and the steam chariot could no longer outpace them. The Sarmatians whipped their horses, preparing a last assault, the dust plumes matched the uncaring sky. Heron briefly wondered why they'd picked this time to finally make their attack when she saw the fleshy-greens of the oasis ahead.

A hill rose like a camel hump along side the oasis, protecting it from the worst of the winds and dunes. The water was muckish-brown and encircled with reeds, but the glint of sunlight across it was a welcome boon. The stone arch, worn away by sand and time, rose triumphantly over the greenery, but not as tall as the hill. As the chariot neared, they could see scaffolding around a cave entrance.

It seemed there was an excavation going on inside the cave. Who, she couldn't tell, for no wagons or camp supplies had been left outside. The site appeared abandoned for the moment, which only doubled the mystery. Her mind ticked through the options, even under the strained circumstances.

Hoth recognized it first and shouted back to her. "The oasis from the painting!"

She took the steering from Hoth. Her arms shook with weakness but she held the vehicle straight.

"We must have passed Memphis in the night, gone south of it," said Heron, checking behind her. "And we can't outrun them any longer."

Hoth pulled his curved blades and appeared rejuvenated by the coming fight. He shouldered off his robes and his lithe muscles flexed with anticipation.

"Can we get to the cave? We can make our stand there." He pointed with his curved sword.

She turned the steam chariot from the road and headed across the hardpack. Stray piles of sand tugged at the wheels and slowed them further. She glanced back to see one of the assassins riding ahead, his amber robes flapping in the wind, exposing his scaled armor. They'd chosen not to wear their fearsome dragon masks.

When he neared, the Sarmatian spurred his horse, blade held high. The man rode hard toward the front of the chariot, probably trying to kill her quickly so they could encircle the rest and pick them off with bows at their leisure.

Surprising even Hoth, who had moved to intercept, the man deftly hopped onto his saddle and leapt onto the platform. Hoth engaged the man with his blades before the assassin could attack Heron and the sound of steel filled the air.

With Hoth distracted on the one side, the other horsemen rode up on the other. A rider pulled his bow back, aiming at Punt. Heron veered the steam chariot away and the arrow missed widely. The other three approached Punt on the back, but his long-handled warhammer kept them from jumping on.

Holding tightly to the rattling steering mechanism, Heron barely shifted away from the blade in time. Only Hoth's shout warned her. The sea captain tackled the assassin from the chariot. They landed in a tangle, spitting up dust and sand. The other assassins kept after the chariot.

Punt moved to the location Hoth had vacated and one of the assassins jumped onto the back. The other three rode close, swinging their blades.

The chariot bounced off the rocks, sending bolts of agony through her side as the impact was translated through the steering mechanism. The cave entrance rushed towards them.

Heron fought the steering mechanism to keep it aimed at the entrance. The scaffolding appeared to be holding the cliff face up and the opening at the bottom was barely wide enough for the chariot. If she hit even the nub of a timber, the whole thing would crash down.

The assassins peeled away as the chariot shot towards the entrance. The vehicle bounced and rocked over the uneven ground and Heron fought to keep it on course. Behind her, Punt wrestled with the assassin.

Shooting through the gap, the chariot hitched wildly to the side. The wooden wheel clipped the scaffolding.

The cave enveloped them. Darkness blinded her. She yelled a warning to Punt and threw herself to the platform.

The impact threw her into the bronze shielding. Pain exploded in her chest and she blacked out for more than a few seconds. As she was coming around, she realized the cave entrance was collapsing. Light fled the room as dust and rock rushed in and moments later they were entombed in darkness.

When pain receded enough to move, she thought about calling out to Punt, to see if he was still alive, but then she remembered they'd brought one of the assassins into the cave with them. For all she knew, the man had survived and was now creeping toward her location with his dagger drawn. A footstep echoed behind her.

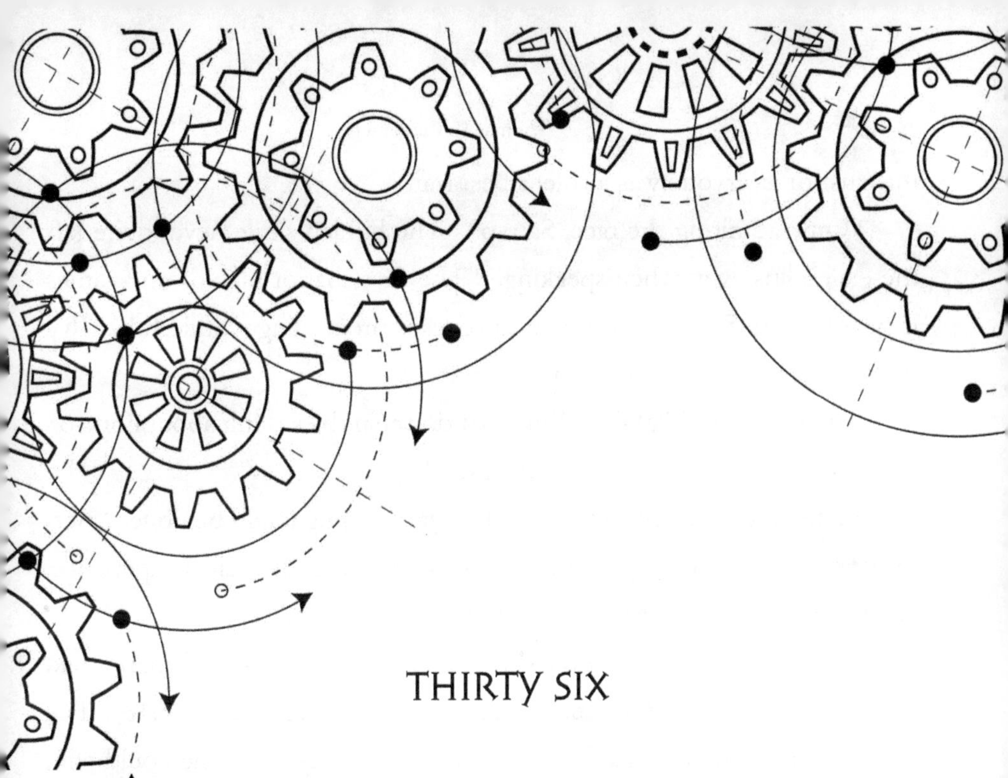

THIRTY SIX

Agog leaned against the railing with both hands, admiring the glittering chariots jostling around the track. The competitors wore helmets with colorful plumes to tell them apart. The horse-drawn chariots were foreign to his countrymen, so the race consisted only of local Alexandrians.

"The games are a wonderful success, Satrap," said the voice of the exile Ramses from behind him.

Ramses, in his Egyptian style tunic and golden ankh necklace, took a place next to Agog. When Ramses inclined his head, his eyes sparkled with thought.

"What is it? I can tell when you have something to say," thundered Agog.

The exile had been invaluable to Agog during his time in Alexandria, helping with the nobles and providing contacts to other kingdoms in the hopes of garnering alliances against Rome. But there was a part of the man that Agog didn't trust, though that was part of the game. A healthy mistrust of everyone was a ruler's best trait.

"Only admiring the race, Satrap." The hidden smile never quite left the exile's lips even when speaking. "The first chariot race of any games is prophetic to future successes and yours is proceeding wonderfully. I've never seen the horses look so magnificent."

Agog frowned slightly. "But what do the nobles think about none of my countrymen participating in the race?"

Ramses waggled his fingers as if to say nothing could be done. "Better not to have one of your men cause an accident in their inexperience. Chariot racing takes years to learn and a lifetime to perfect."

A host of cheers went up in the arena. The azure plumed chariot had taken the lead, while the emerald and crimson were close behind. The azure plumed chariot racer was one of Vestalis' men. If he could win, Agog would take that as a fortunous sign, since he'd invested so much in the man.

"It's good that the *Michanikos'* machines don't take as much skill," said Agog, though he regretted bringing up Heron's name since the man was out of the city. It'd been risky to send him to Old Babylon but the reward was too great for him to pass up. Maybe next time he might send Quadi in his place or one of the other scholars from the Great Library. It was foolish to send his most important ally away.

"The Romans can drive them just as easily," Ramses said, almost apologetically.

"My biggest fear," Agog grumbled.

Another cheer went up as Vestalis' chariot lost its lead. The race was little more than a third over, so there was plenty of time to recover, but he didn't like that Baruch's emerald chariot was now in front. The business with Sepharia complicated the situation. He'd made the noble turn her over for safe keeping and he knew it would cost him later.

"Worry no longer, Satrap," said Ramses. "Your man, Jarngard, will acquit your countrymen well in the wrestling contests."

"I appreciate your confidence, but I'm worried. He hasn't wrestled in years."

Ramses softly clapped his hands once. "Then he hasn't lost in years, either."

After a pause, Agog remembered why he'd called the exile to the Royal area. "Have your men driven away the bandits harrying the southern roads? I cannot lose any more trade. Vestalis complains too much already and I fear the man will look fondly upon his former Roman rule. The caravan he lost last week cost him three hundred talents. That's gold we could sorely use."

Ramses gave a simpering smile. "The steam chariots did their job well. The bandits wander the underworld now. Good Vestalis may rest easy."

A wash of cold dread drifted down Agog's back. Something in the man's grin made him feel like he'd just woken from a bad dream.

"And what commands do your men have now?" asked Agog, watching Ramses closely.

"We shall patrol the trade roads and keep them scoured. Even a single bandit will not take breath upon your roads," said Ramses.

Agog felt a heavy weight on his chest and wanted to sigh, but it would not come. "With the job complete, I'd like to see the steam chariots back in the city where they're safe."

The exile held a hand to his chest in mock injury. "Do you not trust me, Satrap? I have been your loyal servant."

"The support of your men has been most helpful," said Agog. "Between preparations for the Roman navy and providing security for the games, my soldiers are stretched thin. Especially ones I can trust. But bring the steam chariots back soon, we don't want them falling into Roman hands."

"It is the *least* I can do, Satrap. Your men cannot be tired for their matches," said Ramses. "It's imperative they do well to show the vitality of the men from the north."

"No need to remind me again. They're well placed in the games."

Agog nodded thoughtfully and grabbed a handful of spiced figs from an attendant. They were slightly tart and overspiced, but watching the chariot race made him hungry. He washed it down with watered down wine.

The arena rumbled with the soft chatter of thousands, marked by frequent shouts and cheers. The stone rail vibrated with humanity and reminded Agog of the first day he'd entered the city. He'd wished to yoke the city to his needs, but it felt more like a wild horse barely contained. He stared at the scattered empty seats, far too many for an event put on by the Satrap. The outer settlements had thinned as common folk moved away from the city. Mercenary companies had taken up some of the empty areas, but he didn't trust them, no matter how much coin he promised.

Ramses sidled close and whispered, before moving to the far side of the balcony. "Baruch Tanzen approaches. He comes about the inventor's daughter."

Agog barely turned before the noble born Baruch Tanzen was in his face. "When will I have justice for my daughter, Shayna?"

Agog gazed at Baruch until he took a step back and cleared his throat. "Careful with your tone, good Baruch. I agreed to the match between your man and mine. The consent a luxury I would have given no other, but for your circumstances."

"My daughter, your betrothed, rots in the earth because you failed to protect her," said Baruch with a venom that teetered on insolence.

"My life was in the balance that day, as well. I say again, we have struck our deal. Let us enjoy the day and the games instead."

The excess folds from Baruch's plainly adorned toga hung loosely from his arm, swinging slightly as he clenched and unclenched his fist. There was a hint of bloodshot madness in his eyes and Agog thought he detected the smell of strong wine.

"You promised you would punish the thieving girl and I just got a report she is here in the arena enjoying herself at your leisure!" The creases around his mouth deepened and his brow furrowed.

Agog responded, keeping his tone level, for he did not want his anger to race away from him. "Most of the guard is here in the arena or in the city preparing for the Roman navy, I did not wish to leave her alone, lest an accident happen. If you recall, we're preparing for war. While I see your grievance for what it is, I cannot waste my men's time doing extra duties these days."

"Then chain that girl in a slave pen or let me watch her," Baruch said. "I never should have let you take her from me. The girl's conspirator must have paid you off."

Agog raised his meaty fist like a bow coming level. "Mind your words, good Baruch, my temper grows shorter like the day."

A raucous cheer went up behind them and Agog was sorely tempted to turn and see the status of the race. Baruch's gaze did not even so much as flicker in the direction of the chariots.

"What is one girl to my support," said Baruch.

The words welled up in Agog's chest like a mightly bellows preparing to spit forth a gale. He held back, only briefly, before astonishing Baruch with volume.

"I will not be blackmailed in the city I claimed without your help. The *Michanikos* is my friend and ally and his support goes far beyond simple men that *anyone* can supply. Without him I could not have taken the city."

Baruch seemed only momentarily affected by this statement. "So you place that girl above me?"

Agog clenched his fists and controlled the urge to strangle the man.

"Not at all. Your grievances are fair and should be heard. You did, after all, find her on your premises with a scroll of great value in her hands."

On second thought, Agog decided he should be strangling Jarngard for putting him in such a position, no matter how many times his lieutenant claimed the girl was only supposed to be a lookout. Agog bit his tongue in frustration.

"Then why is she here freely enjoying the games?" Baruch asked.

Agog leveled his gaze at Baruch, as he slowly realized the man was going to stay steadfast in his complaint, no matter how much he tried to dissuade him. The poisonous leer in Baruch's stare did not appear to be one ready to accept reason.

The calming breath Agog took wasn't so calming, but it allowed him to remember that Baruch held a sizable portion of the nobles to his sway. As much as he hated to admit it, he needed the man. But he also needed Heron and so he could not endanger the girl.

"For you, I shall send my men to corral the girl and bring her to a more secure location and one without a view of the games. And now that it is decided, let us enjoy the rest of the race."

Agog swept his hand around, indicating they should look down upon the chariots. Another cheer from the crowd announced a lead change, though Agog had no way of knowing who had passed who since he was focused on Baruch.

"She should be back in my care," said Baruch, "paying for the crime of murdering my daughter. Life for life, though I'll happily cut off her hands for stealing from me before she'd be put to death."

"I am the Satrap," growled Agog, feeling his anger loosen its bonds. "I am done discussing this subject."

Instead of answering, as Agog expected the man to do, Baruch fled down the stairs, his face cast in a grimace. Agog nearly called his guard to apprehend the man, but the cheering of the crowd distracted him. Baruch was well away before he thought of it again.

Beneath him on the oval track, the glittering chariots were spitting up dust on their way around the final lap. The crowd had passed frenzy and was now screaming like a horde of Gauls. The azure and the emerald plumed charioteers were side by side, wheels banging against wheels on the last stretch.

Agog gripped the railing and wished that one of his companions was with him on the balcony. Instead, he was surrounded by Alexandrian guards, none of them men he'd brought from the north.

With only half a stadium to go, the two chariots bounced together and then split apart. Agog's keen eyes saw the wheel shatter and be thrown into the crowd. Screams quickly overtook the cheers as the chariot on the inside of the track catapulted into the dirt as the broken wheel dug in.

A cloud of dust enveloped racers and horses screamed in terror as the chariots behind the leaders smashed into the fallen one. Agog felt cold dread wash over him as the dust cleared.

Trotting around the other side of the track, the emerald plumed chariot - Baruch's chariot - made its victory lap. Behind him on the finish line, men in togas with stretchers ran onto the track. At least four chariots had broken in the crash. Men lay lifeless in the ruts and even from a distance, Agog could see blood forming around the head of the first rider.

The crowd was silent, except for dying horses braying in the empty air. A soldier with a sword silenced them with successive thrusts. It felt like the whole world had quieted and the only thing Agog could see was a bronze and broken object near the finish line—the azure plumed helmet.

THIRTY SEVEN

The darkness of the cave surrounded Heron like a blanket. Her heartbeat thrummed in her ears, still racing from the crash. The numbness in her arm was turning to tingles. She shook it, trying to get the pain to disappear.

The *clump* of a footstep on the planks of the steam chariot made her freeze. She gripped her dagger tightly and tried to calm her breathing. The steam mechanical was ticking loudly, like tapping a hammer against a brass pot. The sound of steam escaping could be heard above the tapping.

A noise from behind made her jump slightly and she might have let out a squeak. She bit her lip, hard, and hoped that whatever was lurking in the darkness hadn't heard.

The covering noises and the darkness made waiting difficult. She kept thinking she heard things moving just out of reach but she wasn't sure if it was real or her imagination. She kept her dagger before her like a shield.

After a while she realized that she could see the edge of the guarding on the front of the chariot, but she couldn't figure out how. It should be completely dark in the lightless cave.

When she oriented herself toward the back of the chariot, she realized why. Coals from the steam mechanical, though well guarded, reflected against the metal and created enough light for her to make out the outline of the chariot. The shielding was blackened from burning or it would have shown brighter.

She moved to the steam mechanical. The bottom of the chariot was cracked in the center and she leaned as she stepped onto the middle section. A rag wiped away the blackened soot.

With her eyes adjusted, the room was painted with a warm, orange glow. No one lurked nearby. In fact, she couldn't even see Punt, which worried her as much as not knowing if the assassin was lurking in the dark. Punt could be unconscious and bleeding and her caution could cause him further injury.

"Punt," she whispered through gritted teeth, readying the dagger to thrust toward any sudden movements.

"Punt," she said again, this time a little louder.

She glanced around. She saw nothing. Not her blacksmith, or the assassin.

She decided that if the assassin was going to attack her, he would have done so already.

This time when she yelled, it was loud enough to cause an echo.

"Punt!"

The room sounded much larger than she first thought. The sound of her voice bounced deep behind her.

Heron stuck the edge of the rag she'd found into the coals and held it up to see. Circling slowly, she saw the assassin first. He was crumpled awkwardly onto the rocks near the crashed chariot. Dark liquid leaked from his skull.

Heron breathed a sigh of relief and turned faster, desperate to see her friend.

"Punt!"

The blacksmith was face-first on the other side of the chariot. The warhammer was still clenched in his fist. Heron struggled to climb down from the chariot, realizing with the first step that her leg was injured. Using the lighted rag, she quickly examined herself, only to find a large gash in her thigh. Her knee was slick with blood.

"First, Punt," she muttered.

She limped to the fallen blacksmith and put a hand to his back. He was breathing, but shallow.

She shook his shoulder lightly. "Punt? You'd better wake up on your own, because there's no way I can flip you myself."

Punt answered with a groan. She took that as a good sign.

A few moments later, Punt rose to his knees. He looked like a dog stretching from a long nap.

"Where are we?" he asked, his injuries still evident in his shaky voice.

"In the cave."

When the light from the rag began to dwindle, she retrieved some fuel and a blanket and started a larger fire near the chariot.

As black soot puffed from the growing fire, Heron grew worried that they would choke on the smoke. But as the light reflected off the distant walls, she realized the cave was even larger than she first thought.

Using the light, she repaired her knee and a few cuts on Punt's shoulder. He sulked as she pulled the thread through and tied it off.

"Am I that much of a monster to you now that you know the truth?" she said finally.

He hung his head. The fire shimmered off his skin. Shadows collected beneath his eyes.

"I don't know what to think, Master..." His voice trailed off in question. "What do I call you?"

"Heron," she said forcefully.

The doubt in his tone hurt. She rubbed her still tingling arm and shook it a few more times.

"I'm still the same person, Punt. That I'm a woman changes nothing."

His eyes told her that he thought otherwise. He glanced away.

"Does this mean you won't work for me?" she asked.

The conflict passed across his face like a cloud. He opened his mouth more than once, but said nothing.

"I can still change the world," she said. "Even as a woman."

When he spit his answer out, she could hear Astrela in his words. "Is this why the gods cursed your work?"

It might have hurt had she not known how Astrela dogged him on this point, so she laughed instead. "I told you once before, Punt. Those miracles failed because Philo was sabotaging them and because I was pushing the edges of science."

She could see he didn't believe her, but he wasn't going to argue, either. Typical for Punt, who brewed thoughts long and deep.

Heron rubbed her shoulder absently. "Do you think Hoth got away from the Sarmatians?"

Punt grunted softly. "If the fall didn't kill him."

She shook her head. "I saw him get up, still grappling with the assassin. Right before we hit the cave."

"What does it matter?" He shrugged. "We're stuck here."

Heron tried to contain a smile. Even the little bit of conversation was reassuring. She almost reached out and patted him on the shoulder, but held back. His wheels were still turning and she didn't want to knock him back into silence.

"Together we'll figure out how to escape," she told him. "Or Hoth will make it back to Alexandria and bring help."

In another time, she might have felt despair at being trapped in a cave, but after her gender had been revealed to Punt, figuring out how to escape gave her a tangible problem to work on.

They made torches using lantern oil and blankets. The room was pleasantly warm so they had no need of them.

The floor of the cave had been smoothed flat. The rocky outcropping they'd crashed into curved around and opened up to a much larger cave behind. Using the lantern, they found a large cache of supplies in boxes and sacks.

At first, Heron thought they were for the builders of the scaffolding outside the cave. She peered into an open box to find bundles of cloth. Then she noticed the black wheel stamped onto the side.

"Vestalis' goods," whispered Heron, trying to make sense of why they were in the cave.

Punt furrowed his brow in the thought. "Is this a secret storehouse?"

"I'd hardly think so," she said, circling the boxes with the lantern held high in her right hand. Her left arm tingled and the older wound on her chest throbbed. "The cave is not on the main roads and those arrow wounds are fresh."

Punt indicated a broken arrow. There were six similar holes around it.

"That arrow pattern looks familiar." Heron ran her fingers across the holes.

Punt cleared his throat. He was facing away from the boxes. There was another area behind them. When she lifted the lantern the words caught in her throat.

A glistening steam chariot complete with an arrow launcher waited between the rocks. The Northmen called this version the Manticore like the mythical beast.

The bronze shielding had been polished recently and hundreds of arrow fletchings stuck out of the tubes near the launcher. Heron examined them to find they were Alexandrian made.

"How did this get here?" asked Heron. "Agog controls the Manticores tightly for fear of Rome."

"Much could have happened since we left, Master...Heron," said Punt.

Heron might have smiled, but for the revelation before her. Someone had betrayed them.

"We need to search this cave further. You take one of the torches and try the other side. We must find who stole it."

Punt didn't race off as she expected him to. Instead, he shuffled from foot to foot and stared at the dirt. Eventually the words came in a slow trickle. "What good will that do us? We're trapped in the cave."

His doubt made her clench her fists reflexively. "I'm working on that, good Punt. By the time we figure out who betrayed us, I will have the answer."

In the workshop, Punt always trusted her when she said things like that, and she always followed through with her words. As he walked away, his shoulders slumped and he seemed already beaten.

Heron searched until a shout from Punt brought her ambling his direction. The back of the cave pinched down to a hole they had to duck under. The passage opened up into a wider room. A shrine had been carved into the back of the cave.

The visage of Alexander the Macedonian was carved into the stone. Hieroglyphics surrounded the image and Heron recognized the tone of the message. Here was a shrine to the man-god Alexander. Memory of the painting in the maze came back to her in full.

"Why would the temple of Alexander want to attack Vestalis' caravans?" she asked.

Punt didn't understand, so she explained the painting she'd seen in the maze. The blacksmith could make no sense of it.

"If the temple truly opposed us," said Heron, "then they would have killed us in the maze. I do not believe it's them, though I cannot prove this."

There was a stone before Alexander, flat like a table. Faded writing covered the surface. It was written in Macedonian and in an older style than she was used to.

"Hold your torch high," she asked.

The blacksmith moved closer. The fire light flickered across the stone, pushing shadows to the corners.

As she read the words, her head grew light as a feather and her face grew warm. The inscription on the Alexander Temple in Old Babylon fell through her thoughts like hot coals. The writing on the stone was nearly word for word, except for the beginning and a few extra sections through out the middle. She read it out loud:

"I, Alexander the Macedonian, son of Zeus-Ammon, and the one named in the greater destinies, do hold myself, or whoever comes after me, to change this world, from the farthest sea to the farthest sea. For flesh is weak and men need a shining light like a beacon in the fog. Would I conquer with word and deed rather than spear and horse? Though endless battles stretch out before me to the horizon, I will take whatever course necessary to mold the future to the thoughts of our greatest thinkers."

She waited in silence for a time. The numbness of her arm and the pain in her leg seemed distant.

"A vain and bold man. If he had an heir, that person would have an impossible legacy to uphold," she said, shaking her head in disbelief. "In certain ways, his words here, at this time, mirror the others, the ones in the temple. I wonder how his endless war changed him."

"But we are still trapped," said Punt, low and deep.

"The answer to our escape will come soon enough. I am close," she lied.

Punt wandered back the other way, ducking back into the other cavern. Heron gazed a moment longer on the shrine before following. Seeing the handwriting of Alexander the Macedonian affected her differently than when she'd seen the words in the temple in Old Babylon. It almost felt like a message directly to her, even though she knew that thought was foolish, smacking of prophecy or religion.

Even Alexander the Macedonian had seen the need for other ways of conquering. Of stealing hearts and minds without having to put a spear in them first. The plan of action on the inscription at the old temple was an indication of how his thinking had changed. At this oasis, in the back of this cave, he scrawled his vision upon the rock. Who knew if he thought anyone would find it or if he hoped it would stay hidden. Doubtful of the latter given his vanity.

The Oracle at Siwa must have affected him greatly. Maybe he'd seen that he was to conquer the world and how much blood he would spill? She hoped, as his countryman, that he desired to reduce that spillage. Though, his history was littered with destructive campaigns when his enemies opposed him or caused him some slight. He was ever vengeful.

The flickering torch reminded her of the waning time and she left. She found Punt in the first cave and he held a small shield with an ankh and sun stamped onto the front. A cache of weapons were piled into the corner. Some had the ankh on sun symbols.

"Egyptian made," said Punt, holding a sword and running his finger along the blade.

"Egyptian bandits with an Alexandrian Manticore steam chariot," mused Heron. "And for what purpose? Simple thievery or something greater?"

The symbol tickled Heron's mind. She knew she'd seen it before but the long journey to Old Babylon and back had erased her recent memories of Alexandria.

"These were made on the southern edges of Egypt," continued Punt. "The ore makes the blade a lighter color, though more brittle."

"Ramses made his exile in that region," said Heron, finally remembering where she'd seen the symbol before. "His friends from the old families protected him from the Romans."

Punt shrugged and put the sword back on the pile.

"Why would Ramses attack Vestalis' caravans? For profit or revenge or opportunity?" Heron asked the questions, but she knew no answer would come. "All the more reason that we need to escape this cave and return to Alexandria."

"The Satrap trusts the exile," said Punt plainly.

The corners of Heron's lips turned down. "Does he trust him well enough to give him a Manticore? I truly hope not, but then again, much may have changed while we've been gone."

Punt's arm dipped and she could see the defeat in his downcast eyes. The blacksmith probably thought himself cursed for associating with a woman.

She eyed the broken chariot. The front wheels were shattered from the impact and the structure twisted in the middle like a giant had thrown it. They had the other steam chariot, the Manticore, but she doubted it could gather enough speed to ram through the fallen entrance. Besides, it would probably kill the driver and neither she nor Punt was expendable.

And even if she was able to miracle them from the cave, Punt knew the secret of her gender and appeared willing to spill it, if only to remove the taint from himself. Her secrets or the cave itself seemed more a danger to her and their plans than the possibility that the exile Ramses was against them. Even one Manticore could do nothing against the whole of Alexandria's army. They had more to worry about from the Roman navy in a few months, another reason to get back soon.

But still, it weighed on her mind that the exile might be false. Sepharia was still in the Palace and anything that happened to Agog would affect her daughter.

Heron examined the fallen rocks around the entrance. As far as she could tell, the fall-in was a few lengths deep. More than they could remove by hand and they had not scaffolding to keep the walls from collapsing further. Unless she could devise a way through, they were stuck here, and if Ramses was against them, even Hoth's escape wouldn't help.

No, she couldn't think like that, she decided. She had to figure out a way through. Nothing was impossible, only increasingly more difficult.

Heron wandered to the broken chariot and stared at the motionless steam mechanical. The pistons were bent and the coals a deep black with specks of orange. This chariot wouldn't help them escape, not at all. Heron crossed her arms and hoped inspiration would come soon, because even she was beginning to feel a little despair and once she gave up, they would be as good as dead.

THIRTY EIGHT

Sepharia picked at the whitefish on the terra cotta plate. Thin white bones threaded the flaky flesh. She pushed the food away and stared at the ceiling. The stone room was barely wide enough for the table. At one time, the room had been a cell, but the bars on the door had been removed, though the holes still remained, half-filled with dust and cobwebs.

She glanced at the rumbling cheer. The stone carried the vibration and the noise, but not the result. Then she glanced at the empty door. It would be a while until he came to visit. Too long.

She peeked down the hall. A lone guard leaned against the wall and idly picked his teeth. He had the bronze skin of an Egyptian but an equine Roman nose. The stamp on the front of his leather jerkin was an ankh across a blazing sun.

"Salute. The fish was delicious," he said when he noticed her. His Greek was heavily accented with an Egyptian dialect she wasn't familiar with. Possibly he was from further south where Ramses had lived his life in exile.

"I have more if you want. I'm not hungry."

The guard glanced cautiously the other way. "Bring it here."

She left the hard bread but brought him the fish. The guard scooped the fish up with his hands and started gnawing on the floppy meat.

"Did he win?"

The guard shrugged. "I know as much as you," he said between bites.

"What about my father," she asked hesitantly, "has he returned to the city?"

"I'm not your spy," he said abruptly, making her feel small.

Sepharia tramped back to her room, wishing it was one of the Northmen guarding her and not the Egyptian. She picked up the hard bread but didn't eat it. It was still warm.

Jarngard appeared like a ghost. She nearly dropped the bread.

"Wha—?"

"Is that how you greet your champion? I expect as much from the common folk," he said.

He was bare-chested and a sheen of sweat coated him. He tossed a date in one hand, catching it easily without keeping his gaze on it. He had the swagger of a winner.

"Then you won?" she asked hopefully.

"Only one match left."

He glanced away, looking at the dirt, and Sepharia took that as a sign. A sign of what, she wasn't sure. These men from the north were hard to read.

"You're dirtier than the last time."

He shrugged. "A longer fight."

"Can you beat him? Little Hercules sounds formidable."

He briefly glanced away again, and a stone formed in her gut. "Every man can lose."

"Do your dice tell if you win?"

Jarngard strolled to the table and plopped into the chair, tossing the date as he moved.

"The dice tell me I have a chance. But better if I had a sword in hand rather than without."

He tossed the date high into the air and neatly caught it with his mouth, barely chewing and swallowing immediately.

"Has my father returned?" she asked.

He curled his lips downward. "No sign, but he's not due yet. Maybe in a few days, unless Hoth found a temple whore along the way."

His words were clearly meant to be reassuring, but Sepharia detected a hint of concern.

Jarngard belched and put a fist to his chest.

"Serves you right for eating your food like a crocodile."

He moved to smile, but the corners of his lips twitched and turned into a grimace. He groaned and convulsed once. Jarngard tried to stand, but his knee buckled and he fell onto the stone floor.

"The date!"

She rushed to his side. Jarngard was nearly cross-eyed in pain. Then he surprised her by shoving his hand into his mouth and started gagging. Sepharia grabbed his arm and tried pulling it away to keep him from choking. She'd never heard of a poison that drove a man to asphyxiate themselves. Jarngard shook her off as he reflexively gagged, even going so far as kicking her in the shin to keep her back.

She was about to start shouting for the guard, or maybe even tackle him, when there came a retching sound and the barely-chewed date flung out of his mouth, covered in spit and stomach bile.

Jarngard fell onto his hands and knees and coughed. The guard outside came running to the door, called by the noise. Between labored breaths, Jarngard said, "Run to the training room. Tell them not to eat the food. Poisoned."

The guard nodded and left. Sepharia helped up the Northman when he motioned to her. His skin was pallid and clammy. She imagined he'd be dead if he hadn't vomited up the poisoned date.

"To the Satrap."

With his arm around her shoulder, they moved upward. Her holding cell was deep in the basement of the stadium. After three flights of stairs, Jarngard made them stop.

"I'm slowing us down. Go and warn him. Do not let anyone stop you." His brow was knotted with worry.

She sprung up the stairs, taking them two at a time. The Royal area was on the other side of the stadium, so Sepharia took the servant's passages, hoping to avoid Baruch's followers.

Halfway around, after dodging servants in togas carrying trays of food, Sepharia realized she was lost. She crept up a flight of stone steps hoping to find her location when she heard the sound of two men talking in Latin.

Sepharia fled onto the level. Another cheer erupted in the stadium, reverberating through the stone. She scurried down a hallway and hid in a pillared storeroom behind a rack of chains and hooks they used for gladiatorial matches. The room smelled of mold and leather and human sweat.

When she heard voices, she shrunk behind the rack, making herself as small as possible. It sounded like the two men who had been coming up the stairwell behind her. They closed the door and spoke in hushed tones, though she could make out their words quite easily.

"The men are in place," said the first. "Are we safe to bring them into the city?"

When Sepharia heard the second voice, she thought it sounded familiar. It was higher than she heard in the stairwell.

"You're late," the second voice growled. "Events are moving too quickly. I needed them weeks ago."

"You never answered our message," responded the first.

"I never *received* your message."

The second speaker became instantly recognizable once Sepharia realized she smelled lilacs. Polyxena wore the scent everywhere.

Sepharia peered through the racks to see the woman dressed in soldier's gear. Her hair had been tucked beneath a ridged helmet.

"It doesn't matter now," said Polyxena. "Right now we need to eliminate the exile. It's our only shot."

Sepharia hadn't been completely sure what the two conspirators were talking about, but hearing the last part pulled the conspiracy into focus. When she combined the poisoning of the Northmen and that Polyxena was hiding in a soldier's uniform, along with killing the exile, she knew what was going on. Polyxena was going to overthrow the Satrap. Maybe she wasn't Macedonian at all and was a Roman spy. Why else was she speaking in Latin? All that talk about "fellow Macedonian" was just a front.

Sepharia ground her teeth and clenched her hands. She'd strangle the woman if she got the chance.

"I'll send in the assassins," said the man.

"And I'll go after the Satrap," said Polyxena. "Go ahead and leave, I need to change so I can make it past the guards."

Sepharia's eyes widened and her palms grew sweaty. Polyxena was going to kill the Satrap. When the door closed, leaving Sepharia alone in the room with Polyxena, Sepharia realized she had her chance.

Polyxena was unclamping the buckles on the leather armor as Sepharia snuck up behind. Once she neared, Sepharia wished she'd grabbed a chain off the shelf as a weapon.

Focused on the diminutive woman, Sepharia scuffed a sandal against the stone and Polyxena wheeled around with her dagger drawn. Polyxena's expression went from surprise to welcome in a heartbeat.

"What are you doing here?" smiled Polyxena.

Sepharia thought about rushing the older woman, but the way Polyxena confidently held the knife kept Sepharia from acting.

"I heard what you said," said Sepharia.

"I suppose it doesn't matter now," said Polyxena calmly, letting the dagger point drift to the floor. "Win or lose, everyone will know today."

It made Sepharia angry that the woman wasn't even apologetic about being so false.

"Did you lie about being Macedonian to get me to trust you?" Sepharia questioned angrily.

Confusion passed across Polyxena's face. The dagger came up slightly.

"Of course I'm Macedonian. I come from an important line in our royal history," said Polyxena. "But I don't have time for this now. I must get to the Satrap quickly, or none of this will matter."

When Polyxena sheathed the dagger, Sepharia seized the moment and leapt forward. The Macedonian woman put her hands up to defend. Instead of attacking, Sepharia dodged around and pulled the door open. She felt a hand grasp at her chiton, but yanked free in her escape.

Polyxena shouted something, but Sepharia couldn't hear with her heartbeat laboring in her ears. If she could reach the Satrap first, she could warn him of the danger. Polyxena probably meant to poison him again or shove the knife in his side while her troops entered the city. There wasn't much time.

Nearing the royal area, Sepharia heard a familiar voice from the hallway. He would be able to help her get through the royal guards without being detained.

Instead of heading up the stairs toward the royal area, Sepharia followed the voice. She found him standing with a group of unfamiliar soldiers with the ankh and blazing sun emblem on their jerkins. Weapons were drawn.

Ramses' darkened eyes narrowed at her approach and for a instant, Sepharia thought about fleeing the other way. The paint around his eyes formed tiny arrowheads. Then he smiled and spoke and she remembered she was here to save the Satrap.

"What is this girl doing?" asked Ramses.

Sepharia stood before him and the soldiers shared strange glances. Their weapons glinted in the torch light.

"The woman Polyxena," said Sepharia, out of breath, "she means to kill the Satrap. I overheard her in a storage room."

The exile seemed genuinely surprised and put a hand to his chest. The golden ankh on his necklace shimmered. The creases around his painted eyes deepened, stretching the arrowheads into longer points, even as his smile widened.

"What a delicious turn of events," said Ramses. "Ammon-Ra must be with us. I always knew that Macedonian bitch would be a problem."

Sepharia was about to explain that Polyxena had troops outside the city when she realized that the soldiers had their weapons drawn and they'd been drawn before she'd warned them.

The look of realization on her face must have been plain to see because Ramses made a quick motion and one of the soldiers grabbed her. His smile turned to a sneer.

"This girl should have trusted her first instinct and fled when she saw me," said Ramses lazily. "Not that it matters now. I shall own the city before the day is out and then this girl's fate is mine to give. I am certain that Baruch Tanzen will be quite pleased."

Sepharia pulled an arm away from the soldier's grasp and struck Ramses across the jaw. Ramses barely flinched and showed his teeth briefly before he marched up the stairs with his squad of soldiers.

The royal viewing area was right above them. She'd nearly run up there to warn the Satrap. A hundred thoughts flashed through her head, including all the times she'd talked to Ramses. Why hadn't she seen his falseness?

Outside in the arena, the people applauded some contest. A chariot race, maybe, those brought the most cheers.

Sepharia waited for the inevitable screams and she was not disappointed. A cry of alarm ended in a gurgle. She cringed and tried to pull away but the soldier held her with rough, calloused hands. His warm breath washed over her back.

Shouts and death cries echoed down the stairs. The clash of steel was brief and complete. Sepharia felt her knees weaken, but did not give in. She would need to save her strength. She would need it—all of it. The exile Ramses had killed the Satrap and taken Alexandria.

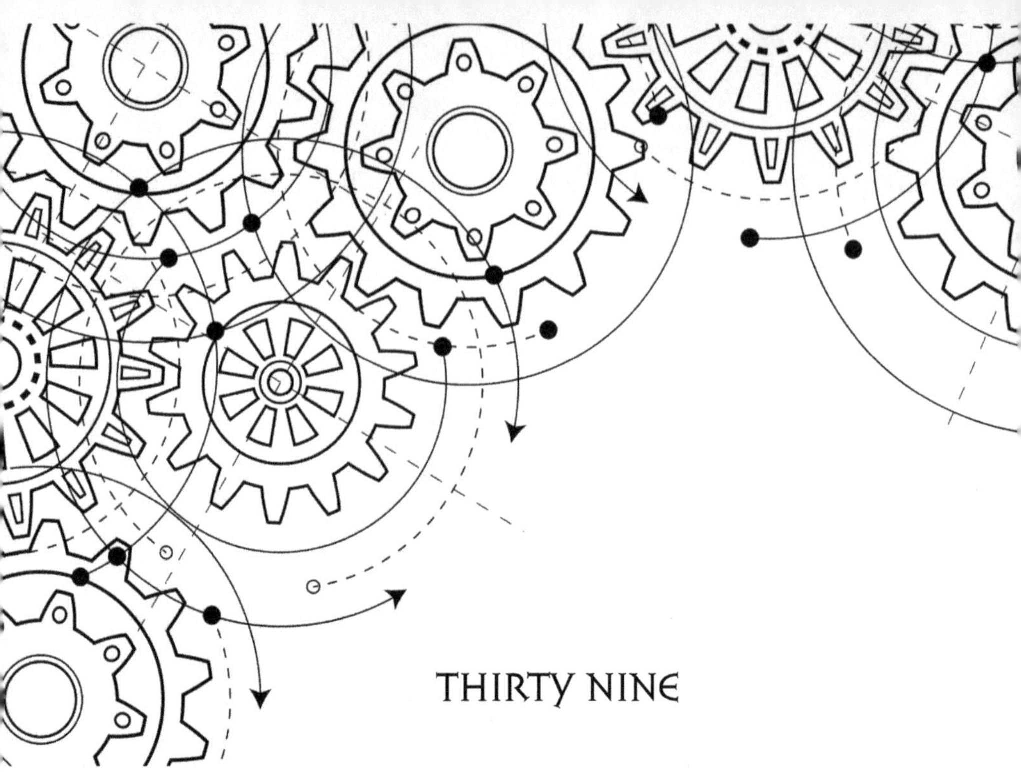

THIRTY NINE

Hoth rode the dying horse with his feet light in the stirrups in case it collapsed beneath him. It'd been nearly dead even before the assassins had attacked them near the oasis. He wanted to get as close to Alexandria as he could before it fell. It was his best shot to save the *Michanikos*, if he wasn't dead, crushed by the falling rocks when the cave collapsed.

One of the Sarmatians had been killed by a rock when he rode too close to the steam chariot. Another took a glancing blow, but survived. Hoth had killed the assassin he'd been grappling with and then taken his horse. He killed the other two before they could get their bows.

It didn't take long for Hoth to realize that Heron and Punt were either trapped or dead and a quick ride around the hill confirmed there were no other exits from the cave. He'd have to ride hard to Alexandria and get help, bringing workers and engineers to dig them out. There hadn't been much food or water left, so he didn't have time.

The first horse died within an hour of leaving the oasis. The Sarmatians had ridden them hard. The second died not long after, but the third, the one he rode, was still going, though he could see white crust around the corners of the horse's mouth.

When the horse's head dipped low and it started weaving across the trail, Hoth quickly dismounted. He walked the creature for a little while, until it fell to its knees and then onto its side, dust puffing out beneath it. There was no death cry like the others. This horse just laid its head on the sandy soil and expired.

Feeling fortunate that it didn't keel over in mid-run, Hoth took another drink of water and began jogging. At least they'd been ambushed at an oasis. He'd drank his fill and topped off three water pouches before he left.

Hoth had been riding on the steam chariot for days, so his legs were rested. His eyes, though puffy from the sun, were clear. He picked out distant scrub brush and ran until he reached it, and then picked another, and kept going. It reminded him of charting a sea course.

Eventually, the old caravan trail met with a larger, well worn one. The path had many tracks upon it. Most signs were recent, even within the hour, so he counted himself unlucky not to have encountered anyone yet.

Hoth knelt in the dirt and pondered why all the horse hooves and wagon tracks led away from Alexandria. Had a large trading caravan passed this way? He hoped it was not more people fleeing the city. He knew fear of the Roman navy would convince the poorer souls to leave, but it wasn't the navy they had to fear. The navy might blockade the city and keep trade away, but it couldn't affect the land routes.

He was busy discarding a finished water pouch when he saw the glint of riders in the distance. They were headed his way. Hoth resumed his steady jog. He would find out who they were soon enough.

As they neared, he could make out that they were soldiers. The sun reflected from their steel weapons and bronze helms. They wore unfamiliar leather jerkins. He knew Jarngard would know what soldiers these men were. Probably mercenaries who hadn't found the gold they desired in Alexandria and were headed south to fight for warlords on the plains, where beautiful dark-skinned women and jewels were said to be as common as rain.

When the soldiers surrounded him, he could see the ankh and sun emblems on their chest. The squad was entirely Egyptian.

"Hail, friends," said Hoth in Greek with his arms folded in front. "It's good you came along when you did, I was getting rather bored of my desert run."

The soldiers circled around him. Hoth wasn't sure which one was their leader. A few exchanged words in Egyptian once he was done speaking.

"Did you not find the coin you desired in Alexandria?" Hoth smiled, though his eyes did not. He sensed their animosity by their hardened eyes and sharp words. He knew enough that they were discussing his fate.

Hoth unfolded his arms and put his hands comfortably on his hilts. He would take a couple with him to his ancestral lands if they decided to attack.

"We will not kill you," said one of the soldiers in accented Greek. Their leader was as plain as the endless blue sky. Sometimes Hoth wished he could blend in with his men like this one did. Too many times the enemy sought him out in battle or on his ship, to prove their glory.

"I never said you would." He faced their leader, circling slowly as the horse sauntered around him. "Hoth the Black has never been bested in battle."

Maybe he could goad one into single combat, he thought. Then he could seize the opportunity to grab an untended horse and escape. That mercenaries would turn to banditry so close to Alexandria worried him about its current state.

Their leader met his gaze with a steely one of his own. Hoth could see the man had experienced battle by his cold stare. A soldier spoke in Egyptian and the others laughed.

"Recognize my name, do you?" smiled Hoth.

The leader smiled, white teeth against bronze skin. "He said you smell like a whore and you're called the black because your cock is rotting off."

"Tell him to come down here and I'll show him the strength of my cock."

They circled him and the dust coated his tongue, but he could not spit or frown or even wipe his tired eyes. They watched, and he waited.

"Best you scurry south," said Hoth, "before an Alexandrian patrol comes this way with one of its Manticores and leaves arrow fletchings in your behind."

When the whole crew of them burst into laughter, Hoth knew he was sunk.

"We own Alexandria now," said the leader. "Where is the miracle worker? Ramses said he would be with you."

Hoth did not know this Ramses well, but he'd heard Agog speak of the man more than once. He thought him an advisor or lackey, not a man with ambitions for the city. The best kind of treachery, he supposed.

"I know not what you speak of." Hoth's smile twitched and he cursed himself for it.

"Liar," said the man. "Tell us that and how you came to be walking on the old caravan road. We expected you east and north of here between Alexandria and Memphis."

"Heron ascended to the gods in Old Babylon and I flew on a dragon's tail here. The *Michanikos* assembles an army of mechanical soldiers and will march when he is good and ready. It was planned for the Romans, but I guess you'll have to do."

A few of the men glanced nervously at each other. The Egyptians were a superstitious lot.

"Don't believe him, you fools," said the soldier and then to Hoth. "No matter what you believe, I'm taking you to the city. The new Satrap has plans for you in the arena."

Hoth had been readying himself to attack. He could kill their leader easily and maybe a second or third soldier, but he would die just the same. The gods did not favor him in this fight.

But the arena, that was a fairer chance. Better to fight for glory and the chance to live longer, maybe even be freed, if the stories he'd heard about their gladiators held true.

Hoth yanked his swords free and the sound of a steel wind followed. He flipped them in the air and deftly caught them blade first, holding them only by his fingertips. He handed them to their leader.

"I'll show you sand people how a Northman fights."

The soldier derisively snorted. "You'll show us how a Northman dies. Tie him to my horse."

They bound his hands and threw him over the back of the soldier's horse. The ropes cut his wrists as the horse bounced and more than once the soldier led them across rougher terrain, just to cause more pain. Hoth silently memorized the man's Egyptian name, Akiiki, spoken amongst his men.

As they approached the white stone walls of the city, Hoth could see black smoke drifting from the harbor. He could not imagine that the exile Ramses would have burned the Library or the docks. When he saw the catapults on fire, he knew the new Satrap meant to give the city over to the Romans.

He spit into the dirt, silently cursing the witch woman's words that had led him to the city of Alexandria. When they passed the golden lions, Hoth found their roars not as sweet as he had when he first heard them. This city of wonders had turned into a death trap and all its clockwork marvels mere toys.

They pulled him from the horse and untied his hands. Blood pounded back into them, bringing stinging needles. Hoth kept his face blank despite the pain.

"So your master's bending over for the Roman cock?" taunted Hoth when Akiiki readied to address him.

Hoth caught a backhand and tried to hide his smile beneath his dirty, knot-bound hair.

"You Northmen were fools to think you could stand up to the might of the Roman Empire. The entire Roman navy will be here in three weeks. Do you think a few catapults and steam chariots would repel them?"

"Three weeks?" Hoth pinched his face in thought. "Have I been gone that long or are they early?"

"Consul Aulus Plautius fooled you idiots into thinking that he was delayed around the mouth of the Mediterranean."

The truth hit him in the gut. The Roman navy would have taken them unawares, even if they hadn't been overthrown. They were dead twice over.

Akiiki motioned for him to follow. A guard of six soldiers walked with him. He was led to the bowels of the arena, where the lowest prisoners were usually kept. Hoth heard the voices of his countrymen murmuring when they saw him. He tried to glance through the bars as he passed, hoping to see faces he knew, but they walked too fast and the gaps were too narrow.

The goaler's key rattled in the lock and the hinges screamed open. They shoved him into the darkened cell. Hoth could see the feet of another prisoner half in shadow.

"I'm looking forward to seeing you in the arena," said Akiiki.

"You want to see how a real warrior fights?" he asked.

"No," said Akiiki, "I want to see how a perfumed man-whore dies."

The other soldiers laughed and Hoth even heard a few of his fellow

Northmen chuckle at the comment. His fellow prisoner said nothing.

"Hail, friend," said Hoth the Black when his Egyptian taunters had left. "Do I know you?"

He stepped into the middle of the cell and blinked long, hoping to force his eyes to adjust.

"Lose something on your journey?" asked the prisoner, the tenor voice weak like watered down wine.

Hoth knew he recognized it, but he couldn't place it. He stepped forward to cross into the shadows and know the man. When he saw the gaunt face and sunken eyes, he didn't know if he should call the guards for a surgeon or greet him.

"I may look like death," said Jarngard, clearly reading the expression on his face, "but I'm still going to kill you for stealing Nessa from me."

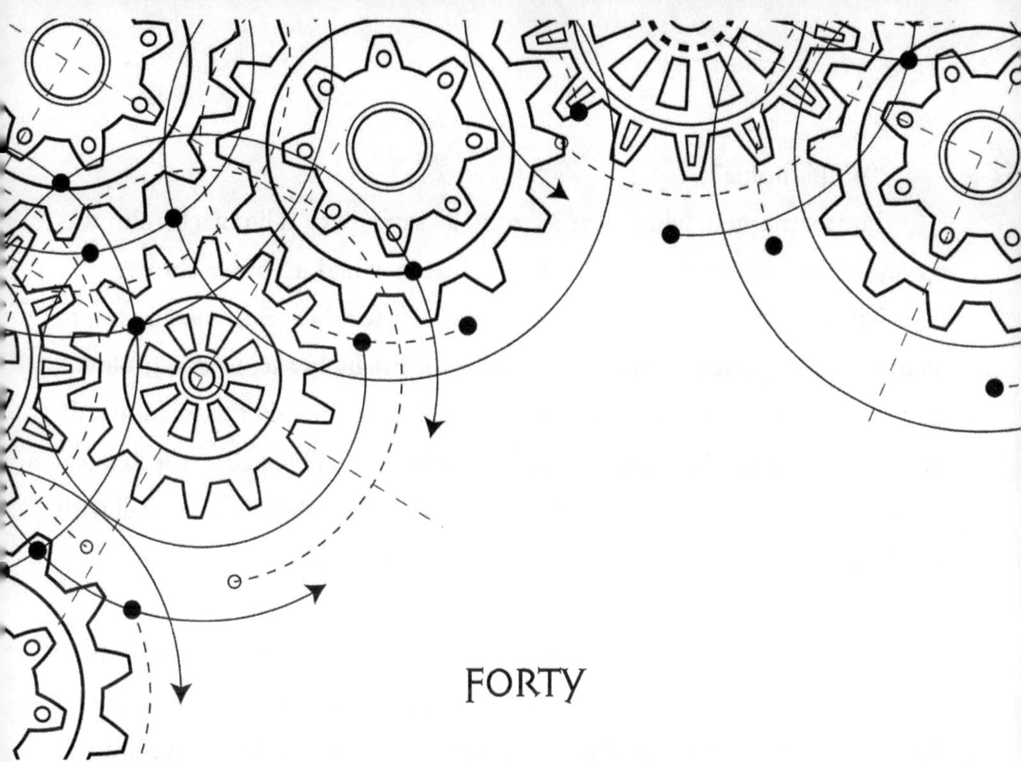

FORTY

Heron was running her fingers across the stone at the shrine when Punt retrieved her. She wanted to look upon its words one last time before they made their attempt at escape.

"I bent the piston," said Punt by way of greeting.

He returned to the front of the cave immediately, not once meeting her gaze. She sighed before leaving the shrine, trying to convince herself things would be different once they were back in Alexandria.

The intact steam chariot rested next to the fallen rocks. The floor raised slightly on the right side of the cave, so they had to shove rocks under the wheels to keep it from rolling backwards. Heron's hands still ached from moving rocks and debris. Her fingernails were black with rock dust.

She climbed onto the chariot and carefully examined the bend in the piston. Without his blacksmith tools, Punt had used his warhammer to modify the iron piston. A slight, jagged line ran across the bend.

"The iron is cracked."

"One of Nektam's," said Punt fiercely. "Mine never crack."

"Will it hold?"

Punt shrugged, which was as good as saying no. The blacksmith was always right when it came to his craft. But they had no other choice.

The bent piston had to hold long enough for the steam mechanical to gain enough speed and energy that when it finally broke, it would blow a hole in the wall, just like the failed mechanicals in the other workshops. If they thought it might break early, they could always engage the mechanical to the gear and hope the impact would tear it apart and the cave wall with it. A risk that would surely result in their deaths.

Heron's biggest fear was that the whole cave would collapse. Dust and pebbles had fallen on them the whole time they moved rocks away from the front. She spit out the dust continuously and grit lay lodged in her teeth. The wall seemed to sense their nearness and like a live animal, it readied itself to pounce.

"Add more fuel," she said and he obeyed. She took that as a good sign, though it was probably more from habit or exhaustion than respect. She'd tried to breach the subject of her gender more than once while they were moving rocks, but she couldn't do more than open and close her mouth like a dying fish. His muscled shoulders, flexing as he easily lifted ragged stones, had been a constant reminder of his gender. A world she'd existed in until a few scant days ago.

The fire crackled and spit flame from the shielding. He'd packed it overfull and sparks leaked out like water, spilling onto the stone floor. Irregular shadows danced across the wall as the pistons gathered speed. Others might see those shadows as evidence of gods or demons, but Heron took them as reminders of the study of optics and thought fondly of Archimedes' writings.

They hid behind the furthest outcropping of rocks and Heron silently hoped that if the cave did collapse, it killed them outright and did not trap them in a sightless pocket. Punt dared once more to pump the bellows and like the mythical dragon, fire belched from the steam mechanical and the pot ticked and rocked like a possessed drum.

The iron whined and screamed, as the bend put more pressure on the metal, threatening to tear itself from the moorings. When it sounded like the wails of a thousand dying blackbirds, Heron readied herself to run out and engage the drive, fearing the mechanical would break before gaining more speed.

When she leaned around the outcropping, the wailing took on a new octave, spraying dust and rock on them as the whole cave seemed to be shaking. Punt held her back with his meaty hand, throwing her onto the ground only moments before the steam mechanical finally failed, spitting its parts and fire - and most importantly - its energy in every direction.

Coals rained upon them, followed by the rumble of an avalanche and small rocks pinged off their backs. Heron swatted out a small fire on Punt's tunic.

When at last the destruction ended, Heron felt the cool whisper of a night breeze on her back. The wall had collapsed and a hole the size of a small shield let soothing moonlight into their cave, a tonic for the harrowing events.

Broken pieces of the mechanical ticked as they cooled. Scattered coals shined in the dark like a thousand tiny red eyes. Heron scrambled toward the hole, ignoring the pain in her gut and knee, concerned the rest of the cave would collapse before they escaped. Punt was on her heels and after a few knee scrapes, they crawled out into the desert night.

Standing far from the broken cliff, an outcropping of rock that looked like a giant had punched it, Heron breathed deep with a hand on her side and let the fresh air fill her lungs until it almost hurt. She was about to thank Punt for his skillful adjustments of the steam mechanical when the rest of the cliff fell upon itself and the hole they'd climbed through disappeared in dust and rock.

They filled their bellies at the oasis and though the water was muddy and bug-ridden, it tasted like nectar. The Sarmatian bodies were easy to spot, but Hoth had picked them clean. No food or water. Not even a water pouch. The sea captain hadn't expected them to escape.

Then they set off on the old road, the one Alexander the Macedonian had traveled after the Oracle of Siwa. But unlike him, they traveled on foot.

The night was cool and the land seemed to absorb all sound of their passing as if they weren't supposed to exist. Night birds hooted from a distance. They set out a rhythm like the slow rising and falling of pistons. Heron imagined herself as an automata, marching endlessly through the desert. She pushed hard, even though Punt seemed to be barely shambling along behind her, feet whispering across the sand. Once the sun rose, they would not be able to travel fast, so she wanted to make up as much time as possible.

The blacksmith's weakness was a boon and a curse. It buoyed her heart knowing that she was outlasting him, but also, he was her friend and seeing him stumble after her with his mouth half-open struck her heart like a heavy stone. She reminded herself that she had been recovering from the chest wound under the sun shade while he alternated shifts with Hoth.

When the rising sun painted the horizon with pale pinks and tired oranges, Heron found them an old dead tree to sit beneath. The ancient wood creaked when Punt leaned against it and soon he slipped over and was snoring. Heron pulled her knees to her chest, careful not to pull out her makeshift stitches, and closed her eyes.

When she opened them, it didn't feel like she'd slept long, but the sun had traveled over the dome of the sky and was headed toward the other side. She rubbed the sleep from her eyes with her knuckles and held her stomach as it rumbled.

"Up, Punt," she said and they resumed their march.

Punt was no better for the rest. His eyelids drifted closed at each step. His shoulders were hunched.

Heron was worried they would not make it much further when she saw the dust trails headed their way. Rather than waste energy, they sat on the road and waited.

She checked the stitchings in her side only to find them bleeding. A white pus leaked out the side. Heron took it as a sign that her humours were out of adjustment.

She greeted the caravan with an outstretched hand. Riders in desert robes encircled them with hands clenched on weapons. The wide-eyed men with curved swords, Meroenians she assumed, glanced nervously to the surrounding desert. One clucked his tongue, reminding her of Agog, and spoke to her in Egyptian.

"Bandits?" he asked, pulling the dusty cloth away from his wrinkled mouth.

"To the east." Heron pointed back the way they had come. "Dead, now."

The leader nodded, seemingly relieved. He barked commands to the others and Heron saw them relax the grips from their hilts.

"Could we purchase food or water from you? I can pay," said Heron, shaking the pouch at her side. She knew it was possible they could decide to take her coinage and leave them dead in the sand, but they would die without food or water, either way.

The Mereonian leader pulled a water pouch from his saddle and threw it to her. He spoke again to his companions and a rider produced hard bread. She moved to pay him and he sliced his hand through the air, stopping her.

"For killing the bandits."

"*Dua Netjer en ek,*" she said using the formal words.

"Which way does the road take you? Your servant has the build of a blacksmith and we have room on our wagons."

Heron tensed, hoping Punt would not take offense, but the blacksmith was still wavering on his feet, chewing on the hard bread.

"We head to Alexandria."

When the Mereonian leader's eyes widened, she knew there was trouble.

"The exile Ramses has taken the city from the Northmen and prepares it for the Romans," he said. "Not a good place for trade."

Her stomach tightened with worry for Sepharia and Plutarch and the others of her workshop. Her association with the Northmen could be dire for her daughter and friends. She felt a twinge of guilt for not being more sad about the loss of the Northmen; she liked Agog and the laughing Jarngard, but they were conquerors and history was littered with the corpses of their kind.

That the exile Ramses was the traitor was unsurprising, given the findings in the cave, though she wondered how he'd done it so easily. Heron quizzed the rider for details but he gave little since he'd been outside the walls when it had happened. The only rumor he could pass along was that the barbarian Agog was going to fight in the arena for his life on the last day of the games.

Heron hefted the weight of her coin bag. "Troubling news, friend. I must get to Alexandria in haste. Could I purchase a mount from you?"

She threw him the purse and he pulled out a few coins and bit them. It was more than enough. He nodded and a horse was brought around. Its limp was apparent, but she had no room to barter now.

Astride the horse, she called to the Meroenians as they rode away, Punt's arms cautiously around her middle. "*Senebti!*"

The Meroenians made whooping noises as the caravan drove away. In a different time, she might have asked Punt if he thought the gods had blessed them, but she was pleased enough he had not refused to ride with her, especially after being called her servant.

When the saber moon hung in the sky, they reached the city of Alexandria. The fires around the shanty town flickered as men and women passed amongst the tents. Heron was careful to watch for patrols.

In the camps, Heron found a pair of Gaul traders ready to head into the city. She traded them the horse to be smuggled into the city.

Once again, Heron found herself trusting strangers, but she had little choice. At the Moon Gate, Heron shifted under the blanket and listened to the Gaul's words as they spoke to the guards. When the wagon lurched forward, she heaved a sigh.

The Gauls left them near the Temple of Saturn on the west side of the Great Library. She bade them farewell and huddled with Punt in the darkness of an alley.

Heron sent Punt to the workshop, but warned him to be wary. The exile Ramses knew she was an ally of the Northman and might be waiting for her there.

She left for the dock district on a hunch, staying to the shadows and avoiding the infrequent patrols. When she found the warehouse with the black wheel against an ochre background, she rapped her knuckles lightly against the door.

Not long after, it opened and an unfamiliar face regarded her, holding up a hooded lantern. She saw the glint of steel in the man's fist.

When the strong voice called out from behind the doorman, she relaxed. "It's Heron, you idiot. Let him in."

With the door barred behind her, she strode into the warehouse. "Greetings, Vestalis."

She was moving to clasp arms with him when a woman in a hooded cloak moved out from the shadows. When she pulled back the hood,

Heron couldn't help but gasp. Once she'd heard the news that the exile Ramses had taken the city, she'd assumed that Polyxena had been a part of the plot, but seeing her with Vestalis changed everything.

FORTY ONE

The city was lost.

Vestalis, the former Roman military commander, explained as much in his steely voice, occasionally running his scarred hand across his salt and pepper chin stubble. Polyxena added to the tale, and Heron found it hard not to be mesmerized by her green and blue eyes. Alexander the Macedonian had similar eyes, Heron remembered from the scrolls.

Poison and treachery had been the cause. The barbarian's games had taxed the city's soldiers and Ramses had used it as an excuse to bring his men into the city to help bolster the defense and patrol the streets. The exile had also commandeered a few Manticores. Heron did not bother telling them about the one from the cave, it was buried under a hill's worth of rocks now.

Vestalis seemed as much disappointed in himself as Agog for letting the exile beguile them. The grey eyed man explained that he'd been the one to council Agog to take the exile's soldiers and lend him the Manticores to drive away the bandits that were harrying the trade roads.

Who better to ally with than the enemy of my enemy had been his advice. Sage words, Heron agreed, but Ramses had been playing them false. At least she knew Vestalis' loyalty, though it would not matter. The pair were planning a retreat from the city.

The diminutive woman, Polyxena, Heron knew less about. She explained in quiet, forceful tones that she was a representative of the League of Corinth. In the time of Alexander, the League had been a political hegemony under the rule of Phillip II of Macedon, to battle the Persians. Polyxena explained that the League now plotted the overthrow of Roman rule and when Agog had taken the city, the League had covertly sent her as an ambassador.

Polyxena claimed the League had two thousand troops stationed on ships in the Mediterranean. The ships and soldiers had been intended to support Alexandria against Rome, but now that the city had been taken, they waited on her word. She spoke with such authority about the matter that Heron privately wondered if the woman was more than just an ambassador.

The two argued, with reasoning Heron found it hard not to agree with, that even if they could take the city back from Ramses, the Roman navy would arrive in less than three weeks and without the defenses along the water's edge, Alexandria couldn't even repel the Roman sailors.

"Truth in every word." Heron grimly nodded, keeping her hands clasped behind her back. Her exhaustion was bone deep. She could use a touch of the violet dust to mask the feeling of thinness, but the last of it had been lost during the flight from Old Babylon.

"The city is lost," said Heron. "Our friends are captured, my daughter is imprisoned by Baruch Tanzen." Polyxena flinched away from Heron's gaze. "We have every reason to flee. Rome will not be merciful."

Polyxena tried to give a comforting smile. "We have enough resources to get your daughter back. Maybe a few of the others. And Macedon will gladly accept a former son back into its bosom."

Heron could not return the smile. Alexandria was her home. In Macedon, there'd be no way to practice her trade, or the Romans would find her.

"If we give up now, the Romans will capture the city, and most importantly, the workshops, and gain the technologies necessary to expand their empire."

Vestalis leaned against the wheel of a wagon. The three of them had been talking through the night, and even the old soldier appeared worn. His eyes were sunken and doubled by the shadows of the dimly lit warehouse.

"My fate is tied to the Northmen," said Vestalis. "Rome will not forgive me for siding with them. But even if I cannot stay in Alexandria, I can also see the benefit of Rome gaining this technology. Who better to spread its use?"

Her exhaustion was replaced by a spike of anger. "Not Rome. They will only use it to enslave more peoples. Conquering the known lands in every direction and taking their people as slaves."

Vestalis shrugged. "Such is the way of the world. I fought many long campaigns against the Gauls and the Germanic tribes. And though the wars were terrible, when I passed through those lands years later, I found them more civilized. Roman roads brought new trade. Laws provided stability. No more attacks on their villages by rival factions."

"And all those people sold into slavery. What of them?" Heron spit into the dirt. "I did not create my machines so they could enslave others. I created them so men and *women* could be free."

Heron caught Polyxena's brief smile, like a hint of moonlight peaking through a clouded sky.

"You could create new ones," said Vestalis. "Better machines. Ones to rival the Roman machines."

"But where? They would know me as soon as the first machine was crafted. And how would I craft them at all? The men of my workshop cannot be found anywhere in the world. Without Punt to cast my images into metal, I would be nothing but a poor scribbler."

In that moment, she knew that she could not run. Her life would end at the first step away from Alexandria.

"We must take the city back," she said. "We *can* take the city back. You said it yourselves."

Vestalis shifted, his stern face and tightly held lips wrestled with her challenge. Polyxena seemed more agreeable. Her eyes twinkled with mysterious thought, suggesting she was contemplating her own plans.

"But what of the Romans? Even if we are victorious, we will have to repel their armada of ships," he countered.

Heron allowed herself a knowing smile. Where it came from, she could not fathom, but a gathering boldness bloomed into her chest and she felt the possibilities thrum from her fingertips as she clenched them together.

"We only need to free the sea captain," she said, imbuing her words with confidence. "The plan we devised on the journey back from Old Babylon will carry the day. Rome's navy will be nothing more than splinters after we are done with it."

She smiled and so did they. In truth, she had no plan. Hoth and her had never worked one out. Sure, they had discussed plans, some even half-workable, but nothing that would ensure the destruction of the Roman navy.

But as they slowly came around to her thinking, Heron had an insight about the man she'd been tasked with investigating—Alexander the Macedonian. Time and time again, the man had used the "will" of the gods, or prophecy, or even his own doggedness, to signal to his troops and followers that he would be victorious. His actions caused a reaction and that rippled outward until he met his goal.

Heron thought back to the Hermes machine. It was a clever machine, but one that no one but herself could understand. Vestalis himself had mocked her for it. When she'd been in debt to Lysimachus, she'd invented ever more clever machines to free herself, only to find them sinking her deeper when they sometimes failed. Alexander the Macedonian had changed the world because he'd been bold, not clever, though the man had an abundance of the latter.

The pair of them, Vestalis and Polyxena, doubted her, but as they worked out the details of retaking of the city, they began to come around to her side. That they thought it was possible was enough to get them thinking, moving forward. Heron's own limbs trembled with the importance of this lesson. Once they had the city back, she would not let this lesson go unlearned.

They counted their resources: the two thousand Greeks outside the city, Hoth's ships and the men on them, scattered pockets of loyalists, other Northmen that hadn't been captured, and a steam chariot that Vestalis had hidden in his warehouse. The plan appeared like a web between them as they each spit out threads, until it formed a cautious and fragile symmetry. The only thing they needed was someone to lead the attack on the arena during the last day of the games. Vestalis could not, he would be leading the scattered Northmen against the wall's defenders to allow the Greeks to enter the city. Their discussion ground to a halt as they fretted about the identity of the raid's leader.

"Can your blacksmith lead?" asked Vestalis, arms crossed and eyes bloodshot.

"He's deadly with a warhammer, but not made for leading other men. There's a reason I made him a foundry that needs no assistants," said Heron.

Vestalis nodded and they drifted into quiet contemplation once again.

"What about one of the sea captain's men?" asked Polyxena.

"The stone halls of the arena are no place for a sailor," said Vestalis, rubbing his grizzled chin. "They'd get lost in its labyrinth trying to free their countrymen."

"I could sketch them maps," offered Heron. "When the lower quarters of the animal holding pens needed to be expanded, I drew the plans after studying the architectural diagrams. Give me ink and papyrus and I can draw them a way."

Vestalis made an amused grunt. "Ever try running into battle with a map in hand? When the battle lust falls upon you, the mind forgets things like maps. Whoever leads the raid must know the arena inside and out."

When she caught Polyxena staring at her, she knew what the diminutive woman was thinking.

"No," said Heron. "I cannot. I know nothing of battle."

The heat of both their gazes warmed her cheeks. Heron imagined herself rushing into battle with a sword held high, screaming until her lungs ached. She nearly laughed out loud.

"You need not be the spear head in every attack," said Vestalis, "but bring them through the maze of the under arena safely. Who else should save the daughter but the father?"

Her first thought was of Archimedes, who was killed by a Roman soldier. She'd always believed that she would never be so foolish as to die like him. Though she studied and admired the great inventor, she thought she'd be smarter when it came to the practice of war; staying in the back and lending only her inventions, and never putting herself before a confused soldier.

But her second thought was of Alexander, and the lesson she only hours before convinced herself that she'd learned. Boldness was necessary if you wanted to change the world. But who was she to thrust herself into battle like a deranged fool? The *Romances* were filled with Alexander's injuries from battle.

Her final thought was of Sepharia. If anyone else led the raid, then her rescue could be in jeopardy. Heron closed her eyes and imagined the sweet smell of Sepharia's flaxen hair as she brushed it in the secluded safety of her room. If Sepharia did not make it through safely, then what good was her promise to her twin to protect his daughter?

In the silence of the morning, when Heron saw that there was no other choice, even though she had no experience in battle, or skill with a weapon, she agreed to lead the attack on the arena. And as the realization trickled into her flesh like a thousand bees waking to the day's duties, she wondered if that was how Alexander the Macedonian felt on the morning before he fell upon his enemies.

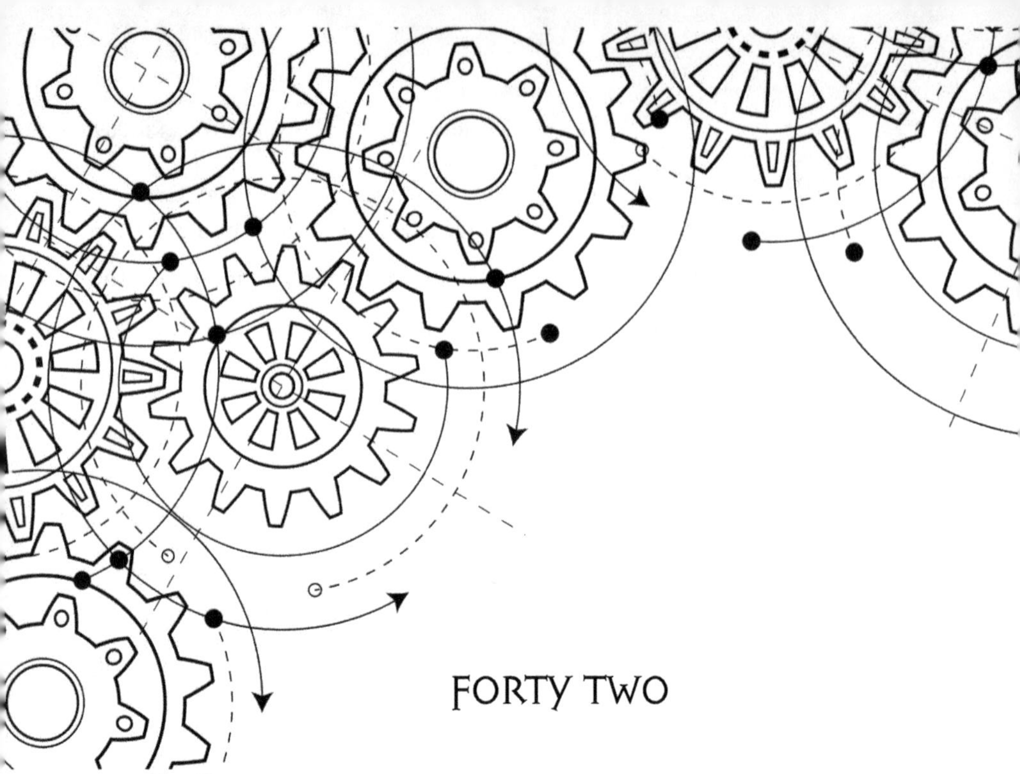

FORTY TWO

Nessa. He tasted her name on his lips in the darkness of the prison cell. She was a heady wine, full-bodied and rich; eyes dark and lips full. He dined on her memory, feeling the soft brush of her touch against his neck as she wound around him, thighs eager, mouth wanting.

Outside the cell, keys rattled in a lock - not theirs - and rusted hinges wheezed open. Jarngard was forced out of his memory and into the present. He heard voices, his countrymen, speaking to their captors on the way out.

The cells were being slowly emptied. Northmen in groups of two or three or five, were led into the arena and given weapons. No one came back.

Jarngard grasped the leather bag around his throat and cursed the gods. His Egyptian captors mocked him by putting Hoth in the cell with him. He'd willingly die by any man's side from the North except the sea captain. If he had a knife or the strength to strangle the man, he would, but the poison had leeched the energy from his limbs until they were like a young child's.

Hoth the Black, a fitting name for a cutthroat and wife-stealer. They'd been brothers-in-arms, adventurers, soldiers in far off lands—but then his supposed friend had stolen his wife while he lay bound and stitched under piles of fur in the cold halls of the north.

"What a tragedy for you," said Jarngard, "that here I am fallen without a wife for you to steal."

The sea captain sat by the door. His normally pale hair was gray with dust and loose strands formed bars across his troubled eyes. Hoth's pain might have comforted Jarngard had he been the one to give it.

"I failed you, my friend. I've failed everyone."

Jarngard pulled himself up until he sat against the wall. He wanted a clear view of the sea captain.

"Quench your worries. We never expected you to actually help. Wodanaz just wanted to use you for your ships," said Jarngard.

Hoth shrugged away the comment. "I would do the same if I were him. He knew my vanity and the words of the wood-witch. He used my expectations against me."

This revelation interested Jarngard, but he did not want to help the man work through his struggles. Jarngard wanted pain, not forgiveness.

"Why did you leave the miracle maker? You were tasked with guarding him."

Hoth nodded in tacit agreement. "I failed him as well, and the blacksmith. Now they're both trapped in that fallen cave and I fear we shall never see them again."

The sea captain picked at the dirt on the floor, gazing past the walls of the prison as if he could see the desert outside. "I should have listened to Heron. I should have brought a bow so I could fend off the Sarmatians from the steam chariot. I shouldn't have been caught so easily outside the city."

Hoth glanced to Jarngard with a real need in his eyes.

"Yes," spit Jarngard, "but your failure was expected."

The words fell flat between them and were less cathartic than he'd hoped. Hoth's gaze drifted to his feet.

The unrelenting silence annoyed Jarngard. He wanted to rage, wanted to thrash out at Hoth the Black, but his admissions disarmed those emotions.

"What did the wood-witch tell you?" Jarngard asked, hoping to draw out some truth he could mock him with.

Hoth smirked derisively, but not at Jarngard. He could see the admonishment was directed inward.

"I was a fool to believe the keys of prophecy. I thought fate but a lock and with only the proper key could I be greatly rewarded."

"You're as vague as you are vain," said Jarngard roughly. "Be clear about your words."

"I went to the wood-witch in the time of the deepest winter, hoping my struggle would convince her to give me a favored reading. I brought the young ram as it is told, and honeyed-wine and other gifts required."

Hearing Hoth's words brought back the smells of their country. The city of Alexandria was a potent mix of human sweat and oily industry while the north was fresh pines and crisp snowy winds. Jarngard missed the comfort of heavy furs resting on his shoulders and deep drifts to struggle through. He missed the smell of hearth fires. He missed Nessa.

"Fuck your prophecy."

The sea captain blinked and sighed into a regretful nod. "If only you'd been there to smack sense into my head. It was the wood-witch's words that convinced me that I should take your wife."

The words were like a strike across Jarngard's face. And once they had settled on him like hot ash, he wanted to lash out, to be angry, but the feeling in his chest was empty. Like those words had sucked out the anger and left only cold breath inside.

He found speaking difficult, so he swallowed away his barb. A cleared throat gave Hoth the space to continue.

"Have you ever been to the wood-witch?" asked Hoth.

Jarngard shook his head. He had no faith in prophecy.

"She was a vile woman. Wrinkled as an old man's balls, and rotten and smelling of old, dead meat. Her hut was filled with smoke. The air hole had grown over during the summer season and she was too old to climb up and cut it open."

Hoth's face was lost to that time, grimacing in remembrance of awful memories.

"She wanted more than the gifts I brought for my prophecy." His eyes filled with regret. "She wanted what all women want of me."

Jarngard reacted out of horror. "You did not—?"

Hoth nodded slowly. Jarngard tasted bile and spit into the dirt to clear his mouth.

"I wanted to know how to become the greatest sea captain, one re-membered through the ages, like an Alexander of the sea. I was willing to do anything," said Hoth, full of conviction.

There were many things that Jarngard would do, but not that. Not even if the wood-witch was beautiful. They were creatures better not tam-pered with. More wild beast than human.

"And what did she say?" he found himself asking despite himself.

Hoth shook his head as if he were trying to erase a bad memory. "When I visited her, I was afraid that I wouldn't be able to remember the prophecy, if I was lucky enough to receive one. Remembering has been the least of my worries. That day is etched bone deep."

Both men paused as the sound of soldiers returning filled the stone hall. Echoes grew louder until keys were loosened from a ring. Jarngard did not flinch. He was ready to fight, even weak as he was, but he did want to hear the rest of Hoth's tale.

The cell door nearest them opened. Jarngard knew the men there: Byrge and Dorn. He hoped they would get a chance to die well.

When the sounds of their countrymen being taken to the arena faded, Hoth resumed speaking. His voice was filled with the biting sarcasm Jarngard was used to hearing, except now he knew who it was directed at—Hoth, himself.

"She made a grand thing of it, while I sat across from the smoky fire and tried to wash the taste of her from my lips with a mug of watered down beer. I wanted to rub my tongue with coals, and my mind. There are some things you can never forget. And when she spoke her prophecy, her voice turned gravelly..."

Hoth drifted off like a stone idly rolling down a hill until it came to a rest and then he looked up at Jarngard. "Did you ever know Grat? He lived in that bay village with the statues and when we fought those Gauls, his throat was partially cut. The wood-witch sounded like that—but deeper and louder. Snow shook from the smoke hole and scattered ashes. I hesitated from putting hands over my ears for fear of not hearing the prophecy. Little did I know that the words would sear themselves into me like a brand. Her lying wood-witch words to me were: *Slumber with Midas' daughter in the stone halls of her forbearer; and claim victory from the seaward eagle.*"

Hoth paused, laughing, his mirth unhinged and bordering on madness. His words tumbled over each other, faster and faster, almost blubbering. "How could I not believe it? The eagle is the Roman military standard. When I saw her there in the inn, the one her father owned, one made of stone and mud, and I thought you were dead, or at least convinced myself that it would come soon, your wound was grievous, and the wood-witch's words flamed in me like a banked fire fed with fresh dry fuel. She bent to my touch and though she was injured by your wound, I persuaded her that she would need a new husband by morning."

"But she is no daughter of Midas."

Hoth shrugged. "Her father loved gold. It was enough for me. I would have done anything at the time to fulfill the prophecy. It was a madness inside of me. One that has proved false and I shall go to my grave a liar, and a thief, and a fool."

The moment was punctuated by the slamming of a door. Soldiers moved quickly through the holding area and keys jangled with purpose. Byrge and Dorn must have died quickly. Jarngard wasn't sure if he felt envy or sorrow for them.

He didn't have long to think about it when the soldier's helm appeared in the window of the cell door. There was a rattle and a grinding of hinges and a command to stand. Eight guards waited outside, ready for trouble. Jarngard didn't remember eight coming to visit the others and felt a twinge of pride.

"Four for each of us," remarked Jarngard, feeling better than he had in days.

The soldiers glanced nervously and clamped manacles around his wrists.

"Better to practice our trade in the arena and earn a place in our ancestral lands," said Hoth the Black, as grim as his earned name.

Jarngard nodded toward his countryman and before he could say another word, the soldier yanked on the chain. They marched from the deeps, up to the sun and sand, and the cheering of the crowds, up to endless blue sky, and to the ghosts of steel singing and men dying. Up they marched, up they marched to die.

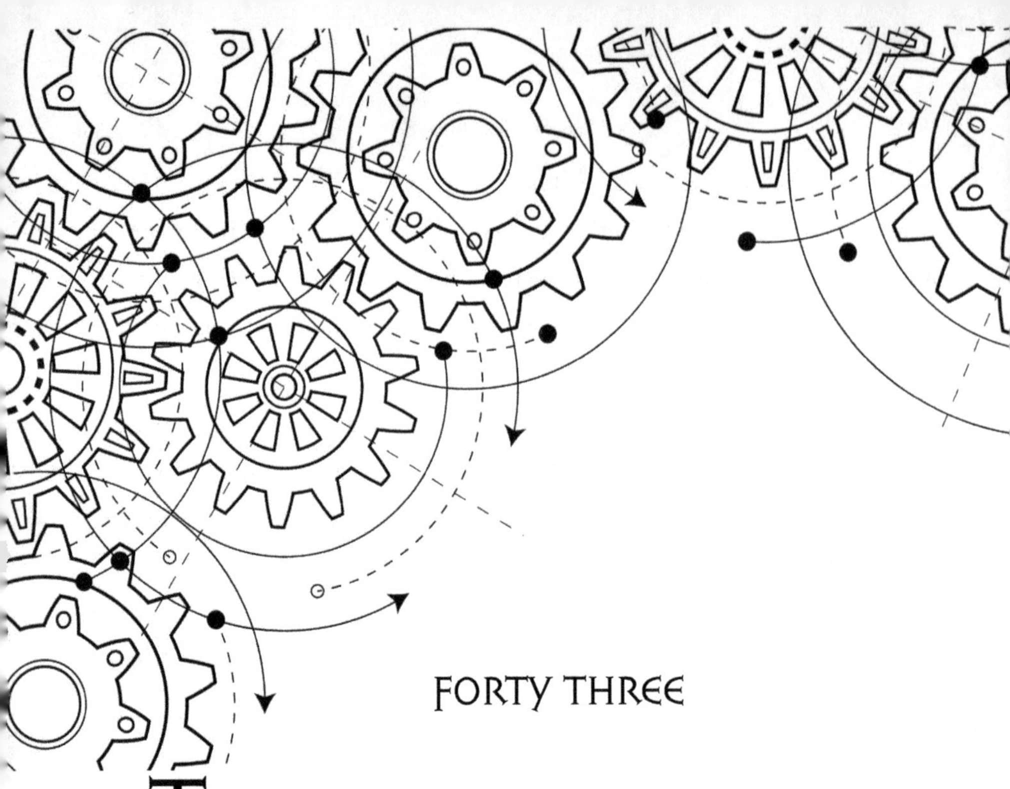

FORTY THREE

There were lessons to be learned under the hot sun of Alexandria, Sepharia decided. She glanced at the exile Ramses in his finely cut tunic, covered in gold and jade and rubies, laughing along with Baruch Tanzen. They had goblets in their fists as they watched the Northmen die in the arena.

Sepharia tugged at the tether around her neck. She did not watch the men fight and die like the others. Nor did she cheer or cry. She stood silently like a statue and watched Ramses and Baruch out of the corner of her eye, and meditated about what she had learned.

Trust none of the nobility, for they are liars and thieves. She'd thought Ramses her friend. She'd been excited to be included in his little game, spying on Polyxena. Even the horrible misstep with the brooch had not made Sepharia entirely afraid. She knew Heron and Agog would protect her. Now she knew different, that no one was truly safe.

The binding around her wrist dug into the skin. She slipped a finger beneath the rough cord to relieve the pressure, but the sweat rolling from her arm only made the cut sting. Ramses and Baruch and the other nobles that had sided with them sipped their drinks beneath a wide sun shade. Sepharia's tether barely allowed her room to scratch her nose with her bound hand.

Parched from the heat, she smacked her cracked lips and tried to swallow, only to feel a knot get caught in her throat. She coughed and hoped a bit of saliva would form to loosen her tongue from the roof of her mouth.

Beneath her on the white sands, the sounds of steel clashing rung beneath the steady chanting. Egyptian soldiers in steam chariots hunted along the edge of the arena, parading the stolen military equipment as if they'd made it. The thrum of pistons could be felt through the stone blocks of the arena.

The Northmen fought well, but they were outnumbered, out armored, and armed with inferior weapons. A hulking white-haired warrior that Sepharia had seen a time or two in the palace broke away from the press of blades and ran for a steam chariot. Maybe he hoped to surprise them and commandeer one.

The Egyptian soldier on the back of the Manticore, wearing plated bronze armor and a plumed Roman helm, aimed the arrow launcher at the Northman. Even with the crowd noises, Sepharia could hear the steam mechanical churn as it spit a hailstorm of arrows at its attacker. The Northman warrior crumpled backwards displaying a chest feathered with a dozen arrows.

"They're not as fearsome as they make themselves out to be," said Ramses, who had appeared by her side, but out of reach.

"I'm sure if you armed them with edged swords and not cracked slabs of iron, they might show your soldiers what a real warrior can do."

Ramses seemed amused by her outburst. "Does this girl forget she's an Alexandrian? These are Alexandrian soldiers fighting against the Northern barbarians. Her answer perplexes me so."

"You're going to give us back to the Romans," seethed Sepharia.

"Clever enough to figure that one out," he said. "But not clever enough to know why."

"I know why," she said, "because you're a coward."

Ramses put a hand across his chest in mock injury. "This girl wounds me. I'm hardly a coward. A coward does not wander into the bear's den and trick the great beast out of its prized carcass. I am delightfully clever, but not a coward."

"Then keep Alexandria for yourself. Why give it to the Romans?"

He snorted derisively and took another sip of his wine. Sepharia had to keep herself from letting her mouth wag open in thirst. Over Ramses' shoulder, Sepharia noticed Baruch staring in her direction, a look not unlike a butcher getting ready to slaughter his prized cow.

"Foolish girl, these barbarians were never going to keep the city from the Romans. Do you know the size of the armada? Of course not. This girl was playing foolish games with that Greek woman." Ramses leaned close, but not close enough.

"Thousands of ships," he said. "Never before has the Mediterranean seen so many ships. The sea rises with their bulk! And by taking the city from these fools I accomplish two things." He leaned in close and Sepharia resisted the urge to claw him, barely. "I wipe my debt to the Romans clean and I save the people the hardship of siege and war. Think about that, girl. Do you wish your fellow Alexandrians that misery?"

His words stole the argument from her tongue. Her clenched hand drifted to her side. She had no answer.

"Remember, girl," he continued, "we Egyptians are an ancient people, proud and with long memories. These Northmen who swoop in and think they can take this jewel from us are mere pretenders."

"Rome won't let you keep it," she told him, ignoring the sounds of the last Northman dying below. They'd killed a dozen so far this morning and the gladiatorial games were set to last all day.

He glanced at her with his painted eyes, amusement and scorn cutting her. He pulled a vial from his tunic, from a secret pocket near the waist. The tube was the size of a finger and the liquid sloshed inside and clung to the glass like rot.

"We call this the 'fiery poison'," he said, "because it burns the person from the inside out. Undetectable and dissolves in water. Best administered by a friend."

"Shayna," whispered Sepharia.

Ramses made a crooked grin. "Don't worry. You won't live the day to tell him. At this point, I don't think he'd care, either. Rome's favor is worth one daughter. You women are a useless lot mostly, except to have babies. And Rome, they can be my friend too, until I find the right opportunity."

Ramses lifted his vial as if he were giving a toast and then slipped it into the hidden pocket above his belt.

"This girl and her father were said to be the cleverest people in Alexandria," said Ramses. "I guess they were wrong."

The Egyptian returned to the party. Sepharia yanked impotently at the tough cord. The pain in her wrist was almost cathartic.

When she felt she was being watched, she glanced up through her hair. Standing at the back of the party, cautiously sipping wine, was the Kushite woman, Bani. Her wide eyes stretched even wider, in what could only be pity. Sepharia turned away, curling upon herself and tried not to watch them drag the limp bodies of the fallen Northmen away.

"I can make the end easy," whispered the sultry voice of Bani from up close.

The woman risked much to talk to Sepharia, but she couldn't turn and look at her, even though she was not angry. Sepharia understood that even as a princess, Bani was as bound as a slave, but in gold and silks rather than chains.

Sepharia spoke over her shoulder, away from the party so she was not overheard, not that it would matter, a new set of Northmen had been released onto the sands. Sepharia cringed when she heard the roaring of lions released from their cages.

"Don't pity me," said Sepharia.

"I don't," said Bani, this time harder, "but I know what a man like Baruch does. I've heard the whispers. Let me bring you something sweet to drink. It'll be just like sleeping."

The death screams of a man tore right through her, curling her toes. She clamped her eyes shut and tried to block her ears, but the tether kept one hand just a finger width away.

"Grow up, girl. I offer an easy way out," said Bani.

Sepharia cracked an eye. The nobles were enthralled by the spectacle. Ramses had his arm around Baruch's shoulder and they were gleefully pointing to the carnage below.

"Decide quickly, I cannot stand here forever."

"Bring your poison, but not for me." Sepharia nodded toward the nobles. "Give it to them."

The sound of the woman's breath, blown hastily from her nose was sign enough of the answer. "I'm not a fool."

Sepharia wracked her brain, trying to think of something to say that would get Bani to help her kill Ramses, to enact her revenge.

"I leave now, girl. Remember my mercy when you visit your gods."

Sepharia heard the shuffle of feet moving away, and spoke loudly through gritted teeth. "Wait!"

A noble in a maroon toga glanced over and Sepharia felt her opportunity falling away as if she were slowly crumbling over the edge of a great cliff. The noble turned his attention back to the fighting below.

Sepharia hung her head. The Kushite woman was surely gone. Her chance wasted.

When the cool hand touched her lower back, Sepharia nearly jumped.

"Quickly, girl. Do you want what I offer?"

"Not that. I need something else," said Sepharia.

"I will not poison them for you," the whisper shot back.

Sepharia shook her head tightly, careful not to draw attention.

"I need something else and it won't get you into trouble."

Bani's breath hit her on the back of the neck as the woman stepped closer. Sepharia wiped the sweat away from her side. Her chiton was nearly soaked through.

She turned and met Bani's gaze, swimming into her wide eyes. She leaned forward and mouthed the object of her desire. *A vial.*

Bani didn't quite know what to make of the request, clearly trying to decipher if it were a weapon or not, but eventually she nodded and left. Sepharia didn't know how long it would take her to find one, but she hoped it was soon. The rate at which they were killing Northmen, the games would be over by mid-afternoon and she would be the focus of their attention once again.

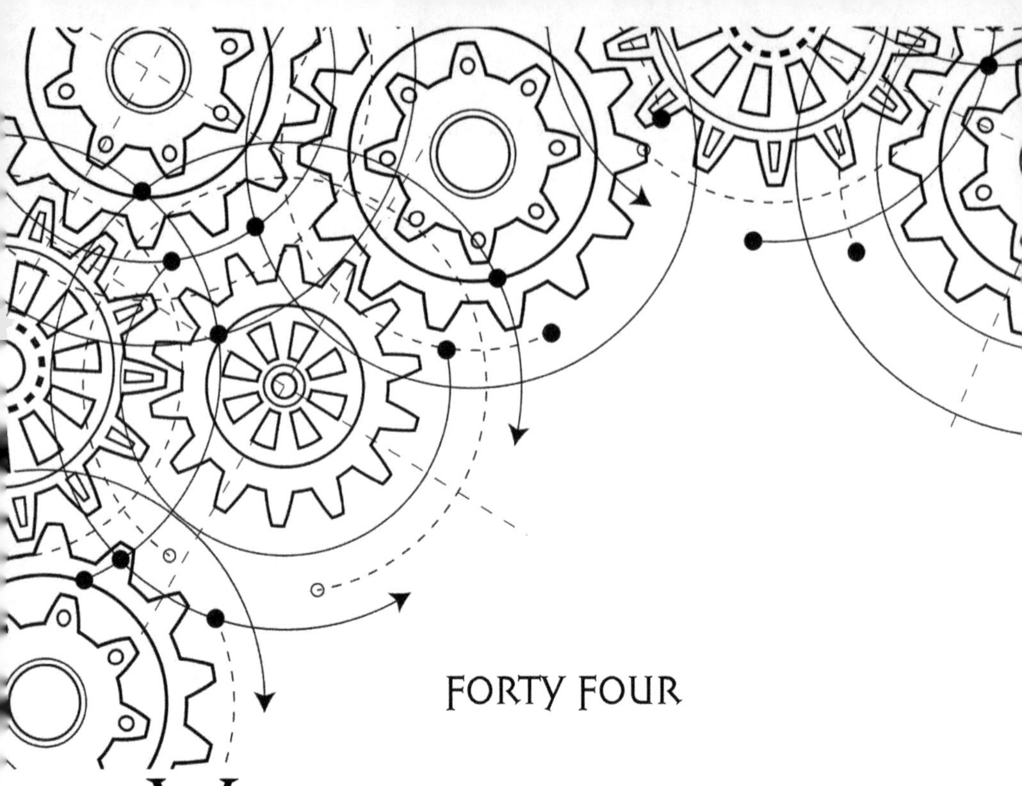

<h1 style="text-align:center">FORTY FOUR</h1>

Waiting in the shade of the warehouse was worse than her fitful sleep last night. She couldn't imagine that Alexander the Macedonian had dreams about being run through with a spear before battle. She wiped the sweat from her nose. When the door opened, she hoped to see Punt standing there with his bald head and warhammer grasped tightly in his fist.

Instead, it was Tormod. He'd scouted ahead to make sure no Egyptian soldiers were about. She tried to give him leadership of the squad but he declined. Said that if Hoth the Black didn't trust him to lead, she shouldn't either. She found little solace in that.

Tormod shook his head, indicating he'd seen no soldiers. The gruesome scar running through his salt and pepper beard reminded her of the upcoming dangers. He hefted twin axes and smiled as if he were waiting for a mug of ale. Heron smiled back and thought about Archimedes and the Roman soldier. At least she was armored.

Buckles on the plated leather chest piece dug into her side, right near the recovering sword wound. The chest binding she wore to hide her womanly breasts had slipped on the right side. Without Sepharia to help, she'd done a poor job rewrapping. Heron tugged it back into place, knowing it'd probably slip back on the run to the arena.

After another fretful glance toward the door, she swallowed, trying to appear calm for the soldiers in her service. Punt should have arrived with his squad of men already. They'd sent word to him and the messenger had returned, so she knew he'd seen the message.

She wondered if he was reconsidering coming to her aid because she was a woman. Heron leaned toward the window to gauge the sun. Either Punt was delayed, stopped, or he wasn't coming. If it were either of the second two, there was no point in waiting. The sounds of a crowd cheering could be heard through the walls. Every moment they waited was another death in the arena, another second past that could mean some horrible danger for Sepharia.

"We must go," she told them.

Leather creaked and snapped as two dozen men stood. Tormod banged his axes together, producing a spark along their deadly edges.

Heron carefully eyed the bronze helm before slapping it on her head. Vision was limited and she turned her head from side to side to check on the others.

Vestalis had secured a warehouse on the east side of the district, right on the edge of the Juden, so they wouldn't have far to run. The warehouse was owned by another trader with no connection to Vestalis. Smack in the center of the district was the arena.

They ran through the Alexandrian streets silently, except for the scuffing of feet against the hardpack. Most of the nobles were at the arena, so the walled dwellings were empty except for slaves tending the gardens. Heron didn't believe the blank stares from the servants, but she knew they had no choice but to hide their feelings beneath a veneer of calm.

The men ran with their weapons drawn. Sweat ran down her forearm and made gripping the hilt slippery. She had to push her helmet back every dozen steps.

Punt's absence was a knot in her chest. They could use the additional soldiers and she wanted to know her friend hadn't given up on her.

The sun was her enemy, filling her armor with an unbearable heat. Heron squinted against the constant reflections from the carried steel. An elderly woman ambled back inside when she saw them.

Heron could feel it building, like a steam mechanical churning to full. The tall stone structure could be seen over the building tops. Flags fluttered in the high breezes, screams and shouts carried. Roast meat and human sweat was rich in the air. Heron felt nauseous as they approached their target.

They were to attack the lower gate. The entrance they used to bring in large animals or wagons stuffed with slaves. They paused at the corner and Heron vividly remembered seeing an elephant being led into the tunnel by a pair of mahout handlers from the Indus lands. The tunnel ran right under the arena and then up to ramps.

She'd only been there to expand the pens, but she remembered the gray bulk of the elephants, the musky scent, pungent and up close. Heron removed her helmet and peeked around the corner. She almost expected to see the elephant waddling into the tunnel, but it was open and lightly guarded.

Heron wiped the sweat from the leather cushion in the helmet and prepared to don it when men in the back murmured with alarm. Her hand went to her sword - a foolish gesture she realized as she had little skill to use it - but then the murmurs turned to agreement.

Punt and his men had found them. He only had seven and they seemed less capable of using a weapon than her. But her heart loosened at the sight of the Egyptian blacksmith.

"I was not worried," she said.

He nodded, and glanced meaningfully at her. Heron couldn't quite decipher his purpose and they lacked the time for her to inquire. She knuckled away the stinging sweat from her eyes and shoved the helmet on, grimacing slightly when the edge bent her ears back.

"Once we breech the gate," she whispered, "we must head straight to the royal balcony. We're late to our purpose and Vestalis should be attacking the Canopian gate soon."

She lined them up behind her, taking the front position. Tormod waited directly behind and Punt at his side. The race to the gate would be critical. If the guards were able to close and bar it, their plan would be over and Sepharia's life forfeited.

As she readied herself for the short sprint, it was not the looming battle that filled her mind. Not the fear of sun-warmed steel sliding between her ribs. Nor of the imagined screams of horror from the sands of the arena, a perverse echo to the screams of delight by the crowd. Instead, it was the structure of the arena that filled her mind like a sack overfilled with Nile grain.

The arena in miniature built itself up in her head, level by level. She saw the holding pits and the animal cages clearly, with shadowy men and beasts mulling between the bars on the lowest level. Stone pillars climbed upward, stacking stone upon stone with steel rods to reinforce. Tunnels and stairs wormed through the levels. She imagined the dirt and sand dumped into the bowl at the center of the arena, creating the field that would absorb so much blood and sweat. Stone slabs connected together forming a honeycomb of chambers for both purpose and strength. Higher above the main levels, the royal balcony burned red in her mind like a glowing ember. Threads of intention ran through the arena as she considered the many ways to approach the chamber. From Polyxena's information, she knew the location of Ramses' soldiers. No matter which way they went, men would die.

Was this what Alexander saw before battle, once the lines were drawn and the weapons set? Did he see them as tools rather than men? Was it merely a problem to be solved?

On her right, Punt wiped the sweat from his palm and regripped his warhammer, nodding in her direction. Punt was ready. The others were ready, as well. Restless to begin. They were waiting for her command.

Getting to the royal chamber wasn't going to be as simple as fighting their way to the top. She didn't have enough men and she didn't want to lose the ones she had. Alexander had been known for his boldness, but was it bold to rush into overwhelming odds? Or madness?

No, she realized, they would need something else to get them up to the royal chamber. She just needed time to figure it out.

Tormod placed his hand on her shoulder. In broken Greek, he whispered into her ear so the others couldn't hear. "Fear is normal. Once you start the run, it turns to battle lust. But we must move soon, or we lose advantage."

"I'm not afraid," she murmured back and she said the words a second time in her head, to confirm the truth. Fear was not the emotion coursing through her veins, even though her hands shook with anticipation. What she felt, she had no name for, but there was no more time. Any plans would have to be improvised along the way.

She turned and spoke to the men, using the voice she used in the workshop when she needed their attention. "Ready yourselves and run like Mercury."

If their smiles were optimistic or full of fear, she did not know, because she pushed off, ignoring the tearing of stitches in her knee. No one yelled, but she heard grunts and scuffed feet behind.

Four guards milled by the open gate, looking disinterested in their duty. One head slowly rose and his face broadened in shock. He dropped his spear and moved toward the metal bars.

Sunlight glinted from her rising and falling blade. The endless distance between her and the gate seemed to grow with each step. There were shouts. The first Egyptian soldier had made it to the gate and was pulling it closed. The other three hesitated, glancing at their weapons and the gate, indecision as clear as the pale sky.

The gate swung around. Heron and her men were only halfway across the street. Tormod grunted and something shimmered through the air, spinning like an aeolipile. The soldier at the gate flew backwards, a wooden handle sticking from his face.

Two soldiers moved to replace the first, while the third still stared at his spear as if were a useless stick. Her helmet slipped down and she pushed it back, feeling twisted slightly in her headlong rush.

Metal clanged into place and the soldiers lifted the heavy iron bar. Heron readied herself to crash into the metal. The soldier staring at his spear seemed to wake and thrust his weapon through the bars, protecting the gate blockers.

Heron tensed as the spear tip slammed her in the middle. She flew forward, hitting the metal bars with her shoulder. The men behind the gate struggled to place the iron bar into the cradle. Like the sea rising up and crashing into a beach, they hit the gate and knocked the soldiers back before they could bar them out.

Heron was on her hands and knees, a burning pain in her stomach. The Egyptian soldier who'd speared her only made it two steps before Punt hit him with his warhammer.

Hands helped her up. Punt appeared, his face wracked with worry, dark fluid dripping thickly from his warhammer. Heron checked her armor, expecting to see a gapping hole in her stomach, but the leather was only creased. The soldier had barely thrust it through the bars.

Blood, however, leaked from the wound in her side, never quite healed. Punt moved to help her with it, but she shook him off. Tormod appeared after wrestling his axe from the man's skull.

"Jam those gates," she told them, ignoring the pain in her side. "And hide the bar. We want this entrance to stay open."

Punt looked almost embarrassed to speak, but when he did, she understood why. "Next time let me lead the assault. You're too valuable a *man* to lose."

He nodded on the word 'man' for extra emphasis. A veiled apology and she assumed, a promise to keep her secret safe. She was about to thank him when one of her workers returned from deeper in the tunnel.

"There's a Manticore back there," said the man excitedly.

Tormod scoffed. "Not up the stairs. We hew our way to the top."

The presence of the steam mechanical gave her an idea. "It might provide a distraction, though."

A heavy cheer erupted in the arena, louder than any previous. Something important was happening, something she knew she didn't want to happen. An hourglass turned over in her head and she felt time working against her.

"We can't fight our way to the top. We just don't have enough men. But if we can pull some of them away, give them something else to worry about, we might be able to make it," said Heron.

"What do you have in mind?" asked Tormod, grinning, and Heron found his smile disturbing.

"There's a storage room right up these stairs. Bring down all the chain you can find. Punt, start up that Manticore. We're going to need its strength to do some pulling." Heron pointed to her workers. "I'll need you six to operate it and keep it safe. One of you manning the arrow launcher should be enough to repel any surprises. The rest go up with me."

"You should stay here, Master Heron, and supervise the Manticore. It's safer," said Punt.

Heron put her hand to his shoulder. "I need to be up top. Sepharia is up there. But you can take the lead once we get this operation going."

The beating of drums rumbled to life in the arena. Heron sent them to their duties and waited nervously as the stone vibrated with energy. Whatever was going on in the arena, it was shaking the very foundation. She hoped to do more of the same.

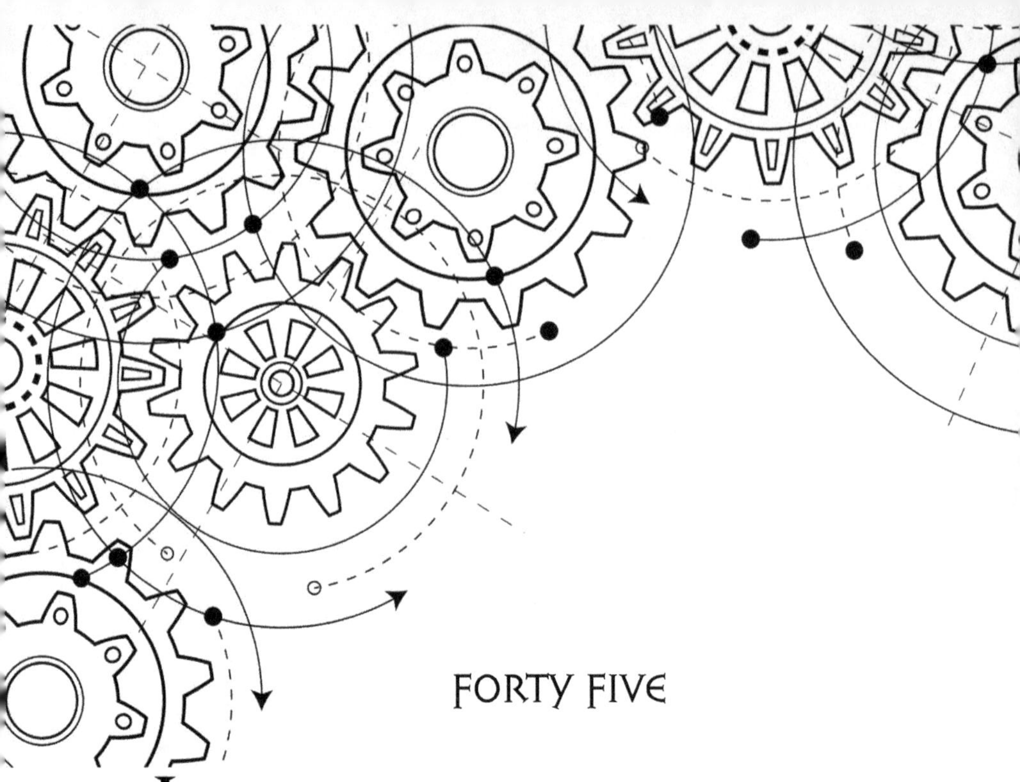

FORTY FIVE

Jarngard touched the leather pouch around his neck reverently and grinned at his coming death. Hoth the Black smiled back, his mirth mostly contained to his eyes, as his lips were clamped together.

The arena shook with their presence. They were the last battle of the day. Tomorrow would be Agog's death, but today was theirs. Jarngard circled slowly, absorbing the jeering and taunting as if it were laughter.

The sky was as pale as tears, but he did not feel sorrow. Carrion birds circled high in the late sun. Golden banners on the high walls had fallen still as the hot winds from the south paused to watch the spectacle.

Jarngard loosened his arm, swinging it across his chest, feeling the weight of the battered sword. The edge was chipped and worn, but the balance held true. He could still take a man's arm off with it.

Three Manticores patrolled the edge of the sands. The crowd jostled restlessly as they waited for the next round of entertainment.

A crimson flag was waved from the speaker's podium. Jarngard was familiar with the customs. He'd attended a match in Rome on his way down to Alexandria.

"Ave, good citizens of the Roman Empire! Here we stand together with our beloved and loyal Satrap to watch these barbarians receive justice!"

The speaker was a heavy man with a gold and crimson toga. His voice boomed across the arena.

Hoth the Black snorted with momentary laughter. "He'd make an excellent captain with that volume."

"His belly rivals Agog's."

The sea captain leaned on his sword while the speaker continued his announcement.

"For the Empire demands justice, not just for the taking of its prized jewel, but of the slaughter of certain upright citizens! Baruch Tanzen's daughter was slain with poison by the devious and malicious Sepharia!"

The girl was thrust against the railing of the royal balcony. Even from the sands, her chiton appeared torn and dirty. Jarngard shared an ominous glance with his fellow Northman. This would not be an ordinary gladiatorial match.

"Because the killer of Baruch Tanzen's daughter cannot fight in the arena, and her father has fled the city ahead of his crimes, these two barbarians will fight for her cause!"

There was a mix of hissing and cheering. Jarngard wondered if they knew she was the *Michanikos'* daughter, if they would react the same. The speaker had conveniently left out that part.

"And if the gods should allow them to prevail! She shall receive a gentle death, and if not, then to the lions with her!"

On three sides of the arena, there were dramatic openings of gates. Wagons with cages were hastily pulled onto the sands and in each cage was a full grown lion. The one nearest to them gave a throaty roar. Even from below, Jarngard could see Sepharia staring blankly at her grisly death.

A drum beat began. Long and heavy like the thundering of giants. From the furthest opening, a squad of six men in bronze armor, shield, and gladius, ran onto the sands in tight formation. The crowd clamored to their feet.

Jarngard strolled across the arena, sword hung lazily at his side, feeling the warm sands and gaze of the crowd soothe his injuries. Hoth matched his pace, keeping his blade resting on his shoulder like a hunk of wood carried to a pleasing fire.

"The village of Yohan," said Hoth suddenly.

Jarngard turned toward Hoth, stretching out an ache in his side. "Village of Yohan?"

"Village of Yohan." Hoth nodded towards the approaching soldiers.

Jarngard searched his memory. It could have been familiar, but he was getting older and those adventures were lost in the mists of time and ale.

The six soldiers surrounded Jarngard and Hoth. The Northmen stood back to back. Hoth had his weapon at the ready, Jarngard's was pointed to the sands while he thought.

"Village of Yohan?" Jarngard asked aloud, as much to himself as to Hoth.

"Aye. The village of Yohan. Don't you remember?"

A pair of soldiers darted in and Jarngard was forced to parry, using the thrust of one to block the other. Steel ringing on the other side announced similar tactics for Hoth. Jarngard expected a drawn out match, otherwise the six soldiers would have attacked as one.

"No, I don't."

Hoth grunted. Steel rang like bells at a feast. Jarngard stabbed at a shield and blocked, feeling the effects of being poisoned slowly wear off. Something about battle always brought life to his tired arms.

"The village that Wodanaz slept with the wicker man's wife."

He remembered now. "Yohan? That wasn't Yohan. That was Gordic."

"Ah...yes, you're right," said Hoth, as simply as if they were drinking by a fire on a cold winter's night. "I remember now, Gordic. Yohan was the place I warmed the sheets with that druid's daughter."

"Druids don't have daughters," he responded.

"Oh yes, right again. Well it was someone's daughter, anyway."

Jarngard blocked a high attack and kicked a man in the chest. The exhaustion from sitting in the cell seemed to fade away. Hoth bumped into him as he performed some maneuver, but Jarngard was focused on his half of the circle.

"They're all *someone's* daughter."

Jarngard paused, remembering there was a point to it. The draining sun wasn't helping him think.

"So what happened in Gordic?" Jarngard asked.

"Don't you remember? While Wodanaz ran off, we got caught by those six men. In a circle just like this."

The memory drifted back to him. It was hard to concentrate, with all the shouting and the occasional sword thrust, but eventually the memory shimmered into his mind like a reflection on the water.

When the next soldier attacked, Jarngard let the man through his guard, and the man's blade cut him along the thigh. Not deep, but enough to cause a fair amount of blood. The crowd cheered.

Jarngard fell to a knee, hanging his head, hands clasped over the faded leather of his sword hilt in semblance of prayer. The soldiers hesitated, as Jarngard thought they would. The soldiers had been clearly instructed to draw out the death.

While avoiding a feeble attack, Hoth backed over Jarngard's out-stretched foot and fell upon his back like a turtle, sword flailing in the air. The crowd broke into laughter. The soldiers looked to each other, the confusion as plain on their face as the ankhs stamped into their chestpiec-es.

Hoth made a show of climbing to his feet as if he'd drank too much wine. He rolled onto his hands and knees. His sword swished through the dirt like an eager tail from a dog. The laughter of the crowd raised in crescendo and a few of the soldiers looked back, clearly trying to deter-mine if they were the source of the laughter, despite the foolish barbarians kneeling in the dirt. One soldier even glanced at the blade of his sword as if he thought it might have been poisoned.

When Hoth swung his sword around and hit Jarngard in the ear with the flat of his blade, the whole crowd cheered with eye watering hilarity. He glanced upward at the royal balcony. The laughter did not extend there.

The hesitant smile of the nearest soldier turned to a tight-lipped grimace. His arms flexed with intentions and he stepped forward, swinging his sword like a headman's axe. The blow wouldn't hit the sea captain cleanly. It would strike across the head like splitting a melon.

The soldier's eyes grew wide with victory. They were meant to draw out the battle, but surely killing the barbarians would bring a few extra coins from the nobles. Even from his kneeled position, Jarngard could see those spinning coins reflected in the soldier's wide-eyed stare.

He'd seen many like him. Overconfident. Trusting to what they saw with their eyes. Like the village of Gordic, when six men had descended upon a pair of drunken barbarians.

And like that day, Jarngard was the first to strike. He burst upward, knocking away the headhunting blow, and chopped the soldier's neck on the down stroke. Men wheeled away, but Hoth was upon them, sliding his keen blade past surprised blocks in double fashion and two more fell.

The last three, who'd clearly thought the odds in their favor, and the killing easy coin, bunched together in an awkward defense. Jarngard could see they had no real experience fighting together by their cautious steps.

The noises of the crowd were distant. Jarngard recalled that there might have been drums, but he could only see the beating of his enemy's heartbeat on his neck, see the naked fear in the man's eyes.

Hoth head faked and stomped his foot. Jarngard whirled past like autumn leaves and the soldiers swiped at empty air. Three fell dead and the two barbarians remained, much to the delight of the crowd.

"Village of Gordic, yes, I'm remembering that more clearly now," said Hoth at his side, barely breathing.

Jarngard put a hand to Hoth's shoulder and squeezed. "I don't suppose that was it?"

"It never is."

To neither man's surprise, the drums increased their rhythm as soldiers on horseback flooded into the arena. There were six again, wearing the colors of Ramses' elite guard, and an ankh stamped on their bronze chestpieces. The six formed up near the main entrance to the arena floor and a seventh rider burst out.

Jarngard recognized him immediately. It was the wrestler they called Little Hercules. He carried a short black bow and a quiver on his back, filled with bright fletchings.

"You know," said Hoth wryly, "when we get through these seven, we'll still have to get through the Manticores."

Jarngard laughed grimly and glanced up at Sepharia. She gripped the railing and stared directly at him.

"Maybe he'd just let me wrestle him? It seemed like a good idea before," said Jarngard.

Hoth chuckled. "Judging by the look of him, I think I'd take my chances with dodging arrows."

"I hide my muscles under this layer of fat to confuse my enemies," remarked Jarngard with a smile in his eyes as he remembered battles past with Hoth the Black at his side.

The horsebacked soldiers began to form up again, so Jarngard leaned over to Hoth.

"Do you remember the valley with all the apple trees and the strange rock formation that looked like a woman's breast? The time we took that Gaul town?"

Hoth turned to him with a quizzical look on his face. "I do quite clearly. We overran them. It was a bloodbath. What tactics are you suggesting?"

"Tactics? No. I wasn't suggesting any. I just thought this situation reminded me of that day," said Jarngard.

"Is the heat going to your head?" asked Hoth with a chuckle. "We'll be lucky to survive their first charge. We're hardly in control here."

Jarngard spoke quickly while the soldiers spurred their horses. "I wasn't suggesting we were. I was saying we're the Gauls this time."

Hoth grunted his agreement. Jarngard locked shoulders with his companion and set his feet for the charge.

High in the pale sky, carrion birds circled lower, drawn by the scent of battle and the arena inhaled, like a great lung, tensing for the impact. And in the silence between, horse hooves beat the ancient song of battle while two proud warriors prepared to die.

FORTY SIX

Sepharia wanted with all her being to look away. Her fingers dug mercilessly into the smooth wooden railing, until they found a splinter, not yet shaved away by the endless touch of soft hands. The sliver of wood pierced the end of her finger and a noise slipped out, shame for having to watch the Northmen fight so she could have an easy death.

A pawing hand floated beneath her elbow. Painted eyes and a smirking smile regarded her like a mouse.

"They fight well for you," said Ramses with considerable delight. "But I think this girl will find herself fed to the lions in the end."

Sepharia stole a glance at the dagger by his side. He caught her looking and smiled wider. He set his wine goblet on a nearby table and held his arms wide.

"Go ahead if you think you can."

She didn't bother. The tether around her wrist kept her reach limited. She held her stomach and bowed her head, feeling the empty vial Bani had brought her. It was tucked into her chiton around the waist.

"Let us watch this battle. It does have a certain importance, right?" he asked with faux interest.

At his urging, Sepharia moved to the rail by his side. On the sands, Jarngard and Hoth were fighting well. The one they called Little Hercules was still circling out of range with his bow while the horsemen charged the two barbarians. They killed one by cutting his horse's legs out from under him and then pounced on his fallen form. The other five horsemen learned from the first's mistake and threw short javelins while the Northmen dodged.

"This girl shouldn't worry too much about the lions. Being a weakling girl will bring about a near death from fright. And the lions haven't been fed in a day or two. They'll tear you limb from limb before you can even scream a second time."

Ramses' eyes glowered and Sepharia shrunk beneath his gaze. There was a burst of movement below and they both looked down. The Northmen were running across the field with recovered javelins in their fists. Two horsemen rode hard to catch them. With identical movements, Jarngard and Hoth planted a foot and launched their missiles. The horsemen flew off their saddles with spears through the throat. The crowd erupted.

Sepharia felt a sudden pain in her arm. Ramses was pinching the skin on the back of her elbow. He was clearly unamused by the battle below. The two barbarians had taken the soldiers' horses and rode together while the remaining four combatants grouped up and began to strategize.

"This girl shouldn't be so smug. Either way, you die," said Ramses intensely. "I might just throw you over the side and watch your brains splatter on the stones below. It's quite a drop."

Ramses took a hasty drink of his wine, spilling some on his Egyptian-styled toga before setting it back onto the table. She couldn't reach his dagger but she could reach the wine.

The new Satrap seemed distracted by the other nobles. Baruch Tanzen was staring in their direction. His jaw pulsed with the implied insult that his daughter's killer would receive a merciful death.

"Oh, all right," mumbled Ramses and he waved to the speaker in his colorful toga. Drum beats increased momentarily and more horsemen appeared in the gates. Along with Little Hercules, the Manticores joined them and now the odds were twenty to two and the crowd began jeering and throwing food onto the sands of the arena, voicing their displeasure at the unfair fight. Crowds wanted victory to hang on the skill of the combatants, not the whim of the nobles. Ramses shrugged and gulped his wine, keeping his gaze level with Baruch.

Hoth and Jarngard spurred their horses and took position on one side of the arena. The Egyptian elite guard took position in the middle, forming up in battle lines with the Manticores on one side and the horsemen flanked on the other. Little Hercules took the middle and pulled out a huge two-handed sword to scant applause.

There were cries of mercy from the crowd, building until it was a chant. Baruch glanced once more at Ramses, filling his gaze with unspoken threats. Sepharia wondered how tenuous their power sharing arrangement was.

Ramses shook off Baruch's gaze and thrust his fist over the railing. The crowd stilled. A thumb up would mean the Northmen lived, and maybe she received an easy death. A thumb down would be death. Sepharia watched his outstretched hand and held her breath. A lion gave a throaty cry and bumped against his cage.

The arena fell to a hush. And in the balls of her feet, Sepharia felt a rumble. The drums were quiet and the citizens in the arena still. Ramses' gaze wavered and his head tilted slightly.

Sepharia noticed the horses in the arena dancing restlessly on their hooves. The crisp battle line had become jagged with half-turned horses. Even the crowd began looking to their feet as if the stone had oozed out scorpions.

Ramses shook his fist as if reminding everyone they should be paying attention to him. A knot formed at his brow and Sepharia knew the direction his thumb would point.

He jammed it downward angrily and held high his other arm in victory. The crowd, confused by the shaking and the unmerciful Satrap, made scattered cheers and boos and whistles.

A hole formed in the middle of the arena, spitting up a puff of dust, like a small, dark mouth exhaling. Sepharia thought it might be a trick, but when it grew like spilled wine on a white cloth, Sepharia knew it was not intentional.

There was screaming and the horses panicked. Before they could escape, the hole, moving like a wave, swallowed the soldiers in the middle of the arena. The center collapsed, spitting dust and stone in a great cloud.

The crowd, fearful that the arena was falling in on itself, stampeded toward the exits. The nobles turned to and fro and called for their guards that had been housed below, but none came rushing up.

Ramses grabbed angrily for her. Digging his long fingernails into her arm. "This girl is supposed to die."

"Maybe the gods believe otherwise," snapped Sepharia.

He was reaching for his dagger when Heron appeared at the top of the steps with Punt and other soldiers. Blades were stained and faces were dirty. Heron had a certain grim demeanor that Sepharia had never seen before.

Ramses slipped his arm around Sepharia's stomach and the cold blade kissed against her neck. The other nobles backed away. Some held weapons limply in their hands. Others dropped them to clatter on the floor. The chaos in the arena had been forgotten even though screams of terror still echoed behind them.

"We've taken the city back," said Heron plainly. "Vestalis takes the gates while we stand here."

"I'll kill your daughter," said Ramses and Sepharia knew he meant it, even if it meant his death.

"You might," said Heron unwaveringly. "But I think you'd rather return to exile."

Ramses spit. "You'd never let me go back to Memphis."

"I never said exile in Memphis. You'd have to leave Egypt altogether. Go east past the Indus river or south to the Bantu peoples. Either way, Alexandria is mine and I want my daughter alive."

"Yours now? Are you taking it from Agog?" asked Ramses.

Heron visibly sighed. "So he's alive? Good. No, I do not want the city. I am an inventor, not a war captain."

"You'd best be both. The Roman navy arrives in two weeks. But you can't win. It's impossible," said Ramses confidently.

Heron smirked as if Ramses had made a joke. "Impossible, yes. But that's not for you to worry about. I'll even let you go, give you food, water, and a horse, and you can ride as far as you want. Or even wait for the Romans to win."

"I would ride. If I cannot trade Alexandria for my freedom, then the Romans would see me dead just as you," said Ramses before his tone changed. "But I do not believe you would let me ride. Your face betrays your lies. So I think I would rather just take your daughter's life and be done with it."

Heron paled and gripped at her sword. Sepharia put her hand on the empty vial hidden in her chiton. The nobles waited and watched.

Sepharia spoke, as softly and as carefully as she could, "What if I rode with you? I would be your willing slave until you were a safe distance away."

"No, Sepharia," barked Heron. "He would just kill you when he was safe."

"Better than to die here. To die now."

Ramses made an amused noise. "A touching exchange between father and daughter. This simple girl is right. She could die here, or maybe she could live later. This option is agreeable to my ears."

"I would be your faithful servant until you were safe," she said with all her honesty.

Heron's face broke with betrayal. Her jaw hung open in mute agony and the sword in her hand tipped into the dirt.

"Yes, I could use a *faithful* servant," said Ramses, growing excited against her. "But do not think that you could deceive me, for I am the master and you would be my slave."

"Yes, Master Ramses," said Sepharia.

"The words sing sweetly from your lips," said Ramses. "Fetch me my goblet, for I thirst. And then we will be away. I may have lost the city, but I prefer my hide." He nodded toward the defeated Heron. "I expect a pouch of gold as well, so I can keep your daughter in luxury while we travel. Maybe even a few of my men for guards?"

He took the goblet from Sepharia while he smiled victoriously at Heron. Even Punt appeared visibly wounded by the deal. Heron had taken back the city but lost her daughter. What a cruel bargain, the people would say after they were gone.

Sepharia relaxed into Ramses as he downed his cup. He made smacking noises when he was done and threw the cup at the nobles dismissively.

"Let us go, girl."

As they moved forward, the vial in her hand slipped out and bounced across his foot, spinning into the space between them. Ramses glanced down and ignored the vial at first, but then his whole body tensed and he scrambled for the vial in his own tunic.

"You bitch! You've poisoned me!" he cried angrily as he pawed at his chest not even trying to hold onto Sepharia.

When he brought the full vial of poison out of his tunic and held it up questioningly toward her, she hit him in the chest with both hands, knocking him over the railing. He tried to grab the edge, but his hand still gripped the dagger and his fist skidded off the smooth wooden rail.

He hit the stone benches below and Sepharia forced herself to make sure he was dead. Blood spilled out from his lifeless body. Heron appeared at her side and put an arm around her shoulder.

"I guess I can play this game after all," whispered Sepharia to herself as she let Heron lead her away.

FORTY SEVEN

In the upper chambers of the Royal Palace, the Antirhodos, as it was named by the Greeks, Agog waited in the Star Chamber surrounded by oil lights. The room served as a royal viewing area for the night sky.

Agog gazed at the dim stars in the heavens and wondered what the scholars of the Library would tell him about their placement in the deep bowl of the night. His people named them Horse-Thief, and Signard the Sailor, and the Three Wives, and many others. Stories carried them through the long winter nights when the sun left for months.

He rested his tired bones on the cushioned seat, silently grumbling that his friends had not yet arrived to take his mind from his sore backside. The stars seemed uninterested in his problems, and as he realized it, they contributed to them as well.

The ledgers from the time of the Ptolemies reminisced about the scholars that taught the royal family in this room. Hipparchus himself, one of the greatest astronomical scholars, had instructed Ptolemy, though Agog could not remember which, since they named themselves the same.

The air pressure in the room changed slightly as a door was opened below. Heron appeared at the top of the marble stairs that led into the center of the room. Black iron fencing surrounded them to keep star gazers from harm. Jarngard, Hoth, Polyxena, and Vestalis appeared right after.

"Conspiring against me, my friends?" asked Agog, chuckling.

Jarngard fidgeted with the leather bag around his neck as he spoke. "Your doorman was insistent that no one bother his royal royalness. Something about recovering from battle wounds. Only Heron's appearance saved us from waiting below with that man. He has horrible breath. And since when is being fat a battle wound, Your Grace?"

Vestalis cleared his throat angrily. "You should not speak to your Satrap or your commander this way."

Agog restrained a sigh. "Enough already, we don't have time for it." He gestured at both of them. "But you are correct, I labor too long on the bench and I've forgotten the faces of my ancestors. When Rome brings its armies to us, I must be ready to lead."

"Forgetting the navy?" asked Hoth. "Or did something change while I was recovering from Heron pulling the floor of the arena out from under me."

Before Agog could respond, Jarngard spoke up, "Hoth is right. Long before you can have your glory against Rome, he needs his chance on the sea."

A raise of his eyebrow wouldn't be enough to express his surprise at the defense of Hoth by Jarngard, so he choked instead. Agog had heard the two had fought together on the sands of the arena, but he hadn't expected they'd buried their past.

"That's why I sent you two to Babylon, to figure out how to beat the Roman navy."

The *Michanikos* stepped forward, but hesitated with his words. "No, you sent us to find something for you and—"

Agog made a cutting motion with his hand. "That's for another time," he said, glancing at Vestalis and Polyxena. Each of his new companions knew the purpose of the trip to Old Babylon, though each thought it a secret with him. There were certain aspects of his plans that needed to wait until they were ready before he announced them. If the five of them began to talk, they would know his mind and secrets were only secrets if no one knew them.

"But what of the strategy?" he asked.

Hoth, who seemed far more recovered from his battles than he let on, pinched his chin in thought. His pale hair was brushed straight, and the resurgent strand of black rested against his jaw.

Agog wrinkled his nose at a flowery fragrance thick in the room. "Is that you?" he asked Hoth, and the sea captain shrugged.

"I have an idea on how we might approach this naval problem," said Heron finally, with some reluctance.

"Do not hold back," said Agog. "A thousand ships arrive in a week. Every second we talk is another second wasted."

"How willing are you to let me build steam mechanicals without those cursed protections? Another workshop had a minor accident yesterday," said Heron.

Agog sighed and imagined his royal treasury growing lighter. "I'd hoped you fixed that problem."

Even in the dim oil light, Agog could see the change in the inventor. Heron seemed less manic and more thoughtful, maybe even more purposeful. The man had not made one mention of his confounded Hermes machine since they'd taken the city back.

"I have, but probably not in the way you desire."

His stomach rumbled, partially in hunger, partially in protest to whatever Heron would say. He would have to get used to his empty stomach.

He needed to get back in fighting shape. Agog motioned for the man to continue.

"It's not the steam mechanicals themselves that matter, but how we use them," said Heron.

"Yes, and as easily as we can use them, so can the Romans. I do not see your point."

The inventor cocked a smile, a much different reaction from their exchange over the subject a few months before. Agog was intrigued.

"When Alexander the Macedonian conquered the world, did he use anything special? Anything equivalent to the steam mechanical?"

Vestalis spoke first, his piercing gray eyes staring directly at Heron. "Of course not, but he had his sarrisa troops and unstoppable Thessalian cavalry."

"Ah yes." Heron raised a finger. "But couldn't anyone train their troops in those manners? Did the Macedonians have a special treaty keeping others from using the sarrisa spear or cavalry? Polyxena, has the League of Corinth ever heard of such a thing?"

The petite woman shook her head. The woman watched intently and seemed to be taking stock of Heron. Agog had business with her later after the others were gone.

Heron spoke louder this time and Agog noted how musical his voice sounded. He wondered if that was a function of his creative genius or something else, something unfathomable. But Agog had little time to ponder because the inventor was speaking.

"Alexander had no special troops or steam mechanicals. He had access to the same things that everyone else did, but he used them in ways that no one had ever considered. Filling tents with grass to float his army across a wide river. Building a mole across the bay at Tyre so he could attack the city, even though it took him a year. Climbing the cliffs of Siagdon Rock to take the impenetrable city. These steam mechanicals are nothing more than tools. We can use them the same as we did yesterday and the Romans can overwhelm us with superior numbers, or we can remove the protections, free the men and women of Alexandria, and encourage the spirit of the Great Library to find new ways we can use the steam mechanicals to fend off Rome, and even build a new empire if we so desire."

"Stirring words, but Rome is nearly upon us. We have no time for innovation. No time for new ideas, except those that destroy those blasted ships." Agog threw his arms in the air.

That same smile crept upon Heron's face, and Agog felt another rumble in his stomach.

"We have everything we need to destroy those ships, but we're going to need a city full of new unprotected steam mechanicals to take on the Roman army next year. I cannot take the old ones from the workshops without promises for new steam mechanicals, ones that do not explode when they get out of balance."

Agog took a heavy breath. "If I just say yes, will you explain your damned plan?"

Heron nodded.

"Fine," said Agog. "Tell me everything. I want to know how we're going to win."

Heron began to tell them. At first, there was skepticism from everyone except Hoth. The sea captain seemed to accept the inventor's ideas quite readily, no matter how far fetched they seemed.

Polyxena was quick to offer her ships and Vestalis much slower. They would need to borrow some boats from the locals, and take some from the Phoenicians, and Agog was to promise payment later for them, a fact which made his stomach twist even more.

There was also business about some magic rocks from the Curiosity Rooms in the Library. Hoth seemed to understand them, but no one else did, so he agreed to go collect them. It would cost gold, of course, and

Agog would have to hand over another heavy pouch, reluctantly.

In the end, they agreed to Heron's plan, because no one offered an alternative. When Agog retired to his spacious room for the evening, he had an odd feeling that he'd unleashed something more dangerous upon the world and it wasn't the steam mechanicals, or the new Alexandria that he could see in their eyes. It was the ideas of Heron of Alexandria.

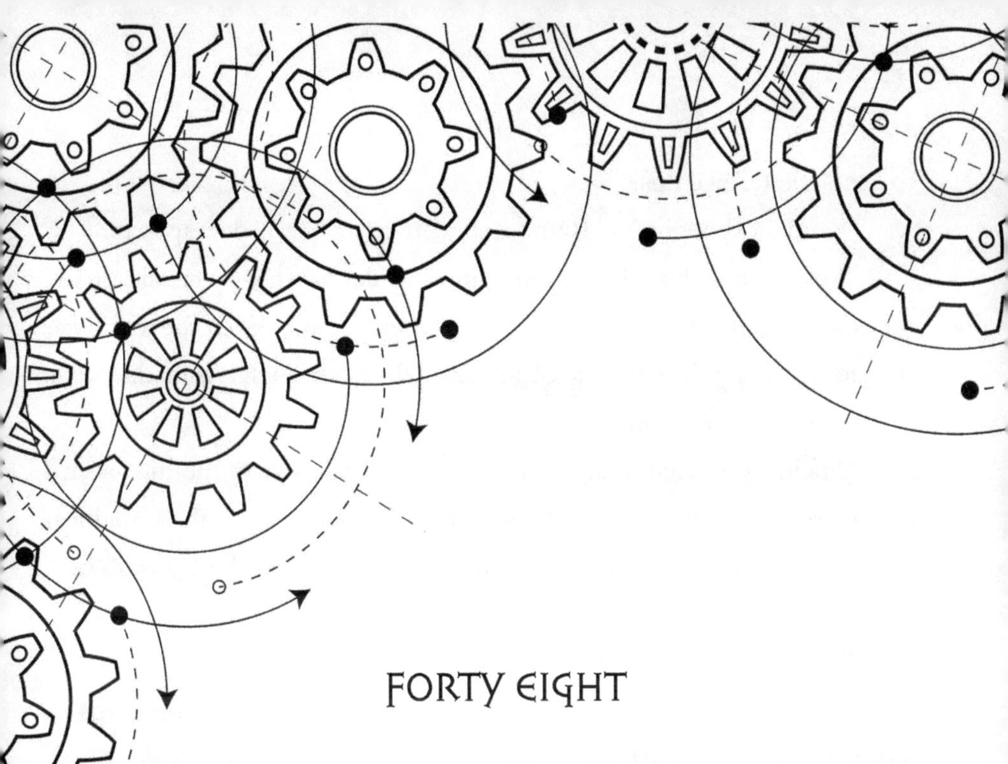

FORTY EIGHT

Aulus Plautius, Consul of the Roman Navy, stood on the bow of the *Mars Valliant* clutching a folded parchment. Stars were thick across the sky. He smiled, wondering if the gods looked down upon his fleet and thought the same thing. Maybe those distant lights were ships sailing towards battle as he. Aulus nodded toward them, feeling suddenly nostalgic.

"Falling asleep on the day before battle?" said Vespasian, his trusted legion general, who had come from below deck.

Aulus chuckled. His mood was triumphant and he felt like indulging in a little banter. "Do you see the lights of the ships around us?"

Vespasian indicated as much with a simple creasing of his eyes.

"Has a navy as large as this one ever sailed the Mediterranean?" asked Aulus.

"Since the Roman Empire is the largest empire the world has ever known, and this is the largest navy the empire has ever sailed, I would say no. This is the largest fleet to ever sail," said Vespasian briskly.

Aulus shook the parchment in his hand. "Then what prompts a man to send a letter like this?"

"Send? I thought you found it in your room?" asked Vespasian.

"Yes," said Aulus, "I did. On that foggy day when we were sitting off the coast of Britton. The air was as thick as pale mud. Even the water was soaked with fog. That anyone could have piloted through it is madness, yet there was the letter in my room behind a locked door."

"Madness is what it is. Though you've never shown me the letter, I can guess at its tone by your interest in it," mused Vespasian. "Madness to sail in such foul weather and madness to sneak upon the Consul's hexareme to leave a note."

"Madness or magic or something else?" asked Aulus.

"Forgive me, Consul, but surely you do not believe in charlatans or witches?" asked Vespasian carefully.

Aulus regarded his general with half-lidded eyes. "I have seen things on the seas that I cannot explain. Like the kraken off the coast of fallen Carthage or women with tails zipping through the water at dawn."

"But this is not a myth," offered Vespasian, "this is just a man, unless that letter says otherwise."

Aulus held the parchment out, pinched between two fingers and thumb. "You've been angling to read it since I told you about it. Go ahead. We're on the doorstep to Alexandria, anyway."

A lantern was brought near and given more whale oil for light. Black tendrils of smoke slipped from the glass and Aulus wrinkled his nose. Vespasian leaned into the warm illumination, crinkling the parchment noisily as he read:

"Ave, flightless eagle of the seas! I am Hoth the Black, a raven from the North, sent down by gods and prophecy to rip your wings—"

Vespasian glanced up grinning. "These barbarians have a way with words, even though his handwriting is terrible."

"Who would have thought barbarians could even write?" mused Aulus.

The legion general leaned into the parchment and continued reading with a sneer on his lips:

"*—away and swallow you whole. If you wish to keep the bundle of wood you call the* Mars Valliant, *sail to fingerrock, north of Alexandria and hand over a thousand talents for your safety. Only then may you return to Rome. If you choose to ignore my warning, I shall climb aboard your ship and take her myself.*"

"Madness is right," said Aulus.

"Do you really think he'd sell his countrymen for gold?"

The Consul took the parchment and neatly folded it in a practiced manner and tucked it in his tunic. "When we neared this region, I sent four of my fastest triremes to this fingerrock, to scout if his small fleet was hiding in the cove. I did not expect to find anything and I was right. He was only playing a game. And my spies tell me there is no sign of this Hoth the Black's ships, even after they took the city back from that imbecile Ramses."

Vespasian laughed quietly. "I would have liked to have hung Ramses as the Emperor requested. A fool to think his little ploy would earn him favor with the Empire. The city would be taken with or without him."

A streak shot across the sky. Aulus heard murmurs from his sailors.

"A favorable sign from the gods," remarked Vespasian knowingly.

After a pause, Vespasian said, "It's a shame they quenched the beacon fire on the Lighthouse of Pharos. I would have liked to see it from a distance. I've heard it's like seeing Zeus' gaze from the heavens."

"They would have been fools not to, though it won't matter. Without a cloud in the sky, we can navigate to Alexandria quite easily," said Aulus as he leaned against the wooden railing. The salty sea air refreshed him. He breathed deep and thought about the time after his victory when he could rest in Alexandria and bother with war no longer, maybe even take an Egyptian wife and have children. He'd heard they were a fertile people.

"Do you hear that?" asked Vespasian, cocking an ear.

Aulus felt the slightest of vibrations in the rail under his calloused hands, but could hear nothing.

"Your hearing is better than mine," he told his general. "I took a shield to the head on my first battle charge a long time ago and I've never quite heard well since."

Vespasian cupped his hand around his ear and leaned over the rail. Stars and the lanterns on surrounding ships reflected in the inky waters.

"I heard it. It's like distant thunder, but it never fades and I haven't seen any lightning," said Vespasian, perplexed.

There was a distant star that seemed to reflect brightly on the seas ahead. Aulus squinted, wondering if it were the flash of light he'd seen fall through the night sky floating on the surface of the sea.

"I think I hear that sound," said Aulus. "Does it sound like a thousand hammers beating a metal pot? But quiet like a hush, and..." He leaned out over the rail like Vespasian and hoped none of his sailors were watching. The pair of them looked like children spitting into the water as they were. "...and there are more than one of them."

Aulus looked back at his fleet that traveled with the *Mars Valliant*. Each ship kept a comfortable distance from the others so there were no naval mishaps. The *Poseidon's Breath* rode heavily in the water to starboard. The ship carried a hundred Roman marines in its hold. On the port side, a pair of quadremes cut through the water, the *Antilla* and the *Caligula*, roiling white foam beneath their wake. Aulus hated to see any ship named *Caligula* but it had been named a decade before and had survived long enough that the crew thought it a lucky name. He'd heard them say it was a different Caligula that it was named after.

He couldn't see the ships behind well enough to know their names, except for the massive hexareme *Eagle's Claw*, but there were another four or five sailing in his wake. He glanced ahead to see the strange light still ahead and growing larger. The odd rumbling had grown louder, enough that Aulus could see men on the *Poseidon's Breath* moving to the bow to determine what it was. Fears of the kraken or other mischief from the myths twisted his gut momentarily. Surely there was nothing even the gods could throw at them that would keep them from their task. He was the Consul of the Roman Empire, and besides the Emperor, the Empire's most powerful man.

Aulus heard calls of, "It's a boat!" before he could see it himself. Before long, he could make out the rounded bow of a small fishing vessel tacking against the wind with black sails. There was only one man on board and he seemed to be stoking a strange bellows.

The vibration in the railing grew more pronounced and Aulus knew it came from the fishing vessel. He wondered if it were an envoy of Alexandria, but the man wore nothing formal that would indicate him as much. The sailor of the boat was tall, and blond, and he wore a simple tunic and belt.

The man in the boat passed between the *Mars Valliant* and *Poseidon's Breath*. It was close enough Aulus could see the machine on the boat, churning away at an awful rate, but for what purpose, he could not determine.

"Is that one of the *Michanikos'* famed steam mechanicals?" asked Vespasian, who like the others, seemed mesmerized by the appearance of this solitary boat.

"Maybe he's stolen one and wishes to trade it for gold," pondered Aulus.

"If so, he doesn't seem to be stopping. He's heading for the *Eagle's Claw*," said Vespasian with a trace of worry in his voice.

"Shoot him and take his prize," Aulus commanded, as he tried to ignore the ominous feeling in his gut.

Before the bowmen could reach the railing, the man did something to the boat and dove into the water like a dart. By the man's lean, arcing dive, he was no ordinary sailor. Aulus noticed a streak of black in the man's hair as well. Aulus was about to shout orders to the *Eagle's Claw* to capture the shipping vessel when he decided that he didn't trust it.

"Avoid that boat!" he yelled across the water.

The steam mechanical on the boat had begun to whine precipitously and Aulus had to put a hand to his ear.

"What devilish thing is that?" asked Vespasian.

Before either could utter another word and as the crew of the *Eagle's Claw* was hooking the sailing lines of the boat, it exploded into flame and shrapnel, punching a hole in the side of the huge hexareme.

Aulus ducked behind the railing. "What in the Empire's name?"

The *Eagle's Claw* was taking on water fast and dipping to one side. Flame licked up the sides and danced across the water in oily pools. The men that had been leaning over the railing were floating in the water. Aulus was about to shout for his messengers when he heard the sounds of more vibrations. Only this time the clankings of steam engines filled the air like a thousand bees.

Aulus ran to the bow and peered over the edge. Reflecting in the starry water were the hulls of numerous small boats, each with a steam mechanical on it.

He was about to turn and yell for a messenger when one appeared at his side. "Good, I need you to take word to the fleet."

Aulus realized the man was not one of his own. "Hail to the Empire," said the man. "I bring word from the north edge of the armada. Centurion Malus of the *Hermes' Daughter* sends word that they are being attacked by a quick moving fleet of a ship design he has never seen."

Aulus growled. "Take word back to him that he should deal with it. We are over a thousand ships strong. He can take a few dozen."

The messenger swallowed. "He said it was a hundred."

"A hundred? It's still ten to one. Tell him to deal with it and to watch out for small boats with steam—" Aulus didn't get a chance to finish because there was another explosion to his starboard and then another further down.

"Tell him to watch out for those!" he screamed.

Aulus grabbed Vespasian's toga. "Get every man on the ship and tell them to carry the word to the others. Even if they have to swim to the other ships."

He pointed to the rapidly sinking *Poseidon's Breath*. "There are men in those boats, get them to bring the message to the rest of the fleet. Send every last one, even if you have to empty the ship."

He could hardly believe what was happening. He gripped the railing tightly and resisted a flinch as more boats exploded against his ships. White sails on either side listed into the dark waters. Flames ate hungrily at his tender boats. The water no longer reflected the sky. Orange flame danced on the surface like ghosts.

His captains were waking to the danger and firing at the boat pilots. Most jumped in before the boats exploded. Some tore apart between the boats where there was no danger.

Sinking ships screamed as the wood tore apart. Further into his fleet, fires bloomed like the stars and still the sounds of hammering bees surrounded him. Men swam through the water and Aulus could tell neither friend nor foe. The air was brighter, like a burgeoning dawn, but lit from the tinder of his fleet.

He felt a presence behind him and turned to ask Vespasian why he wasn't sending messengers. While this attack wouldn't destroy his fleet, he hated taking losses, especially when he hadn't expected it.

The man was dripping and held a sword. The blade was wet. Aulus recognized it. He'd given the rapier to Vespasian as a gift for his service last year. The hilt guard was fashioned into a lion's head.

"Aulus Plautius?" asked the man in tortured Latin.

Aulus did not answer. He stared back, hoping to delay long enough for his bowmen to see the intruder. Then he remembered he'd sent them all away.

"You cannot win," Aulus told him. "Our fleet is too numerous. Our ships are larger and stronger than yours. Alexandria will be back in the Roman Empire in less than a week. Let me go and I will give you all the gold you desire."

The man snickered and set the tip of the blade against Aulus' stomach. "I offered you a chance at life already and you turned it down. Your four ships came and went and never left the thousand talents. I would have been merciful, but I guess the gods have other ideas."

"Hoth the Black?" asked Aulus. "I cannot believe it."

"Believe it and more," said Hoth. "But do not worry. Your name will be remembered throughout all of history with mine. Yours will be the name of the man who lost the greatest naval battle of our time, while mine will be of the victor."

Aulus opened his mouth to protest, but he felt a sharp pain in his gut and he found he couldn't speak. The lion's head hilt was resting against his belly. Aulus slumped to his knees, sliding from the blade, and fell over. The world dimmed and his last memory was Hoth striding away from him, backlit by distant flames.

"For the Empire..." Aulus muttered and died.

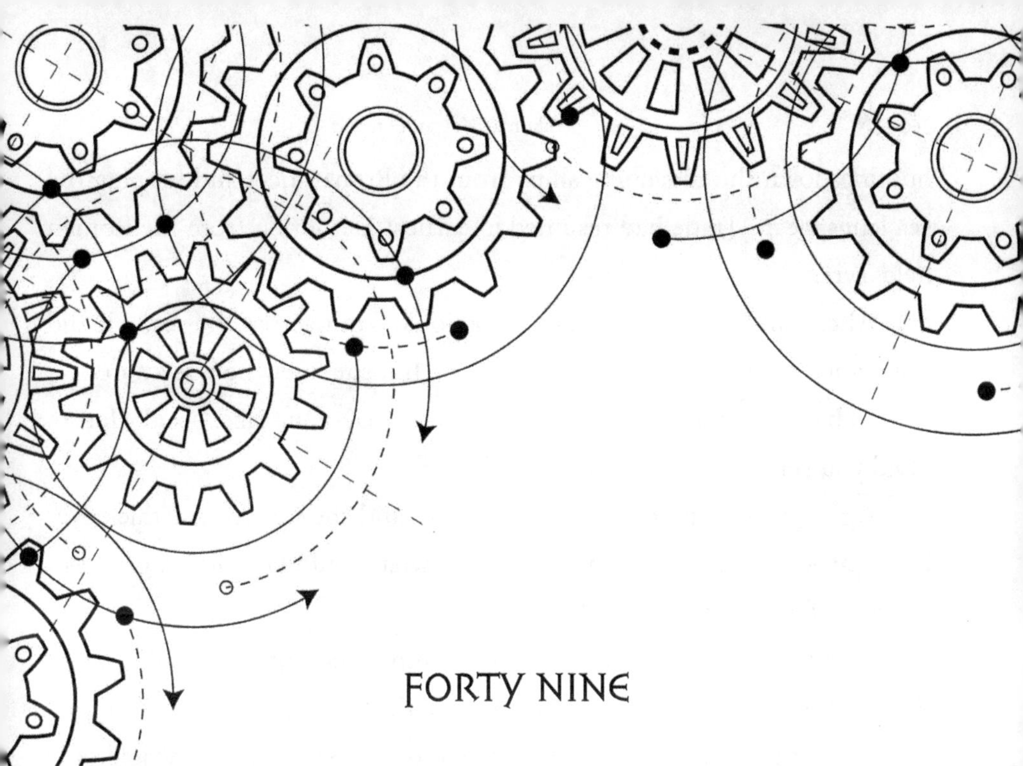

FORTY NINE

The docks bustled along the great harbor of Alexandria. Heron looked down upon them from the royal pier as she rode to meet the Satrap. The charred hulks of anti-siege weaponry had been torn down. Future enemies would not approach from the sea now. Rome would be forced to march around the Mediterranean to attack Alexandria. They'd bought themselves half a year or more with their naval victory. The Romans would be hard-pressed to march during the winter season, especially after a devastating loss. The Senate would be furious and political squabbling would delay them more. Alexandria would need it. Defeating the navy was one thing, but the Empire existed because of the legions. Even with Alexandria's superior technology, it would be a challenging road ahead.

Heron did not see the *Mars Valliant* at the docks and it was hard to miss. The hexareme had been the largest vessel in the Roman navy. It looked like a pregnant whale, three times larger than most of the ships in the harbor.

But it wasn't there, which meant that Hoth the Black was out again, hunting down the remaining ships from the Roman fleet and keeping the sea lanes clear. Trade had resumed in earnest, detouring from the Roman held Tyre.

Ahead and astride his horse, Agog looked out across the sea. He did not glance in her direction as she rode up, but she knew he was aware.

"That seems a proper horse for a man of your size," said Heron. "Did you send for it from the North?"

Agog glanced at her with his dark eyes and she noticed the thick eyelashes around them. His lips broke into what could be called a grin, but the rest of his demeanor said otherwise.

He patted the roan stallion beneath him. The horse flicked its tail at the buzzing flies. A northerly wind blew the hair from Agog's face and sent goose bumps across her arms. The morning was chill and would only get colder as the days marched toward winter, though she knew it would still be a summer's day for the Northmen.

"It's a breed from the east. They say there are giant men who ride them far to the east and then north, where the mountains reach the black sky above," he said.

"When a man your size calls another giant, they must be big."

Agog chuckled, clearly coming out of his thoughts from when she approached him. Heron nodded toward the bruising on his arm.

"Gifts from the exile Ramses?" she asked.

"Nay. Sparring with a few of Hoth's men this morning. I offered a talent to who ever could put a weapon on me." His eyes sparkled with amusement. "Tormod won the only coin, but I think he regrets his foolish maneuver. He'd be a dead man if it were battle. What men will do for coin."

Heron narrowed her gaze briefly. "Like turn their backs on the Empire for a chance to be the city's new Alabarch?"

The roan sauntered to the side and Agog flicked the reins to right the horse. "Has word already leaked?" he grumbled.

"Tamp your worries. I only guessed it because it seemed logical. Though I should have seen it earlier when you became flush with gold. Vestalis' sudden loyalty made it clear," she explained.

"The man loves gold more than he loved the Empire," said Agog. "He's also a keen judge and believes he'll be on the winning side at the end of all of this."

"All of this? How far are we going?" asked Heron, though she knew the answer.

"When you rattle the chains of the Roman Empire, you should be prepared to go the distance. The world has taken notice of our business down here and that naval victory has opened up doors that were previously closed," he explained.

"New allies?" she asked.

He shrugged and his gaze reeked of caution. "Maybe they are interested in joining us, or maybe they only wish to solicit more coin from the Empire. There is gold and influence to be made in a time of war, on both sides."

A black-hulled Phoenician trader tacked into the harbor. Heron watched as men scurried across its deck, yanking lines and adjusting sails. She could hear their throaty cries, carried by the crisp wind. The air was salty clean and helped her forget the pains in her knees.

"So what did you learn about our city's namesake in Old Babylon?" he asked finally.

"Babylon is a moldy ruin of a town," she said, "and visiting it illuminated nothing about Alexander's heir."

The barbarian seemed displeased by the news, but only gripped his reins tighter.

"There was nothing in Baruch's scrolls, either," said Agog.

The roan turned and Heron faced the Satrap. She noticed for the first time a golden brooch on his tunic.

"Is that the one Sepharia made?" she asked.

He nodded and touched it reverently. "A skilled piece of craftsmanship. It is my honor to wear it."

"What does Polyxena think of it?" she asked carefully. "Since you're planning a marriage to her."

The Satrap's face lifted in surprise. "Why do I have secrets if you always suss them out? What gave me away this time?"

"I divine the airs and the entrails of pigs," mocked Heron.

Agog shook his head and smiled. In truth, Sepharia had learned of it directly from Polyxena. Since their previous mistrust had been upended by the business with Ramses, her daughter and the Macedonian woman had been as thick as thieves.

"With no real heir, will she claim Alexander's heritage?" she asked.

"You know me too well," he replied.

"The fires investigation taught me that. Truth to you is like metal to Punt. Easily shaped and used for your purposes." And after a long pause. "I suppose you will not free the slaves then, even as you misuse the knowledge that I returned with."

"Many in the city know the great inventor himself went to Old Babylon in search of the heirs. When I announce that it is Polyxena, they will believe me," he said.

"Why bother with me going all the way to Old Babylon? Why not just lie?" she asked. "It would have saved me a lot of trouble."

"Because they would not believe it otherwise. With your name attached to the investigation, and the hallowed name of Babylon, an ancient city even before the world was old, they will readily believe it." He tugged on the reins and pointed the roan toward the water. "And who knows, maybe you would have found the real heir."

Heron lightly heeled her horse to move it parallel with the Satrap. She had to be careful with her words.

"Then why did you offer alliance with the League of Corinth and marriage to Polyxena before I left?" she asked.

He was not amused by her question and his bearded jaw bristled with anger.

"Is nothing private with you? How did you learn this? I must know, no games," he said coolly.

"I acquired a coded scroll before I left Alexandria. I mistakenly intercepted it from a messenger who mistook me for someone else," she explained, leaving out that she'd killed the man. Once she'd learned what was on the scroll, she was doubly regretful.

"But it was coded. Or at least Polyxena told me so," he countered. "She claimed it was unbreakable."

"And partially ruined from being dropped into a puddle. I shouldn't have been able to break the code, but I realized that it was a portion of the golden ratio, a sacred number to mathematicians. These were numbers well past the decimal that makes whole numbers small. Once I knew that, I made a request to the scholars in the Library, the ones I'd made the counting machine for. They were able to dig deep into that number and find the sequence for which I only had partial numbers. They divined numbers that no tables have seen before, except for the League's sources, of course. Once I had that, uncovering the message was simple."

Agog slapped the horse. "Once again I am reminded why I'm glad you're on my side."

"So if I would have found the heir, would you still have married Polyxena? It seems you were solidifying an alliance even before I left for Old Babylon," she asked. "And would you have really freed the slaves?"

"I would," he said quickly. "But you didn't. So there's no need to worry."

"If you freed them anyway, then Alexandria would become a counter to the Empire, who traffics in human flesh," she said.

He dismissed her words with a wave of his meaty hand. "And we'd find our potential allies suddenly skittish. The world runs on these slaves and they would not want them taken away."

"The world can run on my steam mechanicals, instead," she countered.

"And I've already agreed to your requested changes to the mechanicals. A change I already regret," he told her.

Heron decided not to push him further, but she wasn't done with the subject. She just needed a different tack.

The Satrap glanced at the sun, rising in the morning sky. "I must go. Polyxena waits and we have plans to make."

Heron felt a twinge of jealousy, but she pushed it down deep. She had nothing new to offer Agog that he couldn't get with Polyxena. Her inventions were more important than her emotions, anyway.

The sun warmed her arms as she flicked the reins. Agog brought his horse along side and handed her a bundle of three bound books from his saddlebag.

"These came from your messengers," he said. "With the trail dead in Old Babylon, I don't suppose they'll say anything new, but I thought you'd want them."

He left and Heron found herself alone. She ran her fingertips across the leather bindings. The Satrap had left her with a lot to think about, but she felt naked on the pier. There was a better place to think in the city, one she'd promised herself to visit before she left for Old Babylon and an appropriate place to read the books brought back from Greece. Heron flicked the reins and turned her horse toward the Broucheion District.

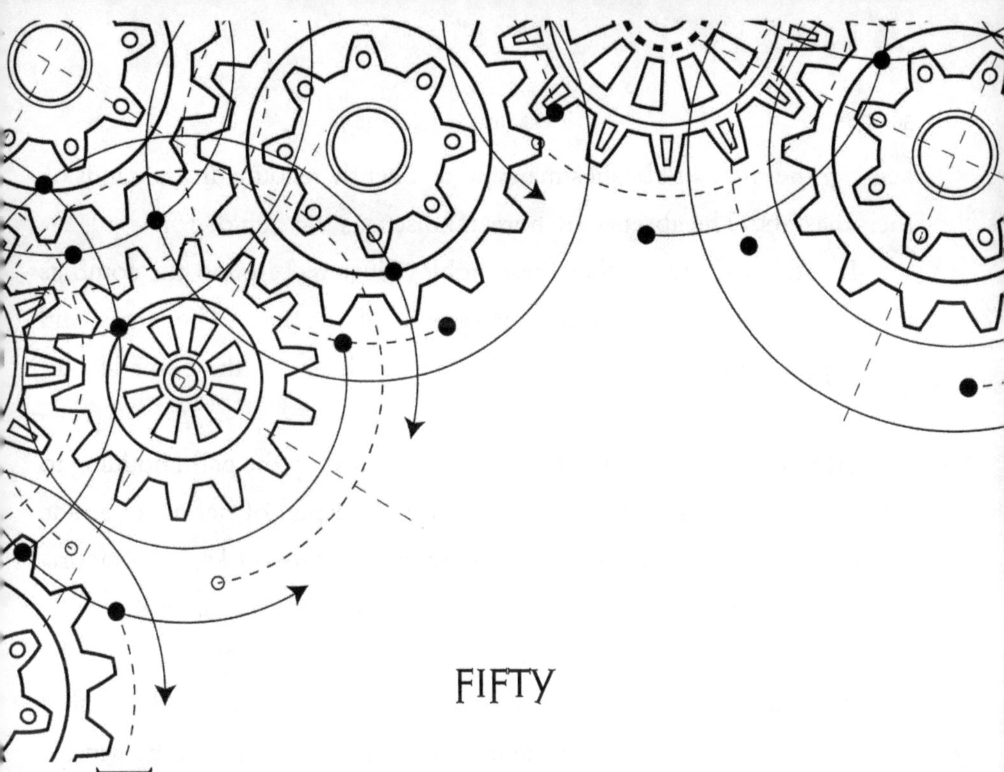

FIFTY

The streets of Alexandria, when first imagined by its great King, were orderly like soldiers before battle. Three hundred years after his death, the streets in the Broucheion District had become those same soldiers after the first press of sword against shield.

In the lesser parts of the city, the government had been firm enough to keep the streets from wavering from their intended paths. The Broucheion housed the wealthiest Alexandrians who could afford bribes and purchase their neighbors plots when misfortune befell them.

The way to the Soma of Alexander the Macedonian led Heron to multiple dead ends. She could see the high colonnades beyond the noble dwellings, sitting on the rise and surrounded by mature trees.

This district was nothing like the others. Heron always felt a tangible energy when she shouldered through the Emporium in the Rhakotis district, or watched the dock runners take papyrus and books from ships for the Library.

These cobbled streets were stilled by the quiet daily death of slaves, keeping the trees and bushes manicured. Silently tending the demands of their masters. The absence of human noise was the sign of rot.

It saddened Heron that these nobles clustered around the tomb as if proximity would give them some essence of the man. The largest and most opulent mansions crowded the flowered lawns of the Soma like tumors.

Heron left her mount at the gate and strolled up the path, nodding to the attendants that kept the Soma. She heard whispers of her name, so she was known to them. These were paid men, for whoever kept Alexandria must keep the tomb of Alexander or feel the people's wrath.

Stepping onto the grass was like the night she climbed from the smoke-filled cave into the brisk night air. A rabble of colorful butterflies swarmed a broad leafed sycamore making it appear to blow in the wind.

An attendant appeared at her side as she tried to pick out individual butterflies, but there were too many to even begin to count. The Egyptian man spoke with the cadence of practice and she could tell he'd recited this bit of knowledge to other visitors before her. "Every year they come to the Soma around this time and visit the sacred sycamore before flying south. Some say it is Hathor, the Lady of the Sycamore, paying homage to Alexander. Others claim Zeus-Ammon reminds the world the legacy of his son, while others say it's the Sycamore of Turquoise mentioned in the Book of the Dead, but only when the butterflies visit."

"And what do you believe?" she asked.

She looked to him for the first time and found he was an old man, though his voice was young. He had that ancient quality that most Egyptians had that always reminded Heron that they were an ancient people.

"I believe it's Alexander's *ren*. And it visits here because his name is still spoken with reverence," he said.

Heron stood with him for a bit and then smiled respectfully and slipped him a ha'penny. He bowed and shuffled off to another part of the Soma.

She climbed the steps, feeling the weight of history bearing down on her. It was an atmosphere she hadn't felt anywhere else on her investigations of the man. Maybe it was exhaustion from the last few months finally coming to rest on her like heavy cargo in the belly of a ship.

There was new artwork in the corridor leading down into the main chamber. She smiled, knowing it was Agog's work. The scenes displayed Alexander's greatest battles.

The side chambers did not interest her, so she skipped them, instead heading directly for the burial chamber which housed the sarcophagus of Alexander the Macedonian. When she reached the room, her breath fell silent.

The stone sarcophagus was larger than one of her Manticores. Scenes of Alexander's most famous battles were carved onto the sides, including his defeat of Darius. The steepled roof of the burial stone was inset with designs of Macedonian sunbursts and Egyptian symbols of Zeus-Ammon.

How long Heron stood in front of the resting place of Alexander, she did not know. But when she realized her knees and ankles ached from standing, she pulled the books from the bag she'd carried and unclasped the bindings.

The books were musty and old, but well-kept. They'd come from the royal library in Macedonia from the scholar Gratis, an acquaintance by letters only. There was a folded note in the first book and she read it to find instructions from Gratis. He'd guessed at her inquiry and explained which sections of the books to review.

She also had the book given to her by the priest Derdas in the temple of Alexander. The scent of urine was still strong. Opening the wood-bound book released the smell, and pages threatened to flee from the binding. She held it open carefully and reread the listing of Alexander's last known heir through the amazon Queen Thalestris, though she already knew it by memory. The name Andromeda was written in neat script. The page she was listed upon had a folded edge on the corner.

With the book of heirs set aside, Heron paged through the listings Gratis enumerated. Contained within the tiny script was nothing of interest in the sections he noted. Gratis' suggestions were well traveled by other scholars.

Curious to her own history, Heron paged through in search of her parents. It was possible that Gratis had not sent the books that contained her family line, but she found them eventually. Her father, Karanos, and mother, Cynna, were listed. Ada and Heron were noted beneath. She touched both names, feeling in that moment like two people inhabited her body.

Notes by her father explained he had left Macedonia in search of family fortune. Strangely, nothing was mentioned next to her name, but it was possible the scholars had not yet made the connection between that Heron and the famous Heron of Alexandria. Or her name had not traveled as widely as she thought. Unlike the butterflies of Alexander's *ren*, her name was contained within the walls of the city.

Then she traveled backwards, climbing the heredity out of curiosity. Some of her ancestors had markers next to them explaining a point of history. Her forbearers had done well, but nothing special stood out.

After a while, her knees were aching and she desired to get back to her workshop. She'd barely been there in months and the workers had run out of jobs. She needed to access its state and speak to the other inventors.

Before she closed the book, Heron turned one more page. A name caught her gaze. Her eyes fell upon it like an axe. There was scribbling next to it, a note of history.

It was the name Andromeda. She married Amyntas, which was a name of kings in Macedonia. Andromeda was not a common name in her country because of the myths associated with it. It was considered great hubris to name a daughter Andromeda.

In the margin it was noted that she came from a nomadic tribe from the east and her mother had been a warrior-woman. Stunned, Heron set the book down.

The specter of Alexander seemed to gaze at her through the sarcophagus. Heron could not believe it, but there it was. Her mind reeled with the implications. Though there could be some error, it appeared she might be the heir of Alexander the Macedonia.

Part of her wanted to run out of the Tomb, and burn the books. Another part wanted to go straight to Agog and show him that she found the heir after all, and it was her. But the repercussions of that were numerous.

If she kept her gender a secret, then he would want to set aside Polyxena and marry Sepharia. A tinge of jealousy twisted her gut. She could not do that to her daughter.

But if she told the world she was really a woman, they would condemn her, even as the heir. That way was wracked with pain and uncertainty.

And would Agog release the slaves as promised? How could she put a price on their freedom? He'd agreed, but now that she had the answer, she doubted his sincerity, just as he'd tricked her with the *gift* of the Lighthouse.

The world both opened and closed upon her. The books sitting on the marble floor at her feet were filled with cursed knowledge. She almost wished she'd never turned that final page and had left, ignorant of her fate.

But another side opened up to her. A thought born from the spirit of Alexander rather than the flesh. Alexander had built his legacy through his actions. Rather than use his name to further her cause, why not build her own?

Though she had not one inkling of what she needed to do, she felt a great welling up in her soul. Heron scooped up the books and deposited them in the satchel. She rested her fingertips on the stone sarcophagus, feeling a moment of communion with her deceased forbearer.

The aches and pains of her wounds faded. She was refreshed and terrified by this new revelation. Those gods she rebelled against, suddenly felt right there at her shoulder, a contradiction of her beliefs, but she could not shake them.

Purpose was like the Great Lighthouse to her. A light shone in her mind. The workshop, her muse of creation, felt too small, too immediate.

Heron floated out of the Soma of Alexander and paused at the sycamore. The butterflies were gone, flown to places beyond Alexandria and to the south. If she believed the attendant, the *ren* of his name had gone with them. For men and women were not remembered unless their name was spoken and Heron could not deny she did not wish the same. For why else did she visit the Demetarium for inspiration?

A delirious shiver descended upon her as she stood in the warm sunlight as she thought of the blood that ran through her veins. Here, she was not just the *Michanikos*, tinkerer of machines and inventor of miracles; here, she was not just Heron the thinker and diviner of ancient secrets; here, she was not just Heron the Alexandrian, its most famous citizen. Here, she was something more, something greater. Here, she was the heir to Alexander the Great.

§ § §

Continue Heron's adventure in Book Three of The Alexandrian Saga

LEGACY
OF
ALEXANDRIA

OTHER BOOKS BY THOMAS K. CARPENTER

The Hundred Halls Universe

SEASON ONE
<u>THE HUNDRED HALLS</u>
Trials of Magic
Web of Lies
Alchemy of Souls
Gathering of Shadows
City of Sorcery

<u>THE RELUCTANT ASSASSIN</u>
The Reluctant Assassin
The Sorcerous Spy
The Veiled Diplomat
Agent Unraveled
The Webs That Bind

<u>GAMEMAKERS ONLINE</u>
The Warped Forest
Gladiators of Warsong
Citadel of Broken Dreams
Enter the Daemonpits
Plane of Twilight

<u>ANIMALIANS HALL</u>
Wild Magic
Bane of the Hunter
Mark of the Phoenix
Arcane Mutations
Untamed Destiny

<u>STONE SINGERS HALL</u>
Song of Siren and Blood
House of Snake and Tome
Storm of Dragon and Stone
Sonata of Shadow and Thorn
Well of Demon and Bone

<u>THE ORDER OF MERLIN</u>
The Order of Merlin
Infernal Alliances
Tower of Horn and Blood

ABOUT THE AUTHOR

Thomas K. Carpenter resides in Colorado with his wife Rachel. When he's not busy writing his next book, he's hiking, skiing, and getting beat by his wife at cards. He keeps a regular blog at www.thomaskcarpenter.com and you can follow him on twitter @thomaskcarpente. If you want to learn when his next novel will be hitting the shelves and get free stories and occasional other goodies, please sign up for his mailing list by going to: http://tinyurl.com/thomaskcarpenter. Your email address will never be shared and you can unsubscribe at any time.

www.ingramcontent.com/pod-product-compliance
Lightning Source LLC
Chambersburg PA
CBHW070542310726

48982CB00010B/1444/J